Caged

Sophie Davis

DEDICATION

To my late Aunt Heidi,
whose creativity and dedication to the arts will truly be
missed.

ACKNOWLEDGMENTS

First and foremost, I would like to thank Baehr, for her willingness to share in the great journey of writing the Talented series. She took on the tedious task of editing *Caged*, and without her incredible attention to detail and inquisitive nature, this book wouldn't make much sense. Between the late-night phone calls and marathon texting sessions, she has spent as much time in Talia's world as I have. Her constructive criticism, heartfelt advice, and never-ending encouragement are invaluable.

I would like to thank Irish for all of her patience, and for indulging me when I asked her questions that likely made little sense to someone who doesn't know how the series ends. A big thank you to my parents, Esther and Henry, for all of their love and support while I pursue my dream of becoming an author. Thank you to Laurel Dabbs, for her wonderful, hand-painted cover art. Thank you to Mary Munsell for undertaking the huge task of proofreading and editing all of the manuscripts in the Talented Saga. I cannot express how grateful I am to have such a wonderful person offering her services. And last, but certainly not least, thank you to all of the readers who have shared, and will continue to share, in Talia's adventures.

Chapter One

The knock at the door came again. Just like the last three times he'd tried to get my attention, I ignored his appeal. Instead, I continued to stare at the metal lock that was barring him from entering.

"Natalia, open the door," his deep voice demanded. Concentrating harder, I watched as the latch switched from the locked to the unlocked position. The sound of the lock engaging and disengaging was barely audible to me, but I knew that he heard the click loud and clear. Confirming my thoughts, he quickly tried to turn the knob again just as I re-engaged the lock.

"Natalia," he warned. His exasperation made me smile. "I will break this door if I have to," he said, his voice low and threatening. The harsh tone left little doubt that he would do just that if I didn't quit playing games. With a heavy sigh, I finally relented, disengaging the lock and leaving it that way. He turned the knob so hard, the metal screeched in protest – I thought that it might break off in his hand – and then Danbury "Mac" McDonough burst into the room.

I sat on my king-sized bed, propped against the fluffy pillows, my arms crossed over my chest, my legs crossed at my ankles and a smirk on my face. Mac, the Director of the Talented Organization for Extremely Interesting Citizens (aka TOXIC), stared at me disapprovingly. "Are the games really necessary?" he demanded, clearly annoyed.

"Am I not allowed any privacy?" I retorted, not bothering to hide the irritation in my own voice.

"No, you are allowed all the 'privacy' you like, but you are not allowed locked doors," he said with mock patience.

"Locked doors, privacy, what's the difference?"

"The difference, Natalia, is that if you have a seizure and the door is locked, these seconds that we lose could prove lethal." His voice was hard, but the tenderness in his eyes touched me. The steely reserve that I'd been holding on to faltered a little, but I quickly recovered.

Pasting on a small smile, I said, "I'm fine, see?" I spread my arms wide to prove my point. He studied me carefully through narrowed gray eyes, inspecting every detail of my appearance for signs of damage. I felt like a child under Mac's hard gaze, but refused to avert my eyes. In addition to my seizures, Mac feared me so depressed that I might injure myself. His unsubstantiated anxiety had landed me in weekly therapy sessions with the Head of Psychoanalysis for the Agency. "You wanted to talk to me?" I prompted when I couldn't take his scrutiny any longer.

"How are you feeling?" he finally asked.

How was I feeling? Where to begin? Expressions like 'lab rat,' 'caged animal,' and 'prisoner' came to mind, but Mac wouldn't appreciate those responses.

"Fine," I replied shortly.

"Fine?" he repeated lightly, raising one bushy eyebrow in challenge.

"Fine. Just like I felt fine yesterday. Just like the day before that. And exactly how I felt the day before that." My voice raising an octave as I punctuated each word.

Mac continued to look me up and down as if the only way that he would believe my words was if he couldn't detect otherwise. Returning his stare, I tried to match the cold glint of his gaze with my own. He was careful to avoid direct eye contact, afraid that I might read his thoughts. As if I needed such contact to access his mind. We both knew better, but we also both knew how much he hated the intrusion, which is why I normally refrained.

"I have been thinking, maybe you would like to help out with some of the classes at School?" He said it like it was a question, but I knew that he wasn't really giving me an option. Mac wasn't in the habit of offering choices; he was more accustomed to barking orders, and few people had the nerve to disobey. I used to be one of his sheep. His approval and praise had meant the world to me, but over the last nine months, I'd distanced myself from the flock. Despite that, option or not, I was eager to do something – anything – besides sit in this room.

"Really?" I replied, almost ashamed by how excited the prospect of leaving my bedroom made me. I tried not to let the excitement show, but I could barely contain myself. I had been locked up in this room, in this house, on the same grounds as the McDonough School, for months. The only time that Mac permitted me to leave was to make the short trek to the School's Medical Facility for my daily blood draw and injections with Dr. Thistler. Even my therapists, Drs. Wythe and Martin, came to Mac's house for our sessions.

Well, maybe locked up was a *slight* exaggeration – the door was only actually locked when I locked it from the inside. And the room wasn't exactly small; it was bigger than most accommodations for teenagers, even bigger than some families' entire homes, and lavishly decorated.

My large bed was covered in a burgundy down comforter with silver embroidered swirls and occupied a space in the middle of my bedroom. One wall of the bedroom was glass and covered with draperies the same burgundy and silver pattern as the comforter. A mahogany dresser stood about waist high, extending almost the entire length of the wall opposite the bed, and a wall screen for watching movies stretched above it. A third wall contained a roll-top desk made of the same mahogany as the dresser.

Huge black-and-white paintings of icy lakes and snow covered mountains, painted by a well-known artist, hung on the three true walls. Next to the desk were giant French doors, made of the same mahogany with an intricately carved design. Behind the wooden doors sat a walk-in closet that stretched nearly half the width of the room itself. Most of the clothes in the closet hadn't been touched in years (two years to be exact).

The shelf that ran around the top of the closet held many shoe boxes filled with pictures of me as a teenager. My curly, chestnut hair highlighted my purple eyes and framed my small face. My smooth olive complexion was marred only by a smattering of freckles across the bridge of my slightly upturned nose. Beside me in most of the pictures was a slightly older boy, a comparative giant, with shaggy blonde hair and clear blue eyes, his skin as light as mine was dark.

The pictures used to decorate the walls and the bedside tables; when I'd moved back into this room, I'd packed them all away, not wanting to see them every day.

"I thought that it would be good for you to get out and rejoin the living," Mac said dryly, interrupting my thoughts and bringing me back to the present.

"Funny, considering you're the reason that I've been denied access to the 'living,'" I snorted. The fact that our house was so close to throngs of students and teachers, but I was barely allowed to interact with them, seemed almost cruel.

"Yes, well, your health has been much better in recent weeks, and Dr. Wythe seems satisfied that your mental state is stable." *Great*, I thought, *the man who overanalyzes everything has decided that I'm not crazy – that's reassuring.*

"I could go back to Elite Headquarters," I replied, hopefully. I knew that Mac approving my return to the Hunters was about as likely as me rehanging those photos, but I had to try.

"You have not been cleared by Medical," he stated, the annoyance from earlier returning. Lately, we'd been having this conversation a lot.

"Medical doesn't seem to be any closer to *clearing* me than Medical was nine months ago," I snapped angrily. TOXIC had access to the absolute latest and best medical research, yet somehow, the exact cause of my seizures still baffled them.

Nine months I was a Hunter Pledge, living at Elite Headquarters, located in beautiful Brentwood Springs, West Virginia. The Hunters are a Division within a government agency called TOXIC, simply referred to as the "Agency". The Hunters devote most of their time to collecting information about the Coalition, the largest threat to national security. My solo mission, the culmination of the Hunters' Pledge program, had brought me in contact with Ian Crane, the President of the Coalition and my parents' murderer. Even though my official assignment hadn't been to kill Crane, I had hoped to do just that if the opportunity presented itself. When I finally did come face-to-face with him, things didn't go exactly as planned; I'd been injected with an unidentified chemical and shot while trying to flee. The drug lingered in my bloodstream now, causing me agonizing – and, at times, embarrassing – seizures.

The Coalition doesn't believe that being Talented is a good thing. They believe that people like me, those with gifts, are unnatural. Their sole mission is to bring down the Agency and put an end to the training of special children. If Crane gets his way, Talents will be ostracized, forced to return to the days when we had to hide our abilities or face ridicule.

"Natalia, we have been over this, we are doing everything we can. I just need for you to be patient. It is best for everybody if you stay here until Medical can isolate the compound in your blood," he said with exaggerated patience. "Besides, even if Medical clears you, there is no guarantee that the Placement Committee will make you a Hunter."

Mac's not-so-subtle reminder that in addition to nearly bleeding to death, I'd pretty much botched my solo hunt, stung. The solo hunt was a necessary mission that each Hunter Pledge needed to complete to actually become a Hunter. Mine had been less than stellar. I knew that there was a very real chance that my performance would prevent the Placement Committee from actually assigning me to the Hunters. Despite that, I was counting on my team captain, Henri, going to bat for me when the time came. Henri would, hopefully assure the Committee that I'd done very well, on all of my group missions and that I was ready to be a full-fledged Hunter.

Still, my proverbial ace in the hole was Mac. As Director of the Agency, he was an important member of the Placement Committee – as far as most were concerned, his word was gospel. If he voted to place me with the Hunters, the others would likely fall in line. At one time, the mutual confidence that Mac and I shared would've left me with no doubt that he would sway the vote in my favor, but the current state of my mental and physical health made it uncertain.

"Fine," I snapped when it became clear that he wasn't going to give me any good news.

"Fine, you will help out with the classes at School?" he clarified.

"Fine, I will help out with the classes at School," I answered grudgingly. Not that helping students at the McDonough School for the Talented was high on my to-do list, but it sure beat twiddling my thumbs in my bedroom.

"Glad we settled that," he said, sounding relieved. "Oh, and Natalia? Keep your senses open," Mac added, seemingly as an afterthought. I could tell that this was his real reason for sending me to the School, and now I was intrigued. Maybe this was more like an assignment than a way to get me to stop brooding. At least, I hoped that was the case.

"Why?" I asked suspiciously.

"I am not sure yet, but I think that we might have a leak in the Agency...a spy."

"A spy?" I asked stupidly, my mouth gaping. How could there

be a spy in the Agency? Didn't we take extreme measures to prevent things like that?

"After studying your official report from Nevada, I can only conclude that we have a spy. Your identity was compromised. Crane knew who you were and, based on the events in his home, I believe that he was tipped off by an Operative on the inside here. I have been quietly investigating this theory, but have not made any progress. I think that it's time that we took more aggressive measures," he paused, waiting for my reaction. I kept my face impassive while I mulled over his words. I had entertained the notion that my identity was leaked to Crane, but I hadn't really considered that it might be from someone within the Agency. Now that I thought about it, Mac was probably right. Crane had clearly known who I was, and it's not like I carry identification on me. He'd also been prepared for my arrival. I guess we really did have a spy.

"Are you thinking that one of the teachers or administrators is selling the information?" I asked carefully, gauging his predictably guarded reaction to my question. If Mac had planned to fill me in on all the details, he wouldn't have broached the subject the way that he did. Ordinarily, he was so direct. The fact that he was beating around the bush could only mean that he was intentionally hiding important details from me. When his expression remained unchanged, I once again considered reading his thoughts. After all, the spy – the traitor – who had compromised my identity had nearly cost me my life. Mac's refusal to divulge details infuriated me.

"Could be," he shrugged noncommittally. "Honestly, I'm not sure. Like I said, I've been quietly investigating this using only a handful of trusted Operatives; those I am positive are not involved. Your specific Talents could be useful since I have all but exhausted my other options."

Great, I'm a last resort. This time, I did read his mind.

His mental barricades were firmly in place, but since I was the one who'd taught him to build the barriers, they were easy for me to knock down. Mac was telling the truth; he really didn't have any idea who the spy was. His inability to make any progress in his search frustrated and scared him. He was afraid that if the traitor wasn't found soon, we would lose more Operatives. But he was most terrified by the certainty that if the interloper got another chance he would make sure to kill me.

"And you consider me a trusted Operative," I teased, trying to lighten the mood. "I feel so special."

"No need for sarcasm, Natalia. But yes, I am confident that you are not the leak," he answered.

"Why do you want me investigating at the School?" I asked, a little confused.

"Here and Elite Headquarters contain the Agency's only Crypto Banks as you know. There are two possible scenarios for how Crane got his information. The leak theory would mean that an individual obtained access to your assignment information and sold that information to the Coalition. The other theory is that we have a Coalition spy working in our ranks. Even in that scenario, the individual would still have needed your mission specifics, and the only way, to do that would be by hacking the records in the Crypto Bank or bribing a Crypto to do so. If there was a bribe that would mean we have several traitors in our midst."

"Why me? Why my records?" I asked with alarm. If Mac was right, wouldn't it have been more advantageous to leak large batches of information? Or Hunting missions where whole teams could be captured or killed instead of just one Operative? And I hadn't even been an Operative when I went on my solo mission; I'd just been a Pledge.

"Most likely because you were going after Crane directly," he answered.

He had been making eye-contact with me up until this point, but averted his eyes when he spoke now. He was either lying or at least only telling me part of his theory. I didn't press the issue this time. If Mac wanted to give me an assignment, I was happy to take it.

"I see. I suppose this is an unofficial mission?" I asked.

"Yes that would be best. I don't want to cause panic within the Agency or tip-off the potential spy by launching a full-out open investigation," he confirmed, meeting my gaze again.

"When do I start?" I asked, with a confidence I didn't feel.

"Tomorrow. You will be posing as an Assistant Instructor, which includes living in Instructor Housing. I've taken the liberty of matching you with several individuals who raised red flags in our preliminary search. By tomorrow afternoon, I'll have each of their files sent to your communicator."

He seemed relieved I'd agreed. As if I'd had an option. Even if Mac had actually presented this situation to me as though I had a choice, there wasn't one. Ian Crane had killed my parents. Ian Crane had nearly killed me. And whoever leaked my identity and mission specifics to Crane was just as responsible as he was for my current condition.

"I'll pack a bag," I said glibly. Mac gave me a hard look.

"I'll take you over first thing in the morning."

"I'm sure I can find the campus, Mac. I don't need a babysitter." Mac's house, my house, was on School grounds; it wasn't like I had far to go.

"I'll take you over first thing in the morning," he repeated. With that, he turned on his heel and left my room.

"Couldn't even bother to close the door," I mumbled.

"If you want it closed, do it yourself," Mac called from somewhere in my sitting room. I stared at the door until I heard a loud, satisfying THWACK. Gratified, I smiled to myself. My pleasure was short lived. A crack, followed by a thud, filled the room. The door had splintered in two when I'd willed it shut. Crap - no more locking the door for me ...Good thing this was my last night here. Unfortunately, this was also my last night in my big comfy bed. Oh, well - my bed was a sacrifice I was willing to make.

Chapter Two

The steady beeping of the alarm clock grew louder with each chirp. I groaned. The only good part about being medically inactive was *not* having to wake up with the birds. Reaching blindly towards my bedside table, I slapped at the offensive machine. After several failed attempts, I finally connected with the off button. I remained lying face down in my bed for several more minutes, my breathing again taking on the steady rhythm of sleep. The beeping began anew.

Ugh, I must've hit the snooze button. Groaning again, I sat up, and rubbed the sleep from my eyes as I swung my legs over the side of the bed. When my feet made contact with the cold wooden floor, I swore loudly, wondering where my slippers were. I padded over to the window and threw open the curtains. It was still dark out ...*Awesome*. Suddenly, I wasn't so sure that I wanted an assignment; sleep sounded like a much better option.

Despite my increasing desire to climb back under the covers, I grabbed my robe and made my way to the bathroom attached to my sitting room. I turned on the hot water, waiting for the steam to fill the white-tiled space before stepping into the walk-in shower. I savored this moment, my last shower without shoes for a while. When I was a student, I'd frequently come up here to bathe, but it was too far to make the trip on a daily basis. The showers at School were definitely NOT my fondest memory from my student days, and I somehow doubted that the teachers' were any better than the students'.

I had enrolled in the McDonough School for the Talented, located on a secure facility in western Maryland, following the deaths' of my parents when I was ten. I'd always known that I possessed the power to hear other people's thoughts and was capable of controlling their minds, but I hadn't known that my ability was called a Talent. I soon learned that Talents came in all shapes and sizes. There were Morphers, people who transformed into various animals; Light Manipulators, those who could turn invisible; Higher Reasoning or Brains, who were like human computers, capable of analyzing information in the blink of an eye; Electrical Manipulators, people who harnessed and controlled electricity; Visionaries, who saw glimpses of the future; and Viewers, who could observe a situation where they weren't physically present; and the list went on.

Our gifts were a result of the Great Contamination, a breakdown of the nuclear reactors all over the world. The United States created the McDonough School to train Talented children in properly using and controlling their gifts. At sixteen, we took placement exams that ranked our abilities and determined the Division of TOXIC that we would be positioned in after graduation. I'd been selected for the Hunters, the only division that I'd ever wanted to be a part of.

Hunters went on Missions to track down people and information that were a threat to either TOXIC or the country as a whole. Most recently, the Hunters have focused on finding and destroying a group, called the Coalition who opposes the *Talent Testing Act*. They don't believe that being Talented is a good thing that Talents are abnormal, and that what we are able do is unnatural. In a way, it is, but the skills that Talents possess help to protect the Nation. We have capabilities that far exceed those of average people, allowing us to both prevent crime domestically and preclude invasion by foreign countries.

The Coalition is so opposed to the testing laws that it staged an uprising, causing seven states to secede from the rest of the U.S. Currently, one of the Agency's main initiatives is to defeat the Coalition before civil war breaks out, hopefully reuniting the country.

"Are you trying to drown yourself?" a woman's motherly voice called as she knocked on the bathroom door.

Sighing, I turned off the water, but didn't respond. I opened the glass door of the shower, the steam so thick that I could barely find my towel and robe. I dried myself off as best I could, considering the amount of moisture in the air, then wrapped my heavy terrycloth robe around myself, cinching the tie around my middle. Bending over, I wrapped the towel around my long wet hair. The robe was so long that I had to hold it up, so I wouldn't trip as I made my way back into the bedroom.

When I opened the bathroom door, steam billowed out into the sitting room, forming warm clouds. The woman who had knocked on the door was sitting at the small breakfast table in the corner with a plate of scrambled eggs, thick white toast and a huge carafe of coffee. I sniffed the air and drank in the rich fragrance of imported dark roast.

"Morning, Talia," Gretchen greeted me warmly. Her clear blue eyes were warm and inviting, a sharp contrast to the cold gray ones of her husband. Despite the early hour, her blonde hair was perfectly coiffed, and she was already dressed in black slacks and a royal blue blouse. "I thought that you could use a good breakfast before your first day of school."

"Thanks, Gretchen," I replied, giving her a genuine smile in return. Gretchen had been like a mother to me since the death of my own as Mac had been like a father to me, and I'd come to love them both deeply. My feelings for Mac had become muddled in the nine months since returning from Nevada even though he had gone to great lengths to aid me in my physical recovery, and I was extremely grateful for his support. But I'd also come to realize that there was a lot Mac had been keeping from me. I knew that as Director, he was privy to highly classified information that wasn't any of my business, but all the secrets were lessening the steadfast trust that I'd always had in him.

After moving to the U.S. to attend the McDonough School, I'd learned that Mac and Gretchen opening their home to me was a highly unusual practice. Since Mac had been a close friend of my father's, he argued that he owed it to him to watch out for me. Mac had recognized me for what I was, a Mind Manipulator, from the first time we met because Gretchen was one of the only other recorded Talents with the same ability.

Gretchen had ranked as a Mid-level Talent during her Placement Exams, and been assigned to the Psychic Interrogation Division. But she had no stomach for the unpleasantness associated with questioning suspects and dreaded performing the interrogations so much that it made her physically ill. She'd requested permission to leave when she was pregnant with their son. Mac wasn't Director then, but he was still well-connected, so her request had been granted. Now, the only role that she played in the Agency was wife to the Director.

When my parents were killed, Mac had offered me the opportunity to learn to use my Talents, something that my parents had discouraged. I'd readily agreed, and Gretchen had taught me all about controlling the powers. She taught me to open up my mind so that I could *hear* everyone around me; she taught me to close my mind to keep out others seeking entrance to my thoughts; she taught me how to create a true connection with another person and about the potential harm in doing so. In no time, I'd surpassed her abilities; I was a much stronger Talent than Gretchen. It wasn't long before I could actively enter someone's mind without making eye contact or touching them. I could control a room full of minds at the same time, bending all of them to my will. Thankfully, Gretchen also taught me about what happens when you abuse your power. She explained to me that Mind Manipulators are so rare because most have driven themselves mad controlling others.

"I bet you're excited. I know how hard these last several months have been on you," she said gently, cutting in on my memories.

I made a noncommittal noise as I began shoveling food into my mouth.

The eggs were covered in a salty cheese and contained mushrooms and onions, my absolute favorite. The thick white bread was warm, covered in butter and strawberry jam; Gretchen had made both the jam and the bread herself. I sighed happily as I chewed. Gretchen's cooking had been the only other perk of my confinement.

"How are you feeling today?" Gretchen continued, eyeing me over a steaming mug of coffee.

Swallowing the too-big bite of my breakfast, I cleared my throat before answering. "Pretty good, but I'll be better once I'm around other people." Gretchen blanched, setting her cup on the table. "Oh, Gretchen that's not what I meant! You've been great, it's just been a little claustrophobic being stuck inside my bedroom all day," I tried to backtrack. I hadn't meant to hurt her feelings. She'd gone out of her way to make me comfortable, and without her companionship, I might've gone crazy.

"I understand, dear," she replied, offering me a small smile. "Dr. Wythe called late last night. He's very pleased with your progress." I groaned. I sort of despised my therapist.

In addition to my physical rehabilitation, Mac had insisted that I see a therapist. Dr. Wythe was the same shrink that Mac had sent me to after I'd witnessed my parents' murders, and I loathed discussing my feelings with him; it reminded me of the months that he'd spent grilling me on what I'd seen when the Coalition raided the hotel room where we'd been staying and killed my only family. This time around, he focused incessantly on the conversation that I'd had with Ian Crane following my capture. The therapy was boring and pointless since he typically disregarded what I said and suggested a version of events that correlated with what the Agency wanted me to believe. It hadn't taken me long to figure out that if I just told him what he wanted to hear, the sessions would end. After I'd agreed that everything said by Crane was a lie, Dr. Wythe declared me healed. He still stopped by Mac's house when he was on campus, but I was no longer required to endure his daily torture.

Though I'd convinced Dr. Wythe that I didn't believe Crane's words, I hadn't convinced myself. I didn't include every detail of our conversation in my official report, leaving out the part where Crane insisted that he'd known my father. I wanted to work through that on my own, wanted to decide if it was a lie without the influence of the good doctor. I wasn't sure what Talents Dr. Wythe possessed, but they seemed like a weaker version of mine. He couldn't read minds like I could, but he had an influence over people, much like my compulsion. His suggestive nature had nearly worked on me in my weakened condition, but my desire to cling to the truth won out.

"Has Danbury told you which Instructors you'll be paired with?" Gretchen continued, a cloud of displeasure darkening her normally bright eyes.

"Um, not yet. He said that he'd have the list sent to my communicator," I said absently, returning to my eggs now that the topic of Dr. Wythe was closed.

Gretchen grew quiet, scrutinizing my table manners. The slight grimace contorting her beautiful features was the only outward indication that she disapproved.

"Danbury is out for a run right now, but he wanted me to be sure that you are ready to go at 6:30," she said, her features reverting back to an easy smile. "I packed a bag of things for you to take to the dorms with you, but call if I forgot anything and I will send it over."

The only response that I could manage was a small nod since my mouth was full of eggs and toast. Gretchen scowled again at my lack of social graces. I swallowed. "This might be the last good meal that I get for a while. You know that the School food is barely edible."

When I was a student, I'd tried to eat in the cafeteria as infrequently as possible, instead sneaking up to have dinner at Gretchen's table. It was just another reason that the other students disliked me.

Gretchen made some small throaty noise that sounded a little like a snort. "The Instructor's cafeteria fare is much better than the students'," she promised.

I spared her a skeptical glance. I'd believe it when I tasted the truth of her words for myself. I quickly scarfed down the rest of my breakfast, gulping my first cup of coffee before pouring a second cup, and sat at my vanity to get ready.

I dried my hair with a blow dryer, then used a big round brush to straighten out all the chestnut strands. When I was satisfied that it was thoroughly dry, I used a flatiron to ensure that no hint of wave remained. Before the last nine months, I'd always worn my hair curly, but lately, I'd been straightening my locks for lack of something better to do. I'd decided that I liked the straight look – sometimes, change was a good thing.

Next, I pulled my hair into a ponytail at the back of my head. I stared at my reflection in the mirror for several minutes before deciding in favor of makeup. My skin was smooth but uncharacteristically pale for me thanks to spending the majority of my time indoors. The dark circles under my eyes were a bluish purple, like I'd been on the losing end of a fistfight.

Rising from the vanity, I retreated to my bedroom, where Gretchen had made my bed while I was in the shower. On the end of the burgundy comforter, in two neatly folded piles, sat several pairs of black stretch pants, white soft cotton t-shirts, and a thin gray sweatshirt. Anticipating my lack of appropriate clothing, Gretchen must've ordered me new outfits. Man, I didn't even have to ask; she always delivered.

My first class of the day was a basic skills combat class, so I grabbed a pair of cotton underwear and pulled them on, followed by the comfy-looking stretch pants. As I put on a matching bra, I caught a glimpse of my reflection in the mirror over my dresser. My back was to the mirror, and over my shoulder, I could see angry red scars, peeking out just above my stretchy pants. Unconsciously, I reached behind me and felt the raised flesh of the scar. My fingers felt the hole where the bullet had pierced my skin, and the places where the Medics stitched me up. I flinched as I touched the flesh even though no sensation came; the Agency doctors said that I may never regain feeling there.

They had offered to remove the scar as was customary, but I was still a little fuzzy on how I'd actually received it. I didn't want to erase the only evidence that it had happened at all. A perverse part of me also liked the reminder that I now owed Crane for more than just my parents' murders.

My recovery had been a long and painful process, including learning how to walk again. I now received a shot every day to stabilize the chemicals that Crane's men had injected, reducing the number of seizures that had plagued me since returning from Nevada. Initially, the doctors were unable to develop an effective antidote, and the episodes were so frequent that I spent most of my time in a drug-induced coma. Eventually, the team of researchers created an equalizer that allowed me to function, but it left me tired and weak.

My primary Medical doctor, Dr. Thistler, had treated me after my parents' deaths as well, but my memories of her weren't as clear as those of Dr. Wythe. Mac told me that she'd been one of the physicians to monitor my condition during my previous stay at TOXIC's Medical facility, but I'd been too traumatized to be aware of my surroundings. She was nice enough, but her involvement in my life served as a daily reminder that I was sick and currently unable to avenge my parents. I longed for a day when she would enter the examination room and proudly declare that she'd found a cure. Unfortunately, the more time that passed, the less confident I became that the time would ever come.

"Natalia, are you dressed?" Mac called from the sitting room, snapping me back to reality.

Grabbing for my shirt, I hastily pulled it over my head. I reached for the insanely bright white shoes and yanked them on as fast as possible. Then I noticed the bag that Gretchen packed for me with the meager personal items that I was allowed to take to the School, and stuffed the rest of my clothes inside. I slung the small duffel over my shoulder and walked out to the sitting room to meet Mac. I didn't look back on the room that had been like a prison for the last nine months.

Chapter Three

Mac and Gretchen's home was located west of the School's main campus. Mac drove me the short distance in a road vehicle that he kept on hand for getting around the compound.

"You really don't need to hold my hand and walk me to class," I snapped once we were seated in the car. Though Mac had been like my surrogate father, our relationship had first become strained while I was in my Pledge year. The past nine months had done little to repair the rift; I was bitter about my current situation and though I knew it was irrational, I blamed him.

"I just want to ensure that you make it there okay," he replied mildly, his eyes fixed on the road. I gave him an odd look; did he forget that I had attended this school for six years? I'd already taken all these classes, and I was fairly confident that I could find them in my sleep. Opening my mind, I risked gently probing Mac's.

"Natalia......" he warned. Mac was one of the few people who could detect when I tried to read him, and he effectively blocked most of my attempts. Mac's uncanny ability to block me was my own doing – I'd conditioned him against mental intrusion.

"Sorry," I smiled sheepishly, only sorry that I'd been caught.

The stone façade of the administration building came into view several minutes later. Mac pulled the car to a stop in the rounded, gravel drive, and he reached for the bags at my feet.

"I'll have these sent up to your new room," he offered.

Now that I was safely on campus, I figured that Mac would bid me farewell, and retreat inside to his office. Instead, he started walking away from the administration building. I quickly followed him.

As we neared the outdoor practice area, Mac sped up. My short legs could barely match pace with his stride. I was so focused on keeping up that I didn't notice when he stopped; I ran smack into his broad back, my head bouncing painfully off the bottom edge of a shoulder bone. *Smooth, Talia,* I thought to myself. But Mac barely noticed. I stood behind him, my view obstructed by his massive frame, rubbing my forehead and waiting for him to introduce me.

"Director McDonough," a deep voice greeted him respectfully. I froze. The morning was relatively warm, and the thin sweatshirt that I was wearing had caused sweat to dot my forehead and upper lip, but that voice raised gooseflesh on my arms and made the fine hairs on the back of my neck stand on end.

My heart raced, images flashed through my mind: fingers light as feathers on my arms, running up my sides, blue eyes so full of longing and desire, soft lips against mine, wind whipping wet hair in my face, glass shards spraying my cheeks, the taste of blood in my mouth, a big hand gripping both my small, blood covered, ones. *Stay with me, Tal, stay with me,* his voice pleaded in my head.

I wasn't entirely sure where that last image had come from, but the other memories were traumatic enough that I didn't dwell, on it. I was torn between two overwhelming desires – one was to run all the way back to Mac and Gretchen's house, bury my face in my pillows, and cry myself to sleep; the second was to attack and viciously assault the boy standing not twenty feet from me.

"Donavon," Mac replied, "I have your new assistant," he paused briefly, "You, of course, know Natalia Lyons." Mac stepped aside, exposing me to Donavon and his students.

Paralyzed, I stood in place as the images swam over and over through my mind. My breathing was labored, my heart beating so fast that I thought for sure everyone could see it through my chest. Mac placed his hand on my shoulder, his touch bringing me back to the present. I tried to smile as I glanced at the seated students, hoping that I looked nervous, but not unstable, which is exactly how I felt.

Finally when I couldn't put it off any longer, I looked directly at Donavon. He was tall like his father, his shoulders broad, body lean, the muscles in his arms and chest were clearly visible through his thin navy t-shirt. His own gray sweatpants were slung low on his narrow hips. His blue eyes looked as shocked as I felt, his shaggy dark blonde hair was messy, like he'd only run his hand through it when he got out of bed that morning. His normally generous mouth appeared thin, his lips pressed together as if he were desperately trying to keep something inside. He was just as beautiful as I remembered, and the feelings swelling up inside of me were just as dark as I remembered.

When Donavon's gaze met mine, the primal urge to strike him was so strong that I had to fight to maintain control. A low guttural growl escaped my pursed lips as a light breeze kicked up, the air growing cold around me and clouds began to gather overhead. Mac's grip on my shoulder tightened painfully. The wind became stronger and a raindrop splashed my cheek. Mac's fingers bit into my flesh, his nails digging in so hard that I thought for sure they'd torn my sweatshirt. The pain reeled in my rage; the winds died down and the sky slowly cleared. The whole scene occurred in mere seconds.

"Instructor McDonough," I hissed through tightly clenched teeth. I tried to give Donavon my most angelic smile, but I could tell from the thoughts he was projecting that I looked slightly crazed.

Confident that I wouldn't maim his son – or start a natural disaster – Mac's grip on my shoulder released. "I'll check on you later in the day, Natalia."

I nodded, so furious at him for springing Donavon on me like this that I didn't trust myself to speak. He gave a short wave to the class and a nod towards Donavon. "Stop by and see me soon, son."

Donavon gave his father an easy smile. "You got it, Dad."

With that, Mac turned and left me to face his son alone. But I couldn't move; my feet felt as if they were stuck in quicksand.

"Talia, please have a seat. I'm going to demonstrate the skills that we'll be working on today, and then we'll break off into pairs to work on them," Donavon said to me, his voice full of unspoken tension. His intense gaze penetrating straight through my skin, piercing my heart.

So many questions burned hot and ugly inside of me. *Why did you cheat on me? Why didn't you have the decency to apologize? Why didn't you ever try to talk to me after everything happened? What are you doing here now?* Yet when I opened my mouth, nothing came out, my unspoken questions handing in the air like a thick fog. Donavon's gaze remained on me.

Until nine months ago, I had trained for hostile situations. Now, looking into the face of the boy who had broken my heart, I could barely contain my emotions or my powers. *Get a grip, Talia,* I scolded myself. *He's not important. You don't care about him, and he doesn't care about you. Sit down and act like a normal human being.* Heeding my own advice, I slowly eased myself onto a cushy mat at the back of the class. Donavan reluctantly dragged his eyes from me and began his lesson.

He began reviewing basic offensive maneuvers, nothing too complicated or advanced. *This must be a remedial class,* I thought to myself. I walked around the periphery, observing the students when it was time to break into partners. I made small corrections in technique when I saw fit, but I was still so distracted by coming face-to-face with Donavon that little else mattered.

During my stay at Mac's house, I hadn't been allowed visitors or communication with anyone besides Mac, Gretchen, and the select Medicals that came to treat me. No one had even mentioned Donavon, let alone told me that he was teaching at the School. Though, the more I thought about it, maybe Gretchen had tried – she'd been nervous and tense when we'd talked over breakfast this morning. Looking at Donavon now, all I could think was that she really should've tried harder.

When I'd left for Nevada, Donavon had been an Elite Operative, same as me, and was stationed at the Elite Headquarters in West Virginia, same as me. He'd also been my boyfriend since I was thirteen, but it ended when I'd caught him naked in bed with another girl.

It now made perfect sense that Mac had insisted on accompanying me that morning. He must've known that, best case scenario, the moment that I saw Donavon I would leave. Worst case scenario, I would cause my own natural disaster right then and there. He'd been right; without Mac's painful presence, I likely would've done something drastic. I'd always lacked impulse control, but lately, my temper was more easily provoked, and reining it in had become harder.

Finally, after what felt like an eternity, Donavon called class to an end. Grateful to escape his unwelcome presence, I turned to leave with the students.

"Talia, can I have a quick word?" Donavon called after me. I briefly considered refusing to speak to him, but then thought better of it. I'd have to face him eventually; now was as good a time as any. Since this assignment wasn't exactly voluntary, it was unlikely that Mac was going to let me opt out just because I didn't want to work with Donavon.

I'd stopped in my tracks when he called my name, and twisted my neck to meet his gaze.

"Hey, Donavon, you got a second?" a female voice rang out from across the paddock. Despite the distraction, Donavon's eyes remained locked with mine, pain and regret visible in their cerulean depths. His mind was unguarded, and the thoughts and feelings that poured freely tore open the wound that his betrayal had created.

"Um, sure," he called regretfully to the approaching woman.

I snapped my head to face forward and swallowed the rage and bitterness that threatened to rip from my throat in an animalistic scream. His gaze bore into the back of my skull.

"*I had no idea,*" his mental voice said inside my head. Willing myself to remain composed, I closed my eyes, slowly exhaled, and counted to three.

When I opened my lids, I forced one sneakered foot in front of the other, away from the boy who'd broken my heart. I could hear the soft murmur of Donavon and the woman conversing, but their words were indistinguishable over buzzing between my ears. A loud, satisfying crack filled the morning air, followed by two strangled yelps as a large limb landed a foot from where Donavon and the woman stood. Pausing briefly to relish in my childish antics, I smiled, continuing to walk away. Maturity had never really been my strong suit.

Instead of going to my next class, I ran to the Headmistress' office. I barely noticed the lush green lawn or perfectly manicured flower beds that decorated the School's grounds. I could not believe that Mac had done this to me – what was he thinking? Forcing an interaction between me and Donavon? Was he crazy? Mac was the one who'd continually insisted that my mental state was fragile; what made him think that being around Donavon was a good idea?? Donavon's betrayal had nearly destroyed me, and now when I was more vulnerable than I'd been in my entire life, Mac was forcing me to relive that pain. What was wrong with him? I continued my mental rant the entire way to the administration building.

Chapter Four

I pushed the wooden door open with more force than necessary, and it gave a satisfying bang as it hit the door jam. The secretary seated behind a sleek wooden desk jumped when I entered.

"Can I help you, dear?" she asked, with a sickeningly pink-lipsticked smile.

"Is Janet in?" I practically growled at her.

"You mean Headmistress Evans, dear?" she replied, her pleasant demeanor becoming disapproving.

"Yeah, whatever. Is she in?" I demanded.

"Is she expecting you, dear?" The smile remained plastered to her face, but suspicion clouded her brown eyes. My temper was already bubbling over and her condescending tone made me want to throttle her.

Whoa, Talia. Calm down, she's just a secretary, I warned myself. Squeezing my eyes shut, I pinched the bridge of my nose and took three deep breaths before answering. Seizures weren't the only lingering effect of my trip to Nevada; my temper had developed a hair-trigger since the ordeal, although that was more likely a byproduct of cabin fever.

I replaced my scowl with a near manic smile of my own. "I would imagine she is expecting me," I replied as calmly as I could manage.

"Your name, dear?" *Ugh, stop effing calling me dear!*

"Talia, Talia Lyons." Pink Lipstick pushed a button on her console. I heard a buzzing noise and then the secretary lifted a handheld unit and spoke into it.

"Excuse me, Headmistress Evans?" she asked. She paused as Janet replied a greeting.

"There is a student here to see you, ma'am. She claims to have an appointment." Pink Lipstick paused again. "Ms. Lyons," she answered.

Awesome, she thinks I'm a student.

"Yes, madam, Talia Lyons," the secretary said firmly. The secretary's face flushed as Janet admonished her for making me wait.

Janet's secretary didn't appear to be more than late forties at best, but her hearing must already be failing if she kept the volume turned up loud enough that I could hear both sides of the conversation from across the desk. She quietly replaced the handheld unit, looked up and gave me another big pink smile. "The Headmistress will see you now."

Marching past the secretary's desk, I twisted the large brass doorknob below the nameplate reading "Headmistress Evans." Janet Evans had become Headmistress of the McDonough School when Mac had been promoted to Director of the Agency. I'd first met her during one of my family's bi-annual visits to the Agency Compound. Janet had been a Hunter then, and along with Mac, had been one of the Operatives assigned to guard my family during our trip, and I'd taking an instant liking to her. After I'd been enrolled at the School, Janet had become somewhat of a role model for me.

After my parents had been killed, Janet left the Hunters to become the Headmistress and keep watch over me. She was one of the few who knew the extent of my abilities; what I was actually capable of. In fact, Janet was one of the only people alive who had seen my powers. She'd been with Mac when he rescued me from the destroyed hotel room that had been the scene of my parents' deaths.

When I walked into her office, Janet was standing behind her large oak desk with her back to me. She was tall - close to six feet - and slim. Her reddish-brown hair was streaked with wisps of gray and cut to just above her shoulders. She wore a tailored navy pant suit and the collar of a white oxford shirt peeked out from underneath the jacket.

"I told him that this was a horrible idea," she stated, her back still to me, her hands busy with something in front of her.

"A horrible idea? That might be an understatement." The anger that had been building since I'd first laid eyes on Donavon was close to boiling completely over. Janet turned to face me, her slim fingers curled around two crystal glasses that were three-quarters full of amber liquid. Her dark green eyes, creased at the edges, radiated concern.

She held one of the glasses out, in my direction. I walked slowly forward and wrapped both of my small hands around the cool glass, tracing the Agency's logo engraved on the side of the tumbler. Janet raised her drink in a mock toast, and I gently clanged my own with hers. I looked down into amber liquid, wishing that I could drown myself in its depths before bringing the cup to my lips. The liquor burned; first my tongue, then my throat, and finally my stomach. Draining half the glass, I felt the tension slowly ebb and the anger dissipate.

I sank into one of the two leather chairs on my side of Janet's desk. The chair was slick, the liquor had gone instantly to my head, and I nearly slid right off. I scooted all the way back, my feet dangling as they could no longer reach the floor. Meeting Janet's eyes, I finally managed my first real smile of the day.

"Better?" she asked.

"It's a start," I admitted.

"How are you feeling?" she asked, the concern still heavy in her gaze.

"In general? Or today specifically?"

"Well, I was asking generally. I can imagine how you're feeling today," she laughed, slipping into her desk chair.

"Generally, pretty good. The seizures are becoming less frequent. I haven't had one in almost a month, so I guess that's good news," I mumbled. Following my return from Nevada, seizures had been a daily occurrence. Medical had worked around the clock to create the equalizer that I now received regularly. Eventually, the seizures had occurred less often, but unfortunately, they haven't ceased completely. Besides the convulsions and loss of bodily control, the episodes left me extremely tired and mostly bedridden for days afterwards.

"Good, I'm glad to hear that. And I see you're up and walking pretty well," she commented, gesturing to my dangling legs with her drink.

"Yeah, the physical therapy really helped. It was slow going at first, but I've been walking on my own for a couple of months now." The rehabilitation had helped, but it had also been torture.

"What'd you make of Dr. Wythe?" she asked with a knowing smile hovering over the rim of her cup. Janet clearly thought as much of therapy as I did.

"He was okay, for a therapist. He declared me 'stable', so that is a step towards me returning to active duty ...I think." Actually, I wasn't sure if a "stable" diagnosis was good enough for the placement committee, but since it was good enough for Mac, I was hopeful.

"It is," Janet confirmed. "Now we just need to find you a cure and you'll be back with the Hunters in no time."

"Yeah, I just hope that the Committee finds in my favor," I replied, examining a small scrape in the leather chair with one fingernail.

"They will. Mac will make sure of it," she promised. "I'll make sure of it."

"Thanks," I said gratefully, meeting her earnest gaze. Knowing that Janet was on my side made me slightly more optimistic. "The way I see it, Mac owes me after springing Donavon on me this morning," I added.

Janet snorted. "When he told me that he intended to bring you in on this spy hunt, I have to admit that I argued strongly against it. Given what happened between you and Donavon last year, I was worried that you might still be too fragile to handle it. If that's true......" she let her voice trail off, the unspoken question hanging in the air. I didn't need to hear her finish her sentence. Janet was offering to have Mac replace me – she was giving me an out.

"No, but thank you. I know that I can't avoid him forever. I was just caught off guard this morning."

Part of me did want to take the easy way out and let her convince Mac that I wasn't ready to work with Donavon. But the proud part of me couldn't let Donavon win. And if I had myself removed from this assignment, Donavon would win.

"For what it's worth, he's been torn up over what happened to you," Janet said, eyeing me carefully for my reaction.

I arched one eyebrow in surprise and then drained the other half of my drink to cover my reaction. Donavon upset about what happened to me? Somehow I doubted that.

"How long has he been here?" I asked finally, extending my cup for Janet to refill its contents.

It was Janet's turn to look surprised, her green eyes full of suspicion. "As long as you have," she answered hesitantly. "Mac didn't tell you that?"

What? Why had Donavon been here for nine months? He was a Hunter. He should've been out on missions, not here doing ...whatever it was that he was doing. The knowledge that he'd been here this whole time without once attempting to see me was like a bucket of ice to the face. He really didn't care about me. The confusion must have been evident in my expression because Janet continued without waiting for me to respond.

"Well, I guess that Mac thought it best you recover in peace," Janet said hastily, refilling her empty glass.

"Why is he here?" I asked, scanning the older woman's mind to find the truth. Janet had her thoughts guarded and I didn't want to push.

"I think that Mac should be the one to tell you."

Well, that's ominous.

I spent the remainder of the day in Janet's office, catching up on everything that had happened during my confinement. She elaborated on what Mac had told me the previous night, about the covert investigation they'd launched to uncover who'd leaked my identity. Janet agreed that there was a traitor in our ranks. She agreed that my mission was targeted because I was sent directly in to Crane's lair. However, unlike Mac, Janet wasn't skilled at blocking me; I found in her mind what I assumed was in Mac's.

Both felt that there was more to it than that. They both believed that I'd been targeted, at least in part because of who I was and what my Talents were. I'd surmised as much even though Mac had been reluctant to share that detail with me.

Janet gently grilled me on my confrontation with Crane, hoping that I'd remember some detail that I'd been unable to recall when I made my official report. I hated to disappoint her, but I couldn't shed any more light on the situation. In nine months, I hadn't been able to determine what I thought about Ian Crane's insistence that he knew my father. I had no idea if that was true or just something that he'd said to through me off balance. If it was the latter, his plan had backfired. His claims about my father were what sent me over the edge, making me attack him.

Spending the day with Janet made me feel bad for losing touch with her during my Pledge year. It also made me realize how much I craved human interaction. I'd always considered myself something of a loner. When I was younger and my parents were still alive, I spent most of my time with adults. My parents had kept me out of the public eye as much as possible. They had both known that I was different. Many people felt uncomfortable around me even though they had no idea what I was capable of. But it hadn't really bothered me. I'd preferred the company of adults to that of children my own age, anyway, so it wasn't until I came to school that I truly made friends.

Well, "friends" might even be an overstatement. I made exactly one friend: Donavon. Donavon was the first person my own age that I'd ever connected with. We'd quickly become inseparable. I hadn't yet mastered my Talents when I first formed a connection with Donavon. We stopped communicating with words when we were twelve. At first, we would sit next to each other, holding hands, having our own private conversations. The only outward sign that we were communicating would be when one or both of us wouldn't be able to suppress a giggle. By the time we were thirteen, we didn't even need to be touching to keep up a continuous dialogue. We were even able to carry on full discussions at night, each in our respective dorm rooms.

When Donavon had cheated on me, I'd felt like I lost half of my heart. I didn't realize how much I depended on him until he was no longer there. I hadn't been able to actually break the connection we'd formed, but the absence of a soft song playing in my head before I went to bed, or a joke when I was called on to answer a question in class, were painful reminders of what I'd lost.

Now, after being forced into social isolation, I found that I was desperate to converse with people who weren't ordered to evaluate me. Sure, I knew that Janet was going to report anything that I said to Mac, but at least she was genuinely interested in how I was feeling and what happened to me in Nevada and didn't view me as a number in a long list of patients.

The light-responsive windows behind Janet's desk and the electric lights in her office slowly became brighter, marking the setting of the sun. My stomach gave a rumble. I'd had three glasses of Janet's liquor and no lunch. Suffice it to say, I was drunk. *Definitely time for me to make my way to the cafeteria*, I decided. Sliding myself to the edge of the slippery leather chair, I stood, swaying slightly.

"One surprise before dinner!" exclaimed Janet. Her cheeks were rosy from the liquor; she'd had also her fair share of the bottle.

"A surprise? You shouldn't have," I teased.

"Mac wasn't sure if it was a good idea, but I figured that if he was going to force you to work with Donavon, you deserved a little reward," she smiled, a mischievous twinkle in her green eyes. My curiosity was definitely piqued.

I followed Janet out of her office, through the lobby, past Pink Lipstick, and out the front door. Even though the sun was low on the horizon by this point, the air was warm, and my workout clothes were still sufficient for keeping me toasty. Or the liquor might've been the real culprit. I concentrated hard on my feet and not falling as I ran to keep up with Janet. We finally came to stop in front of the Crypto Building, one of the few places on the School's compound that I'd never been inside.

"What are we doing here?" I asked suspiciously.

"Be patient, you'll see," she smirked.

Curious, I waited while Janet entered her security information in the keypad by the door. Once she was cleared, the huge glass doors opened and we entered a giant sterile room, several white leather couches in the middle forming a square. A glass coffee table sat in the center of the square, a fluffy white rug underneath.

Janet walked past the waiting area and down an equally white and sterile hallway. We passed several closed doors that would have been undistinguishable from the walls if it weren't for the chrome door handles. Our footsteps echoed loudly in the empty corridor. We walked for what seemed like hours before the floor began to slope ever so slightly downwards. Two chrome handrails appeared and I instinctively reached out for one, holding on as the ramp became steeper.

The spotlessly clean building was so impersonal it reminded me uncomfortably of Medical. The air was cool and felt stale. I wrapped my arms tightly across my chest to ward off the unpleasant feeling. Janet appeared oblivious to the eerie emptiness of the Crypto facility as she marched forward.

At the bottom of the slope sat a large room covered with computer screens and barricaded by a thick, glass wall. When we were a foot away from the glass wall, two panes slid apart, allowing access to the main Crypto Bank. A tall girl, so thin that she could only be termed gangly, with bright red-orange hair turned in her swivel chair at the sound of our approaching footsteps. She jumped to her feet and covered the distance between us in three strides. Her lime-green eyes were shining with excitement. She flung her arms open and engulfed me in a huge hug.

"Penny!" I exclaimed as I stood on my tippy toes to return her embrace. I hadn't seen Penelope Latimore, my best friend since leaving Elite Headquarters for my ill-fated mission. Mac had forbidden communication with anyone since I'd been hurt, so I hadn't even been allowed to call her. Penny had been the same year as me in school, but we hadn't become friends until we were both Pledges. One night, I'd run into her in Hunters' Village and she'd invited me to hang out. She had been the first person besides Donavon to go out of her way to befriend me. I'd felt an instant kinship with Penny and we'd been best friends ever since.

"What are you doing here?" I squealed. I was so excited to see Penny. I'd missed her terribly over the past couple months, but I hadn't realized just how much her presence comforted me until her arms were around me.

"She's been so worried about you that she pestered Mac and me to death." It was Janet who answered. "I figured that if we didn't let her see you soon, she might explode."

"No one would tell me anything," Penny said, sounding exasperated. "Erik and Henri wouldn't talk about what happened, and everybody else kept telling me it was classified." Her eyes were wide with concern.

"I figured that we needed a Crypto here to go through the

personnel records, anyway, and since Mac needed a person we could trust to be discreet, I suggested Penny," Janet said, grinning at both of us. I beamed back. After my solitary confinement, I was overjoyed to have her again. Gretchen was great and all, but she was no Penny.

"And this," Janet declared, gesturing to a small brunette with a pixie cut and hazel eyes, "is Gemma Samuels. She will be here mostly as back up. She will still be responsible for her regular work, but since time is of the essence, she'll be able to assist with anything extra the two of you need."

"Hi, Gemma." I smiled at the slightly older girl and gave her a small wave.

"Hey, Natalia. It's nice to meet you," she replied shyly.

"Well, I'll leave you two to catch up," Janet smiled at me and Penny. "Talia, tomorrow you go to all your classes, no more freebies." I rolled my eyes, but nodded my understanding. Penny looked at me questioningly. I just shook my head. *Don't ask*, I mouthed.

"I was just about to get some dinner. Would you guys like me to pick up anything?" Gemma asked, standing to go as well.

"No, thanks, I already ate," Penny told her. I shook my head, even as my stomach grumbled.

"So, tell me EVERYTHING." Penny turned to me as soon as Janet and Gemma made their exits through the glass doors.

"I don't even know where to begin," I said, shaking my head.

"If you don't want to talk about it......"she trailed off. The look of open curiosity on Penny's face told me all that I needed to know. She wanted desperately not to pry, but her curiosity and longing were written all over her face. I was going to tell her that I didn't want to talk about it, but before I could communicate the thought, my mouth began to form the beginning of the story.

Penny had been part of the Crypto team that intercepted the information regarding Crane's trip to Nevada, and therefore knew the basic details of my assignment, so I decided to start with meeting Kyle, the guy I'd manipulated into taking me to Crane's temporary estate. Once on the grounds, I'd ordered Kyle to stay in his bedroom while I searched for information. In Crane's office, I downloaded the contents of his computer to my communicator. When I finished pilfering the office, I moved on to the basement. I told Penny about the strange resistance that I'd encountered when I tried the basement door. It had been like trying to reach into a blocked mind – my Talents had been ineffectual against the security.

I took her through my physical attack on one of Crane's men in the basement hallway, rage mingled with shame nearly consuming me when I recounted how I hadn't seen the second man until he plunged the syringe into my neck. That was the chemical injection that now caused my seizures. I relived the panic that I'd felt waking up shackled to a bed, staring at the man who'd killed my parents. Penny listened with rapt attention as I told her about my conversation with Crane, gently probing me on the exact nature of our exchange. Despite my earlier resolve to work out the meaning of Crane's words on my own, I told Penny about his claims that he'd known my father. Her eyes grew rounder, but she didn't comment.

I faltered in my story when I reached the part about being shot. That was the last thing that I remembered. I couldn't really recall my escape. Everything that had transpired from the time the bullet entered my back until right before I lost consciousness was blurry. No matter how hard I tried, I couldn't grasp the memories that eluded me; it was like trying to collect raindrops in my hands.

I had no recollection of stealing a hover vehicle from Crane's home, but the extraction team had found and disposed of one. I had no recollection of driving nearly one hundred miles to the clearing where I'd been found. I had no recollection of cutting the tracking unit out of my hip to activate it, but I now had a two-inch scar to prove that I had, and that was the signal that the team had used to locate me. I had no recollection of stumbling into the woods and covering my body with wet leaves. These were all details that Mac pieced together for me over the ensuing months.

Once I'd activated the tracking unit, a signal had been sent to the Crypto Bank at Elite Headquarters. The Crypto on duty had immediately contacted Mac, who sent out an extraction order to all of the Operatives in the area. Luckily, a medi-craft with cloaking capabilities had been able to respond in under an hour. Later, Mac had told me that I'd lost more blood than the medi-craft had on board. He'd arranged for the craft to land in a small town in Kansas with a fairly advanced Medical facility.

The doctors in Kansas had done everything in their power to stabilize my condition. But the loss of blood, coupled with the internal damage from the bullet, had left me in a precarious state. Two weeks passed before I was deemed "fit-to-transport." I'd been flown on one of the Agency's luxury crafts, complete with my own entourage of medical personnel, back to Maryland, to the McDonough School. Once on campus, I remained in the Medical facilities for nearly three months. The first couple weeks had been touch-and-go as the medics fought to neutralize the effects of the foreign drugs in my blood stream and stop the seizures.

I spent the following weeks slowly gaining the strength back in my legs. The medics on the hover craft had saved my life, but they didn't have the resources or the technology to repair the nerve and tissue damage caused by the bullet. The Medics at School had done everything they could, too, but too much time had passed for tissue regeneration. It had been up to me to slowly learn how to walk again. After several long months of intense regeneration therapy, Mac took me home to his house, where I'd stayed until this morning.

There was one part of my long journey that was seared into my mind: Erik's letter. I'd thought a lot about his words while sitting in my old bedroom, but Erik's letter was not something that I had shared with anyone. It wasn't part of my official report. I didn't want to share his past with others. It would be a gross violation of his trust. I might have been willing to trust Penny with Crane's admissions about my father, but I couldn't bring myself to tell her about Erik's letter.

Penny listened with rapt attention to my whole story, her eyes wide and unblinking the whole time. Her green eyes filled with tears that began to spill over and mascara streaked down her cheeks like black snakes. Her front teeth bit into her lower lip so hard that blood began to pool around them.

"Don't cry, Penny," I said softly. "It's over. I'm better."

"You could have died," she sobbed, smearing her makeup further.

"That's a risk with any mission I go on," I said evenly, reaching out to take her hand. "Besides, I was foolish. I let my guard down when I thought I was in control of the situation. It won't happen again." This only made her cry harder. I reached over and hugged her.

"You smell like liquor," she choked, her voice muffled by my shoulder.

"I had a little meltdown this morning and Janet thought that a drink might help me relax," I replied, laughing.

"What happened?" she sniffed.

"Donavon," I replied, rolling my eyes in an attempt to cover my unease. Penny pulled away and looked at me, shock written all over her face.

"Donavon is here?" she asked, wiping her nose.

"Uh......well...yeah. He's an Instructor at the School. I think he's undercover trying to figure out if one of the other Instructors is the leak. He's part of the same team we are."

"Oh, I didn't know. The Director just called me two days ago and said to pack my bags, that I'd been temporarily reassigned. I met with him briefly yesterday, but he didn't mention Donavon. He just told me what I was supposed to do. I didn't even know that he was forming like a team or whatever," Penny explained.

"When did Donavon leave Headquarters?" I asked uneasily.

"I don't know," she said, averting her eyes. "He was on a mission when you were hurt, and he never came back. Harris told me that he'd been suspended from the Hunters for a while. Some people are saying that he was too upset to come back after what happened to you."

"Upset? Over me getting hurt?" I laughed at the absurdity of the rumor even though Penny's words nearly mirrored the sentiments that Janet had expressed earlier.

"Well, it's no secret that you two dated, and a Pledge was assigned to Harris and Arden's team at the beginning of the year, so......," she let her voice trail off.

"Right, but after the breakup, we didn't speak. He couldn't have been that upset." The breakup had ended in me destroying the cabin that he shared with his Hunting teammates, so I seriously doubted that my injuries caused him to leave the Hunters. Donavon had wanted to be a Hunter for even longer than I had.

"I don't know, Tal. There are a lot of rumors swirling around about what happened to you and why Donavon left, but no one actually knows the truth." Penny searched my face as if the reason for Donavon's presence was written in the wrinkles on my forehead.

I let Penny's words sink in. *What was the truth?* Sure, if the situation had been reversed, I would've been worried about Donavon, but I wouldn't have left the Hunters.

My stomach was starting to feel queasy, reminding me that I hadn't eaten since breakfast with Gretchen. Or maybe it was a reminder of how much Donavon's presence had affected me that morning. It was only been the second time that I'd laid eyes on my first love since the night I'd caught him with the other girl.

"How's Erik? Have you seen him much?" I asked hesitantly. After Donavon and I had broken up, I'd gotten involved with one of my teammates: Erik. Much like my relationship with Donavon, it had sort of ended in disaster. Right before I boarded the plane to Nevada, our other teammate, Henri, gave me a letter from Erik.

That was the letter that I'd read just before passing out in the clearing. Unlike with Donavon, I desperately wanted to see Erik, but I wasn't positive the feelings were mutual.

"I've seen him a couple of times," she answered with a small smile.

"How's he doing?" I repeated. He was the only person I missed more than Penny. My inability to get Donavon out of my head had led to a colossal fight between me and Erik, culminating in him storming out of my room the night before I'd gone to find Crane.

"He's good. You know, he's Erik," she shrugged, but didn't offer any further explanation. She didn't need to; I knew what "being Erik" entailed.

"So he's frequenting the city, boozing and womanizing?" I laughed even though I didn't find any of that the least bit humorous. In fact, the thought of Erik with another girl twisted ugly knots of jealousy throughout my entire body, causing my peripheral vision to go red. I knew that it wasn't exactly fair. I'd been the one who was still hung up on my ex-boyfriend, but I couldn't help the way that I felt. Erik hadn't tried to contact me at all. I guess that his attention span really was as short as the rumors claimed; as soon as I was out of sight, I was out of his thoughts.

"Um, well, he goes into the city a lot," she answered evasively. "But I think that he really misses you."

The weight that had settled on my chest lifted slightly, and a glimmer of hope broke through the sadness like a ray of sunshine. "Did he say that?" I asked.

"Well, not in so many words, but he's been really mopey, and he asks about you whenever I see him," Penny admitted, bobbing her head up and down encouragingly.

"That's good, I guess," I tried to match her enthusiasm, but Erik asking Penny about me and Erik actually calling me were very different things. Petty as it was, I wanted him to be pining in his room, missing me.

"How's Harris?" I asked, wanting to change the subject to something more pleasant.

"He's good ...I guess" Penny said regretfully. "We kind of broke up a couple of months back."

"I'm sorry to hear that," I said honestly. She'd really liked him when they'd first started dating, and they were really cute together, so I was bummed the relationship hadn't worked out. "What happened?"

"Oh, you know ...it kinda just ran its course. We're still friendly and all, but Harris wasn't really looking for a serious relationship," she rolled her eyes. "Besides, there are too many other great looking boys running around Elite Headquarters to stay tied down to just one." Penny winked at me. Since becoming friends with Penny, I'd noticed her fondness for crushing on guys; even though she said that it was Harris who didn't want a serious relationship, it wouldn't surprise me to learn that Penny really hadn't been looking for one either.

We sat for a couple long moments in silence, neither of us really sure what to say to the other. It wasn't uncomfortable, we were both just absorbing the revelations of the evening.

"I should probably be heading back to my room." I smiled apologetically at Penny.

"Already? You just got here!" she protested.

"I know, but I haven't eaten, and I need to run by Medical," I replied. She looked so disappointed, I almost told her that I would stay a little longer, but the hollowness in my stomach made me change my mind. I was pretty sure that the ache I was feeling had nothing to do with my lack of nourishment and everything to do with my longing for Erik.

"Tomorrow night?" she asked hopefully.

"Of course, I'll be over after dinner." I smiled at her reassuringly. I gave Penny one last hug before making my return trip through the glass doors and down the sterile white hallway.

Chapter Five

The evening had grown cool and damp, the moon just a sliver overhead but clearly visible in the cloudless sky. I kept my eyes titled upwards, gazing at the stars as I made my way to Medical. It was late and the receptionist was long gone. I wound through the corridors and found Dr. Thistler in her office.

"Hello, Natalia," she greeted me when I knocked lightly on the open door. "You are late."

"Sorry, I've been busy," I mumbled. She pursed her thin lips in disapproval. She rose from her desk and gestured for me to sit in an empty chair. I did as I was told and watched as Dr. Thistler opened a cabinet and withdrew several vials. With deft movements, she filled a syringe with my medication. I rolled my sleeve back and rested my arm on her desk. Dr. Thistler bent over me and plunged the tip of the needle into the crook on my elbow.

I sighed. "Thanks."

"Please come earlier tomorrow," Dr. Thistler responded. I nodded and scurried out of her office.

The School grounds were deserted. It was past the student curfew. I reached the Instructor's dorm quickly and climbed the three flights of stairs and found my new room. As promised, my bag of clothes sat on the end of a small bed that was covered with crisp white sheets and a thin white blanket. I realized how tired I actually was as soon as I laid eyes on the bed; this was the longest that I'd managed to stay awake in months, so this shouldn't have come as a surprise. I wasn't sure if my perpetual fatigue was a result of my health or extreme boredom.

Rummaging through the bag for something to sleep in, I sent waves of gratitude toward Gretchen when I pulled out a faded gray t-shirt and a pair of navy sweatpants that were devoid of any shape. I quickly shed the workout clothes that I'd been wearing all day, leaving them in a heap on the floor, and exchanged them for the comfortable pajamas that Gretchen had rescued from my room at Elite headquarters.

The sheets were cool and scratchy against my exposed skin. I curled into a ball, hugging my knees to my chest, trying to conserve body heat. My last conscious thought of the evening was to have Gretchen send a real blanket.

The next morning, I woke before the sun was in the sky and tried in vain to go back to sleep. All of the thoughts and feelings that the alcohol suppressed the day before began swimming to the surface of my mind: the unease from seeing Donavon, the anger at Mac for making me unknowingly walk into that situation, the pain of reliving the events in Nevada, the frustration from the memories that still eluded me, the longing to see Erik, and the worry that feelings weren't being reciprocated. After several failed attempts to quiet the scenes playing in my head, I got out of bed and dressed for a run.

I donned the first workout clothes that I found in my bag and gathered my hair into a tight ponytail, then left my room.

Bright stars were still scattered across the ink-colored sky, forming a dazzling map of unexplored territory. The chill in the air brought my senses to life. I inhaled deeply, filling my lungs with the early morning dew that hung in the air, and moisture bathed my face and arms like a cold blanket.

Over the past few months, my weakened condition had caused walking to be an unwelcome chore and jogging to be torture. Now, with my head bursting from the overload of emotions, my atrophied muscles craved the exercise; the physical exertion and pain felt liberating. After only ten minutes, my breathing was labored, and my t-shirt clung to me, damp with sweat.

I cleared my mind of my current surroundings, and the trees, already shedding their leaves in preparation for winter, disappeared. The thick green grass beneath my feet ceased to exist. Instead, my mind cycled through images from my memories like a slideshow.

I saw myself positioned between two handrails, the effort of lifting one foot excruciating, the muscles in my leg tensing, readying themselves for what they knew was next, but next never came. I ran harder. *I saw the hallway of Crane's basement and the man with the syringe. I felt the chemicals heavy in my veins.* I ran harder. *I saw Donavon cowering in the corner of a room, hands over his head, pleading with me to stop, electricity crackled in my fingers and toes.* I ran harder. *Mac squatting next to my hospital bed, our eyes locked as he told me what I already knew: Ian Crane killed my parents.* I ran harder. *I saw myself crouched in a closet, peering through the wooden slats at the men in black mercilessly murdering my parents.* I ran harder. *I saw the hotel room, windows blown out, bodies of faceless men scattered around me, enclosing me in a circle; all dead.* I ran harder.

The Instructor's dorm was in sight. My lungs were on fire, every breath felt like a knife plunging deeper in to the flesh between my ribs. My legs screamed in protest as I pushed them each additional step. The memories had been replaced by white electrical snow accompanied by an increasing buzzing sound. The weight of my sweat-soaked clothing was threatening to drag me under the tidal wave of exhaustion I was riding. Salt stung my eyes as I attempted to wipe it away with the back of my dirty, slippery forearm. I was mere feet from the back entrance when my legs finally won the battle with my mind and gave out completely.

I wrapped my arms around my torso, trying to get my breathing under control. My head spun so fast that I wasn't entirely sure which way was up anymore. I fell over, my cheek pressed against the cold grass, letting it draw the heat from my body. The world began to right itself and I took a couple of deep breaths for good measure before pushing myself up on all fours.

I felt his presence before he spoke. "Go away, Donavon," I said quietly, hoping that I sounded threatening.

"You don't look so good, Tals," he replied, sounding like he actually cared. "You need help getting up?"

"I said, go away." This time the undertones in my voice were definitely closer to pleading than threatening. Donavon came up behind me. He hesitated, but I knew that his intention was to guide me to my feet. As soon as he made his move, I summoned the last of my strength and kicked my right leg straight up and back. My foot made solid contact with his chest, and he lost his balance, stumbling backward.

"Suit yourself," he mumbled as he walked away. I smiled. I might be totally out of shape, but Donavon would definitely have a bruise. Sometimes, it's the little things in life that are the most gratifying. My satisfaction was short lived; I could still feel Donavon's presence when I began vomiting.

I was so busy regurgitating the previous day's breakfast that I didn't even notice Janet until I felt her hand on my back. I tensed.

"What happened to you?" Janet asked worriedly. I relaxed at the sound of her voice.

"Oh, you know, I just went for a little run." I smiled weakly up at her, wiping my mouth with the back of my hand.

"You're soaked through. How far is a little run?" she asked alarmed. Her hand gently stroked my tangled curls.

"I left at sunrise," I replied sheepishly. Janet grumbled, then wrapped her arm around my waist and carefully lifted me to my feet. I felt a little weak in the knees, but managed to stay upright with her help. I leaned against her gratefully, letting her support most of my weight.

"You might want to have somebody clean that up." I nodded

to the grass.

"I'll get right on it." She rolled her eyes.

Janet guided me up the stairs and into my room before demanding I shower. I still had a small part of my dignity left, so I refused her help to the bathroom. As soon as the cool water hit my face, the stomach queasiness subsided, the cold sweat trickling down my back warmed, and the uncontrollable shaking in my limbs slowed. I stayed in the shower until Janet banged on the door, forcing me out.

When I finally exited the small bathroom wrapped in my fluffy robe, I found Janet sitting at my desk with coffee, water, and a plate piled with slices of toast.

She rose when she saw me and motioned for me to sit. I dutifully complied and wasted no time replenishing the calories that I'd unwillingly purged from my body. The bread was soaked with butter that poured into my mouth with each bite. The coffee was too hot and a little on the bitter side, but I was too impatient to wait for it to cool or to bother with sugar. I felt the last hints of uneasiness leave my stomach and my head pounded a little less. By the sixth piece of toast, I was as good as new.

Janet watched me devour my breakfast without comment. Instead, she picked up my brush and began winding my long dark hair into a braid down my back. The motherly gesture comforted me. By the time she finished, I had consumed the entire loaf of bread.

"Better?" she asked once I'd wiped the excess butter from my hands.

"Like a million bucks." I smiled.

"Good, get dressed. Be downstairs in ten," she directed in a gentle voice.

"You don't need to walk me. I can find it on my own," I replied. Now that I was once again in control of my gag reflex, I was more than a little embarrassed at the condition she'd found me in.

"I'm not worried about you finding it. Get dressed." Her voice had a slight edge to it now. She'd expected my reaction to Donavon's unwelcome presence yesterday, but like she'd promised last night, no more freebies.

I dressed quickly in black stretch pants, a tight white tank top, and sneakers, still damp from my morning run. Grabbing a light jacket, I set off to meet Janet out front. At the last second, I remembered that Mac had promised to send the personnel files of the Instructors that I was assisting. I hurried back to grab my communicator before leaving the room.

Janet escorted me just far enough to ensure that I arrived at Donavon's class. I could feel her gaze until she was sure that Donavon had seen me and my opportunity for escape had passed.

Donavon gave a slight nod in my direction as I approached. I didn't reciprocate. Instead, I took a seat on the ground in the back of the mat, folding my legs underneath me. Donavon began by describing, in excruciating detail, each move that he wanted the students to work on. He droned on for so long that I actually thought he might break down the name origin of each skill. I guess my musings were louder than I'd intended because Donavon stopped mid-sentence.

"Enough talk," he said, smiling at the class. "If I could get my *assistant,* Ms. Lyons, to come up front, we can demonstrate each of these maneuvers." I would have known, even if he didn't have a shit eating grin on his face, that I was about to be sorry that I hadn't kept my thoughts to myself. I slowly made my way to the front of the class, giving a small wave and a half-smile to the seated students. They stared back, wide-eyed.

Standing next to him, the two of us made quite the pair. Donavon was lean and muscular, biceps straining the sleeves of his shirt, his forearms corded with sinewy muscles. I was small and wiry in comparison. Prior to being shot, I'd actually had a fair amount of muscle; now, I was practically skin and bones. Donavon's height was impressive next to an average-sized person;

he must have looked larger than life standing next to me. More than a few of his pupils looked skeptical about Donavon using me as a demonstration dummy.

"Do you want to suit up, Lyons?" he asked once I'd taken my position opposite him. When students at the School practiced, they often wore suits made of a synthetic material that had been developed in some Agency test facility. The suits thin and fit the body like a second skin. The fabric wasn't exactly breathable, but was nearly impossible to penetrate; it dulled the sensation of a hit, so it felt more like a hard pillow than a fist or foot. The suits allowed students to practice with weapons ranging from attack batons to small knives without causing each other too much bodily harm.

While on missions, Hunters wore a high-tech version of it called an adapti-suit. These both prevented injury by being nearly impenetrable, and camouflaged the wearer by replicating the surroundings. On my first Hunt, I'd found one of the exceptions for piercing the fabric the hard way; nothing keeps out a poisoned tip dagger.

For practice drills like the one that Donavon wanted to run, the partner being used as a punching bag often won't wear a full suit, but rather pads on their thighs and core. The pads serve the dual purposes of both giving the attacker somewhere to aim and protecting the wearer. I knew that I should at least put on the pads. But after Donavon found me in such a vulnerable position just hours earlier, I felt the need to show him that I was every bit as hardcore now as I had been before my incident. So, instead of moving to pull on the pads, I met his eyes and answered, "I don't need one."

Outwardly, Donavon's eyes gave a small flicker of something that looked almost like concern. Inwardly, he was all irritation. "*Don't be stupid, Talia,*" he mentally chastised me.

"*We spar all the time without suits,*" I mentally shot back.

"*You haven't sparred in almost a year. You're not conditioned to take hits anymore.*" His mental voice sounded impatient.

"*How's your chest feel?*" I snapped, my eyes darting to the space where I'd kicked him. Baiting him was probably a bad idea, but I couldn't help myself.

He scoffed with irritation, then turned his attention to the class and began going through the motions of the first combination of kicks. He first demonstrated each one in the air, then faced me and demonstrated what each one looked like when it made contact with another person. He was clearly still annoyed with me, for ...well, honestly, probably for a lot of things.

His first kick struck my thigh with a force so jarring, it reverberated through every bone in my body. My face remained neutral, not betraying any of the pain I felt, but inside, I screamed, and a long string of expletives escaped my mind.

"*Should've worn the suit,*" Donavon shot back. His tone was haughty, but his blue eyes were wary. A brief flash of tenderness warmed his harsh expression. I felt a small flutter in my stomach; damn, I really hated him.

I guess he decided that I'd learned my lesson after the first kick because he let up on me for the rest of the demonstration. While the students practiced, I wandered through the pairs, correcting technique and trying not to limp. My thigh was throbbing. After what seemed like the entire morning, though actually only ninety minutes, Donavon finally dismissed class. If I'd been an ordinary assistant, I would've stayed to help put away the practice mats and pads. But I wasn't. Both my leg and my pride were stinging, so instead, I just left along with the students.

Chapter Six

Students at the McDonough School have six classes a day, alternating their days between physical and intellectual lessons. The students that I had in class this morning would continue on to small weapons training and defensive combat techniques before lunch, then offensive combat techniques class, large weapons, and finally Talent training after lunch.

Unlike the students, my second period was not a physical one. Instead, I was assigned to assist Annalise Cleary in her *Prevalent Languages of the World* class. On the short walk to her classroom, I glanced through her record. I immediately noticed the red flag in her file; Annalise's husband, Jerald Mathias, defected to Colorado five years after their marriage to join the Coalition. Annalise had been thoroughly investigated at the time and cleared of any wrongdoing. She'd reverted back to her maiden name and continued working for TOXIC.

I found her room with mere seconds to spare. I quietly walked through the doorway and ducked into the back of the classroom. Not wanting to interrupt, I decided to wait until after her lesson to introduce myself. I leaned against the wall, surveying the class, and immediately felt self-conscious.

I had forgotten that there was a reason why the students alternated days between physical and academic classes. My stretchy pants and tight workout shirt had fit right in during

Donavon's combat training, but I looked wildly out of place in this classroom, where all the students were wearing khaki slacks, crisp white dress shirts, and navy blazers. Instructor Cleary was wearing a red skirt suit with the collar of a floral-print shirt peeking out from under her formfitting jacket. *Well, crap*. Not only was I inappropriately dressed, I was willing to bet that I smelled. I'd have to remember a change of clothes tomorrow.

Annalise Cleary began class as I wrapped myself in the lightweight jacket that I grabbed on my way out of my room. She gave brief instructions in Spanish, then the students opened their bags and began working from glossy books. After she was satisfied that all of the children understood her directions, she finally turned her attention to me. She motioned me over to the desk with a wave of her hand.

"You must be Natalia Lyons," she said warmly. Up close, I noticed that she was much older than she'd appeared from the back of the room. Lines crinkled around her blue eyes and the corners of her mouth when she smiled. Her nearly black hair, pulled back in a tight bun at the nape of her neck, had a handful of gray streaks interspersed.

I held out my hand. "Yes, you can call me Talia." I returned her smile, grateful for a friendly face after my encounter with Donavon.

"Are you proficient in languages?" she inquired. Hmmm, I didn't know. Was I supposed to be? Mac didn't really specify.

"Actually, I am." I decided that answering truthfully was best, and languages had been my best classroom subject. I was fluent in most major languages as well as some that were more obscure; it was easy to learn languages when you were a mind reader.

"Very good. I'll give you the answer key for the assignments that I need you to grade, and you just have to see if the student's answers match mine," she replied, still smiling.

"Great," I tried to match her enthusiasm, but the thought of being relegated to grading papers made me feel more like crying. I failed to see how this was a productive use of my time. I reminded myself that remedial tasks were an unfortunate, but necessary, part of this assignment; I set to work.

I spent the rest of the class sitting at Annalise Cleary's desk, comparing test papers to the answer key. Every red mark that I made on a student's paper made me wonder how this was helping find the person who leaked my identity.

Once Instructor Cleary's attention was diverted, I risked skimming the rest of her file for pertinent information.

Annalise Bernice Cleary was born forty-two years ago in Atlanta, Georgia, the only child of Jonah and Eloise Cleary. The report listed her as an Elite-level Electrical Manipulator. In her junior year, she'd taken three placement tests for the Hunters, the Crypto Division, and the Weapons Division. She'd placed with the Weapons Division and received a position there after the successful completion of her Pledge year.

After four years of developing and manufacturing advanced weapons, Annalise requested a transfer to the School after her husband's defection. The transfer had been approved since she was cleared of any involvement.. Following her reassignment, she put in her dues as an assistant Instructor before being receiving own class seven years ago.

The students seemed to genuinely like her, always giving her favorable reviews. Janet also appeared pleased with her teaching abilities and had nothing but praise for the woman in her annual reviews.

Annalise had never remarried after her husband's defection, and I can't say I blamed her. After a betrayal like that, I wouldn't have either. Other than her ex-husband having proven to be a traitor, there was nothing suspect that jumped out in her file. Well, nothing except her Talent Ranking.

Elite-level Electrical Manipulators weren't rare, and I'd come across a handful in my time at School and with Toxic. They all shared a unique brain pattern, one that I hadn't felt in my brief interactions with Instructor Cleary. All exceptionally strong Talents gave off a signal of sorts, emitting a crackle that felt like a tiny shock to my system. When I formed a strong enough connection with someone to read their mind, the impulses were stronger and sometimes even uncomfortable. Annalise didn't radiate so much as a spark. I made a mental note to double check the information with Penny later that evening.

After World Languages, I was off to aid an Instructor named Cadence Choi in her defensive combat techniques class.

From a quick look at Cadence's file, I learned that she was a twenty-four-year-old Mid-level Light Manipulator from Brooklyn, New York. She was the youngest of Clarence and Raven Choi's three children. Her middle brother, Daniel, was a Low-level poly-morph who currently served as a guard for one of TOXIC's weapons facilities. Randy, her oldest brother had been a guard at Tramblewood Corrections Facility, the prison where Toxic housed the highest-priority offenders. He'd been charged with treason and jailed after helping an inmate escape. The inmate had been Ian Crane's sister. Interesting, very interesting.

After Randy's fall from grace, the entire Choi family had been scrutinized, but they'd all been found innocent of any nefarious deeds. Despite that, both Cadence and Daniel's movements were still heavily monitored. I would have to remember to ask Penny to pull Daniel's file for me.

Thankfully, I arrived at Cadence's class with plenty of time to spare. I walked straight up to her and introduced myself.

"Hi, Cadence? My name is Talia, Talia Lyons," I said, extending my hand to her in greeting.

"I was expecting you yesterday," she replied, pointedly staring at my fingers like they might bite her.

"Sorry, my paperwork had some problems," I lied. My personal situation with Donavon was none of her business.

Cadence Choi was not much larger, or much older, than I was. She wore baggy gray sweatpants and a white short-sleeve shirt. All of her facial features were scrunched. Her eyes could only have been described as beady, her pupils so large that they looked like black orbs, set deeply in her face. Her nose was small and very turned up at the end, like she had once made a face in reaction to something malodorous and her nose had subsequently been stuck that way. Her mouth was small and puckered, like she was ready to kiss somebody at any moment.

"Were you in the student's Offensive Combat Techniques class this morning?" she asked. I nodded in reply. "Good. We will be learning the defensive maneuvers that correspond to the combinations Donavon taught this morning."

I didn't need to delve into Cadence's mind to know that she had a major crush on Donavon. Her beady little eyes lit up like a firework when she said his name. I had an overwhelming urge to giggle.

"Roger that," I said instead. She gave me a hard look, trying to decide if I was mocking her.

I hadn't established enough of a connection to get much from her mind, but I could almost see the waves of dislike rolling off her body as she looked me up and down. I was definitely off to a slow start making friends.

I studied Cadence as she demonstrated several defensive moves, grudgingly watching her fluid motions and perfect form. I hated to admit it, even to myself, but she was very good. The mastery of her skills wasn't lost on the students either; they all observed her with rapt attention, seemingly unable to tear their eyes away.

"Ms. Lyons, if you could help me out?" she called to me.

"Um, sure," I mumbled, moving to the front of the practice mats.

"I need you to walk through the skills Donavon taught this morning. Can you handle that?" she asked in a short, clipped voice.

"I can," I snapped before remembering that I needed to gain her confidence, not make her dislike me more than she clearly did.

Starting slowly, I aimed light jabs at her midsection, letting her block my weak attempts. As the demonstration progressed, I realized that she was fast – really fast. And she was responding to my slow movements with more force and aggression than necessary. Her attitude irritated me and I picked up my game. Soon, we were sparring for real, both of us panting and sweaty. Not only was Cadence fast, she was almost as good as I was. Fearing that she would get the best of me, and not wanting to be shown up in front of a bunch of students, I decided to show her exactly how good I was. My next movement landed her flat on her back.

Normally, I wouldn't have stopped there; I would've pinned her to the ground until she conceded my victory. However, the audible gasp from the pupils in attendance brought me back to reality. So, instead of claiming my win, I reached out my hand in an attempt to help her to her feet. Her beady black eyes were murderous as she stared up at me from the ground. I recoiled at her open hostility. She reached for my hand but instead of grasping it to let me help her up, her own arm – from fingertips to shoulder – disappeared in front of my eyes. My fingers grasped air. I'd braced myself to pull her to her feet, and her trick had caught me off guard, and I stumbled.

Several of the students snickered. Cadence's lips curled into a snarl as she glared at me through the pieces of her black hair that had escaped her ponytail during our scuffle.

"Light Manipulator," she said quietly. I'd known that; I just hadn't anticipated her using her ability to embarrass me. Cadence moved from where I'd fallen on my hands and knees and began assigning practice partners to the class. I had to bite my lip as the anger and humiliation at her having gotten the last word threatened to cloud my better judgment. Taking three deep, calming breaths, I plastered a smile on my face. I spent the remainder of class suppressing my desire to attack the girl.

After class, I made my way to the Instructor cafeteria.

Gretchen had assured me that the food here would be better here than the students', but I wasn't optimistic as I entered and saw long plastic tables anchored to the floor by long plastic uncomfortable benches.

I joined the end of the line of teachers and assistants waiting to load their plates with mystery meat and crispy lettuce from the food bar. The chicken was covered in thick, brown gravy, and actually smelled amazing. My mouth watered and my stomach rumbled as I searched for an empty table. I knew that I should join some of my colleagues and try and dig around a little, but I wasn't really in the mood. Finding all of the tables already occupied, I chose the least hostile looking option: a small blonde boy with his nose buried in a book.

"Mind if I sit?" I asked, approaching his side. The boy looked up at me and his eyes widened, taking on a glazed expression.

"Sure," he squeaked in reply. "I mean, sure, it's okay if you sit. Not sure, I mind if you sit," he felt the need to clarify.

"Thanks," I smiled, regretting my choice. *This kid was definitely in the Crypto department*, I thought to myself. If his stringy, blonde hair and paler-than-normal complexion weren't dead giveaways, his rambling lack of interpersonal skills were.

"Talia," I said, holding out my hand to him as I slid onto the bench. "I just started here as an assistant."

"Ernest Tate," he replied, extending one freckled hand. "I am an Instructor for Advanced Crypto Techniques class." Ha. I knew it.

"Ah, so you're a Brain," I said, giving him a knowing grin. Brain was a slang term for a Higher Reasoning Talent. I hadn't taken any advanced crypto classes – or any at all – while I was in school, but Penny obviously had. I added Ernest's name to my growing list of files to be pulled. A Brain could definitely be the leak.

"Yeah, I guess I am," his face reddened with embarrassment. I decided to take a look into his thoughts.

"How long have you been teaching here?" I asked as I took a bite of my ranch-drenched salad and latched onto his hazel eyes.

"Just a year," he answered.

"Where were you stationed before that?" I continued. Ernest looked young, but I didn't think that he was young enough to have only graduated the previous year.

"A computer development facility in Scranton, Pennsylvania," he answered.

"How long were you there?" I pressed, swallowing the lettuce and picking up my knife to cut the chicken.

"Two years," he replied, playing with the gravy on his own plate. With every answer he gave, I got a better feel for his brain patterns. Like Electrical Manipulators, Higher Reasoning Talents had unique patterns. Ernest's synapses fired so rapidly that it made me dizzy, and the overactive brain functioning was exactly what I'd expect from a strong Higher Reasoning.

"Why did you leave?" I asked. If he thought that I was being noscy, he didn't let on; he actually seemed pleased that a girl was taking an interest in him. I gathered that Ernest didn't have a lot of friends.

"The pressure was too much," he admitted, his face going scarlet as he averted his eyes. I smiled sympathetically at him. He was an easy read, not much of a mental guard, and was telling the truth, at least about the pressure being too intense.

"What did you do before you came here?" he asked, visibly sagging with relief when he no longer had the added weight of my mind on his shoulders.

"I was ...well, I was a Hunter Pledge," I answered after a long pause.

"Man, you must know all about pressure, then, huh?" It wasn't really a question as much as a statement, but I felt the need to answer anyway.

"Yeah, I guess you could say that's why I left my previous post, too. I basically broke down on my solo mission." I tried to look like the admission made me uneasy, which wasn't hard because it was basically the truth; I had broken down on my solo mission, at least physically.

After lunch ended, Ernest walked with me to the academic building before saying our goodbyes. He might be a suspect, but at least Ernest seemed to like me. That was more than I could say for some of the others whom I'd encountered thus far.

Chapter Seven

My first class of the afternoon was Talent History taught by Thad Wietz. My interrogation of Ernest had left me little time to search Thad's file for his red flag. I walked into the classroom and made my way to the front of the room to introduce myself, blind to Mac's reasons for including him on my short list of suspects.

The first thing that I noticed about Thad was his size. He was huge. Next to Thad, even Donavon would've looked like a child. He had a mess of reddish-brown hair, pulled back in a short ponytail, and his piercing green eyes bore down on me as I went to shake his enormous hand. When he spoke, he had an odd accent that I thought might be Scottish. I was willing to bet that his lineage was what had landed him on my suspect list.

Thad seemed friendly enough. He asked me to sit in the back of the class and just observe for the day. Happy to oblige, I tuned out his lecture on the Great Contamination, and observed the students in the class instead. Nobody stood out as being particularly devious, but I imagined that listening to history lectures probably dulled even the sharpest of criminal masterminds into a near comatose state.

Thad dismissed class when my own mind had been sufficiently numbed and my eyes burned from the effort of trying not to blink, for fear my eyes might not be able to force themselves back open. I nearly knocked over my desk in my eagerness to leave the room. History had been my least favorite subject while in school, and I truly believed that Mac chose this class for me more as punishment for my attitude since the incident, and less because he actually suspected Thad.

Thankfully, my last two classes of the day were both physical. The first was a small caliber weapons class, which happened to be my specialty. Guns were never my favorite, less so since being on the receiving end of a bullet. Despite that, I could hit a moving target from further away than most thanks to Henri's master tutelage. I was proficient with a bow and arrow, but rarely had the patience to put such weapons into practice. Hand knives, throwing stars, and daggers- that was where I excelled.

The Small Weapons Instructor was Griffin Knight, and no introductions were necessary; Griffin had been my Small Weapons Instructor when I was a student. I had been looking forward to this class all day. Griffin had been a teacher at the School for decades, and I'd started training with him when I was just eleven.

When I first saw Griffin's name on my schedule, I'd been shocked that Mac assigned me to assist in his class. I desperately hoped that I wasn't here because Mac really thought that Griffin was the leak, but instead because he thought that I deserved a treat after all the crap instructors I'd endured. I'd always liked Griffin.

My fears were put to rest the moment I opened his file. Instead of personnel information, Mac's secretary had included a note, indicating that I was actually to be an aide for Griffin. It also said that Mac wanted me to assist Griffin because I would be an asset to his students, most of whom were extremely strong Talents, likely to be placed with the Hunters or the Military Police.

Griffin's face lit up when he saw me. "Class, we have a real treat," he exclaimed, clapping his big hands together in a gleeful gesture. "The Director and Headmistress have found an assistant Instructor whose experience will be invaluable to us." Griffin's white head bobbed up and down enthusiastically as he spoke.

"Don't make promises that I can't deliver on," I teased

Griffin.

"Everyone, I would like to introduce you to my star pupil, Natalia." I waved at the class, feeling more than a little embarrassed. I surveyed the doubtful faces of the seven seated Talents. No surprise there; they were skeptical. Apparently, Griffin saw the same thing that I did.

"I think a little demonstration might be in order." He winked at me.

"I'm a little rusty," I warned, fearing that my weapons skills had gone the way of my running abilities. At least I hoped throwing knives was unlikely to make me vomit.

"Duly noted, my dear," he replied, with a knowing smile. He thought that I was being modest; little did he know. "Pick your poison."

Griffin had laid out a number of small weapons on tables set up behind him. I walked slowly from table to table, drinking in the varying choices. After making a complete circuit, I opted for a belt that I secured around my hips, with two six-inch blades. The knives had hand-holds and weren't ideal for throwing but great for lashing out at an opponent. Both hand-holds had a thumb release button that snapped open, allowing you to either throw the blade or just drop it if necessary. Next, I selected an ankle holster with four throwing blades and a thigh holster with an additional four blades. A Hunter was only so heavily armed in practice; all of that weaponry weighed you down in the field.

Behind the tables of weapons was an obstacle course. The course hadn't changed since the first time I attempted it years ago. It was rigged with scarily lifelike dummies that popped out at every other turn. The dummies didn't actually attack, but you had to deliver an incapacitating blow to get past them. The obstacle course had just that - obstacles: rope swings over water, rock walls, rope bridges, and mud pits. It had always been one of my favorite activities.

I crouched at the beginning of the course, waiting for Griffin to signal me to start. As soon as he blew his whistle, I sprinted for the first rock wall. Clearing it with relative ease, I took off across the rope bridge at the top. The first assailant stood halfway across the bridge; I stabbed him in the neck with my blade and continued on.

After taking part in actual missions with the Hunters, facing real enemies with real weapons, the course was a breeze. Even though I was out of shape and sucking wind, I finished in record time, even for me.

"Amazing as usual!" Griffin exclaimed, clapping me on the back as I stood doubled over, my hands resting on my thighs, trying to catch my breath.

"Thanks," I panted, twisting my neck to smile up at him through sweat-soaked curls. Behind Griffin, I could see the astonished faces of the students. Their skeptical stares had turned respectful, and I couldn't help but feel immense satisfaction. Donavon might have bruised my thigh – and my ego – and Cadence might have humiliated me in front of her class, but at least I knew that I hadn't completely lost my touch.

The final class of the day was Telekinesis Training with Ursula Bane. As with Griffin's class, Mac actually wanted me to aid Ursula's students since they all possessed telekinetic powers. Unlike Griffin, Ursula did have some suspicious incidents in her past.

Her parents hadn't submitted her for mandatory testing when she was five, which wasn't a huge deal in and of itself. However, both of her parents were outspoken members of a rebel group that opposed the testing laws. The Agency hadn't actually discovered a connection between them and the Coalition, but openly disagreeing with the law was only one step removed from being branded a Crane supporter, and a traitor.

TOXIC first became aware of Ursula when she was arrested with her parents at an anti-testing rally when she was thirteen. When the members of the Interrogation Division had questioned her, they'd realized that she was a very strong Telekinetic. Afterwards, they offered her a place at the McDonough School, which she readily accepted. Until she'd met members of the Agency, Ursula had never realized her ability to move objects with her mind was actually a Talent.

Since attending the School and then becoming a member of the Agency, Ursula had proven herself to be a loyal Operative. But while she was establishing her allegiance, her parents became increasingly more outspoken. As a result, they were both currently serving time at Affelwood Correctional Facility, a low-security prison in D.C. The red flag in her file was because Ursula had been to visit her parents in prison numerous times in the months prior to my mission to Nevada. Those visits were undoubtedly monitored. I just needed to get copies of the recordings – another job for Penny.

Unlike Cadence, Ursula was thrilled at my presence. At least until she realized that my Talent was stronger than hers. From her file, I'd learned TOXIC considered her to be an Extremely-High level Telekinetic. I immediately registered the smugness she felt in her abilities. Her arrogance irritated me to no end, even though I also had a certain amount of pride in my own powers, which may have been the reason our personalities conflicted. I had to keep reminding myself during her class that my primary objective was learning whether she was a spy, not showcasing my clearly-superior skills.

After my classes wound down for the day, I jogged back to the Instructor's dorm. My stomach grumbled with hunger. I couldn't wait to get to dinner, but I was fairly certain that Penny wouldn't appreciate it if I showed up without showering first.

Hurrying through the front of the dorm, I took the stairs two at a time to the third floor. I mentally switched the door lock to open as I rounded the corner to my room. I quickly shucked my clothes and made for the shower, wishing that I was back at my room in Elite Headquarters, where I could just program my wall sensor for maid service. No such luck. Here, I was my own maid.

The warm water felt great on my already-beginning-to-ache muscles. I desperately craved more time for the warm water to ease the lingering tension from earlier in the day, but I knew that I needed to hurry if I was actually going to eat before meeting Penny. Full of regret, I turned off the water with a sigh and reached blindly for the fluffy white towel hanging on the bar attached to the back of the door. I quickly dried off and dressed in a pair of lightweight navy blue drawstring pants, a soft white shirt, and well-worn leather sandals. I glanced at the clock on my desk. "Crap," I said out loud. I was as per usual, late. Grabbing a lightweight zip-up jacket, I headed for the door.

I made it halfway to the cafeteria when I ran into Mac.

"You forgot to go to Medical today," he said as soon as he spotted me.

"Evening to you, too," I replied.

"You know how important it for Medical to sample your blood levels every day, Natalia. Not to mention, you need your injection." Mac ignored my glib comment. His cold eyes surveyed me disapprovingly.

"My day was great, thanks for asking." I smiled as though he'd actually inquired.

"Medical. Now," he barked. Mac had no sense of humor.

"I was just on my way to dinner. Care to join me?" I asked.

"Natalia ...," he warned.

"Mac, I am staaaarrrving," I whined.

"I will have dinner sent to you and Operatives Latimore and Samuels at the Crypto Lab." Without another word, Mac turned and walked away. I grumbled to myself as I altered my course towards Medical, my stomach protesting loudly.

After my routine blood taking, chased down with my daily injection of experimental medicine, I finally made my way to the Crypto Building. As soon as the glass doors slid open, granting me entry to Penny's inner sanctuary, my olfactory senses lit up. I inhaled deeply, drinking in the wonderful scent of Gretchen's cooking.

"Roasted hen," I called. I breathed in again. "Mashed sweet potatoes with honey butter." Sniff, sniff, sniff. "Greens with roasted pine nuts?"

"You got it!" Penny exclaimed, smiling at me. "Mrs. McDonough had it delivered a couple minutes ago. It's delicious," she added, glancing guiltily to her plate, already piled high with large helpings. Gemma also looked shamefaced for starting to eat without me. I sat down and helped myself to equally large portions of the feast, and the three of us sat in companionable silence as we gorged ourselves with Gretchen's cooking.

"Food coma," I muttered, licking the last remnants of potato off my plastic fork. I looked sideways at Penny, who was staring glassy-eyed at the bank of computers. She nodded her agreement. A wave of exhaustion hit me as I began to digest the enormous meal.

"The Director gave me the list of Instructors that he paired you with as a starting point," Penny began just as my eyelids were becoming too heavy to keep open. Shaking my head, I tried to jostle myself awake. "I did a more thorough background search of each," she continued. "I printed you the in-depth reports." Penny handed me a stack of thick folders.

"Thanks," I answered.

"You learn anything useful today?" Penny asked hopefully.

"Not really," I said, absently flipping through the first folder. It was Annalise's, reminding me to ask Penny about her Talent ranking. "Actually, there was one thing I was curious about. This first Instructor, Annalise Cleary, is listed as an Elite-Level Electrical Manipulator."

"Yes, why?" Penny looked confused.

"Will you double check that?" I asked. Penny narrowed her eyes at me, but wheeled her chair several computers down. Her fingers flew adeptly across the keys.

"Annalise Bernice Cleary," she read from her screen. "Elite

levels of Talent consistent with Electrical Manipulation," Penny confirmed. That was what my printout said, too. I stared down at the file, twisting my face in concentration.

"I assume you disagree with that diagnosis?" Penny asked dryly.

"Disagree might be a strong word," I replied. "More like, question its accuracy?"

Penny laughed. "Okay, lay it on me. Do tell, Dr. Lyons, why do you question the accuracy?" she said, sarcasm dripping from her words.

"Well, for starters," I began, putting a slight effect on my words, trying to match the tone used by highly educated Medicals and Psycho Medicals. "Ms. Cleary exhibits none of the brain patterns consistent with an individual possessing such levels of Talent. Additionally, Ms. Cleary does not exude electrical impulses, which she would if she were, in fact, capable of electrical manipulation to the degree you so claim." Penny couldn't contain herself and her body shook with silent laughter. Even Gemma burst into a fit of giggles as I mocked the Medicals' haughty mannerisms.

"Care to repeat that in dummy speak?" Penny asked, wiping a tear from her eye.

"What" I exclaimed, "the brilliant Penelope Latimore doesn't understand technical jargon?" I brought my hand to my chest and took in a gasp as I feigned shock.

"Ha ha, I don't know everything," she shot back, her face flushing slightly. I suppose when your IQ is off the charts, you don't like having your intelligence questioned.

"I'm just saying that her mind doesn't feel like other strong Electrical Manipulators," I said.

"What do you feel when you read her thoughts?" Penny asked.

"Nothing really." I shrugged. "She feels like a normal person."

"Interesting," Penny mused thoughtfully. "I'll pull her placement exam records and see if there are any inconsistencies."

"Thanks."

Penny and I spent the remainder of the evening dissecting the other Instructors' profiles. I committed every seemingly-important morsel to memory, making a mental checklist of every fact that I wanted to verify with each teacher. By the time that I noticed the clock on Penny's desk, it read 11:53 p.m. I yawned.

"I need to get to bed," I announced. "Need to be bright-eyed to kick Donavon's butt tomorrow morning."

"I'll call you a car to take you back." Penny hit a button on her console, a tired voice answering on the first ring. "I need a car to take Talia Lyons back to Instructor housing," Penny said by way of greeting.

"The vehicle will be outside in five minutes, Ms. Penny," the voice replied. Penny thanked the man and hit a second button on the console, ending the call. I tucked my files under my arm and said goodnight to Penny and Gemma.

"Oh,! I almost forgot! Will you do me a favor and check out a guy named Ernest Tate? He teaches Advanced Crypto something or other," I said.

"Sure thing, I'll have a profile on him when you get here tomorrow night," she readily agreed. I smiled in appreciation and gave her a small wave as I left.

Chapter Eight

As tired as I was, sleep still eluded me. My mind buzzed with thoughts of Donavon. Why was he really here? If this morning was any indication, it appeared that his sole purpose was to torture me. In reality, I suspected that Mac had recruited him to covertly investigate the other Instructors as well. But why hadn't Mac told me? His omission unnerved me and I couldn't let it go, much like a dog with a bone.

Once I'd exhausted that train of thought, my mind wandered to Erik as it so often did. I replayed the words from his letter, words that I'd committed to memory. It was a good thing that I had since I no longer had the letter. When Mac had finally let me read the entire incident report on my mission, I'd noticed that Erik's letter had not been listed among my personal belongings. I prayed that it was because the letter hadn't been found and not because someone had found it and turned it over to Mac. The rational part of my brain knew that the words had likely torched along with the blood-soaked leaves that had nearly been my burial shroud, but I couldn't shake the anxiety that I'd failed Erik and unwittingly divulged his secrets. Protocol dictated that if an Operative bled during a mission, anything contaminated had to be burned, and that letter had been smeared with my blood.

I considered calling Erik. Mac hadn't explicitly lifted the moratorium on interactions with non-approved people, but I figured that I was now back among the land of the living, the restrictions were no longer applicable. The problem was I had no idea what I would say to him if I did call. Our last encounter had been less-than-friendly. Yet he *had* sent Henri with that letter, and his desire to confide something that was so personal felt a lot like a peace offering. Still, I couldn't muster the courage.

What if he didn't want to talk to me? Penny said that he was back to being his old self. What if he had a girlfriend? What if he had several girlfriends? The notion tore at my chest like razor blades slicing open old wounds.

I finally fell asleep before my subconscious could conjure up anymore unpleasant scenarios.

The next morning, I woke before my alarm. Like yesterday, the tension running through my body made it impossible for me to continue sleeping. I turned my alarm clock off and quickly dressed in running clothes. This time, I added a thick nylon belt with bottle holders to my ensemble. I filled three bottles with water from the tap in my bathroom and secured them to the loops at my waist. I chalked up yesterday's embarrassing display to dehydration, and was determined not to repeat it.

Setting off at a slow jog, I replayed the events from the previous day in my mind. I analyzed my interactions with each individual in light of Penny's more in-depth profiles. Next, I mentally scripted the questions that I would ask each teacher. When I exhausted that task, I moved on to recalling the highlights of each profile.

All of the Instructors, except for Thad, had some family member who was either affiliated directly with the Coalition or who was strongly suspected of supporting their cause. Thad was also from a different country, a fact which warranted a little mistrust on its own, but not much. Many other countries didn't have schools to train Talents, so it wasn't uncommon for foreign children to come here for education. Part of the deal was that if they were educated here, they stayed here after graduation and worked for TOXIC. Many thought that it was a good alternative to being ostracized for their abilities in their countries. Thad had been a Hunter, which meant he would've come in contact with Coalition members and turned spy as a result. But Thad had a good record and hadn't raised suspicion in all the years that he'd been a Hunter or an Instructor with the Agency.

Annalise Cleary, at best, seemed like a fake. Her Talent Ranking was listed as 'Elite', but I had serious doubts that it was, in fact, true. However, I also doubted that made her a spy, and chalked the inconsistency up to a mistake during her ranking tests. Until I delved further into her psyche, or questioned her extensively about contact with her ex-husband, I wouldn't know for sure whether she was one of the good guys.

Cadence Choi stunk of desperation to prove that she was better than her ranking. Penny's report indicated that Cadence had taken the Hunter's Placement Exam. She'd been rejected because her Talent ranking was too low since the Hunters only accept Talents with a ranking of Extremely High or Elite. She'd requested several transfers to the Hunters in the six years that she had been teaching at the School, and each had been denied. Personally, I thought that she was lucky to have been granted an Instructor position at graduation as opposed to an assistant one; new graduates were seldom awarded such a noteworthy post. Despite our instant mutual dislike for one another, I had to admit that she was really a very good fighter, and not a bad teacher.

Ursula was a surprisingly hard read. Aside from her extreme arrogance where her Talents were concerned, I'd been unable to get much of a feel for her. Luckily, she was her own favorite topic of conversation, so I doubted that it would be difficult to get her talking about more intimate matters. Thinking about Ursula made me realize that I'd forgotten to ask Penny about getting the recordings of her visits with her parents at Affelwood. I really needed to start writing this stuff down.

Even as I repeated the Instructors' statistics in my head,

thoughts of Donavon crept to the surface. Penny's more extensive background reports gave a detailed history of past relationships, and known acquaintances at each posting. If casual friendships and known hook-ups had been immortalized in their files, I was confident that my own high-profile relationship with Donavon had been carefully documented. The realization made me incredibly uncomfortable, and slightly desperate to read our files.

TOXIC did not prohibit Operatives from marrying and having children with one another, even encouraging the idea in some cases. Though scientists hadn't conclusively proven that Talented parents begot Talented children, it was more common if at least one of the parents was. Donavon was an Extremely-High-level Morpher, and I was an Elite-level Mind Manipulator; it was almost a certainty one of our children would have strong powers. Mac had encouraged our relationship for this reason, and he wasn't the only one. Many believed that a pairing such as ours would prove extremely beneficial to the furtherance of TOXIC's objectives.

As the Director's son, Donavon was slated to follow the same course as his father. After his stint here, as an undercover spy hunter or whatever his actual assignment was, I assumed that he would return to Elite Headquarters and the Hunters. In a few years, he would be promoted to team captain. Like Mac, he'd become Headmaster by the time he was forty. Donavon would likely be appointed Captain of the Hunters, or the Liaison to the United Nations International Talent Education Division after leaving his mark at his namesake, the McDonough School. Finally, he would become Director; every McDonough had followed the same path since the inception of TOXIC.

This wasn't Donavon's life plan so much as it was his fate. Not that Donavon didn't want to do all those things, too, he just didn't really care about receiving accolades. What Donavon did care about was making his father proud. So if Mac wanted him to follow in his footsteps, Donavon would.

The more my thoughts clouded with Donavon, the madder I

got at myself. My life had come full circle. It had been just a year ago that Donavon and Erik interfered with my ability to concentrate on more important issues. I was here to do a job. Not just any job. I was supposed to find out who'd leaked my identity to Ian Crane.

Had it been about money? Was the Coalition paying for information on Operatives? Or worse, was this personal? Operatives' deaths weren't infrequent, but an Operative being targeted specifically had to be rare.

Just as I was beginning to think that my brain couldn't process one more coherent thought, the Instructor dorm came into view. Every inch of my body was slick with sweat. I briefly wondered if it was possible for every part of your body to sweat, or if you sweat only in certain portions of your body and it just dripped to the rest of it.

Coming to a halt in front of the entrance, I leaned against the cool stones. I hoped that the coolness would seep into my exposed skin, but instead, I had a feeling that my body heat warmed the smooth surface. I reached for a water bottle, only to discover it was empty. I looked down. Ugh. All of my water bottles were empty. I took a deep breath.

My head pounded so loud that it blocked out all the sounds of nature around me. My stomach was queasy and my legs shook slightly, but I was still standing upright and last night's dinner hadn't seen the sunlight that was now peeking through the trees. Considering my morning run a success, I grinned as I opened the front door to the dorm and headed up to my room for a shower.

I arrived at the practice arena in good spirits, still pleased with myself. Since we would have a different set of students today we would be repeating the drills from yesterday. I inwardly groaned as I thought of my bruised leg, but still firmly insisted that I didn't need a suit when Donavon suggested it. Pride was definitely a sin.

Donavon gave me a hard look in response. His light blue eyes clouded over and somehow became darker, like when a sunny, cloudless sky begins to fill with thunder clouds. I swore that I could hear his back teeth grinding together as he clenched his jaw. He turned to the class and began taking them through the movements he was about to demonstrate. I stood perfectly still beside him, feet shoulder width apart, hands clasped behind my back.

I glanced sidelong, trying in vain to not look at the silky blonde hair that fell in his eyes. It was longer than I'd seen it in years, like he hadn't cut it since leaving Headquarters, and he kept pushing it back with one hand. His skin was a little tan from all the time that he spent outside; usually, the most color he had was pink tinges since he tended to burn easily. The muscles in his arms moved fluidly with each gesture he made. His hands were large and calloused from training, fingers long and slim. I watched his mouth move as he spoke, his lips looking even fuller from the side. I had seen many girls in D.C. who used lip gloss injected with insect venom in an effort to make their lips swell slightly, trying to achieve the look that Donavon had naturally.

Donavon's dark eyelashes were so long, they brushed the hollows of his cheeks when he closed his eyes. When we were in school, Donavon and I would sneak out at night to lie on a blanket under the stars. I would lie on my back, my head on Donavon's arm. He would lie next to me, his head resting on my shoulder close enough so that his lashes would kiss my cheekbone, sending tingles through my whole body and nervous giggles out of my mouth every time he blinked. Butterfly kisses, he'd called them.

I was so lost in the memory that I didn't even realize that Donavon had stopped talking and turned to face me expectantly. My throat was dry and I nearly choked when I tried to swallow my unease.

"You okay?" he sent, concern warring with irritation at my daydreaming.

"Yes," my mental voice snapped back at him. I was angry with myself for recalling those memories, so naturally I took it out

on him. He cocked one dark-blonde eyebrow, and I wondered how loud my thoughts had been projecting. Blood rushed to my face, and my pulse roared in my ears. Of course, this totally physical reaction, that I couldn't help, angered me even more.

"Let's start this," I growled. I threw all of my concentration into the exercise. Granted, all I was supposed to do was stand there in a defensive stance, and not really try to deflect the blows. Still, I readied myself for the physical contact, and I didn't even feel Donavon's first kick make contact with my body. I steeled myself against his second, which I knew would land on my bruised leg, but the pain never came.

At least, the pain never came to me. As soon as Donavon's foot hit my thigh, he doubled over holding his own leg. My eyes widened in surprised. It took me several seconds to react while his mental voice screamed expletives in my head. Closing the distance separating us, I knelt down, not sure whether I should touch him. Donavon writhed in agony.

"Get a Medical," I yelled to no one in particular. The students all stared, frozen. "Now," I snapped. The compulsion behind my command was so strong that several kids took off at a run.

"What happened?" I asked shakily, my hand hovering over his shoulder.

"I don't know," he replied out loud, his teeth gritted. He let out several long, hissing breaths, and squeezed his eyes shut to ward off the pain.

We stayed like that, him lying on the ground and me kneeling beside him, for what seemed like an eternity. I wanted to touch him, soothe him, but I was scared he'd reject me. When he opened his eyes, he looked murderous, and I had a bad feeling that his anger was directed at me. I recoiled, sitting back on my haunches in case he decided to release his aggression.

Finally, a Medic arrived with Janet in tow. As soon as Janet saw me kneeling on the ground, she quickened her pace, fear shining in her eyes. When she glanced down at me, she did a double take. Her eyes grew big as saucers. I followed her gaze; my gray pants were darkening to a reddish-black.

"Oh," I cried out loud. As soon as I saw the blood, a loud crack resonated in my head. Oh, no, I knew what had happened. Suddenly *I* was the one writhing in the grass. My leg burned, flames shooting down my thigh to lick my toes. My pants clung to my skin, sticky with my blood. I was vaguely aware that Donavon had stopped panting, his breathing returning to normal. His eyes found mine, the blue irises swirling with accusations and fury. Donavon scrambled back, putting as much distance between us as he could manage with the all the people crowding the area.

Janet motioned a Medic closer to where I lay paralyzed with fear and agony. He scooped me up in his arms and began running, cradling me to his chest. I squeezed my eyes shut and tried to breathe through the pain. I wanted to deflect it or block it, but the last thing I needed was to transfer the pain – I certainly didn't want the Medic to drop me.

When we arrived at the Medical building, a team was standing by. The Medic carefully deposited me onto a stretcher waiting at the entrance. I still had my eyes shut, but I felt and heard people cutting my pants away from my thigh. I swore loudly as one peeled the sticky fabric from the wound. Terrified that the sight of my blood would send me into hysterics, I kept my eyes scrunched shut and tightly gripped the handrails of the gurney until the skin over my knuckles turned white. *Don't cry, don't cry*, I chanted silently. *You've been through worse.*

The stretcher came to a stop, and I felt four simultaneous pricks several inches above my knee. A heavy chemical feeling flowed through my veins, and my leg went numb.

I chanced a peek. The same Medic who'd carried me from the practice field was sopping up the blood with clean towels while another prepared sterilized pads to disinfect the area. I averted my eyes; watching the needle thread stitches through my skin was the last image that I wanted burned into my mind. Unfortunately, I still felt the pull of the fiber as he threaded the stitches to close the wound. It took every ounce of my willpower not to retch.

"Good as new," he pronounced when he was done.

"Thanks," I mumbled, lying back on the stiff white sheets of the gurney. His footsteps retreated from my bedside.

"How are you?" Janet's voice asked.

"Didn't you hear him?" I replied. "Good as new."

"You only needed ten stitches. Dr. Remy said there was only so much blood because of the bruise," she explained. "What happened? Why weren't you wearing pads?"

"Please don't lecture me," I moaned. I felt stupid enough as it was. I had no one to blame for this except myself, my own stubborn nature.

"I wasn't going to lecture you," she replied. I peered up at her through one squinted eye. She looked exasperated; she had definitely been gearing up to lecture me.

"Did you bring me some new pants?" I asked her.

"Yes," her lips were pursed in a disapproving grimace, but she was carrying a pair of loose-fitting navy sweatpants.

"Thanks," I muttered, holding out my hand to take the clothing.

"Dr. Remy says that you don't have to stay here if you don't want to, but no physical activity for the rest of the day," she warned.

"Did Dr. Remy say when I can do physical activity?" I assumed Dr. Remy was the unknown Medic who had stitched me up.

"Preferably not for a week, but if you promise to be careful and wear a protective suit, tomorrow should be fine."

"Tomorrow it is," I snapped, immediately feeling bad. Janet was just trying to help, and she wasn't the person I was angry with. I was angry with myself for being stubborn.

Janet helped me slide off of the stretcher and into the sweatpants, then handed me three green pills and a small plastic cup of water.

"Prevent infection," she said as she handed them to me. I nodded my understanding and cupped the pills in my palm before throwing them into my mouth.

If I'd insisted, Janet would've let me mull over my stupidity in the solitude of my own room. Somehow, I didn't think that was a productive use of my time, and I knew that I'd feel even worse if I didn't have something to distract me. So instead of heading back to my dorm room, I limped to Ms. Cleary's language class.

I arrived just as her previous class was letting out.

"Ms. Lyons!" she exclaimed. "You're early!"

"Um, yeah. I had to visit Medical, so I left a little early from my last class." That was mostly true. There was no way that I was explaining my refusal to wear protective padding just to prove to Donavon I was tough.

"I have plenty for you to get started on." She smiled, motioning me to her desk. Inwardly, I groaned. Paperwork - just what I wanted to do. Outwardly, I matched her smile and limped pathetically to sit in her chair.

The opportunities to engage Annalise in conversation were few and far between, so I jumped on them. Mostly, I made small talk asking about what she did in her free time and if she ever got the chance to leave campus to enjoy Baltimore or Washington. I was even so bold as to chance asking about her personal life.

"Oh, not much chance for that," she laughed. "My duties here at school keep me very busy."

"But you don't want to date? Start a family? That's the great thing about being a teacher, right? It's easy to get married and settle down. I've even heard that if you're married you can request to live off campus," I pressed. Sure, I knew that the questions were indelicate, but after my morning, tact was not a priority. The sooner I found the spy, the sooner that I could get away from Donavon.

"Yes, that is true, dear...but the students here are my family. I don't need more than that," she answered. Her eyes took on a faraway look and I knew that she was caught in the memory of her failed marriage. Her thoughts were sad, regretful. Annalise had truly loved her husband, and his actions had cut her deeply. But through the pain, I felt her determination to personally right the wrongs of her husband. Her inner turmoil saddened me. I couldn't imagine living with the knowledge that someone you'd loved had betrayed you so severely. I wasn't positive that she wasn't a spy, but she was coming close to being a strike-through on my list of suspects.

The rest of my school day was blessedly uneventful. I followed Cadence around, observing the students and making small suggestions on form and technique. She seemed irked at my presence, and took every opportunity to disagree with my advice. I tried to engage her in conversation several times, hoping to establish a connection so that I could delve into her mind, but she wasn't having any part of it. She answered my inquires in a short, clipped manner that suggested she'd rather be clawing her own eyes out than talking to me. By the end of the period, I wanted to claw her eyes out for her.

I ate lunch with Ernest the Brain and actually enjoyed myself. The previous day, he'd been so nervous around me that he'd barely been able to keep up his end of the conversation. Today, we bantered easily, and I realized that he was actually pretty funny. I felt bad that my motivations for befriending him weren't genuine. Under different circumstances, we might've even become real friends.

After lunch, I made small talk with Thad while his students worked on group projects. I subtly threw in questions about his life back in Edinburgh. He was wistful when he talked about Scotland, smiling at the memory of his childhood. I asked about his family, and he seemed hesitant to talk about them. From what I could glean from his mind, he wasn't hiding anything, but rather felt guilty for having left to come to school here. Thad rarely went home to visit even though he missed his birthplace. I knew the feeling; rarely a day went by that I didn't miss Capri. I hadn't been back since my parents' deaths.

Griffin's class was one of two in which I would see the same Talents every day. Mac had asked me to keep a close eye on each of them and wanted to be kept apprised of my impressions. Almost as much as being tasked with hunting down the traitor, this made me feel like I had purpose again, and not so much like I was living in limbo.

Griffin and I worked individually with each student as he or she threw a sampling of small weapons at a target. Most of the kids were actually very good already and needed little coaching. I didn't get a chance to speak with Griffin very much, but since he wasn't a suspect, I wasn't too bothered by the fact.

Ursula's Telekinesis class was the other one where I would see the same Talents on a daily basis. The fifteen students in the class varied greatly in ability level. Several had extremely developed Talents while others had virtually non-existent abilities. I made a mental note to ask Penny to run profiles on all the students in the class, so that I would know what I was dealing with. Ursula concentrated her efforts on the stronger gifts, leaving me to work with those less capable. I didn't really mind. I found that I liked teaching others how to better use their powers.

As I walked, practically dragging my throbbing leg behind me, to my room to change before dinner, I mentally compiled a list of the intel that I needed Penny to help me gather that evening. My stomach grumbled in anticipation of food, and I longed for a hot shower; the antiseptic smell of the disinfectant the Medic had used to clean the wound filled my nostrils every time I moved my leg.

"How dare you!" Donavon's mental voice screamed in my head just before I reached the entrance to the dorm. I stopped dead in my tracks, whipping around to face him. His cheeks were bright red with anger and his eyes were more gray than blue.

"Me?" I exclaimed mentally. *"I'm sorry, did I miss*

something? Because last time I checked, I was the one with STITCHES in her leg!" I screamed back. As exhausted as I was from my eventful day, I wasn't going to take his accusations lying down. I could feel a vein in my neck straining as the blood rushed to my face.

"You had no right," he shot back. *"You knew that you could transfer pain to me. You knew how easy it was with our connection being so strong!"*

"Oh, and you think I would purposely let you kick me so hard that you broke the skin just so that I could transfer the pain to you?" I mentally demanded, refusing to back down.

"The way you've been acting? I wouldn't put it past you," he retorted.

"Get over yourself, Donavon. I wouldn't put myself through that pain just to hurt you." He looked doubtful, indecision warring with ...panic. Donavon was scared of me, I thought, the realization only slightly curbing my anger.

"Do you think that I manipulated you into kicking me so hard you drew blood, too?" He didn't answer. *"Oh, my god, you do."* I blanched. Rage consumed me. Now I wanted to hit him hard enough make him bleed. I advanced on him so quickly that he barely had time to react. His eyes grew wide in alarm, his fear written like lines of text in his creased brow. The horrified expression that Donavon wore stopped me in my tracks. What was wrong with me? I was out of control. I needed to get my temper in check. He had every right to be scared of me; I was scared of me right now.

"FUCK YOU," I screamed, a million emotions bursting out of me at once, like water from a dam. The urge to attack Donavon was so strong that if I didn't leave right then, I feared that I might not be able to suppress it. Turning on my heel and ignoring the throbbing in my leg, I took off at a dead sprint to my room. What was wrong with me? Sure, I was rightfully angry that he'd accused me of something so ridiculous, but I'd come within inches of assaulting him. And for what, blaming me for something that I didn't do? Even given my usual, somewhat irrational behavior, physical violence was extreme under the circumstances. I barely made it to my room before the first tears wet my cheeks.

Chapter Nine

A quiet beeping in my ear woke me. Disoriented and
confused, I opened my eyes and jumped when I found my nose
inches from bright red, glowing numbers. My neck was stiff and
one of my feet tingled when I moved it. I sat in the desk chair in
my dorm room, a soft light illuminating the surface of the desk.
Stretching my arms over my head I looked to the left, the shade on
the window was up and a sliver of moonlight shone on the rough
beige carpet.

The beeping continued. "Crap!" I exclaimed out loud when
the numbers on the clock came into focus. I'd slept through dinner.
Shoot, I hoped that I hadn't missed my meeting, too; Mac was
going to be pissed.

When I'd returned to my room after the confrontation with
Donavon, I had a message on my communicator from Mac
requesting my presence at a status meeting. Glancing at the
communicator, I realized that it was the source of the incessant
beeping. Mac must have programmed the meeting into the
communicator because not only was it beeping, it was also
alternating between flashing "Mac" and the time.

I had ten minutes to make it across campus. I was still dressed
in a robe, my hair a wet rat's nest on top of my head. Grabbing the
first clothes that I could get my hands on and the black jacket off
the back of the desk chair, I set off at a jog across campus. My leg

ached worse than earlier, and falling asleep sitting at my desk hadn't done me any favors.

The Director's Office came into view with only two minutes to spare. When I tried to turn the door handle, it wouldn't budge. Frantically, I looked around, and found a key pad staring back at me. One-by-one, I pressed my fingers, starting with my thumb, to the scanner. Two high-pitched beeps assaulted my ears, and then a glowing green light washed over my skin. I waited for the light to extinguish, and entered my ten-digit personal identification code. The lock clicked open, rewarding my efforts. The main lobby of the Administration Building was empty, so I opened my mind. A flurry of mental activity greeted me from the end of one corridor. I followed the buzzing to a door marked "Conference Room # 1". I had hoped that this meeting was for just me, Mac, and Janet. Apparently, I was wrong if we were using the conference room instead of Mac's office.

Tentatively, I pushed the door open, cognizant of the fact that I was now officially late.

Mac spared a moment to glance up from the stack of papers that he was rifling through. "Nice of you to join us," he said dryly.

I smiled apologetically, and scurried to take a seat. Three people sat around a large oval table with three additional chairs; one for me, one for Mac, and one for –

"Sorry I'm late! I got held up." The voice was so ingrained in my brain that I didn't need to turn around to know that it belonged to Donavon. Great. After our fight, I had promptly run home and sobbed in the shower until the water ran cold. Then, I had sat at my desk, and cried myself to sleep like a child. My eyes were swollen reminders of the earlier breakdown, and if I'd looked in a mirror, I'm sure that I would've seen that they were red rimmed as well. Good thing I hadn't found a reflective surface on my way here.

Without turning to look at Donavon, I squeezed into the empty chair between Janet and the Agency's Deputy Director, Mitch Rice. Mitch was older than Mac by at least ten years. He'd chosen the dignified route and shaved his head when he'd begun to bald. Since forsaking his Operative status, and becoming a TOXIC figurehead, he'd let himself go. He was now quite rotund and jolly looking. He offered me a warm smile that I returned, grateful to have another friendly face at the table.

To my surprise, and relief, the third person was Penny. She, too, shot me a huge grin.

"No, problem, Donavon. Take a seat so that we can get started," Mac directed his son.

Donavon scanned the group, pointedly skipping me. His face was an unreadable mask, but he was projecting his thoughts so hard that he might as well have spoken them aloud.

The PG version? He still believed that I had coerced him into hurting me, so that I could, in turn, project the pain on to him. As if that weren't enough, after my earlier display of nonsensical rage, he thought that I was coming unhinged. His condemnation invoked my earlier feelings of shame and anger. The anger won out, and before I could think it through, I forced his gaze to meet mine. I concentrated on the noise that bees make – an insistent buzzing. Slowly as though turning the dial on a radio, I cranked the volume louder. Donavon's right eye began to twitch involuntarily and he tried to break the connection, but I was too focused. He wanted manipulation? I would show him manipulation.

"Talia!" The tone of Mac's voice indicated that it wasn't the first time he'd said my name.

I reluctantly severed the tie to Donavon's mind and turned to face Mac. "Sorry, I'm ready to start whenever you are." I smiled, doing my best imitation of innocence.

Several minds pressed on mine, but I blocked them, not needing the mental chastising to know that I was being childish.

One did break through my walls. *"Jesus, Talia, act your age."* Trying to keep Donavon out was like trying to run between raindrops without getting wet – impossible. Yup, he definitely thought that I was losing it.

Mac's gray eyes narrowed, but didn't comment on my silent torture of his son. Instead, he started briefing our small group on his current theories. He began by reiterating the theories that he'd expressed to me several days prior; he believed that we had a spy on account of Crane knowing that I was coming and knowing my identity. Mac explained that I was likely targeted because my mission involved Crane directly, keeping his speculation that the reason was more personal to himself.

"What about the Cryptos who intercepted the original intel?" I interrupted, glancing sidelong at Penny. She'd been one of the Cryptos who had intercepted the intel. Her face remained impassive. I almost felt bad about asking, but they would naturally be the first people I'd investigate if I were him.

Mac gave me a hard look, annoyed at my disruption. "The Crypto team in question consisted of two Operatives and a Pledge. As you are well aware, Natalia, Ms. Latimore was that Pledge. She and the two Operatives have been questioned extensively by a member of our Psychic Interrogation Division. I was present during the interrogations as was Captain Alvarez. After an exhaustive investigation, we've determined that they were not involved. That is why I have asked Ms. Latimore to help with this inquiry. Does that satisfy you, Natalia?"

"Just asking," I muttered, appropriately abashed. He made it sound as though I was accusing him of not doing his job, but I wasn't. I was just curious for goodness sake, trying to be thorough.

Mac continued, effectively dismissing me. "As you are all aware, we have two Crypto facilities. One is located here, and the other at Elite Headquarters. The information about Natalia's mission would have been logged into our system, and only someone extremely adept with computers would have been able to access it." He paused, meeting each of our eyes in turn before continuing. "Naturally, I have had Raj Anderson, Head of the Crypto Division, identify any of his personnel that accessed Natalia's file. We have come up empty-handed thus far, but we are still pursuing that avenue. In light of our lack of progress, I have decided to take more aggressive measures and launch a full investigation of every person at both locations. Operative Latimore is combing the network to determine if the data was hacked while also aiding Natalia in identifying suspicious individuals. Janet identified several Instructors here at the School that have family members that are known associates of the Coalition." Mac paused to take a breath, and I jumped at the opportunity to interrupt asking another question that had been plaguing me.

"Why is Donavon here?" I blurted out.

Janet coughed into her hand, but when I glanced in her direction, I saw that she was trying to suppress a snicker. Mitch shifted uncomfortably in his seat. Donavon gave me an exasperated look. Only Mac looked unfazed by my question; I think that he'd been expecting it. To my surprise, Donavon was the one who answered.

"Because up until very recently, *Talia*, you've been indisposed, and my father needed someone who could pose as an Instructor to keep his ears open for any rumblings that would lead us to the spy." Donavon enunciated my name, his voice like a razor. The only word that I really heard in his rant was "indisposed".

"Indisposed?" I shrieked, swinging my chair around to face him for the first time since he'd entered the room. "I was shot, you ass. I almost died. I had to relearn to walk. Sorry that my torture inconvenienced you." My temper rose with each word, like mercury in boiling water. Donavon at least had the decency to flush and shrink back slightly in his seat at the venom in my voice.

"Your personal conflicts aside," Mac started to say, but I interrupted him again.

"We don't have personal conflicts," I spat, my palms slapping the top of the conference table.

Janet couldn't suppress her snort of laughter this time. Mac shot her a warning look, but Janet just shook her head as if to say,

"I told you so."

"Fine. The reason that Donavon is here is because I knew that he wasn't the spy. Vetting another Operative to come in and play Instructor would've taken too much time, and time is not something that I want to waste. We need to find the leak before another Operative is hurt or killed," Mac said shortly. His tone had a note of finality and his eyes blazed, warning me that he had nothing further to say on the topic. I wasn't ready to let it go.

"What about Erik or Henri?" I insisted. "I'm sure that you've vetted both of them since they knew about my mission?" I met Mac's eyes dead on, daring him to contradict me even though I regretted the words the moment they left my lips. Taunting Mac was kind of like baiting a hungry tiger – never a good idea.

Donavon scoffed and shook his head. "Really, Talia? Erik? He'd just sleep with all of the students. We'd never find the spy if he went undercover." Donavon sneered. His words were meant to hurt me, and they did. I bit my lip, fighting the stinging in the corners of my eyes at the thought of Erik with another girl.

"Enough!" Mac shouted, banging his fist on the pile of papers in front of him. "Natalia, yes, both Mr. Kelley and Mr. Reich have been vetted. I am confident that neither of them is the spy. While it is not any of your business why I chose Donavon, I'll tell you. He is my son, making him the Operative who would draw the least amount of suspicion here. Satisfied?" I flinched as Mac fixed me with his cold stare, his eyes boring holes in my head. I sat up straight and nodded my head that I was indeed satisfied with his explanation. In truth, I was. It actually made perfect sense; Mac was nothing if not logical.

"And Donavon," Mac continued, training his hard gaze on his son. "Stop baiting her. You two could at least act like professionals instead of petty children."

"Sorry, Dad," Donavon muttered, embarrassed by his father's reproach.

If I were a bigger person, I might've felt badly for him since, after all, I was actually the one being petty and baiting Donavon. His comment about Erik was a low blow, but it paled in comparison to some of the antics I'd pulled in the last couple of days. Despite admitting the truth to myself, I wasn't the bigger person, and Mac's admonishment of his son gave me a perverse sense of satisfaction.

"Now that we are all on the same page, let's get back to what is important. Natalia, it is imperative that you keep your mind open. I want you looking into the head of every person that comes in contact with you. I want to know the minute that you feel something is off. I don't care if you just have an inkling; I want to know. Are we clear?" he asked me. I swallowed hard and nodded, afraid to speak again.

"Penelope, I want you to do everything in your power to determine whether the system has been hacked. I want you and Natalia to look through every Operative's file, and if you find anything that seems off, I want to know." Penny nodded, her eyes wide. She also appeared to be too afraid of Mac to speak.

"Donavon, continue to become friends with as many of the other Instructors as you can. Keep your ears open and let me know if you hear anything that needs further investigation."

"Yes, sir," Donavon replied quietly.

"Janet, Mitch, and I will continue to follow up on some leads. I want daily reports, and we will have weekly status meetings. I want this matter to be taken care of as quickly and quietly as possible. Are we all clear?" We all nodded. Then, mercifully, Mac dismissed us, not a moment too soon. The tension between me and Donavon was palpable, and the conference room had quickly become too small to hold us both.

Donavon made a run for the door as soon as Mac dismissed us. I remained firmly planted in my chair until I was sure that he was out of the building. I didn't have the energy to go another round with him.

"You look like death warmed over," Penny said, leaning

towards me.

"I've had better days," I replied softly.

She scrutinized my appearance. "Do you know you're wearing two different shoes?" she asked, her voice edged with both amusement and concern.

I looked down. Sure enough, I was wearing one brown leather sandal and one black. "Oops," I replied sheepishly. "It's been that kind of day."

"Come on, let's get over to the Crypto Bank. I got the file that you wanted on that Ernest kid. I also got your message about needing the profiles for the students in your Telekinesis class." I'd managed to send Penny a comm sometime between my shower and crying myself into exhaustion.

"Great, thanks."

"Don't thank me yet. I haven't gotten started on those profiles, I figured that we could do them together tonight."

Penny and I made our way out of the conference room with no more than a wave to Mac, Mitch, and Janet, who were so lost in conversation that they barely noticed our departure. We were halfway to the Crypto Bank when my portable communicator started beeping.

"Medical," a mechanical voice said between chirps. I'd forgotten. No wonder Mac had programmed it. I turned to Penny.

"Meet you there in five?" I said apologetically.

"Want me to come with you?" she asked, still looking concerned about my mental state.

"Nah, I'll be okay," I answered. I really appreciated her offer, but I needed a few minutes alone to collect my thoughts; I was still reeling over Donavon's statements about Erik. I hated myself for falling into Donavon's trap. He'd been trying to cause me pain, wanted to hurt me. Donavon figured that I'd caused him physical pain earlier, so he would cause me emotional pain now.

Only, I wasn't the only one of us who'd been emotionally stung by his words. When Donavon had felt my reaction to his claims about Erik, he'd been hurt, too. The fact that I cared enough about Erik to be so upset by the thought of him with another girl tore Donavon apart inside. No matter what he said, or how he acted, Janet and Penny were right – Donavon still cared a lot about me. He knew that I'd been involved with Erik before I left for Nevada, but he'd assumed that it had been a rebound. He thought that I'd done it to get back at him.

Donavon hadn't realized that I'd had real feelings for Erik; that I still had real feelings for him. As mad as I was at Donavon, his pain weighed heavily on my shoulders. What a mess.

"See you shortly." Penny smiled before heading to the Crypto Bank alone.

Dr. Thistler not only took my blood and gave me my medication, but provided me with more painkillers as well. I was feeling much better, and kind of high, half an hour later when I entered the sliding glass doors to Penny's home-away-from-home.

Chapter Ten

The next day, I vowed to get an accurate analysis of Cadence. Once again I tried to engage her in small talk, but like my earlier attempts, she wasn't receptive. We'd had enough interactions that I should've been able to read her mind, except she was fairly adept at shielding her thoughts. When I pushed harder, I was able to break through her mental barricades, but the only thing that she was concentrating on was class. I cursed her single-mindedness.

As was quickly becoming my daily routine, I ate lunch with Ernest. We talked and joked easily, and the more time that I spent with him, the more I liked him.

"Don't you get bored here?" I wanted to know. I was partially asking to get a feel for what he did in his free time, and if it included selling information to the Coalition, and partly because I was genuinely curious how a person survived sans entertainment at School.

After sitting alone in my bedroom for months on end, I'd thought that coming to the School and being around people would be exciting. For the first day it had been, but now, not so much.

"Not really," he shrugged. "There are plenty of people to hang out with, and sometimes, I lend a hand in the Crypto Bank analyzing data. That keeps me pretty busy." My ears perked up at the mention of his involvement with the Cryptos; he might prove to be a promising lead after all.

"You can do that?" I asked. "Like just go in there and help out?" Keeping my tone only mildly interested was difficult. I was nearly bursting with curiosity.

"Well, not just anybody can." His pale face colored slightly. "I'm an Elite-Level Higher Reasoning, and was actually offered placement with the Crypto Division, but I turned it down. Since I technically have the skill set, they let me fill in if they are shorthanded." From anybody else, I'd have taken this disclosure as bragging, but Ernest was almost embarrassed to admit that he was a highly-ranked Talent, and had been offered such a coveted position.

"Do you fill in often?" I pressed.

"Oh, not often, just every few weeks or so," he replied.

I studied his mind; nothing in his brain suggested anything more than joy at getting the chance to do the work that he really loved. After leaving Penny the previous night, I'd reviewed Ernest's file and found no obvious red flags, but I also didn't remember any mention of his moonlighting as a Crypto Operative. I'd have to double check on that.

That afternoon, I took advantage of Ursula's talkative nature to question her more closely.

"I forgot what it was like to be at school," I began as we watched the students practice using their minds to throw knives at a target.

"You were at Elite Headquarters before this, right?" she responded.

"Yeah, it was so much better. I mean we were allowed to go into the city, and the rooms are so much better than the dorms here." I rolled my eyes.

"I bet. But weren't you just there for your Pledge year? I thought that Pledges weren't allowed in the city?" I winced; apparently, her propensity for over-sharing was contagious.

"Not normally, but there are always ways to sneak off," I replied conspiratorially. There, maybe if she thought that I was rebellious, she'd trust me enough to confide in me.

"I've heard that." She nodded. "A couple of my friends from school became Hunters."

I relaxed; she'd bought my lie.

"Have you ever been to Washington? There are so many cool bars and stuff," I said.

"Yeah, on the weekends I meet some friends down there, if I'm not on duty." She smiled mischievously. "City boys are so much fun to flirt with. They get a kick out of seeing me take shots without using my hands." Ursula winked; Telekinesis came with some fun perks.

I laughed. I bet they did. That sounded like something Erik would do if he could.

"Do you travel much other than that? Like go home to see your parents or anything?" I decided to test the bond that we were forming, and see if she'd tell me the truth about her family.

Ursula's lips pursed together in a thin line, and her body went rigid next to me. "No, I rarely see my parents. They aren't supportive of my decision to join TOXIC," she replied thinly.

"That sucks. Mine weren't really either," I empathized. That wasn't exactly a lie; my parents hadn't encouraged the use of my abilities, but only because they just hadn't wanted me to make people uneasy. My admission seemed to calm her.

"Weren't? Are they dead?" she asked bluntly.

I blanched at her harsh words. Apparently, tact wasn't in her repertoire.

"Yeah, they are," I replied evenly. "That's when I came to the School; after their deaths."

"Really? So you weren't five when you came here?" she asked, seeming interested. Her mental guards were coming down, and I could tell that she liked the idea of bonding with someone who hadn't been a conventional student.

"Nope, I was ten, actually. You?"

"Thirteen. Best thing that ever happened to me." She smiled

fondly. She really believed that coming to the School was good fortune. Like me, she'd felt normal for the first time in her life once she was surrounded by other Talents.

"Yeah, me too," I agreed. At one time, I'd really felt lucky that Mac had been the one to find me. Since my incident in Nevada, I wasn't so sure. Ursula also was falling lower on my short list of viable suspects.

After Ursula's class, I set off for the dorm. My path took me past the targeting range. To my surprise, I saw a small black-haired girl surrounded by an assortment of weapons, practicing – Cadence.

Standing out of her line of sight, I watched her run through a litany of simulation firing drills. Cadence was actually pretty good. Her mental focus was amazing; I could feel the concentration. Cadence was determined to persuade Captain Alvarez to let her try out for the Hunters once again. She was convinced that if she demonstrated how great her combat and weapons skills were, she would be able to make up for the fact she wasn't an Elite. If Cadence hadn't been such a heinous wench, I might've even felt bad for her. There was no way that Cadence Choi would ever become a Hunter.

"You're really good," I called out when she paused to reload a handgun. Startled, she glanced in my direction. Realizing who'd praised her abilities, she rolled her eyes and returned her attention to the bulls-eye. I ignored her uninviting attitude and walked closer to where she stood.

"I know," she snapped. Really, would it kill her to be pleasant once in a while?

"Are you trying out for the Hunters?" I asked, hoping that if I brought up the subject, she might be willing to talk. She lowered the weapon and turned to face me.

Cadence studied me for several long moments. "Yes, I am," she answered finally.

"Would you really want to go through another Pledge year?" I probed. Usually when an Operative transferred Divisions, they only went through a brief training period. But the Hunters' missions were so intense that transfers were required to complete an entire Pledge year prior to receiving a permanent placement. Suffice it to say, there were few who transferred to the Hunters.

"The Hunters are the most highly regarded Division of the Agency, it would be well worth it," she answered shortly. I might not like her, but I did admire her intensity.

"Well, if you ever want a shooting partner, I'm always eager for more practice," I offered in what I hoped was a friendly voice. Not that I was keen on the idea of spending more than the ninety minutes a day that I already did with Cadence Choi, but maybe if we found common ground, she'd open up.

"Don't hold your breath on that," she muttered.

"Well, the offer's on the table," I said pleasantly before turning to leave. The rapid fire of bullets hitting the target provided a soundtrack for my retreating footsteps.

During my nightly session with Penny, I finally had a chance to review the tapes of Ursula's visits with her parents. I found nothing exceptional on the recordings. Mostly, they talked about innocuous topics like the weather and what Ursula had planned for her birthday which had coincided with one of her trips to Affelwood. I briefly entertained the notion that they were talking in codes. If they were, I wasn't really the right person to be analyzing the tapes.

"Penny? I doubt that this will lead anywhere, but could you listen to these tapes and see if maybe they are speaking in code? Or maybe I could ask Dr. Wythe if he could observe the interactions and give me his take?" I asked, removing the headphones that I'd been wearing to listen to the audio that accompanied the security footage.

"Yeah, I could take a look. Unless......" she let her voice trail off, and nodded to where Gemma sat on her other side. I shrugged. Gemma had been given clearance to help me and Penny; I couldn't see a reason not to assign her the task.

"Hey, Gemma?" Penny called loudly. The older girl removed her own headset and looked at Penny expectantly. "Want to help us with something?"

"Um, sure. If you think that would be okay, I'd love to," she replied, pleased at the opportunity.

"Yeah, it would be okay," I confirmed, making an executive decision. Then, I explained what I wanted her to do. Gemma began scrutinizing the same footage that I'd just watched. Once she was engrossed in her assignment, I decided to ask Penny about Ernest's claim that he "filled in" when the Crypto Bank was short staffed.

"Hmmm, I wasn't aware that was a normal practice," Penny narrowed her eyes in thought. "We should probably say something to the Director," she advised. I nodded my agreement, hoping that Ernest wasn't involved with anything treasonous.

Over the course of the next week, I fell into a routine. Every morning, I woke before the sun and either ran or went to the gym to train with a punching bag. If I ever got the chance to plead my case to the Placement Committee, I wanted to be in tip-top shape.

I dutifully assisted in all my assigned classes, keeping my mind open for any signs of plotting. Ernest became my regular lunch companion, and I found myself looking forward to the time that we spent together. He was easy to talk to and, despite the fact that I was supposed to be investigating him, I found his company calming and uncomplicated. For one hour every day, I was able to pretend that I really was an assistant Instructor and not a disgraced Operative with questionable health.

My evenings were spent with Penny and Gemma, tirelessly working through electronic files for other potentially untrustworthy Operatives. The task was tedious and unproductive.

Most nights, I didn't go to bed until well past midnight, but could never seem to sleep more than a few hours. With the exception of my morning sessions with Donavon, the majority of my day consisted of delving into the minds of others, which, in

turn, kept my own thoughts from obsessing over Donavon or –
even worse – Erik. At night, alone in my room with nothing to
distract me, they were the only thoughts that crossed my mind.

As far as Erik was concerned, to call or not to call, that was
the question. If I did call, would he talk to me? If he did talk to me,
what would he say? What would I say? Would he tell me what I
wanted to hear? What exactly did I want to hear? Did I want him to
say that he was sorry about what happened between us? I already
knew that he was. Did I want him to say he missed me? Would I
believe him if he did? Surely, if he did miss me, he would've
called.

With Donavon, the question was to hate, or not to hate.
Sometimes, I definitely hated him. Like when he accused me of
manipulating him into kicking me just so I could transfer my pain
back to him – what a convoluted theory. And he thought that I was
the unstable one. Other times, I knew that I didn't hate him at all; I
was just still hurt by his betrayal. Unfortunately for him, the
former usually outweighed the latter.

What. A. Mess.

The more time that I spent with the Instructors, the more
convinced I became that Mac was having me bark up the wrong
proverbial tree. Sure, they all had some, albeit tenuous, tie to the
Coalition. But honestly, with Crane's influence spreading
eastward, infecting the Nation like the plague, there were a lot of
Operatives with extended family in his employ. The only
difference between my suspects and the other Operatives was that
my suspects happened to be in close proximity to a Crypto data
bank. As far as I could tell, not one of them had the wherewithal to
infiltrate our encrypted records, except one – Ernest.

Ernest lacked the motivation though; nothing about him
suggested that he was involved with the Coalition. If he couldn't
handle the stress of his previous post, then there was no way that
he could handle the stress of being a double agent. His story could
be a lie, but if it was, then he was a better manipulator than me.

Annalise Cleary showed no signs of being any more adept at Electrical Manipulation than I'd first observed. In fact when I'd used my own Talents to persuade her to show me how hers worked, she was barely able to make the lamp on her desk flicker. No matter how deep I dug, I couldn't find any other inconsistencies in her file.

I asked Penny about Annalise's lack of Talent, but even her overly analytical brain couldn't posit a theory. Collectively, the best that we could come up with was a mistake during her Talent ranking exams.

I asked Mac about it, and he'd just attributed her low-level ability to lack of use, but that explanation bothered me. For a Talent, using her abilities was second nature. It was just like using any other sense; it was done subconsciously. So even if Annalise hadn't been actively practicing for the past however-many years, I was willing to bet that she used it without thinking on a daily basis. Something about her was definitely off, but I doubted that "something" was duplicitous. In general, she appeared to be on the level. She was a loyal supporter of TOXIC, and believed that the *Mandatory Testing Act* was a solid law.

Cadence Choi disliked me more and more by the day; unfortunately as Mac pointed out every time I mentioned the fact, disliking me didn't make her any more suspicious. She took advantage of every opportunity to contradict me in front of the students. Even though she wasn't always technically right, I usually let her snide remarks roll right off. Her less-than-friendly welcome was partially due to her jealously over my placement with the Hunters for my Pledge year, and partially over my obvious relationship with the Director. Her crush on Donavon didn't help either.

I'd dealt with her type since coming to the McDonough School and refused to let her bother me. While she was definitely jealous that I'd been asked to pledge the Hunters, she also took a great deal of satisfaction in the fact that I'd not been permanently assigned there after graduation. Since the official story was that I'd failed my solo mission – I guess that was technically true – she felt assured that I was no better than she was.

Mac felt that it was best that no one knew what had actually happened on my assignment, so I swallowed my wounded pride and let her continue believing that I hadn't had what it takes to be a Hunter. Unfortunately, her honest belief that the official version of events was true also meant she was unlikely the spy. The person who'd leaked my identity to Crane would definitely know why the Hunt had failed.

As for Thad Wietz, he felt guilty about leaving his parents for what he thought would be "a better life"; it consumed his every thought. The more that I pushed for details about his past, the less willingly he divulged them. I used our daily conversations to establish a strong connection, and superficially believed that he was telling the truth. However, he was fairly adept at blocking his deeper memories. Despite Mac's insistence that I be more forceful, I refrained. Thad was definitely at the top of my suspect list, but that wasn't saying much since he only landed there by default.

Then there was Ursula. There wasn't much to say about her. She was confident in all her Talents – and I do mean all of them. She constantly pranced around the Instructor dorm scantily clad, her ample cleavage on display and her curves hugged by the minute pieces of fabric that she favored. Her male admirers included any guy with a heartbeat. Of course, there was one in particular she was gunning for: Donavon.

When we were in school, I'd had to contend with a lot of school-girl crushes on Donavon. He was a good-looking guy and the Director's son, which made him a hot commodity. I supposed the same still held true. The number of attractive male Instructors under forty was limited, making Donavon stand out even more.

Both Ursula and Cadence's attractions irked me. I knew that I had no right to be upset; he and I could barely be in the same room without me losing my temper. But I hated the way that they both flirted with him. Even more, I hated the way that he indulged their advances. Donavon lapped up every opportunity to engage in flirtatious conversation when I was present. His behavior made me want to kick him.

Gemma finished her in-depth examination of the visits with Ursula's parents and determined that they were not using codes. I decided to pursue one last avenue regarding the tapes; I submitted them to Dr. Wythe asking him to give me a report on the interactions. Mac agreed because Dr. Wythe had been my therapist since my return from Nevada, and was well versed in the events that had transpired there.

The tension between Donavon and I grew exponentially by the day. I half-wondered if others could sense it and were just too scared to mention it, or we were the only ones who understood how precarious our situation really was. I hadn't even told Penny about the fight, my stitches, and what Donavon had accused me of. I wasn't sure where my hesitancy to confide in her came from – was I embarrassed by my reaction to his accusations? Or maybe a small part of me worried that they were true, and if I told her, she might make me confront that uncomfortable realization.

I *had* been concentrating really hard. And I *had* been trying to block the pain. And I *had* been anticipating that he would land a really hard blow. Had I been concentrating so hard that I'd actually been manipulating him to do it? Had I actually been deflecting the pain instead of trying to block it? No, that was absurd. At least, that's what I told myself every time I considered it. There was no way that I'd do something so ridiculous ...or would I? Admittedly, my temper had been even more out of control than usual lately, and Donavon's mere presence fueled the flames of my rage-driven fire.

It was one week to the day after my arrival on campus that the tension finally broke. Afterward, I couldn't recall what precipitated the altercation. One minute, I was in Donavon's class, helping students with their offensive moves. Donavon's mental voice was disagreeing with what my actual voice was telling someone, and something inside of me snapped. I don't remember what I mentally yelled at him – I probably repressed the words to save myself later anguish – but whatever it was, it must've been ugly.

Donavon immediately dismissed class, but the students seemed to realize that something was amiss between us. Several of them stuck around, pretending that they were lost in their own conversations. At first, it wouldn't have mattered whether they were listening in; the entire fight was mental, insults flying back and forth ...until it wasn't.

"You want a fight, Talia?" Donavon's mental voice screamed at me. *"Then let's do it. Hit me."* Apparently, I didn't need to be asked twice. I literally flew at him. Launching myself into the air, my entire body went horizontal to the ground. He hadn't anticipated that I'd take him up on his offer quite so quickly, which gave me a split second of surprise. It was all I needed.

I hit him square in the chest, knocking him to the ground. His reflexes were fast, and he recovered quickly. Grabbing my wrists as I fell on top of him, he used his superior upper body strength to throw me over his head. I anticipated this and used his momentum, in addition to my own, to flip my feet completely over my head, landing neatly on my toes.

Donavon was quick though, and before I could even turn around to face him, he was upright. We backed away from each other and began circling. I was positive that we had an audience, but I no longer cared.

My peripheral vision reddened. In that moment, my only care was hurting Donavon – physically hurting him for all of the emotional pain that he'd caused me, making him suffer the same way that I had. I wanted him to pay.

Usually, my biggest advantage in a fight was that my opponents underestimated me, but it was an advantage I didn't have with Donavon; he knew better. Every minute that I'd spent training as an adolescent, he'd been right there beside me. The only benefit that I had over Donavon was my anger, my unqualified, nearly primal urge to attack. Donavon might not have liked the way that I'd been behaving lately – and being a Morph, his blood tended to run hot – but he lacked the epic levels of animosity toward me that I harbored for him.

I flew at him again. This time, I used my momentum to cartwheel through the air so that my feet were over my head when I landed beside him. My hands made contact with the ground close to his feet. Summoning all of the strength I had, I vaulted myself upwards and was rewarded for my efforts when my foot made contact with the underside of his chin, throwing him off-balance. I finished the rotation and landed on my feet, in time to see him stumble and lose his footing. I was about to press my advantage when he miraculously stabilized himself and reached out, grabbing my arm. Instead of pulling away, I used his arm for leverage and kicked off the ground. My right foot made contact with his shoulder, and my left should've followed suit to make contact with his head.

But I'd kicked off too hard, and Donavon, realizing what I was going to do, added his own strength into my swing; when my feet were over my head, I was much further off the ground than I'd anticipated. Donavon and I were locked in the awkward embrace when it happened.

I was completely upside down, his fingers encircling my wrist as my fingers frantically clawed at his. Suddenly, I became disoriented, losing awareness of my surroundings. I was no longer in control of my now-flailing limbs. Time slowed to a stand-still as gravity fought to return me to the ground. I didn't fall back to earth gracefully as I had so many times before, but rather with legs floundering in a desperate attempt to get them underneath me.

My fingers would no longer obey my command to hold on to Donavon, and my grip slackened. My body began to convulse, arms and legs twitching as the seizure racked through my entire being. I wanted to cry out, but I was no more in control of my vocal chords than the rest of my muscles. My last conscious thought was that I hoped I landed on one of my fleshier parts, like my butt.

Chapter Eleven

"I always forget how amazing it is to watch her fight." Janet's voice cut through the haze that was clouding my brain.

"I don't even know where she learned some of those tricks," Mac responded, something like pride in his tone.

"Dr. Thistler says that the levels in her blood have dropped drastically," Janet commented.

"Thank goodness for that," Mac replied.

"I don't mean to say I told you so ...but well, I told you so," Janet said sternly.

"I know that there was some tension initially, but they have been fine for the better part of the week. It wasn't Donavon's fault; it was the extreme physical exertion," Mac snapped.

"Fine?! Fine?!" Janet sounded exasperated. "Were you in the same status meeting that I was? They aren't 'fine' Mac. She's been on edge since Day One. In light of what just happened, I suggest that we get another Operative in here, one with less emotional attachment to Talia."

"No. Donavon stays. Natalia stays. They are both professionals. Hopefully, this little episode will demonstrate just how important it is that they put the past behind them and learn to be civil," Mac retorted.

"Mac, they're teenagers. You can't expect them to act like adults – they aren't adults," Janet replied flatly.

"I can, and I do," Mac said angrily.

I couldn't stand to hear them talk about me like I wasn't there. I had to intervene.

"Invalid trying to sleep over here," I announced loudly.

A large hand gently covered mine. "Shhhh," Donavon's voice said soothingly.

I froze. Slowly, licking my extremely dry lips, I turned toward the sound of his voice.

"If you want me to leave ...I understand," his mental voice said softly. He raised my hand, still enclosed in his, and rubbed it against his stubbly cheek. My throat ached as I tried to swallow my unease. I wanted to tell him exactly where he could go ...but something stopped me. As upset as I'd been over Donavon's betrayal, I really missed his friendship. Going through the intense physical therapy alone had been agonizing. Penny was great, but she wasn't Donavon; she didn't know me like he did, she didn't comfort me the way he did. And Mac was right. I was a professional. Age-wise, I might still be a teenager, but I'd been through more in my short existence than most people experienced in their entire lifetime.

If we wanted to catch the spy, I needed to start acting like the Hunter that I'd trained to be even if I wasn't technically a Hunter anymore.

"Stay," I croaked out loud, my voice hoarse. *"Water?"* I added mentally. The straw hit my bottom lip, and I opened my mouth, guzzling the refreshing liquid as quickly as the straw would allow.

"Easy, easy," Donavon chuckled. *"I don't want to be blamed for you choking to death."*

"Will you tell Janet and Mac to go in the hallway if they're going to talk about me?" I urged him.

"They are in the hallway. Down by the nurse's station, actually," he replied, sounding a little uneasy. *"Can you hear them?"* he added hesitantly.

"Of course, I can hear them," I snapped. *"Their voices woke me up."*

Donavon didn't reply, but I could tell that he thought that I was confused. I assumed that he could make out their words, but his Morph hearing was naturally much better than mine. I wanted to tell him that I wasn't confused at all, that I could hear Janet and Mac loud and clear, but I hesitated. If they were really all the way down by the nurses' station, there was no way that I should've been able to hear them without concentrating. Superior hearing was not among my many Talents. I had better-than-average senses, due to the sensory-deprivation training that I'd done, but they were nothing compared to a Morph. If Janet and Mac were really that far away, how on earth could I hear their conversation?

For some reason, that thought took a tangent and brought up the day that I'd been admiring Donavon's eyelashes in class. He'd been a solid ten feet away. Sure, if I focused all of my mental energy to the task, I *might* have been able to hone in on his eyelashes, but I hadn't been doing that. How had I picked up on the detail from so far away?

I must not have been keeping my thoughts private; no sooner had I begun to ponder his lashes, I felt them softly brush my cheekbone. As his face leaned closer to mine, I inhaled his familiar scent – soap and clean linens. Tingles traveled down my whole body, and goose bumps sprang up on my arms and legs. My head felt heavy, and I was glad that I was lying down; surely my legs would give out if I tried to stand.

Donavon's mouth rested right next to my ear, and my body tensed at the proximity to his. What was happening? I didn't want to feel like this. His breath tickled my ear as he whispered out loud, "butterfly kisses."

My heart was pounding so loudly that I could hear each accelerated "thump." Forgetting all my early anger, I nuzzled my face against Donavon's. His mental voice hummed softly in my head. It was a melody that I knew well, the words that accompanied it long forgotten. I smiled, feeling truly at ease for the first time in months as I fell back to sleep listening to Donavon's comforting song.

When I woke up next, Dr. Thistler was the one holding my hand. I looked at her and groaned. "Am I dying?" I asked dryly. I definitely felt like I was.

"No, despite your best efforts Natalia, you will live to fight another day," she replied, irritation and disapproval flickering in her gray eyes. I had a bad feeling that I was in store for a lecture.

"Give it to me straight, Doc. I can handle it," I replied, trying to sit up.

"Easy, Natalia," she replied, adjusting the pillows behind my back to better support me. "It was a little bumpy at first. The adrenaline elevated the levels of the compound in your blood, but I increased the dosage of the equalizer. It took a couple of days, but you are stable now." She smiled, pleased with her work.

"I've been out for several days?!" I exclaimed, not caring about her efforts to stabilize me. I'd be pleased when her efforts actually cured me.

"I felt that it was best to heavily sedate you while I stabilized the compound in your blood. It was necessary to prevent further seizures."

"Great Did it work?" I snapped. The liberties that she'd taken with my consciousness irked me; she was treating me like some experimental lab rat.

"It did, actually," she replied, smiling and seemingly oblivious to my ungrateful attitude.

"Where's Donavon?" I demanded. After spending the last week avoiding him, I craved his presence now.

"Mr. McDonough is teaching, but Headmistress Evans is waiting outside to see you once I finish checking your vitals," Dr. Thistler answered pointedly.

"If you could hurry, that would be super," I snapped. She shook her head and rolled her eyes, showing me just how much she appreciated my impatience. She quickly finished her appraisal of all my vitals, then opened the door to allow Janet to come in.

I waited for Dr. Thistler to leave before I interrogated Janet. "What exactly happened?"

Janet studied me through narrowed green eyes assessing whether I was prepared for this conversation. She apparently decided that I was. "Several students saw the altercation between you and Donavon," she explained. "Fearing the worst, I called Mac."

I sighed. "So, you were there when ...I had the seizure?" I asked quietly, staring at the machine that monitored my heart rate like it was the most fascinating contraption in the world. The beeps came more quickly as color raced to my cheeks. Up until now, the only people to witness my seizures were Mac, Gretchen, and the Medics who treated me. The episodes were embarrassing and painful, and I hated for others to see me so vulnerable. I was supposed to be strong – a fighter, a Hunter.

Janet cleared her throat loudly, ignoring my anxiety. "Yes, Mac and I arrived shortly after it started," she said gently. "Donavon realized that something was wrong as soon as you started to convulse. He caught you before you hit the ground."

Thank goodness for that. He probably saved me a broken bone or two.

"The trembling didn't subside," she continued shakily. "When we finally got you to Medical, Dr. Thistler gave you the equalizer immediately, but it didn't work. She had to give you a sedative."

"How long?" I asked, keeping my eyes trained on the red spikes that blipped across the monitor screen.

"How long?" Janet repeated, sounding confused.

I turned to meet her gaze. "Yeah, how long before the seizure stopped?" I asked.

"An hour," she whispered.

An hour? That was the longest yet; my condition was deteriorating. I blinked furiously, trying to hold back tears.

"You were agitated and kept screaming in your sleep. Mac was so worried that he refused to leave your bedside," Janet pressed on.

"What did I say?" I grimaced, worried that my night terrors might have been a little too telling.

"Nothing coherent," she assured me, "mostly just screaming."

"I see. Is that why Dr. Thistler kept me comatose?" I asked quietly.

"Even after she sedated you, she couldn't quiet the nightmares. It wasn't until Donavon started sneaking into your room that you finally calmed down." Janet watched me carefully for my reaction.

"Donavon? Really?" I arched an eyebrow in surprise. The more that I thought about it, the more her statement made sense. Donavon's presence had always calmed me, eased my tension. The familiarity between us made me feel safe and secure.

"Natalia, do you want me to have you replaced?" she asked bluntly. "Because I will. Mac is against the idea, but I'm honestly not sure that you're ready for this."

I stared at her while carefully measuring my next words. She didn't know that I'd heard her conversation with Mac, and I didn't want her to know that I'd unwittingly eavesdropped. "No, Janet, I'm ready for this. I want to do this. Donavon and I are adults. We're professionals who can put our issues aside – this assignment is too important."

My words did nothing to dispel her concerns, but she didn't argue further. She knew me well enough to understand that once I put my mind to something, there was no changing it.

Just then, Mac stuck his head through the doorway of my room. "Thank goodness you are finally awake," he said, by way of greeting.

"Sorry to have inconvenienced you," I replied sarcastically. "I'm feeling great, thanks for asking."

"You are awake, Natalia. Therefore, you must be feeling

better," he replied absently. He apparently wasn't overly concerned as long as I wasn't dying.

"Did you come down here just to see my smiling face?" I asked. Mac's indifference to my physical health annoyed me. I had to remind myself that Mac went out of his way over the past few months to aid my recovery. Still, the building animosity that I'd been experiencing since the previous year didn't soften my irritation now.

"No. I need you to get dressed and come with me, now," he answered. He wasn't wasting any time. My displeasure grew, but I was itching to get out of Medical. After the extensive rehabilitation and current daily visits, I was none too keen to stay here any longer than absolutely necessary.

"You don't have to tell me twice. Where are my clothes?" I asked brightly.

"Wait just a minute," Janet interrupted, "she has suffered a traumatic event, Mac."

"Dr. Thistler said that her vitals are fine, and I need her to interrogate a suspect," Mac snapped, baring razor-sharp canines. Janet and I both flinched at his open display of aggression. Like his son, Mac was a poly-morph, but he rarely displayed his Talent anymore.

"What are you talking about? Who?" I demanded, recovering once Mac's lips safely concealed his teeth again.

"I had Penny dig deeper into Ernest Tate. Just as you thought, not everything adds up," Mac responded, now composed and in control of his emotions.

"Hold on. I never said that I thought things didn't add up. I just thought that maybe we should look into his background." I was suddenly on the defensive. Ernest had been nothing but nice to me. Sure, he was one of the few people that I'd encountered at School who was actually capable of hacking into our network, but that alone didn't make him a traitor. I honestly didn't believe him capable of such deception.

"And that is exactly what I had Ms. Latimore do. She looked into his past – he has family in California. After monitoring his parents' communicators, we've determined that his father is still in contact with them. Now I need *you* to do what you do best and find out where Ernest's loyalties lie," Mac replied.

My stomach sank. I genuinely liked Ernest, even considered us friends. I really hoped that he wasn't a Coalition spy.

Sensing my trepidation, Mac spoke softly. "Sometimes, the people closest to us are the best at deceiving us." He gave me a pointed look. "You, of all people, should know that."

Suddenly, I loathed Mac. Just when I'd resolved to try moving past Donavon's infidelity, Mac threw it in my face. Donavon had been the person closest to me until he betrayed me.

Janet shifted uncomfortably as she took in my distraught reaction to Mac's hurtful words. "Can this not wait?" she asked him in a low voice.

"No. It cannot," Mac replied shortly, refusing to even look at her, his gray eyes fixed on mine.

"Janet, would you mind running to my room and getting me something to wear?" I asked, determined not to be the first to break the silent battle of wills between myself and Mac. Out of the corner of my eye, I saw her nod her agreement. After giving Mac an if-looks-could-kill stare, she walked noiselessly from the room.

Mac held my gaze, his stare so intense that if I'd known what was good for me, I would've backed down. After all, he had the advantage; he loomed over my hospital bed where I lay, still shaken from Janet's account of my seizure. Sensing my resistance, Mac moved closer, a low rumble starting in his chest that was meant to intimidate me.

"Why is this so urgent?" I demanded, still refusing to give in, even though the weight of his mind bore down on me.

"Natalia, we have a SPY in the Agency," he spat back, eyes flashing angrily and menacingly.

"I understand that, but what did Penny find that makes you so confident that he is our spy? I've talked to him, and he is a truthful person. I bet there are plenty of Agency Operatives with family members in the Coalition," I said, gritting my teeth.

"Exactly, you have *talked* to him. You have not dug into his mind to see what he is hiding."

"We don't know that he's hiding anything!" I yelled.

"No, you are right, we don't. But we also don't know that he is not," Mac replied pointedly. "I did some further checking into Ernest's claim that he 'filled in' for sick Operatives in the Crypto Division. That apparently has happened on several occasions over the past year, but an appointment like that needs to be cleared by me, and it was not. I've suspended the Crypto Supervisor here at School, pending an investigation."

His words cooled the blood boiling in my veins; that was exactly what I'd been afraid of. When Ernest confided that piece of information to me, I'd known that it was a serious breach of protocol. I'd hoped that it would prove to be miscommunication somewhere in the chain of command or that Mac would confirm that he'd sanctioned the temporary placement. Apparently, that was not the case.

"Do you plan on having me interrogate everyone that could possibly be the spy?" I demanded, feeling the fight go out of me. Mac was right. Ernest's actions were suspect.

"Natalia, you have been here a week, and have found nothing!" he shouted at me, his cool demeanor cracking like ice on a frozen lake. "I am not going to wait around for another situation like what happened in Nevada! I will not see another Operative brought back from a mission at death's door! I will not lose more Talents to the Coalition. I want this person found and I want him found now."

Shame filled me at the passion in his words. He wasn't uncaring. He had been there when the Medics brought me off the plane in Kansas. Mac had seen me broken and nearly ruined. Mac had painstakingly helped me to recover, both mentally and physically, from what Ian Crane and his men had done to me. Mac was the one pushing the Medical to find a cure for my condition. All he wanted in return was the same thing that I should want – to find the person who'd nearly cost me my life.

"Mac, I'm sorry," I began, biting back the tears that burned behind my eyeballs.

"I don't want sorry, I want answers, Natalia." His voice was just above a whisper, and deadly serious as he leaned his face close to mine. I think that I preferred him yelling. Swallowing any further replies, I nodded my understanding.

Chapter Twelve

Janet returned soon after with a pair of jeans and soft cream-colored sweater. Thankful to shed the gray medical tunic, I dressed quickly while Janet and Mac spoke in loud whispers in the hallway.

"I don't think that you should be pushing her so hard," Janet whispered angrily.

"I don't remember asking your opinion," Mac snapped.

"Are you not the slightest bit concerned about her condition?" Janet's voice raised an octave, her words laced with venom.

"You know what I am concerned with, Janet? I am concerned about the traitor – the spy – that we have in our Agency." I could almost hear Mac's teeth grinding together with the effort of keeping his voice to an audible whisper. "Natalia is the best chance that I have of finding that person. But don't you think for a second that I don't care about her well-being. I brought her into my home, I raised her, and you, of all people, know the lengths that I would go to protect her. So don't you dare accuse me of not caring. She is every bit as much a daughter to me as Donavon is a son." Mac was furious. Tension rolled through the closed door. The air was thick with the vibrations emanating off both of them.

I loudly opened the door to my room and stepped out into the hallway. Both Janet and Mac turned quickly. "I'm ready," I said quietly, effectively putting an end to their bickering.

Mac, Janet, and I set off across the campus. Neither of them looked at the other nor uttered a single word. Both were lost in their own angry thoughts.

Our destination was a small nondescript building on the very outskirts of the compound. I'd never actually been inside the building, but had wandered past it on many occasions. Truthfully, I hadn't been exactly sure what purpose the structure served – apparently interrogations.

My head was still fuzzy from all the drugs that Dr. Thistler had used to sedate me. My body ached with every step I took, making me regret my eagerness to jump out of bed. Janet was right; I wasn't ready for this.

A dimly-lit guard booth materialized in the dark night. I could make out three individuals – two standing outside, and one inside. Penny's flaming red hair was starkly illuminated by the light from the guard booth. Donavon stood next to her, anxiously shifting from one foot to the other, eyes intently studying the blades of grass beneath.

"Hi, there," I mentally called to him. His head shot up and our eyes met across the great distance. He turned and said something to Penny, who turned and looked in our direction. Donavon began closing the gap between us.

"I'm glad that you're here," I sent. Donavon smiled, and I felt relief flood through him. He'd been worried that I'd rethought my earlier feelings of camaraderie. I hadn't. I really had missed him, and I was resigned to making the best of our current situation. After all, it wasn't Donavon's fault that he'd been sprung on me.

"Tal!" he exclaimed, wrapping me in his arms. "Are you sure that you're up for this?"

I glanced at Mac; the hard set of his jaw and coldness of his eyes told me that I'd better be.

"Of course," I lied. No, I wasn't ready for this, but it needed to be done. If nothing else, my interrogation would prove Ernest's innocence. Granted, that would not put me any closer to identifying the actual culprit, but at least I could rest assured that another person I counted among my friends hadn't deceived me.

The four of us made our way to the guard station where Penny waited.

"How did you know that it was us standing here? You had to be like a hundred yards away!" she exclaimed, hugging me.

"Penny, I think the people manning the satellites can spot your hair from space," I replied, only half-joking. My point was valid; Penny's bright red-orange locks were like a lighthouse beckoning to ships in the night.

"Ha ha." She rolled her eyes.

"Natalia has work to do. So if social hour is over, we should really get this over with," Mac interjected. I nodded in response to him, then glanced conspiratorially at Penny and Donavon. Mac was being a little dramatic. Janet kept shooting him dirty looks when he was sure to notice. It felt good to have somebody like her in my corner.

The four of us followed Mac to the front of the building. There was another guard stationed inside, who exchanged a nod with Mac as we passed. We followed Mac to an elevator bank, then waited in silence for the ping that signaled the elevator's arrival. The doors slid soundlessly open, and we filed in. Mac pressed his thumb to a scanner on the front-right panel of the elevator, and a green light flashed, confirming Mac's identity. He entered a two-digit number on to the touch pad and the car sped downward.

The elevator gave another soft ping, indicating our arrival on the designated floor.

The hallway was cool and impersonal, with dreary, gray walls. I shuddered, hugging myself as we followed Mac to a door marked 5B. Inside was a waiting room with a long rectangular table, sitting underneath a one-way mirror. On the table sat several monitors, each displaying a different set of data, and three plastic chairs sat in front of it, facing the mirror. On the other side of the glass was Ernest.

"Let's get this over with," Mac said to me. I nodded and took a deep breath. Janet gave me a tight-lipped smile and nodded encouragingly. Exhaling slowly, I opened the door to the adjoining room.

Ernest was staring nervously at his hands folded in his lap, but looked up when I entered. His hazels eyes darted nervously between me and his reflection. The air was thick with the stench of body odor and anxiety. I fought the urge to wrinkle my nose in disgust.

"Talia?" he said uncertainly. "What's going? Why am I here?"

"I just want to ask you some questions," I said soothingly.

His eyes darted left, right, up, and down. "Did you have to drag me here just to ask me a couple of questions?" He laughed nervously as he wiped sweaty palms on his shirt, leaving damp handprints in their wake.

"I'm sorry. This is just a formality." I tried to keep my voice light. The smell of his sweat, sweet and pungent, consumed the small room. Forcing back the bile rising in my throat, I focused on his face. Beads of moisture glistened just below his hairline. I didn't need the monitors on the other side of the mirror to tell me that his heart was beating much more quickly than normal; I could hear the soft thump-thump with my own ears.

Slowly, I moved to sit across from Ernest. I began with the easy questions: name, place of birth, parents. I read the answers as they popped into his head. Every answer that he spoke aloud matched the one that I read from his mind. Finding my rhythm, I moved on to more personal questions – those that Donavon's mental voice fed me from the other side of the glass. I asked questions about his family in California, and his father's reputed communications with them. I delved into his own personal relationship with his extended relatives.

Hours passed as I dissected every detail of Ernest's life. Finally, when my mental and physical exhaustion peaked, I turned to the mirror and spoke aloud.

"It's not him, Mac."

Donavon's mental voice answered me. *"Search deeper,"* it responded.

I glared at the mirror and thought unspeakable words in Mac's direction.

"We need to be sure, Natalia," Mac's mental voice responded. Scowling, I turned back to face Ernest.

"Give me your hands, Ernest," I commanded in a low voice. He obeyed without hesitation. "Look into my eyes," I ordered. He raised his hazel eyes, the pupils so dilated that they appeared black, and reflected a distorted image of my face. Locking our gazes, I concentrated as hard as I could, and opened my mind to Ernest's. Wading through his most recent memories of teaching here at the School, I saw nothing of use. I systematically moved backwards, pulling every memory and experience that Ernest had ever had from his mind. I felt the last vestiges of Ernest's willpower leave him, and every thought that he'd ever had crashed over me in a tidal wave of memories.

No longer able to distinguish where my mind ended and Ernest's began, I started shaking and gulping air. It was quickly becoming hard to breathe. I truly felt as if I was drowning in Ernest's mind.

"Natalia," a sharp voice snapped in my head. *"Natalia, pull back!"* the voice – Donavon's – screamed. But it was so far away, sounding like a distant echo in a long hallway, and I couldn't pull back. I was in too deep.

"Tal, listen to my voice. Pull back," Donavon frantically ordered. I tried to concentrate on his words, but it was next to impossible with Ernest's memories swirling like a funnel cloud inside of my mind. The interrogation room ceased to exist. I was floating, becoming part of Ernest as I pulled more and more of his life into me.

"Tal, please. Follow the sound of my voice. You need to come back to me," Donavon urged. The intensity of his words, coupled

with the strength of his will, brought me back to reality. I was still entrenched in Ernest's thoughts, but it was becoming easier to separate our minds.

Summoning all of my willpower, I yanked my hands from Ernest, who was now clinging to me with a death grip. I ripped my eyes away, and felt the imaginary rope that had connected us snap. Severing the bond hurt. I collapsed against the chair, feeling disoriented and shaking. I took deep breaths, and tried to calm the trembling in my hands. Donavon burst through the door, but stayed several feet back, scared to come any closer.

"Talia," he said tentatively. I turned to look up at him; his face was blurry, and I blinked several times in an attempt to sharpen the image. All of my senses felt dull and sluggish, like I'd just woken from a dream. He quickly knelt down beside my chair, taking my hands in his.

"Are you okay? What happened?" he asked.

I shook my head, my tongue felt thick and too big for my mouth. *"Can I leave now?"* I asked him mentally. The need to get out of the room consumed me. I couldn't breathe, couldn't think. Dizziness filled my head as bile made its way up my throat. I needed fresh air, now.

"Aloud," he answered. I looked at him, confused. "You need to speak out loud right now. I don't think that you should be communicating mentally – you're too vulnerable."

I looked back across the table at Ernest. His head was slumped against his chest and he was drooling. The scene cut through my haze like a knife piercing my heart.

"Is he going to be okay," I whispered, close to tears.

"Get her out of here." Mac's voice came from the doorway before Donavon could answer.

Behind Mac stood two Medics, and all three entered the tiny room. The Medics each took one of Ernest's arms, lifting him out of his seat and into a waiting wheelchair. I stared blankly after the trio.

"Get her out of here," Mac repeated.

"Still think that this was such a good idea?" Donavon demanded, rounding on his father.

"She will be fine. She just needs to rest," Mac replied shortly.

"What about Ernest? Will he be okay?" I asked, looking up at Mac.

"In time," Mac answered without meeting my eyes.

Donavon rose to his full height and faced his father. Their eyes locked in a silent battle of wills, eerily similar to the one that had transpired between myself and Mac just hours before. Neither spoke, both men standing rigid, electricity crackling in the air around their bodies. Donavon's hands were tightly fisted at his sides and a low growl sounded in his chest.

"Take Natalia back to her room," Mac ordered his son, his words holding so much authority that I flinched. Donavon sagged under the weight of his father's command as he backed down. He never could stand up to his father, not that I blamed him. Mac was not the kind of person that most dared to challenge. Even Janet stood silently in the corner of the crowded room, too intimidated to make so much as a peep.

Donavon gently pulled me to my feet. He wrapped one of his long arms around my shoulders and silently led me from the suffocating interrogation room. Penny quickly fell in step with us as we made our way to the elevator. She looked as tired and drained as I felt. Her eyes were bloodshot, and dark circles colored the hollows beneath.

No one spoke as we made our way back up the elevator and out into the night. I let them lead me back across campus to my room. My mind was so numb that I barely registered my surroundings, and was surprised to find the three of us standing in my bedroom sooner rather than later.

"Why don't I take it from here?" Penny said quietly to Donavon. He looked at me questioningly. I managed to nod my head, indicating that he should go.

"You should sleep in. The first people won't be arriving until lunchtime," he replied.

"Huh?" People? Lunchtime? What was he talking about?

"Career fair starts tomorrow," Penny said tiredly, sensing my confusion.

"Right. Career fair," I mumbled. My medically-induced hibernation period had thrown my sense of time out of whack.

"I have to help set up in the morning, but I'll come check on you afterward," Donavon said as he bent down to place a gentle kiss on the top of my head. Instinctively, I wrapped my arms around him, craving the physical comfort of his familiar body against mine. An overwhelming urge to hold him tighter consumed me, making me hesitate before I pulled back and said goodnight.

Once he was gone, Penny set about finding my pajamas and helping me get ready for bed. I changed and climbed under the covers. Every muscle in my body relaxed as I lay on the now familiar mattress. Penny pulled the chair from my desk over and sat next to my bed.

"Want to talk about what happened?" she asked quietly. Her green eyes were so full of concern that my frozen insides began to thaw.

"Not really," I mumbled. Reliving what had just happened with Ernest so soon might send me over the edge of sanity, on which I was currently teetering. My hands were still shaking slightly. The view from the other side of the glass must have been pretty horrific too because I noticed that, in addition to the bloodshot eyes and dark circles, Penny was also extremely pale. Her hands twitched uneasily in her lap.

"Want to talk about Erik?" she countered mischievously.

"Erik?" I asked, startled. "What does he have to do with anything?" I'd thought about Erik constantly over the past couple of months, but besides initial inquiries into his well-being, I hadn't talked to Penny about him.

"Both Erik and Henri will be here tomorrow for the career

fair......" she replied. "I assumed that Erik had messaged you," she added hastily.

"No, he hasn't," I said wistfully, glancing at my silent communicator. Erik's purposeful refusal to call me stung. If nothing else, wasn't he wondering if I'd read his letter? Oh, God, Erik's letter. His words had fueled my animosity towards Mac during my recovery, yet I still wasn't sure that I truly believed him. Not that I thought Erik was lying. I just thought that maybe Erik had misunderstood the encounter. Or maybe I just hoped that was the case.

"Wait, did he call you?" I asked accusingly. The miserable look on Penny's face told me that he had. "What did he say?" I demanded.

"Erik didn't call me, Harris did," she clarified. I sighed with relief and instantly felt bad for jumping down her throat. "We talk every so often, and he just mentioned that Erik was one of the Operatives chosen to represent the Hunters at the fair."

"Oh, I see," I replied in a small voice. "So, do you think that he might want to see me?" Tears pricked the backs of my eyes as I waited for Penny to give me some sort of confirmation, to reassure me that Erik would want to see me.

"I'm sure that he does," Penny said softly, wrapping her arms around me. Despite the fact that she'd told me exactly what I wanted to hear, I couldn't hold back the tears any longer. The full emotional impact of the day finally hit me, and I sobbed against Penny's shoulder. She rubbed my back soothingly. "I know he'll be happy to see you tomorrow," she promised.

"I don't even know why I'm crying," I laughed shakily as I pulled back from Penny's embrace.

"You've had a really long day. It's a lot for anyone to handle. Why don't you get some sleep? We can talk about stuff tomorrow," Penny offered.

"Do you mind staying until I fall asleep?" I sniffed. Part of me wanted to be alone, but part of me feared that, left to my own devices, I might start weeping again.

"Of course, not, I'll be right here," Penny replied kindly as she settled back into my less-than-comfortable desk chair. Her voice was strained and tired, and I knew that I should insist she go back to her own room; watching such an intense interrogation hadn't been easy on her. But I needed her, needed her strength, and I was too selfish to tell her to go rest. Tomorrow, I was sure that I'd hate myself for being so weak and self-centered, but not tonight.

Chapter Thirteen

Taking Donavon's suggestion, I slept late the next morning. For someone who'd slept for the better part of the past five days, I sure was exhausted. My head throbbed, and thinking of the upcoming day's events did nothing to alleviate my misery: career fair.

Every year representatives from the major divisions of TOXIC came to campus and set up booths shortly before the students chose which Placement Exams to take. The event afforded them the opportunity to speak with representatives, decide what career path they wanted to pursue, and, subsequently, which tests they would sit for. Each student would be allowed to select up to three Divisions for which he or she could attempt placement. The students were encouraged to sign up for demonstrations and get one-on-one advice and assistance from Operatives currently working in the sector they wished to join.

When I was still a student, I'd loved the career fair. I'd loved getting out of classes and seeing the Operatives' demonstrations. In retrospect, it all seemed rather pointless since, in most cases, students' Talents and Rankings dictated their placement. Many students hoping for coveted positions began training as young as twelve, the age when students were allowed to start taking electives.

TOXIC identified strong physical Talents early, and began

training them in combat to develop the necessary skills to become a Hunter. Students with strong Higher Reasoning Talents, like Penny, were often pulled from physical training to focus solely on honing and refining their computer skills. Ordinarily, higher-level mental Talents like me were marked for psychic interrogation and took specialized investigative techniques classes. Mac had insisted that I take several interrogation classes, but had fully encouraged my pursuit of the physical ones as well. He'd never doubted that I would become a Hunter, at least not back then.

Today, I couldn't muster any of my usual enthusiasm for Career Day. What was I going to say to Erik if – no, when – I saw him? He hadn't even sent me a heads-up that he was going to be here. Admittedly, I hadn't called him either. Every time I punched his contact information into my communicator, something stopped me. I wasn't ready to speak with him, let alone face him.

With Donavon, I walked the thin line that separated love and hate. With Erik, I walked the line that separated extreme embarrassment and whatever its opposite was. Part of me was thrilled at the prospect of seeing Erik later today, but part of me wanted to crawl back under my covers and stay there until he left. And still another part of me felt awful for feeling any reaction at all. I had no idea what was going on with me and Donavon, but I somehow doubted that I should be in such emotional turmoil over another guy. It was like being back at the beginning of my Pledge year when I'd first developed feelings for Erik that rivaled – and eventually surpassed – my feelings for Donavon.

A sharp knock at my door brought me out of my tortured reminiscing. I debated staying quiet and seeing if my visitor would leave. Instead, I opened my mind to determine if the person on the other side was someone that I knew; Donavon *had* promised he'd visit me this morning. When I opened my mind, a mental voice, loud and clear, demanded to be let in: Erik.

"Tals, I know you're in there. I can feel you," Erik called. *"Open the door or I will break it down."*

"I'm still in bed," I sent.

"Don't care," he shot back.

"I haven't brushed my teeth yet." I tried another tactic. I could imagine him rolling his beautiful turquoise eyes.

"Tal, I've been around you plenty of mornings," he answered, sounding more than a little impatient. He had a point; we'd shared a cabin for months while I was a Pledge, not to mention several sleepovers the week before I'd left for my solo mission.

"I don't want to see you," I insisted. Even as I sent the words, I knew that they weren't really true. Now that he was here, standing outside my door, I really wanted to see him, wanted to tell him about everything that had happened since the embarrassing encounter in my bedroom at Headquarters. But his rejection was still fresh in my mind. I'd thrown myself at him, offered him something personal and intimate, and he'd refused me.

"I kind of figured you felt that way, but I don't care if you want to see me. I want to see you," he replied.

"Why didn't you call me then?" I demanded. *"Why didn't you tell me that you were coming if you wanted to see me so badly?"*

"Please, Tals. Let me in, so we can talk," he urged.

I let out a frustrated noise that Erik must've taken for acquiescence because I heard the lock click and the door swinging open. The bed sagged under his weight as Erik perched on the edge. He ripped the covers off of my head, and I was left staring at two sparking turquoise gems. The sunlight streaming through the small window next to my bed lit up his dark hair as he nervously ran his long fingers through the heavy strands that hung low over his forehead. Thin lines creased the corners of the tan skin around his mouth. His mouth. I wanted to touch the soft pink bottom lip that he was biting down on.

"Hey," he said softly, anxiety clouding his normally carefree expression.

"Hey," I mumbled back. He stared into my eyes and I felt a hundred unspoken messages pass between us. Finally, after what seemed like forever, he broke eye contact.

"I brought you breakfast," he said, tentatively holding up a bag. I sat up and grabbed the bag out of his hand, then peered inside.

"Chocolate muffins - my favorite," I said grudgingly.

"Peace offering," he answered sheepishly. "Now scoot over so I can get comfy while we eat." I hesitated for a heartbeat before obligingly scooting toward the wall to make room. Erik kicked his flip flops off and crawled in next to me. I handed him one of the muffins, and we munched in companionable silence.

"So, are you going to tell me why haven't called me in nearly a year?" I asked, licking the chocolate crumbs off of my fingers.

"You could've called me," he replied gently. "Last time I checked, your communicator makes outgoing calls."

"That's not an answer," I shot back, refusing to turn and look at him. Now that we were done eating, I was acutely aware of his leg pressed against mine.

Erik heaved a huge sigh. "I really wanted to," he began, brushing his fingertips over the back of my hand. I didn't pull away, but I didn't encourage him either. Erik swallowed thickly before continuing. "At first, I wasn't allowed to. Captain Alvarez refused to even tell us where you were. All he would say is that you were recovering and you couldn't be disturbed." Erik paused, seeming to weigh his next words carefully.

"And then?" I prompted, trying to ignore the feel of his skin against mine. I wanted to be angry with him, but his touch made it hard.

"I don't know exactly. I figured that if you wanted to talk to me ...well, you'd call." He shifted uneasily and threw his muffin wrapper in the metal wastebasket next to my desk. "I mean, Tal, I gave you that letter......" Erik's voice trailed off. He moved his hand from mine and clasped it with the other one resting in his lap.

"I didn't know what to say," I whispered. "Mac wouldn't let me talk to anyone, really, until last week. When he finally let me out of my bedroom to do something other than physical therapy or blood testing – "

"Blood testing?" he cut me off, his body tensing and alarm radiating from his pores.

"Yeah," I answered. "I was injected with ...something in Nevada, and whatever the chemical is has been causing seizures." I chanced a look at Erik out of the corner of my eye. His eyes had grown wide, and his arm twitched like he was going to wrap it around me, but thought better of it.

"What chemical? Doesn't Medical have a cure or antidote or whatever?" he asked.

"Medical doesn't know what the chemical is. And they can't scrub it out of my blood," I replied, shuddering at the thought of the foreign drug infecting my body. Just minutes ago, I'd desperately wanted to tell Erik all about the seizures, but his reaction made me regret my decision. Waves of anger rolled from his mind and he ground his back teeth together in an effort to retain his composure.

"What are they doing about it?" he asked slowly, again measuring his words.

"Dr. Thistler, this high-ranking Medical woman, gives me daily injections. They're supposed to, like, neutralize the compound or something."

"And does that work?" his tense body language belied his neutral tone.

"For the most part. When I get overly stimulated, though, I sometimes still have seizures," I mumbled.

Erik reached for me, wrapping his strong arms around my waist, and lifting me into his lap. I rested my head against his chest and he kissed the crown of my hair. The accelerated beating of his heart thudding against my ear indicated how unnerved my admission had made him.

"I've missed you so much," he mumbled, moving his mouth close to my ear.

Warmth spread from where his lips rested in my hair, all the way down to my toes. I wrapped my arms around his body, running my fingers over the planes of his back and feeling the strength of his muscles through his t-shirt. Snuggling closer still, I tightened my grip on him before replying. "I've missed you, too."

Being with Erik had always been thrilling, intoxicating, and it was now, too, except now I also felt safe. For the first time in months, my world wasn't crashing in on me. The anger and frustration that constantly bubbled under the surface even quieted. The feeling of instability lessened.

Neither of us spoke again for a long time. There was so much that I wanted – no, needed – to tell him, but I didn't want to lose the physical closeness, so I stayed silent. I could tell that he wanted to ask me more, but the news about my medical condition had bothered him and he settled for rubbing my back instead.

"I've got to go help set up for the demonstrations," he said regretfully, much too soon for my liking. He gently extracted himself from my embrace, and I shifted to face him head-on for the first time since he'd arrived.

"Will I see you later?" I whispered, chewing my lower lip nervously. He cupped my face with both his hands, gently stroking my cheeks with his thumbs.

"Of course. We still have a lot to talk about," he promised. I closed my eyes as he softly brushed his lips across my forehead. Electricity crackled through me, like it did every time his skin made contact with mine. I wanted to beg him to stay; instead, I climbed off his lap and watched him go, in silence.

Long after Erik left, I sat in my bed, mulling over the way that I felt when I was with him. I recited the words of his note. I thought about Donavon, and how he'd sat with me in Medical for days even after I'd been so horrible to him. I still felt that he deserved a little of my anger, but maybe I could be the bigger person and get past what he'd done to me.

Finally, when I couldn't stand to be alone with my own

confused thoughts, I showered and pulled on a pair of navy pants and a white cable knit sweater. I left my hair to air-dry, knowing that it was only a matter of time before it was a mass of loose curls. When I looked in the mirror, a pale, drawn face stared back. My purple eyes, normally vibrant and intense, appeared dull and lifeless, the hollows underneath dark and haunted.

I grabbed a bottle of concealer and smeared liberal amounts over my skin. The makeup erased the death pallor, but couldn't rid my eyes of the ghost of Ernest's interrogation. His memories still lingered in my mind; every time that I closed my eyes, I saw his vacant expression, and hated myself a little more.

Deciding that looking human was the best I could do for my appearance, I set off for the Arena. When it came into view, I saw that the entire inside of the stadium had been transformed. Booths had been set up and demonstrations were already taking place. Surveying the scene, my eyes landed on two guys sparring – Erik and Henri. I smiled wistfully. I loved watching them fight, but it made me a little sad, too. I should be out there, I should be with them. Instead, I was here, chasing an apparition and praying that I didn't drop to the ground, convulsing at any moment.

I wanted to say hi to Henri, but I knew that there would be time for that later. He was busy now, so instead, I sought out Penny. I found her sitting at a booth with several portable computers. She had a small group of students clustered around her table, and she was explaining the role that Cryptos played in the Agency, in the broadest terms possible. She glanced up, and smiled when she saw me approaching. I waited patiently for her to finish her spiel.

"Hey, there." She beamed once the students had dispersed. "How are you feeling this afternoon?"

"Pretty good," I replied truthfully. Physically, at least, I felt better than I had in days. Emotionally, I felt raw and unstable after Erik's impromptu visit. When we'd actually been together, I'd been able to forget my predicament and what I'd done to Ernest.

As soon as he'd left, the cruel reality that I now lived in had returned.

"Good," she smiled. "Want to take a seat and help me out?"

"I don't know. I barely understand what you do," I teased.

"You could just sit here and do what you do best." She paused. "Stare at people all creepy-like so that I don't have to keep explaining things to kids who don't understand and don't care." I rolled my eyes, but Penny did have a point. My penetrating purple eyes tended to make others uncomfortable, not to mention the power that Mac said radiated off of me. Those were among the many reasons my friends were few and far between.

"I can do that," I replied, pulling out the chair next to Penny and taking a seat.

Over the next several hours, despite my best efforts, quite a few students stopped by to listen to her presentation. Sitting there with Penny, I felt normal for the first time since Nevada. Talking about boys and gossiping about Instructors and the other Operatives we'd both known from when we were in school, I felt like myself.

"Hey ladies," Donavon called as he approached our table. I gave him a genuine smile. Seeing Erik had brought on a whole host of emotions I wasn't ready to deal with, but I liked the point that Donavon and I had reached, and I wasn't ready to let it go. To my surprise, he bent over and planted a kiss on my cheek and – even more shockingly – I found my smile growing larger.

"Captain Alvarez is hosting a dinner tonight and it's my privilege to extend an invitation to both of you."

Captain Alvarez was the leader of the Hunters, and usually accompanied his Operatives to the Career Fair.

"He's here? Have you seen him?" I asked.

"He is, over at the booth with the Hunters," Donavan answered.

I turned to Penny. "If you can manage on your own, I think I'll go say hi."

"I'm sure I'll get by," she replied dryly.

"Come and get ready for dinner with me?" I asked.

"Will do." Penny's eyes sparkled at the prospect of dressing up for a formal occasion. I could practically see the cogs in her brain working double-time as she debated how to accessorize me for the night's festivities.

I stood and began making my way through the crowd, towards an area where a large group had congregated to watch the current exhibition. Donavon fell in step beside me.

"Why was Erik in your room this morning?" he demanded. I gave him a sharp look.

"How did you know that he was in my room this morning?" I retorted.

"You just told me," he shot back, outraged.

"What!?!" I was in no mood for games.

"I was on my way to see you this morning when I saw him leaving the Instructor housing," he explained.

"And you just assumed that meant he was with me?" I snapped, my own temper flaring. Erik *had* been there with me, but I didn't appreciate Donavon's accusatory tone. I was so angry that I reached out, and retrieved the memory from Donavon's mind, and watched it from his perspective.

Donavon opened the front door to Instructor housing, to see Erik bounding down the stairs.

"McDonough, good to see you," Erik said, extending his hand in a seemingly inviting gesture. Donavon stared down at his hand, but refused to take it.

"I would've thought that you'd be in better accommodations than us lowly Instructors," Donavon replied, eyeing him suspiciously.

"Yeah, I'm actually staying in guest housing." Erik laughed easily. "I just wanted to stop by and see a friend."

"Were you with Talia?" Donavon asked bluntly.

Erik appeared non-phased, his turquoise eyes twinkling

mischievously. He gave Donavon a wide, white-toothed grin. "Gentleman never tells, man," he said, his tone suggestive.

"Talia, stay out of my head," Donavon chastised me, bringing me back to the present.

"Look, Donavon, Erik was in my room this morning. We ate breakfast. That was it," I replied defensively, unsure why I felt the need to justify my actions to him. Obviously, I also left out the part where I'd climbed into Erik's lap and let him hold me. Or the part where I'd been so reluctant to let him leave that I'd contemplated begging him to stay.

"I don't think that you should be entertaining guys in your room," Donavon replied flatly.

"And I don't think that's any of your business," I snapped aloud. Picking up my pace, I left Donavon behind, and staring after me. I wasn't stupid. I knew why he was upset. At one time, I would've been desperate for just this type of reaction out of him. Now, instead of feeling special, I just felt annoyed. He had no right to be upset about Erik. Donavon and I were barely friends again, let alone anything more. Yet, even as my anger propelled me farther away from him, I recalled all of the nice things that he'd done for me over the last couple of days.

I finally arrived at the Hunter's booth. I joined the crowd and watched as two well-muscled guys circled each other. One was extremely tall and lean with light brown hair and warm brown eyes. The other was shorter and more defined, his nearly-black hair held back from his face with a navy bandana, his turquoise eyes shining with excitement. Both were dressed in loose pants and fitted sleeveless shirts.

Glancing around, I realized that over half of the gathered crowd was female. I couldn't say that I blamed them; Erik and Henri were both beautiful, and when they're in action, they were mesmerizing. Surprisingly, Cadence was one of the females in attendance. Sidling up next to her, I attempted conversation.

"They're really amazing to watch, aren't they?" I said to her.

Cadence spared me a glance out of the corner of her beady eye.

"I suppose so," she admitted grudgingly, like it pained her to agree with me.

"Those two are my teammates," I replied proudly.

"Used to be, you mean," she retorted.

"Excuse me?" I said, taken aback by her open hostility.

"They used to be your teammates. Since you failed your solo mission, you aren't a Hunter, and they aren't your teammates," she said slowly, enunciating each word.

Witch, I wanted to scream. She was a horrible, horrible wench. It took every ounce of my self-control to not punch her. Fuming, I turned my attention back to the boys.

The two guys circled each other, making small jabs and kicks as the crowd cheered. Henri's arm span was so vast that he had a terrific advantage over Erik, but Erik was extremely agile. Henri caught Erik in the shoulder with a hard kick, causing Erik to stumble slightly. Without missing a beat, he jumped straight up, both feet leaving the ground, tucked his knees up into his chest, and struck out. Both of his feet made contact with Henri's chest, which Erik used to push off of and flipped his feet over his head. He landed neatly on the balls of his feet.

Henri fell over backwards, catching himself on his hands before hitting the ground. In one fluid motion, he pushed off and flew back at Erik, feet first. He landed in a crouch and swept his leg out in a wide arc, attempting to trip Erik, who did a standing flip to avoid his leg.

"It almost looks like a dance they choreographed, huh?" a voice said in my ear. I let out a startled yelp.

"Hello, Captain." I smiled, looking up into the dark features of Captain Alvarez.

"It's great to see you, Lyons," he said sincerely. "How are you feeling?" His dark brown eyes were narrowed in concern.

"Pretty good, actually," I replied.

"We have the top Medicals working on an antidote," he

promised.

"I know," I muttered, looking at the ground.

"We'll get you back out there before you know it. Besides, those two need you." He gestured to where Erik and Henri were now flying through the air to the delighted oohs and ahhs of the crowd.

Glancing at Cadence and seeing her annoyance at Captain Alvarez paying attention to me gave me way more satisfaction than it should have.

"Thanks. I really want that, too." As I said it, I realized for the first time that I wasn't entirely sure that I did. I had desperately missed the Hunt throughout my long recovery, but for some reason I now felt reluctance at the prospect of rejoining the Hunters.

"Will I see you at the dinner this evening?" he asked hopefully.

"Of course. I'm looking forward to it," I answered honestly.

Captain Alvarez smiled, giving my shoulder a comforting squeeze, then walked back to where Erik and Henri were still sparring. I watched as Captain Alvarez called the session to an end, and the crowd responded with a chorus of "boo's". He announced that if anyone wanted to see more and get a chance to go one-on-one with a Hunter, they should sign up for the small group demonstrations that would take place over the next two days.

"You were invited to the dinner?" Cadence asked, outraged.

"Of course, I was," I retorted angrily. I'd had more of her attitude than I could take in one day.

"Why?" she demanded. "I wasn't."

"I guess you'll have to ask Captain Alvarez since he's the one who invited me. Or you can ask Mac since he's been taking me to this dinner since I was eleven," I shot back. I immediately regretted losing my temper. I was supposed to be gaining this girl's confidence instead of purposely baiting her. It was no wonder that she hated me. Without so much as a reply, Cadence stalked off.

Feeling suddenly exhausted, I, too, turned to leave – the day's events had worn me out. I made it several feet before two sets of slick, sweaty arms encircled me. Erik and Henri were both beaming.

"You guys smell." I wrinkled my nose.

"Every girl here is wishing that she were you right now." Erik laughed. He was right; many of the girls who'd congregated for the show were now glaring at me jealously.

"Only because they don't know you two like I do," I groaned.

"Haven't you missed us even a little?" Henri asked, sticking his lower lip out in a mock pout.

"Maybe this much." I held up my thumb and forefinger, indicating a space that only an ant could fit through. Smiling, I hugged Henri again, his sweaty shirt damp against my face. The truth was I'd missed them both more than I could ever express.

"If you two will excuse me, I need to shower again before dinner." I rolled my eyes and pretended to wipe their sweat off my face. Giving them a small wave, I turned to go. Erik grabbed my wrist.

"Can I walk you back to your room?" he asked, his voice light.

"I have to go to Medical first," I responded.

"Okay. Can I walk you to Medical and then back to your room?"

I looked at him for a long minute before finally nodding. After Donavon's earlier outrage, I didn't want to rock the boat, but he wasn't my boyfriend and had no right to be upset.

We walked for several minutes in silence.

"Please don't provoke Donavon," I finally said, trying to fill the awkward silence.

"Provoke? Me?" Erik feigned a look of shocked innocence. I rolled my eyes.

"Why are you dating him again?" he demanded. When my eyes met his, I saw more hurt than anger in the turquoise depths.

"We aren't dating," I said quickly.

Erik raised his eyebrows, but didn't comment. Silence fell between us, yet I felt surprisingly at ease; Erik's demeanor had changed at my reassurance that Donavon and I weren't a couple. All of the awkwardness dissipated, and I felt comfortable. For a brief minute, it was just like we were back at the Elite Headquarters and Nevada had never happened.

The Medical building came into view and the reality of my situation came rushing back: the shots, the seizures, the spy. The stability that I'd finally established after my parents' deaths was gone. My desire for revenge against the man who'd ordered my parents' deaths wasn't the driving force it used to be. I still believed that Ian Crane had something to do with their murders; I just wasn't sure that it was all so black and white anymore.

"Why so serious?" Erik's mental voice filled my head, interrupting my thoughts.

"I just want everything to go back to the way it was," I sent back.

"We're going to get this all worked out." He reached over and squeezed my hand affectionately, holding it for just a second longer than necessary as we entered the big sterile building that was Medical.

"Want me to come back with you?" he asked. I stared at him a minute, wondering if he was serious. He was.

"No, thanks. I'm a big girl and I've gotten pretty used to the shots." I smiled, touched by his offer. Erik nodded and took a seat in one of the white plastic chairs across from where the receptionist sat behind a huge white and chrome desk.

"Natalia, Dr. Thistler is expecting you. You can come on back," the receptionist said, giving me a small smile. I nodded and made my way to the swinging doors that led into the heart of the facility.

"Back in a second," I told Erik without turning around to look at him. I caught the receptionist sneaking glances in his direction as I disappeared through the doors.

I found the designated room, and it wasn't long before Dr. Thistler appeared. She quickly worked through the familiar routine of checking my vitals and taking a vial of my own blood, then injecting me with the equalizing agent. As she worked, she asked me the same series of questions that she always did: "How was I feeling? Did anything out of the ordinary happen today? What had I eaten? How was I sleeping?" My answers were basically the same as they'd been every day for the past nine months.

"All set, Natalia. I will see you tomorrow," she declared once she'd finished making notes on her ever present electronic pad.

"Dr. Thistler?" I asked, hesitating for a moment before continuing. "How's Ernest?" I was as eager for her answer as I was to experience another seizure.

Now it was Dr. Thistler's turn to pause. Her gray eyes studied me carefully before she finally answered. "He is responsive," she said slowly, measuring her words.

"Responsive?" I repeated.

"Yes, he is aware of his surroundings." She averted her eyes back down to her electronic tablet.

"Oh, I see," I said quietly.

"I am sure that, in time, he will be good as new." She smiled brightly, daring to tear her eyes away from the screen in the crook of her arm to meet mine.

"Does he know who he is?" I blurted out. She shook her head sadly. It was exactly what I'd feared.

"Natalia, this is always a risk with psychic interrogation. The Director never authorizes such an extreme step unless he feels it's necessary," she replied sternly.

Necessary? I thought incredulously. It hadn't been necessary. I should've tried harder to convince Mac that Ernest wasn't capable of such treachery. I shouldn't have pushed Ernest so hard in my interrogation. His current situation was *my* fault. Even the calming effects of the equalizing drug couldn't suppress my rising panic.

"Can I see him?" I asked.

"No, darling, I don't think that is a good idea," she replied gently.

Quickly, I swiped her mind. She feared how Ernest would react if he saw me; she worried that he might go into fits since I was the one who'd actually performed the interrogation.

What had I done? I was a monster. Gretchen had once told me that this was a possibility, but I'd never before invaded another mind so completely that I'd ever been in jeopardy of eradicating all the memories and thoughts.

Swallowing over the lump that had formed in my throat, I slid off the edge of the hospital bed and left.

Erik walked me back to my room, thankfully having the good grace not to ask me what was wrong. I couldn't stop thinking about Ernest. I felt responsible for what had happened. Worse, I *was* responsible for what happened. If only I hadn't pushed him so hard. I should have put my foot down and told Mac that I'd done all I could. After all, I'd known that he was telling the truth. There was no need for me to have gone so deep. What if he never recovered? What if his memories were no longer in there? What if I had ruined the rest of his life?

"Is my company really that bad?" Erik asked, giving me a slight nudge in the ribs with his elbow.

"Huh?" I asked, his question putting an end to my mental chastising.

"You look like you're about to cry. Women don't usually react to me like that," he joked. I rewarded his attempt at humor with a half-smile.

"Just have a lot on my mind," I mumbled.

"I'm here if you need to talk," he replied, his tone turning serious.

We came to a stop in front of Instructor housing. Erik clasped both of my hands in his and squeezed gently. I stared at the ground, avoiding his imploring gaze.

"Thanks. I'll see you at dinner," I muttered, snatching my hands away and turning to leave. Erik reached for me again, his fingers trailed across the inside of my wrist before dropping to his side. A hot flush crept up my neck and burned my cheeks. I paused, my hand halfway to the door handle. I wanted to turn around, wanted to fall into his arms and tell him about Ernest. I wanted him to stroke my hair, to tell me that everything would be all right. Instead, I finished extending my arm and firmly gripped the cold metal of the door handle. Pulling with way more force than was necessary, I yanked the door open and entered without turning back. I'd leaned on Erik too much in the past – I wouldn't let myself fall back into the habit now.

Chapter Fourteen

When I reached my room, there was a huge package lying on my bed. On top of the box sat a plain white envelope with my name scrawled across the front in familiar handwriting. Smiling, I tore open the envelope and found a single sheet of thick white stationary with the TOXIC logo emblazoned across the top, and several lines of text below.

Natalia, Danbury told me that you would be attending Captain Alvarez's dinner this evening. I took the liberty of selecting one of your gowns and having it cleaned, pressed, and taken in. I look forward to seeing you tonight. Love, Gretchen.

Opening the box, I found a dark red gown made of raw silk. It had long, sheer sleeves that kind of belled at the wrists. The dress was designed to rest on the edge of my shoulders with deep V's cut in the front and the back, exposing a great deal more skin than I was used to showing. The waist was cinched and would likely emphasize my drastic weight loss. The skirt of the dress hung all the way down to the tops of my feet. Gretchen had also thought to include a black velvet jacket, perfectly tailored for my small body, to wear over the dress in case the night air was chilly.

Gretchen loved having clothes made for me, and I never minded. It meant that I didn't have to bother with doing my own shopping. Still, sometimes I felt more like a china doll than a person. I made a mental note to thank Gretchen when I saw her later.

I carefully removed the gown and jacket from the box and hung them on the back of the bathroom door. There was no way either, let alone both, would fit in the closet. The mental and physical exhaustion from earlier returned, so I laid down on my bed, and closed my eyes to take a quick nap.

An insistent pounding woke me after what seemed like mere minutes.

"Go away," I called groggily.

"Talia, are you sleeping??" Penny's impatient voice was muffled by the door.

Opening my tired eyes just enough to see the clock next to my bed, I instantly registered the lack of sunlight streaming through the window.

"Crap. What time is it?" I said more to myself than to Penny. "Come on in," I called to Penny, mentally disengaging the door lock.

"Don't you check your communicator?" she demanded. "I've been messaging you for the last hour."

"Sleepy," I replied, burying my face in the pillow.

"We barely have enough time for you to get dressed!" she exclaimed.

Grumbling, I turned to face her and rubbed my eyes trying to clear away the sleep.

"You look pretty," I commented with a grin.

Penny's wild red-orange hair was twisted into a knot at the nape of her neck. She wore a simple long black dress, a matching black shawl resting on her slim shoulders.

"And you look awful," she teased.

"Thanks," I said sarcastically.

"Did something happen?" she asked suspiciously, her eyes growing wide with worry as she took in my disheveled appearance.

I climbed out of bed and made my way to the bathroom to splash water on my face, debating whether to tell Penny about

Ernest. I considered how much better I'd felt after telling Penny about what happened in Nevada, and decided in favor of filling her in on my trip to Medical.

"Do you think I'm a monster?" I asked once I'd explained about Ernest's condition.

"Of course not, Tal!" she assured me. "It's not your fault."

"Not my fault? How could it not be my fault? I kept pushing and pushing. I went too deep into his mind. I should've known better."

"No," she said emphatically. "You were following the Director's orders."

"He didn't mean for me to turn Ernest's mind to mush. He just wanted me to find out the truth," I insisted, quick to defend Mac even though I also felt that he deserved some of the blame.

"By pushing you past the point of exhaustion and forcing you to delve so far into Ernest's mind that you broke his will?" she demanded, an uncharacteristic fire igniting behind her lime eyes.

"Mac had no way of knowing how close Ernest was to breaking. Only I knew, and I still pushed. I pushed him over the edge." My voice cracked when I thought about the way that Ernest had looked after the interrogation. I slumped down in my desk chair, and Penny knelt down in front of me, to look me square in the eyes.

"It's not your fault, Natalia," she said firmly in a low voice. "Let me hear you say it."

"It wasn't my fault," I repeated numbly. For a second, looking at Penny's earnest face, I almost believed that the words were true.

"Now get ready. We're already late." She smiled, her tone switching back to bubbly.

There was no time to shower and straighten my hair, so I threaded a gold headband through the front of my curls to hold them back from my face. I applied a bare minimum of makeup – just enough to cover the dark circles beneath my eyes and to give my cheeks a rosy tint, so that I didn't looking like the walking dead. Penny helped zip me into the dark red dress before I shrugged on the velvet jacket.

Just as I was giving my appearance a last once over, there was a knock at the door. Penny rushed to answer it, so that I wouldn't be distracted. Donavon stood in the hallway. He looked amazing in a perfectly-tailored black suit complete with black shirt and black silk tie. He'd clearly put in extra effort, making his hair shiny and silky, falling neatly to his shoulders.

"I'm sorry about earlier," he apologized as he stepped into the room.

"No need to be sorry," I replied with a smile. I didn't have the energy to fight with Donavon tonight.

"I thought that you ladies might like an escort," he said aloud.

"Thank you." I really was glad that he'd come.

That is until Erik appeared in the doorway a second later. He, too, was wearing an immaculately tailored suit, but had opted for black pants and a white jacket instead with a white shirt and white bow tie. The white set off the tan of his skin. I had to restrain myself from hugging either boy. Worse, I didn't know who I wanted to go to more.

"Guess I should have called," Erik said lightly.

Donavon visibly tensed at the sound of Erik's voice. Penny looked uncomfortably from one boy to the other, chewing on her thumbnail. Inwardly, I groaned. This was already shaping up to be an *awesome* night.

"No, it's fine. The four of us can go together," I replied, giving Erik a hard look. His self-satisfied expression, and smug thoughts, let me know that he'd anticipated Donavon's presence. Erik knew that showing up in my bedroom again would piss off Donavon. From the look on Donavon's face, Erik's plan had worked; to say that Donavon was less-than-thrilled to see him would've been an understatement.

Our awkward foursome walked to the Headmistress's building. Penny and Erik chatted easily about mutual acquaintances back at

Elite headquarters. I trailed several paces behind, trying to ignore Donavon's thoughts, centering mostly on his dislike for Erik. When we finally reached the entrance to the banquet hall, I let out a sigh of relief. The sooner I could get away from the stifling tension between the two boys, the better.

Most people were already there, thanks to my extended nap. The room was decorated in a truly magnificent fashion. A huge rectangular table sat in the middle of the room. The tablecloth was made of a thick gold fabric and embroidered with an intricate floral design. The place settings appeared to be bone china, slightly off-white and rimmed in real gold. All of the silverware was actually gold-ware; real gold, if I had to guess. Huge red floral arrangements decorated the center of the table with red and gold candles intermixed. The candles were emitting a smell that could only be described as fall - cinnamon and pumpkin spice. Carving stations with huge hunks of every type of meat I could imagine – and some that I'd never seen – lined one wall.

Waiters stood, attired in pressed black pants and crisp white shirts, ready to carve tender pieces of meat for the guests. The opposite wall was lined with large, brightly colored fruit: apples so red that they appeared painted, grapes larger than my thumbs, watermelon with bright pink flesh in stark contrast to the black seeds, all emitting a mild sweet smell that mixed pleasantly with the candles.

The back wall had been turned into an ice bar, where more waiters stood ready to wow attendees with their mixology skills. I grabbed Penny's arm harder than I intended to, evidenced by her audible gasp, and steered her in that direction.

"Penny and I are going to get drinks," I called over my shoulder to Donavon and Erik, dragging a protesting Penny behind me. Thankfully, neither boy followed.

"What can I get for you ladies?" a smiling bartender with orange eyes and messily-styled blonde hair asked as we approached.

"Something strong," I replied shortly. Penny gave me a worried look.

"Just some wine for me," she told the bartender without looking at him. "Are you okay?" she asked me.

"Fine," I snapped.

Penny flinched at my harsh tone. I pinched the bridge of my nose between my thumb and forefinger and took several deep, calming breaths.

"I'm fine, Penny," I promised in a much softer voice. Penny relaxed, and gave me a weak smile.

"We're going to have a good time tonight," she assured me, placing one hand on my arm.

The boy who'd taken our order juggled bottles filled with brightly colored liquors around his back and over his shoulders, adding only a splash from each to the chilled glass on the ice bar in front of me. When he finally finished his show, he added two cherries and handed me my drink with a gallant bow.

"Thank you." I smiled appreciatively, and watched while he poured Penny's wine with significantly less fanfare.

After the bartender handed her the goblet, Penny and I moved to the side of the room to make way for those waiting to be served behind us. I took the first sip of my purple drink, and exhaled blissfully as the liquor burned my throat. Calm washed over me, and I sighed. Penny watched me closely, observing the tension leaving my face, and chanced talking.

"Tal?" she asked hesitantly.

"Hmmm?"

"Are you getting back together with Donavon?" She spoke quickly, trying not to lose her nerve to broach the topic.

"What makes you think that?" I asked, sipping more of my drink to cover my unease. Were my confused thoughts projecting that loudly? I wasn't exactly considering getting back together with him, but I'd been thinking about him a lot lately.

"Well, I mean, he was in your hospital room every night while you were ...sick. And then today when he came over to my booth, it seemed like you guys were pretty friendly. And then he showed up in your room tonight......" she ticked off.

I watched Penny gulp her wine, choking slightly when she tried to swallow the huge mouthful. Her eyes remained on my face, like she was trying to read my answer before I gave it. I sipped my drink and mulled over her words.

"I don't know, Penny," I said finally. "I'm not really thinking about dating him again, but he's been so nice to me, and I think that maybe we could at least be friends."

I let my gaze wander over the crowd, feeling uneasy at the way Penny's intense stare was boring into me.

"Just friends?" she pressed gently. "I see the way you two look at each other, Tal. I just don't want to see you get hurt again." I turned to face her.

"I know, Penny," I promised. "I'm not stupid. I'll be careful with him."

"Good." Penny visibly relaxed and sipped her wine, more carefully this time.

Penny's question gave me a lot to think about. Could I ever trust Donavon again? Even just as a friend? I thought that I could forgive him, even move past what he'd done, but would I always doubt everything that he told me? Would I ever really believe him when he said he loved me? Had he told that girl, Kandice, that he loved her, too?

Even as I pondered the cosmic questions of trust and love, I thought about how much Donavon comforted me, how much we'd been through together. He understood how much being a Hunter meant to me and how devastated I was to be stuck here instead of finding Ian Crane. Penny hadn't known me in the years following my parents' deaths. She couldn't understand how much Donavon had helped me. Now that I was vulnerable and lost again, he was here for me.

I was racking my brain for a new topic to lighten the mood

when I felt a tap on my shoulder. Turning to face the welcome distraction, I found Captain Alvarez standing beside me.

"Natalia, Penelope, I hope that I am not interrupting anything," he greeted us. His face was already beet-red, making it obvious the purple drink in his hand wasn't his first.

"Of course, not, Captain," I replied, grateful for his intrusion.

"Great! I was curious if I could ask you two a favor?" he asked conspiratorially.

"Sure, anything for you," I matched his sly tone.

"I was hoping that you ladies might be able to get all the basic background information on a couple of students for me? Natalia, Director McDonough tells me that you have been working with Operative Latimore here to learn our Crypto system."

"We would be happy to," I replied with false enthusiasm. I was more than a little dismayed that the task he was requesting wasn't more interesting. After a week of sifting through personnel files, I wasn't exactly eager to explore more.

"That won't be a problem," Penny agreed.

"Wonderful. I will have the list of names sent over in the morning. Natalia, if you could just come to the gymnasium after you have the information, that would be great." Before I could reply, someone caught his eye across the room.

"Senator Bosica!" he called exuberantly to a man with neatly trimmed gray hair turning away from the bar. "Tomorrow, Natalia." He winked over his shoulder at me as he retreated.

"Looks like Erik found a friend," Penny snorted, pointing across the room to where Erik stood in deep conversation with Ursula. She rested one perfectly-manicured hand on his arm as they spoke. Her navy cocktail dress clung tightly to every curve of her body, perfectly emphasizing her feminine assets. The white tips of her nails gripped Erik's arm harder as he said something that made her laugh, and I noticed that the tiny flowers painted in the corners of her nails matched the color of her dress. Her closeness to him irritated me. I couldn't hear what they were saying above the dull hum of the other conversations taking place throughout the room, but their body language suggested that they knew each other.

"Down, girl." Penny laughed, putting her hand on my arm. I'd absently taken several steps toward where Erik and Ursula were standing. "They're just talking."

"Sorry," I mumbled. "I just wish she'd stop touching him."

"I wouldn't worry, Tal. She's not the one that he rushed to see this morning," she pointed out.

"Yeah, you're right," I agreed, still unable to tear my gaze from the duo. "Wait, how did you know that he came to see me this morning?" I asked suspiciously.

Penny drained the rest of her wine glass. "He told me. I saw him at the fair before you got there." She smiled smugly, and I wondered how much of our encounter Erik had divulged.

My skin tingled just thinking about the way he'd touched my cheeks and kissed my forehead. *"I've missed you so much,"* he'd said while he'd held me. My pulse kicked up a notch and I was slightly breathless, like I'd just sprinted up the stairs to my bedroom.

"So, rekindling my relationship with Erik is acceptable then?" I asked.

Penny shrugged, an amused smile tugging the corners of her mouth up. "Call me biased, but Erik never cheated on you."

I gave a short, humorless laugh; she had a point. Erik might be a flirt, and rumors of his conquests fueled the gossip mill at Headquarters, but he wasn't the one that I'd caught with another girl.

Thankfully, Mac announced that dinner was to be served, and asked us to take our seats before I had a chance to give Erik and Ursula any more dirty looks. I found my place card between Janet and a Senator from New Hampshire, whom I'd met once or twice. He and I exchanged pleasantries, but he was much more interested in ogling the woman on his left. That suited me just fine; after witnessing Ursula throwing herself at Erik and contemplating my future with Donavon, I wasn't in the mood for small talk.

Penny was seated directly across the table between Captain Alvarez and, to my dismay,...Ursula. Penny kept trying to dodge the Captain's wild hand gestures that accompanied his stories.

"You should have seen the look on the poor guy's face when I morphed from the dog he was petting into a naked man!" he exclaimed loudly, throwing his head back as he roared with laughter. As he did, his left hand sent Penny's water flying off the table. The glass slowed its flight just enough for Penny to be able to catch it before water and ice ended up all over the unfortunate waiter standing behind the Captain. I guess that Ursula's close proximity was lucky after all; telekinesis came in handy on occasion.

The waiter gave Penny an appreciative smile as he wiped at the stray drops that had sloshed on the table and her arm.

"Nice catch, Penelope," Janet laughed. For his part, Captain Alvarez seemed oblivious to the near-accident he'd caused.

Donavon and Erik were next to each other, several seats down on the other side of Janet. Their unlucky seating assignments made me wonder who had made the seating chart. *At least Erik wasn't sitting next to Ursula,* I thought. I decided to keep one ear on their not-so-friendly conversation. Then, I glanced around the long table, searching for Henri. To my utter astonishment, I saw him sitting between Griffin and Cadence. Guess she'd finagled an invite after all.

Cadence looked pleased with her fortune at being seated next to Henri, and she was taking the opportunity to talk his ear off. I concentrated all of my strength towards my sense of hearing, and was able to hone in on their conversation. She was attempting to flirt with him in hopes he'd put in a good word for her with Captain Alvarez. *Lost cause, Cadence,* I thought. Flirting with a guy who has a boyfriend was unlikely to yield positive results.

"How are you feeling after last night, Natalia?" Janet asked quietly, drawing me out of Henri and Cadence's conversation.

"Not too bad. Worried about Ernest," I admitted.

"I'm sure that he will regain his memories," she said. She smiled when she spoke, but the expression failed to reach her eyes. Janet didn't really believe that Ernest would ever regain his memories – she just said so to make me feel better. While I appreciated her attempt, the confirmation that Ernest was unlikely to get better further deflated my mood.

"I hope so," I whispered as a waiter placed a plate full of food in front of me.

Dinner consisted of a Cornish hen stuffed with wild mushrooms and rice with green beans on the side. I picked at my hen and tried to pay attention to what was going on around me, but found my mind constantly wandering.

Would Ernest ever be whole again? Could he regain his memory on his own? Did I want to get back together with Donavon? If so, why did Erik's presence affect me so much? If it had been Donavon that Ursula was fawning all over, would I have reacted the same way? Erik said that he missed me, but did that mean he still wanted to be with me? Would I ever come home early from a mission to find Erik in bed with another girl?

My inner musings left me with more questions than answers.

"That fork is real gold, dear," Janet said gently as she closed her hand around my fist.

"Huh?" I looked down, confused, at our hands and found the gold fork wrapped tightly in my fist. I was grinding it into the plate. I guess I'd gotten myself a little worked up.

"Excuse me, miss? Are you still eating?" I looked up and recognized one of the waiters from the meat carving stations. I released the fork hastily, as though it were on fire. Nodding my head no, to too embarrassed to speak, I felt the heat creep up my neck and color my cheeks.

The waiter replaced my picked-over hen with a piece of pumpkin cheesecake topped with cinnamon ice cream. Managing to choke out a "thank you," I dug into my dessert.

Dessert was a long, drawn out affair, complete with coffee drinks heavily laden with bourbon. I tried my hardest to keep a pleasant look pasted on my face even though I desperately wanted nothing more than to get out of the opulent room. Not a moment too soon, Mac finally stood and thanked everyone for coming inviting those who were interested to stay for a nightcap. I quickly said goodbye to Janet and made a beeline for the exit.

I made it as far as the door before I felt Erik's hand on my shoulder.

"Walk you back to your dorm?" he asked hopefully.

I glanced around, looking for Penny. In my haste to leave, I'd temporarily forgotten about her, but now I thought that I should really tell her I was leaving.

"Donavon is occupied being the Director's son," Erik continued coolly.

"I wasn't looking for Donavon," I snapped.

For his part, Erik appeared nonplussed by my annoyance at his having drawn the logical conclusion. He offered me his arm. I hesitated briefly before looping my own underneath his crooked elbow. A grin lit his face as we exited the building together.

"Are you coming tomorrow to show all those Hunter wannabes how it's done?" he teased as we walked across the damp grass.

"I would love to, but I'm not sure if Dr. Thistler would like that. She seems to think that physical stressors bring on the seizures." I rolled my eyes to indicate how absurd I found the notion.

"Are they any closer to finding a cure?"

"According to Dr. Thistler, every day they get a little closer."

"Well, don't worry about being replaced – you'll always be my partner." He winked down at me and my stomach dropped as I read way too much into his words. The way his body brushed against mine while we walked made me always want to be his partner – just not his Hunting partner.

"Sure about that? Earlier tonight, it looked like you'd found yourself a new Telekinetic." The words were out of my mouth before I could stop them. I hadn't meant to bring up watching him with Ursula.

"Jealous much?" Erik laughed.

"No," I snapped. "I just noticed that you two were awfully friendly."

Erik's laughter died in his throat. "I've known Ursula for a long time. We have a close mutual friend. Sometimes, we all meet up in the city," he said awkwardly, taken aback by the intensity of my accusations. He wasn't the only one. I hadn't meant to get so angry, but seeing Ursula touch him infuriated me, and Erik making light of the situation didn't help.

An uncomfortable silence fell between us.

"How do you like being back at school?" Erik asked finally, breaking the mounting tension.

"Eh, it's okay. I can't wait to get out of here." I choked over the lump that had formed in my throat, thinking about Erik with another girl.

"Really?" he gave me a skeptical look.

"You think that I'd rather be here twiddling my thumbs than out there with you guys doing something that matters?" I asked, not quite sure what he was implying.

"No, it's just ...I don't know. Never mind," he mumbled.

"It's just what?" I demanded. He didn't answer. Mentally, I reached out to him. Anger clouded my mind like a haze. "You think that I'm here playing house with Donavon?" I said incredulously, releasing my grip on his arm and coming just short of actually shoving it away.

"When you left, you two weren't even on speaking terms," he mumbled. "And now you two seem awfully chummy. I mean he was in your room when I came over tonight. And he was pissed when he realized that I'd come to see you this morning." I could tell that he regretted bringing up this topic before the words even left his mouth.

"Not that it's any of your business, but Donavon and I are friends. I've been going through a really traumatizing ordeal and he's been here for me!!" I was practically shouting. "I don't have time to worry about dating Donavon, or you for that matter. He at least understands that."

"Hey, I never said I was looking to date you, Talia. I'm just looking out for you because I thought we were friends, too." Erik's temper flared as he hurled the angry words in my direction. The word "friend" stung as though he'd physically slapped me across the face.

"Fine!" I yelled, my voice wavering with the effort of keeping my tears at bay.

"Fine," he shot back.

Kicking off my shoes without bothering to pick them up, I took off at a dead sprint for my room. When I got within several feet of the door, it burst open, and I flew through without missing a beat. I took the stairs three at a time and heard the door to my room fly open, slamming against the doorjamb as I rounded the corner. As soon as the door banged shut behind me, and I heard the lock engage, I collapsed to the floor in a pile of damp red silk. Tears of humiliation burned the backs of my eyes before streaking ugly black mascara rivers down my flushed cheeks.

Chapter Fifteen

The next morning, I woke with eyes so swollen that I couldn't for a second trick myself into believing that the previous night had been a bad dream. My ruined dress was lying in a crumbled heap on the floor of my bathroom. I kicked it aside as I rummaged through my medicine cabinet, trying to find the cream that Gretchen ordered for me in the city. I found it and rubbed the cream all over my eyes, cringing against the burning sensation that accompanied the reduction in swelling.

After a long, hot shower, I dressed in jeans and a thick black sweater. As promised, Captain Alvarez had sent a list of names to my portable communicator. Grabbing the device from my desk, I set off for the Crypto Building.

Penny was already seated in her usual chair with a large cup of coffee when I arrived. As per usual, Gemma occupied one of the other chairs in the room. Both appeared to be analyzing information on half a dozen computers at the same time. I watched silently as four sets of fingers flew across keyboards as random numbers and letters scrolled downs the screens of each of the individual monitors. I marveled at their ability to process the data simultaneously.

"Hey," Penny called without turning around.

"Morning," I greeted her. "Hey Gemma," I said to the other girl. She smiled shyly before returning to her work.

"You ran out pretty fast last night," Penny declared, still facing the computers.

"I was tired," I replied quietly.

"So tired that you needed Erik to help you home?" she teased.

I knew that she was curious, but the last thing that I wanted right then was to rehash my fight with Erik and the accusations leading up to it. Penny would think that I was nuts. I was starting to think that I was a little nuts myself. Last night, I'd felt justified in my actions, but today with no alcohol clouding my judgment, the harsh daylight illuminated just how ridiculous I'd acted. I'd gone into a jealous rage over seeing a guy who wasn't my boyfriend standing too close to a girl that he'd known longer than he'd known me. Then, when he'd called me on it, I practically bit his head off. I was just this side of sanity. If we didn't find the spy soon, I was going to end up in a padded cell.

Penny pressed a key, halting all of the text scrolling across the screens, and swiveled her chair around to face me. Her bright green eyes urged me for more details, but the light dimmed when she saw my distraught expression. Her devilish smile contorted into a sympathetic grimace.

"What happened, Tal?" she asked gently.

"Erik didn't exactly walk me home," I mumbled, looking at my feet.

"Do you want to talk about it?" she asked.

"We got in a fight about Donavon and Ursula, and then, somehow, it evolved into something else altogether."

Penny studied me intently, almost as if she was willing me to tell her more, but I really didn't need her confirmation that I was losing it.

Penny slid a smile into place, but the gesture didn't reach her worried eyes.

"So, want to plug this communicator in for me so I can get the info the Captain wants?" I asked, desperately wanting to change the subject.

"Hand it over." She held out her hand with mock impatience and an eye roll. I gave her a broad smile and gratefully handed her the electronic device.

Penny attached my portable communicator to one of the computers not currently being used. Again, I watched in awe as her fingers flew across the keys, entering information too fast for me to follow. Several times, she told me to hold either my thumb or my eye up to a scanner mounted next to the computer. I obediently complied and after what seemed like an excessive amount of typing, she told me that I was all ready to begin.

Taking a seat in my own swivel chair, I set to work. I spend the next several hours sifting through files on the designated students, downloading and organizing only the pertinent data for each individual. I probably could have just asked Penny, in my special suggestive manner, to do this for me, but I never used my Talents on her. After all, she was the only real friend that I had. My resolve began to waver the longer I stared at the screen.

"Done!" I announced happily. My eyes ached with fatigue and it took me a minute to uncross my vision.

"Got everything you need?" Penny asked.

"Yup, so if you could just disconnect this thing for me, I'll be on my way."

Penny deftly disconnected my portable communicator and handed it to me.

"See you at dinner?" she asked.

"You got it." I gave a small wave to Gemma and set off.

My next stop was Medical. I walked through the sliding glass doors and the receptionist on duty waved me back immediately.

"Room Five, Ms. Lyons," she said pleasantly. Nodding, I continued on through the double doors to Room Five. The receptionist must have buzzed Dr. Thistler immediately because I'd just managed to jump up on the exam table when she walked through the door.

"Hi, Natalia. How are we feeling today?"

I hated when she said "we", like she was somehow part of me.

"Same as yesterday," I mumbled. Sometimes, I wondered why she bothered asking; if I was feeling anything less than "fine" she'd know because I would've been whisked into Medical, convulsing. Her only response was a smile. Pulling my sweater over my head, I waited anxiously as she filled the syringe with the thick liquid out of a bottle from her coat pocket. I gritted my teeth as she plunged the tip of the needle into my arm and depressed the plunger.

The chemicals burned as they entered my bloodstream, and I sighed. The annoyance of receiving daily injections was a small price compared to the calming relief that the medicine provided me. As soon as she removed the injection needle, she replaced it with the one that would draw a sample of my blood. I watched as the syringe filled with my red liquid.

"All set," she said, taping a small piece of gauze in the crook of my elbow.

"Thanks," I muttered, and eased myself off of the exam table to head for the door.

"Dr. Thistler?" I asked, hesitating before I crossed the threshold.

"Hmmm?" she answered distractedly, making notations on her electronic pad.

"How's Ernest today?" I asked quietly.

"Same as yesterday, dear," she replied without looking up.

"Oh, okay. Well, thanks." I wasn't really sure what I'd expected to hear, but I'd hoped for a more positive response – something like, "he's great" or "he's regained his memory." No such luck.

In the hallway just outside the door to Room Five, I paused. Closing my eyes, I swallowed my guilt. I had to see him. I had to know if he was really in as bad a shape as Dr. Thistler said. Surely not. I could understand him being confused or dazed, but the way that Dr. Thistler saw it in her mind, Ernest appeared comatose.

Quickly, I glanced to my left and my right. The hallway was empty. I opened my mind and searched for active brains. I could feel Dr. Thistler's behind me, but she was too busy logging my visit in her files. I could feel activity throughout the entire complex and decided to keep my mind open as I turned and walked to my right.

Winding my way through the corridors of the Medical facility, I searched in vain for Ernest. I was convinced that I'd be able to track him through his mind, but I couldn't seem to get a handle on it. Deeper and deeper I traveled into the bowels of the Medical building, scanning my palm at various locations to gain access to the more secure areas. I was definitely leaving a trail behind me – sloppy for a Hunter.

At last, I reached a door labeled Psychiatric. I took a deep calming breath; I knew that Ernest was behind that door. I still couldn't feel his mind, but I knew in my heart that he was there. Holding one shaky palm up to the scanner, I waited, a small part of me hoping that I wouldn't be granted access. The light on the scanner turned green, and I heard the lock on the door disengage. Dread weighed me down like a wet blanket as I pulled the door open and entered the Psychiatric Ward.

In the first room on my right, I felt an emptiness, a void the size of the Grand Canyon. My feet were forcing me forward before I could register the fact that they were taking me into Ernest's room. I saw him immediately. He was propped up in a large bed. There was a leather belt secured around his middle, keeping him upright. I was barely able to suppress the gasp that rose in my throat. Tears of shame welled in the corners of my eyes.

Ernest stared dully in my direction, but his expression was vacant and unfocused. I stood paralyzed in place, the soles of my shoes feeling heavy, as though I'd stepped in wet cement. One of Ernest's eyes began to twitch, and he made a soft gurgling noise deep in his throat. I swallowed hard and swiped his mind. I didn't bother to suppress the sob that clawed at my windpipe this time.

Ernest's mind was empty. Not confused, not dazed. Empty. I sunk to my knees, my fists balled at my sides as hot tears ran down my face and splashed the linoleum floor. Wrapping my arms around myself, my body began to shake.

"Natalia, I told you that this was not a good idea," Dr. Thistler's voice sounded behind me.

Her white lab coat clad form swam when I turned to look up at her. Dr. Thistler grabbed my upper arm and pulled me to my feet with a strength that I hadn't believed she possessed.

"Can I put the memories back?" I stammered hopefully. Maybe I could make this right.

"No, Natalia," she replied gently. "It's too much of a risk."

"To who?" I asked, already knowing the answer.

"To you," she responded as if the answer were obvious. The answer had been obvious; I'd just needed to hear her say it.

"I don't care!" I insisted. "This is all my fault, I'm a monster."

"No," she said firmly. "No, you are not. And you are much too valuable to this organization to risk a memory re-implementation."

"What about Ernest? Wasn't he valuable?" I demanded.

Dr. Thistler gave a weary sigh, and then gently led me from Ernest's room. Her non-response brought to mind the words that Ian Crane had thrown at me in Nevada, "*You have no idea what your Agency does to innocent people,*" he'd said. Maybe I hadn't known then what TOXIC did to innocent people, but I was starting to realize it now.

Crane had told me that my parents' deaths were a consequence of war; was Ernest's condition now a consequence of war, too? Could I be so callous as to accept that notion? Once again, I was left with more questions than answers. Worst of all, I was starting to wonder how much of what Crane told me was true.

I desperately wanted to go back to my room and pull the blankets over my head, form a barrier against the outside world. Instead, I walked numbly from the Medical building to the Arena to meet Captain Alvarez. I couldn't erase the image of Ernest and his blank stare from my fragile psyche. Ernest's condition was considered an acceptable risk of psychic interrogation, but it wasn't a risk that I wanted to be part of.

I was still distracted when I reached the Arena; so distracted in fact that when I rounded a corner, I ran smack into another person. To top it off, that person was Erik.

"Sorry," I mumbled, sidestepping around him.

"Tal, wait." He grabbed my upper arm. "I'm so sorry about last night –"

"You have nothing to be sorry about," I said, cutting him off. After witnessing the fruits of the destructive side of my Talent, my embarrassment over what had happened with Erik seemed trivial.

"No, you were right, Talia. It is none of my business what does or does not go on between you and Donavon. We're just friends after all ..."

"Right, just friends," I muttered. I hated the part of me that felt the deep bite of disappointment at his calling us "just friends."

"So, we're good?" he asked

"We're good." I smiled tightly.

"Want to help us with the demonstration?" he asked hopefully. I was about to say "no," that Dr. Thistler had said I wasn't supposed to physically exert myself, but instead, I agreed. I decided that what I needed, more than hiding myself under my covers, was a distraction. Erik gave me a big smile and squeezed my shoulder in a buddy-buddy kind of way that he would've done to Henri as he walked away. My mood plummeted so fast that the splat when it hit the ground should've been audible.

Making my way to Captain Alvarez, I linked our communicators like Penny had shown me, so that I could transfer a copy of the information that I'd downloaded. Then I found Erik and Henri and changed from my own clothes into an adapti-suit that zipped up to my neck. I plaited my dark curls into two thick braids, then wrapped a black-and-white bandana over them and tied it securely at the base of my skull. Henri had dressed to match.

Captain Alvarez was speaking to the large group of students assembled in the Arena stands. I followed Henri to the center of a mat and we took up positions facing each other, about ten feet apart. We waited for Captain Alvarez to finish his introductions. The shrill sound of the whistle reverberated throughout the Arena, and I wasted no time in charging Henri.

We ran at each other, but he lunged first, his long body leaving the ground and becoming completely horizontal as his huge hands reached for me. At the last second, I broke to my right, dropping to the ground in a roll. Henri tucked his long body into a roll of his own and we spun around to face each other once more.

Henri rose to his full height, but I'd remained crouching, and I didn't hesitate before I launched myself vertically like a lioness using my Telekinesis to propel myself higher so I would collide with Henri's shoulders. He was ready and caught me, wrapping his long fingers around my waist and flipping me over his head, but not before I'd made contact. I added the momentum that I already had to Henri's flip, and let my feet fly over my head, landing squarely on the ground.

Henri stumbled as a result of my blow and dropped to one knee in an effort to steady himself. He flung one leg out and I felt the front of his foot connect with the outside of my ankle, effectively cutting me down, and I fell.

I should have landed on my face, but my reflexes were quick from years of training. I was able to get my hands underneath me and instead fell in an awkward push up position. I felt Henri close in from behind, and judged the distance to be close enough for contact. Pushing up onto my hands, I kicked back as hard as I could just as he was bending towards me.

My feet caught him first in the stomach and then in his chest, knocking him backwards and off-balance, giving me enough time to get on my own two feet and turn to face him. By this time, we were both breathing heavily, and I knew that I must be sweating terribly in my suit, but the temperature-regulating function kept me comfortable.

We both backed up a couple of feet as we tried to catch our breath. I felt what Henri was going to do before my mind could really register it. The suits could stretch and mold to any body shape, making them easy to morph in.

Henri kicked off the ground and leapt towards me again, but this time, as his feet left the ground his body morphed into his favorite go-to shape – a gigantic bird. Henri flew at me in bird form and I had barely enough time to react. Letting myself fall backwards, I kept my feet planted. I used my own powers to keep my body horizontal, with my knees bent. Henri, as the bird, flew right over me. As soon as he cleared my head, I twisted around and jumped, wrapping my arms around his thick neck. I was unable to get my short legs wrapped around his body because his huge wings were in the way.

He flew low around the Arena with me clinging to his neck. He tilted one way and then the other in an attempt to throw me off, but I held tight. Throwing all of my concentration to my mental abilities I willed him to change back. Within seconds my mental battle won out over his physical one, and we were falling to the ground, a tangle of human limbs. We rolled several times until finally his heavy form landed on top of my much smaller one. He lifted himself up to take the weight off of me and I gave him a wicked smile as our eyes met. I had just a second to see the look of confusion cross his face.

As soon as he had lifted himself off, I tucked my knees to my chest and used all of the strength that I could muster to kick him in the stomach. Henri flew backwards, propelled farther by my telekinetic powers. But I had only seconds of satisfaction before I sensed a new threat coming.

Rolling first to my stomach and then quickly to my feet, I had just enough time to see a huge predatory cat leaping at me. Henri rarely morphed into anything besides the huge bird, but that didn't mean that he couldn't. I dove to the side as the huge cat landed where I'd been standing only seconds before. I stood, and the cat and I circled each other. I again risked using my mental muscles to will Henri to change back to human. I watched as my efforts were rewarded and the huge cat was replaced by Henri's human form, now down on all fours.

Using my mental powers often physically exhausted me. I'd trained since coming to School to utilize them during a fight, but rarely implemented them in a real battle. While I'd had the best physical training available, and could hold my own against a normal person, I was really no match for a Morph. I'd used my mental powers because it was my best defense against a trained fighter like Henri in his morph form, but it cost me a great deal of my own strength.

I stood facing Henri, my entire body shaking from the physical and mental exertion. My skin was dry, thanks to the suit, but sweat stung my eyes and soaked my bandana. Taking several deep breaths to calm myself, I tried to refocus my mental energies.

Henri slowly rose from his hands and knees. I tensed, readying myself for his attack. Instead, he slowly bent at the waist in a deep bow. I let out a huge sigh; he was calling an end to the demonstration. I inclined my head and gave him a small bow in return. He walked over to me and wrapped his long arms around me. I knew that he could feel my body shaking against him, but he didn't comment.

"You're better than I remember," his mental voice filled my head. I knew that he was just being nice, but at that moment, I would take any compliment that I could get. As we drew apart, I opened all of the senses that I'd been directing solely on Henri to the entire Arena. The whooping and cheering of the students filled my ears. Giddy from the physical release of tension, I turned and gave them a small wave. *Dr. Thistler was wrong*, I thought to myself. *Physical exertion was exactly what I needed.*

"Amazing, Tals," Erik said, giving me a hug.

"Thanks." I smiled at his praise.

"Yeah, I might even have a bruise or two," Henri joked. Bruises were unlikely since I'd only hit him where the suit covered.

"They'll make you look more manly," I laughed, playing along. "Frederick will love them."

"Yeah, he really likes it when I get beaten up." Henri rolled his eyes, but his expression softened at my mention of his boyfriend.

"How is he?" I asked. During my time at Elite Headquarters, I'd had the pleasure of meeting Frederick several times, and really enjoyed his company.

"He's good. Really good." Henri smiled fondly.

"Lyons, Reich, Kelley, we're ready for you over here," Captain Alvarez called.

Now it was the students' turn. All Talents took basic combat classes, and many of these kids would have taken more advanced training, but very few of them would have the opportunity to use their abilities in combat. Captain Alvarez broke the students into five groups, and assigned me, Erik, Henri, and two other Hunters that he'd brought with him to a group.

I spent the remainder of my afternoon coaching the teenagers as they fumbled through using their Talents to fight one another. Some had very developed powers, managing to morph on the fly into varying forms while others could barely manage a complete morph standing still. Several students were able to use telekinesis to throw their attackers off course. One particularly skilled light manipulator evaded her would-be attackers by becoming invisible, leaving her opponents confused and defenseless when she reappeared and attacked from behind. Her apparent mastery of her craft impressed me.

In the midst of all of this, there was a tall gangly girl that reminded me of Penny. I recognized her from Ursula's telekinesis class. At first, I'd thought she was a fairly Low-level Talent, but after working with her, I'd noticed that her problem wasn't her

Talent level – it was that she didn't know how to use her abilities.

Physically, her only resemblance to Penny was the fact that she was tall and gangly. She had light brown hair and a smattering of freckles across her pale face – a sharp contrast to Penny's dyed bright red-orange hair. The girl had light brown eyes that appeared to be the same color as her hair, nothing like Penny's color enhanced bright lime-green ones. Still, there was something about her that screamed "Penny" to me. *Maybe it's the fact that she's definitely not a natural fighter*, I thought to myself as I watched her spar against a particularly skilled Telekinetic. The boy adeptly avoided most of her blows using his mind. Her form was good, and no matter how many times he diverted, her she kept coming right back at him. If nothing else, the girl had a lot of heart.

I'd strapped my portable communicator to my arm, and I used it to pull up the gangly girl's file. Talent: Higher Reasoning, Telekinesis. *Interesting*, I thought. Dual Talents were rare, particularly when the Talents were as unrelated as Telekinesis and Higher Reasoning. But I now understood why she reminded me of Penny; Higher Reasoning Talents gave off a very specific brain pattern.

It surprised me that a Higher Reasoning would be interested in joining the Hunters. Her Telekinetic powers made her a possible candidate, but since she had yet to master them, it was doubtful they would be much use on her Placement Exams.

Technically, any student could be assigned to any department during the Placement Exams, but it was rare for Higher Reasoning Talents to become Hunters. I was sure that it had happened at some point in the Agency's history, but a strong Higher Reasoning – and I was confident that this girl was a strong Talent – was better utilized in the Crypto Division.

Her name was Kenly Baker. She was a junior, and therefore due to take her Placement Exams at the end of the year. Instantly, I started to think of the possible advantages of having a Higher Reasoning Talent, who also happened to be a Telekinetic as part of a Hunting team. She would instantaneously be able to compute the probability of success on a mission. She would be able to determine the best exit strategy if a Hunt went south. It would be like having a human computer in the field, one that could think and feel; she was a more proficient strategist than any of us other Talents could ever hope to be. By the end of my day with the students, I'd convinced myself that it was a great idea, full of nothing but advantages ...if she could learn to use her Telekinesis.

I walked back to my room with an extra spring in my step, giddy about my newest idea.

"Talia!" Erik called out to me.

Turning at the sound of my name, I saw him jogging in my direction.

"Where's the fire?" he joked.

"Huh?" I replied, still lost in my fantastic scheme.

"Why did you run out?" he clarified.

"I'm gross, I need a shower, and I have to talk to Mac about something," I listed absently.

"How about having dinner with me?" His big turquoise eyes were hopeful when I met his gaze.

Remembering his proclamation that we were "friends," I not-so-kindly retorted, "I'm having dinner with Penny." I did, in fact, have dinner plans with Penny, although I saw her every day, and I doubted that canceling on her would be a big deal.

"Oh, ...well, okay. But I'm leaving tomorrow evening and I just wanted to spend some time with you." He looked truly hurt by my refusal, and my resolve softened.

Just then, my communicator, still strapped to my arm, beeped with an incoming message. It was from Donavon. I hit the text button option and read only one word: "dinner?" I quickly typed back, simply, "Penny, sorry."

I looked up at Erik. He was still staring at me with his beautiful sparkling eyes. My fingers involuntarily started typing a second message, this time to Penny to break our plans when I realized what he was doing.

"Erik!" I exclaimed. "Do *not* use my powers against me."

He beamed devilishly, not even the least bit abashed at being caught. "I just really want to have dinner with you, nothing special, just the cafeteria," he pouted, pushing his bottom lip out and fixing me with a look that I knew well, the one that had led countless girls to his bed.

"I can't. I already promised Penny. I'll see you tomorrow." With that, I turned and left before I changed my mind without the help of his will.

Chapter Sixteen

I showered and changed as quickly as I could manage, and text messaged Penny to tell her that I would meet her for dinner in an hour. Then I called Mac.

"Danbury McDonough," I said clearly as I depressed the voice button.

"Hello?" he answered his communicator on the first ring.

"Hey, where are you? I want to ask you something."

"I am in my office," he answered.

"Mind if I come over?"

"That would be fine; I am just finishing some work," he replied.

"Be there in a minute." I pushed the end button on my communicator and set off.

I reached the administration building ten minutes later. It was already dinnertime, so Mac's assistant was gone. I walked past her desk and knocked lightly on his door.

"Come on in, Natalia," he called.

Pushing the heavy oak door open, I shuffled into the room.

"I hope this relates to the spy in our midst?" he said, giving me a tired look.

Immediately, I felt bad about approaching him with what I'd thought was a brilliant idea just an hour ago. Now, under his hard gaze, I wasn't so sure.

"Not exactly," I began slowly, gauging his reaction.

"Natalia," he started, but I cut him off before I lost my nerve.

"I want to personally train Kenly Baker to help her become a Hunter." I waited anxiously for Mac to say something. He just stared at me for several long moments with blank gray eyes, causing me to shift uneasily from one foot to the other.

"I don't think that is a productive use of your time, Natalia," he finally answered, turning his attention back to the work on his desk.

"No, but it is, Mac. Kenly is a Higher Reasoning Talent and a Telekinetic. I think that her Talents could actually be really useful in the field, if she could just learn how to fight. If she were adequately trained in hand-to-hand combat and weapons, she'd be an asset," I replied earnestly.

"Natalia, there is a reason that Higher Reasoning Talents are never placed with the Hunters. They don't belong there," he answered harshly, not looking up from his paperwork.

"I know, I know. I know that she'll need a lot of work before her Placement Exams, but I think that she could be really great," I pressed, imploring him to come around to my way of thinking. "And Telekinetics frequently become Hunters."

"Dual Talents are rarely strong in both areas. If she is a strong Higher Reasoning Talent, then her Telekinetic abilities are likely weak," he stated.

"But I don't think that they are. I think she just needs to learn how to use them better. And she only needs to be ranked Elite in one to be considered for the Hunters," I pointed out proudly.

Mac spared me a withering look before returning his gaze to his desk. He apparently wasn't as impressed with the loophole in the system as I was.

"She will never be able to catch up - her exams are at the end of this year. You won't have the time to strengthen her senses and teach her to fight well enough to qualify for placement with the Hunters. And even if you could, by some miracle, manage such a feat, she'll never make it through her Pledge year without continuous training. Besides, her skills are better used in other departments."

I gritted my teeth and held firm. "I know, Mac, but she has a lot of heart and really wants this. It won't interfere with my other duties," I promised. "Maybe I could even stop aiding in Donavon's class?" I continued hopefully.

"The way I understand it, the two of you have been getting along much better in the past couple of days. Why would you want to stop helping him?" Mac asked, finally finding the conversation worthy of looking up from his work.

"It's getting me nowhere," I replied emphatically. "We both know that Donavon isn't the spy, and I haven't heard anything in the minds of his students that seems off. Maybe I could even spend that time in the Crypto Bank with Penny, going through more files," I offered.

"Really? You want to spend more time sifting through files? I was under the impression that you weren't exactly thrilled with that portion of your assignment."

"Well, no, not exactly. But I have a feeling that's the place where I'm most likely to find the spy. If you want, I can even stop helping Griffin since he isn't our guy either."

Mac mulled this over for a long time, and a quick swipe of his mind told me that he was on the fence.

"What is it that you think you will find if you spend more time in the Crypto Bank?" he asked finally. He seemed genuinely curious.

"I don't exactly know," I replied honestly. "I just have this feeling that something isn't right, and that's where I'm most likely to figure it out." Mac nodded his head slowly, processing my sketchy argument.

I kept quiet. I'd already laid all my cards on the table, and at this point he was either going to agree or not.

"Fine. You will stop assisting Donavon and spend that time in the Crypto Bank. You will remain with Griffin, though; I paired you with him because your weapons expertise is very valuable there. I will let you train the Baker girl after the school day ends. But I am warning you right now, Natalia – it is incredibly unlikely that she will even come close to scoring high enough to become a Hunter. I don't want you filling her head with false hope. The girl will take the Crypto Placement Exam in addition to the Hunters' Exam. I implore you to make sure that she is adequately prepared for both. In a fight, her Higher Reasoning will be of no advantage," he warned.

"I suppose that we'll have to agree to disagree on that last part." I smiled triumphantly at him. He made a noncommittal noise in response. Not wanting to give him an opportunity to change his mind, I turned to leave.

"Natalia?" he called.

I turned back. "Yes?" I asked.

"Please stay focused right now. One of your greatest strengths is your focus and dedication to the ultimate goal to TOXIC. Do not lose that now. Let's find this spy and get you better, so that you can return to the reason that you are here." He paused before finishing, but I didn't need him to finish his sentiments; I read the words out of his mind. I took a deep breath and readied myself for him to speak them aloud.

"You are here to avenge your parents' deaths. You made that choice. I gave you the option to return to Capri, but you chose to come to the McDonough School."

"I know," I replied weakly.

"Do you still want to help track down Crane? Do you want another chance to kill him?"

"Of course, I do!" I exclaimed defensively.

"Then find the spy so that we can interrogate him, and find out what we need to know."

"Like you had me do to Ernest?" I knew that I'd gone too far the moment the words were out of my mouth.

"I am sorry about what happened to Ernest. I really am. But we are at *war,* Natalia, and if it means that a few innocent people get hurt in the process, then that is a risk I will take. Every time." His voice was scarily calm.

Once again, Ian Crane's words played in my mind. *"You have no idea what your Agency does to innocent people."*

"That's easy for you to say, Mac; you're not the one who has to live with the consequences of what you personally did in the name of war," I spat back, my temper clouding my better judgment.

"You have no idea of the sacrifices that I have made in the name of war." Mac's voice rose an octave, and I feared that he would bare his teeth the way he had in my hospital room. "Do. Not. Let. Your parents' deaths have been in vain." He punctuated every word in a low voice that sounded more animal than human, but at least no pointy canines flashed over his bloodless lips.

"I will find the spy." I spun and fled Mac's office before he could say anything else, my victory concerning Kenly long forgotten.

Chapter Seventeen

"You're late," Penny declared as I walked into the cafeteria after my meeting with Mac.

"Sorry," I replied absently. "I had to meet with Mac about something."

"What's up? Did you find something about the spy today?" she asked hopefully.

"Oh, no, nothing like that," I said.

I told her all about Kenly, and how I hoped that if I helped her train I could make her into a Hunter. Penny thought my idea was great, and she agreed that having a team member with analytical skills would be an invaluable asset in the field. Her enthusiasm for my plan renewed my own. She too seemed intrigued by the fact that Kenly was a dual Talent. I was thrilled to have Penny as a sounding board, and we bounced ideas back and forth until the cafeteria staff kicked us out.

My day had been such a roller coaster of emotions that I was mentally exhausted, and I returned to my room after dinner. Penny told me that she would be in the Crypto Bank tomorrow evening, and I promised to head over as soon as I finished helping Captain Alvarez.

I was in a good mood when I reached my room. My communicator was blinking and beeping furiously on my side table when I entered. Selecting the voice button, I went in my bathroom to get ready for bed. I listened to Donavon's voice fill the room as I brushed my teeth and washed my face. After I'd finished my nightly routine, I hit the reply button on my communicator and waited. As soon as Donavon answered, a mini hologram of him popped out of the communicator.

"Don't put me on hologram; I'm already in my pajamas," I whined when he answered.

"Exactly what I was hoping for," he replied, the mini-Donavon suggestively wagging its eyebrows. With a pang, I thought of how Erik always wiggled his eyebrows when he was being crass.

"You called?" I asked, hurriedly changing the subject.

"Yeah, just wanted to make sure you're feeling okay," he said.

"I'm good," I answered with a half-truth. Physically, I'd felt great all day. Emotionally, I was still raw from my encounters with Ernest and Mac.

"What's wrong, Talia?" he asked, sensing my dishonesty.

"Nothing," I mumbled, not wanting to recount my taxing day.

"I'm coming over," he declared.

"Not necessary," I insisted.

"I can tell that it is. You should've told me; I would have gone to see Ernest with you." Damn, our connection was still strong enough for him to pick up on my mental projections across the building. It was also a possibility that his father had told him; I felt certain that Dr. Thistler had gone straight to Mac after my breakdown in Ernest's room.

"I don't want to talk about it, Donavon," I warned.

"Then we won't talk. I'm on my way now, though." The mini-hologram Donavon disappeared when he disconnected.

True to his word, Donavon quietly knocked on my door just minutes later. Reluctantly, I opened it and let him in. Donavon said nothing as he came over and kissed me softly on the top of my head. He pulled the covers back on the bed and waited while I climbed in. I scooted all the way over to the side closest to the wall, keeping my back to him. Donavon kicked off his shoes and crawled in behind me. I lifted my head and he slid his arm underneath it. One hand absently played with my hair while his other sought out my hand, threading our fingers together.

Penny's words filled my head, followed by my own promise to be careful where he was concerned.

"Tal, I can't tell you how sorry I am about what happened. I wish that I could take it all back, but I can't. I care about you so much, and I know that there's a lot going on right now. I just want to help you. I will do anything I can for you," Donavon urged. *"You can trust me, Natalia. I will never hurt you again. If it takes the rest of my life, I will make you see that you can trust me, that I am sorry, and that I love you."*

"Did you tell her that you loved her too?" I whispered. I didn't really want to, but I had to know.

"No, I never told Kandice that I loved her. It would've been a lie," he replied, tightening his fingers around mine.

I wanted to believe him, but his mental barriers shot up, letting me know he was lying to me.

"You should go, Donavon," I said quietly, tears filling my eyes.

"No, Talia. I'm not leaving. You can't honestly tell me that you don't still have feelings for me, can you?"

I did still have feelings for Donavon. I still cared so much that knowing that he was lying to me broke my heart all over again. "If you love me, if you still care about me, then tell me the truth, Donavon. Did you tell her that you loved her?"

Donavon swallowed hard. "Yes, I did," he whispered.

A sob tore through my chest and I yanked my hand free from his. "Get out!" I cried.

Donavon sat up, but didn't leave my bed. "Tal, please, let's talk about this," he pleaded.

I shot up and scrambled to lean against the wall. Shadows danced across his features and a thin strip of moonlight illuminated his shiny blue eyes. Hot anger coursed through my veins, and the urge to attack him was too strong to suppress. My hand shot out and I slapped him across his face. Donavon didn't raise a finger to defend himself. His complacent demeanor infuriated me further, and I balled my fists and pounded on his chest, sobbing hysterically.

When my blows slowed, Donavon wrapped his fingers around my wrists and pulled me to him.

"I'm so sorry, Talia, I'm so sorry," he repeated over and over again.

Donavon let me cry until my wails gave way to hiccups and my breath came in ragged gasps. My head spun even as I buried my face in his shirt. Though my cries had subsided, I still couldn't breathe right; my chest felt so tight, and a searing pain accompanied every breath. The trembling in my arms and legs became worse instead of better. The rigidness left my muscles and I sagged against Donavon, a violently quaking puddle of limbs. Then my jaw clenched and air hissed through my barely parted lips.

"Tal?" Donavon asked in alarm.

I couldn't answer him; I couldn't say anything. I couldn't even find the wherewithal to communicate mentally.

"Crap, crap, crap," I heard Donavon chant from somewhere far away.

My vision and hearing were fading fast, and I knew that I would soon be unconscious. Terrified, I scratched weakly at his t-shirt, willing him to understand that I was having a seizure and I needed him to call Dr. Thistler.

The message must've gotten through because I heard him screaming into my communicator seconds later.

"Dad! Dad! You have to get down here - it's Talia! She's convulsing. I think she's having a seizure!"

Then his lips were next to my ear, and my head knocked against his as the spasms racked through my body.

"Hold on, Tal. Help is coming," he promised. His arms were strong and comforting; the more I shook, the tighter he held me. Donavon continued to murmur assurances while we waited for his father to arrive.

Mac must have been close because the door to my room burst open several minutes later. Mac, Dr. Thistler, and Janet rushed inside. Mac pried me from his son's arms, shoved Donavon aside, and laid me flat on the bed, pinning me against the mattress as I thrashed uncontrollably. Dr. Thistler tore the sleeve back from my arm and wasted no time plunging the needle into my exposed vein. The moment the drugs hit my bloodstream, the shaking slowed. Mac stroked my sweaty hair back from my forehead, and I relaxed into the blankets.

"You're okay, now," he soothed.

I still couldn't talk, but I managed to bob my head up and down. Mac wrapped his large hands around mine, rubbing back and forth to calm the lingering tremors. I closed my eyes, exhausted.

"Natalia, are you hurt?" he asked, holding up one of my hands.

Hurt? Like besides the seizure? I wondered.

"It's not her blood, Dad," Donavon answered quietly.

Blood? I thought, managing to muster enough strength to lift my eyelids. Sure enough, the fingernails of the hand Mac was examining were stained red. I looked from my bloody hands to Donavon; the front of his shirt was torn, and long scratches ran the length of his neck and chest. One of his cheeks was slightly darker than the other, where I'd slapped him.

"Did I do that?" I stammered, tripping over the words.

Mac, Janet, and Dr. Thistler exchanged worried glances, but Donavon's sympathetic eyes stay focused on me. No one answered my question.

"Donavon, go change," his father ordered.

"Someone should stay with Talia tonight," he replied, keeping his feet firmly rooted in place.

"She should go to Medical, so I can observe her," Dr. Thistler said pointedly.

"No," I moaned in protest. The only thing that I wanted less than having an overnight babysitter was having a sleepover in the hospital.

"She'll be more comfortable here. I'll stay with her," Donavon answered evenly, boldly meeting Dr. Thistler's gaze. Like his father, Donavon was physically imposing. As he rose to his full height, haughtily crossing his arms over his torn shirt and pinning her with a gaze that was pure ice, I realized just how much like Mac he really was. Dr. Thistler must have realized it too, because she pursed her thin lips and gave Donavon a disapproving look; but then she took several steps back and didn't argue further.

Mac's expression was neutral, but I could feel his displeasure. Donavon tore his eyes from Dr. Thistler, and the warm baby-blue color was back when he fixed them on me. He silently pleaded with me to tell them that he could stay. The doctor might have cowered under his stare, but his father would not. If I insisted on spending the night in my room with Donavon there to watch me, Mac might agree. Truthfully, I wanted to spend the night in my own room alone, but I knew that option wasn't on the table.

"I want Donavon to stay with me," I said, the words sounding garbled and nearly unintelligible since I was still trying to regain control of my muscles.

Mac, Janet, and Dr. Thistler exchanged more uneasy glances.

"Fine, but you have to sleep," Mac finally agreed.

He needn't worry about that; between my seizure and Donavon's admission, I was barely able to stay awake.

Dr. Thistler made me promise to go straight to sleep and check in with her in the morning. Mac tucked me under the covers and said a quick goodnight. Janet leaned down and kissed me on the forehead before following the other two out of the room.

Donavon walked with them to close my door once they'd

gone.

"Don't," Mac told his son in a voice so low that I knew he hadn't meant for me to hear. Donavon threw me a look over his shoulder, indecision and sorrow warring in his mind.

"I won't," he said to his father in the same barely audible whisper. Then he shut my bedroom door in Mac's face.

I was too tired to care what Mac didn't want his son to do; I had a couple of guesses, all of them embarrassing for me. Donavon discussing our personal interactions with his father was *so* not something that I wanted to know about. Given that Mac had found his son in my bedroom late at night, his mind must have jumped to the logical conclusion, but that he'd felt the need to expressly warn him not to touch me after I'd had a seizure was more than I could handle.

Donavon didn't get back into bed. Instead he sat on the floor next to it, leaning against the wall. He propped his elbows on bent knees and rested his face on upturned palms. Tentatively, I reached for one of his hands. He wound his fingers through mine, but refused to face me.

"I'm sorry," I whispered. "I didn't mean to claw you." Gingerly, I touched the raised scratches on his neck; he didn't even flinch as I ran my finger over the wounds. The marks were extremely thin and felt more like they'd been made by a cat's claws, rather than human fingernails.

"I'm the one who's sorry, Tal. I know how badly I hurt you, and now I've given you seizures, too." He sounded close to tears.

"The seizure wasn't your fault," I assured him, although it kind of was. "I helped with that Hunters' demonstration today even though Dr. Thistler told me not to physically exert myself. And then everything with Ernest. So when you said ...well, you know, it was just too much. I overreacted."

"I'm so sorry," he repeated; and when he finally turned to face me, tears were streaming down his cheeks. "I never meant to hurt you. I love you."

Just like I'd known that he was lying earlier, I knew that he was telling the truth now. Donavon did love me; and if he could take back what had happened with Kandice, I knew that he would. Unfortunately, he couldn't - and he also couldn't make me trust him again. I did still have feelings for him and maybe even still loved him in a way, but I wasn't sure that it was enough.

Luckily, I didn't have to make any decisions tonight. In my weakened condition, that was probably for the best.

"I know, Donavon," I replied quietly, raising our joined hands to my cheek. "I know."

Chapter Eighteen

The next morning, I woke tightly wrapped up in Donavon's arms; at some point during the night, he'd climbed into bed with me. The memory of my seizure washed over me when I saw the angry red lines marring Donavon's throat.

"Hey, you," he whispered when he felt my eyes on him. "How are you feeling this morning?"

"Okay." I smiled weakly. "Tired, mostly," I added.

"Why don't you sleep a little longer?" he asked, his brows knitting together with concern.

"I can't," I sighed. "I have to go to Medical before I help the Captain." I pushed the covers back.

"Are you sure that's a good idea?" he asked, fingering his torn t-shirt.

"No, but I'm so tired of these seizures controlling my life. I just want things to be as normal as possible," I said, frustrated.

"I know, Tal," he soothed, running the back of his hand down my cheek.

"What are you doing today?" I asked, shrugging away from his touch.

Donavon let his hand fall. "Helping Dad," he said, rolling onto his back and twining his fingers behind his head.

I crawled over him to get out of bed and started toward the bathroom.

"Want to meet me for dinner?" he called after me.

I turned the cold water faucet on and began brushing my teeth to give me time to make a decision. Did I want to have dinner with him? Before my seizure, I'd briefly hated him, but the way that he'd held and comforted me and kept me conscious during the episode made me not hate him at all. He'd sat on the floor for most of the night just to make sure I was okay.

I returned my tooth brush to the medicine cabinet and turned off the water. Peeking my head back into my bedroom, I answered, "Sure, I'd like that."

Leaving Donavon lounging in my room, I set off for Medical. Dr. Thistler told me that she was increasing the dosage of the equalizer, again, then made me promise that I would refrain from overstimulating myself in the future. I cringed when I read between the lines and caught her not-so-subtle meaning. Like Mac, she assumed that physical contact had precipitated my seizure ...intimate physical contact.

Too humiliated to ask about Ernest, and resigning myself to a life of celibacy, I slid quietly off the hospital bed and left to promptly break the promise that I'd just made. I jogged to the cafeteria in hopes of finding something left over since I'd missed breakfast. Luck must have been on my side that morning; there were baskets of assorted muffins and bagels alongside jams and flavored butters. I quickly buttered a plain muffin with cinnamon spread and happily munched on it while I walked to meet Captain Alvarez.

Today's demonstration would take place in the open-air Arena. An obstacle course had been set up, complete with holographic bad guys.

When I arrived, Captain Alvarez, Henri, and Erik were already there. I stuffed the remaining crumbs of the muffin into my mouth and waved a greeting. Captain Alvarez told me to get ready as the students began trickling into the Arena. I dressed in an adapti-suit just like the day before. The suits are a dark green color; but when an individual's body heat triggers the camouflaging mechanism, the suits blend in with, and adapt to, their surroundings.

Inside, the suit's covering is enough to protect the feet of the wearer; but since it doesn't provide sufficient cushioning outside, I pulled on knee-high boots made of the same material as the suit. Next, I threaded a black belt holding eight small hand knives through the loops around my hips. I zipped the suit up to my neck, but left the hood down since it would be unnecessary for a training exercise. Erik and Henri were dressed almost identically, except for their weapons; two long blades crisscrossed Erik's back, and Henri had a long rifle with a scope slung over one shoulder.

Captain Alvarez was busy explaining to the assembled students what they were about to see. Overnight, the outside Arena had been transformed to include very real looking - albeit fake - trees, rope swings, bridges, and platforms. Approximately twenty flags had been placed throughout the Arena, and the goal was to collect as many as possible in a given amount of time. The holograms would be on motion sensors, triggered when one of us tripped an alarm.

When Captain Alvarez finished speaking, he turned and gave us a slight nod. I held one hand out to Erik and one hand out to Henri. Each took hold and I closed my eyes, concentrating on both of their thoughts. Erik's mental voice filled my head first, but Henri's was only seconds behind. It took several more seconds before all three of our minds were linked. I released each of their hands and we entered the Arena.

"Natalia, right. Erik, left. I'll take center," Henri said, falling into his role as team captain.

"Got it," Erik answered.

"Ditto," I sent.

I, of course, managed to trip the first sensor. The hologram appeared ten feet in front of me. I didn't hesitate: I reached for my belt, grabbed one of my knives, and the dagger found its mark, the hologram disappearing as quickly as it had materialized.

"Okay, Tal?" Henri asked.

"Yup," I confirmed.

"Got a flag," Erik interjected.

"Show-off," I teased.

Carefully, I navigated my way through the next few areas of the obstacle course. I kept my eyes alert, dimming my other senses since it was not as though I would *hear* a hologram. I managed to uncover several flags of my own, in addition to scoring a number of points by defeating more holograms. Erik and Henri were both still working their way through their own paths. I came to a climbing wall with a thick rope dangling down the center and hand- and foot-holds off to each side. I decided to go for the rope. Approximately a third of the way up, I tripped another sensor. The hologram appeared on my right. I had only two knives left on my belt and didn't want to waste them by throwing one from that distance and risk missing. I planted both feet on the wall and shoved as hard as I could. I swung towards the hologram at an alarming pace. I didn't want to collide with it if it could be avoided; the holograms didn't hurt exactly, but they gave you a strong and unpleasant shock when you made physical contact.

I struck out with the knife, releasing it from the handle when I was just inches away, and plunged it into the hologram's chest. The hologram disappeared, and my body collided at full speed with the side of the climbing wall. The force of the impact made me groan.

"What happened, Talia?" Henri's mental voice was full of concern.

"Nothing. I'm fine," I grunted in reply.

"Get to the top of that wall and let's end this in style," Erik sent.

Grabbing one of the handholds in the wall, I released the rope. I scurried up the remaining two-thirds as quickly as I dared. The top was smooth and hard to grip, and my fingers strained as I scrambled to pull myself up and over the wall.

"Tals, be ready to jump in five," Eric's voice said, urging me on.

Hoisting myself the last couple of inches, I was finally able to pull my entire body onto the narrow ledge. From this vantage point, I could see the entire obstacle course. I saw Erik and Henri crouching down on one knee, and I waited for what I knew was coming. Both boys morphed simultaneously into large black birds with beautiful iridescent feathers and long slender beaks. One bird soared over the stands of the Arena where the students were sitting. The other bird, Erik, flew toward where I stood on the top of the wall. I closed my eyes – I hated heights – and focused on my hearing and sense of touch, listening for the quiet flapping of Erik's wings and feeling for the slight disturbance in the air that would signal his arrival.

I crouched when I heard the wings and closed my eyes tightly in preparation to jump. Judging him to be approximately two feet out from the wall and one foot below, I leapt. I landed on my knees between Erik's wing joints. Not the most graceful landing, but hey - at least I hadn't missed! Rolling onto my stomach, I wrapped my arms around the bird's neck. We flew to meet Henri and circled the Arena, flying side by side. Finally, and not a minute too soon in my opinion, we landed on the top level of the stands. I quickly jumped off Erik's back, thankful to have my own two feet back on the ground. The two giant birds disappeared before my eyes, and Erik and Henri materialized in their place.

When I looked down, the crowd was going wild, amazement written all over their faces. I waved and smiled alongside Erik and Henri.

"Show-offs," I teased them even though I, too, was basking in the praise of the students.

"You miss it, don't pretend," Erik joked back. He was right; I did miss being part of their team. Not so much the flying, though; no matter how many times I did it, I never got used to riding on Erik in bird form.

"You were amazing." I smiled as Donavon's voice filled my head.

"Where are you?" I called to him.

"To your right. Down. Down. Now more to the right," he instructed. I finally spotted him, sitting in the stands with Mac. I waved and felt warmth spread through me.

"Excuse me," I said out loud to Erik and Henri, who were still relishing in the attention of the admiring students. I made my way down to where Donavon and Mac sat.

"Not bad for someone who is out of practice, Natalia," Mac greeted me with a backhanded compliment.

"Thank you, I think," I responded, not really sure what else to say. "What are you doing here?"

"I wanted to check out this Baker girl. After all, I did agree to devote one of my best resources to her training. Besides, when Donavon told me that you were defying Dr. Thistler's advice, I wanted to be present in case you had another episode."

I flushed guiltily and shot Donavon a withering glare.

"Sorry," he sent, shrugging apologetically.

Just then, Captain Alvarez joined us. "Director, Donavon, good of you to come," he smiled pleasantly at the father and son duo.

"I am just here to observe, but by all means put Donavon to work," Mac replied.

"Donavon, head on down and Henri will give you a station to man. You too, Natalia," Captain Alvarez suggested.

"Actually, I would prefer that Natalia observe with me," Mac answered before I had a chance to comply. "After all, she has done background on the students and had a chance to observe them yesterday. I would really like to hear her thoughts." I knew that Mac thought a lot of my Talents, even if he was convinced that I'd been unfocused lately. However, he'd never really treated me like a peer, never asked for my opinion; Mac was more of the type to give you your opinion. I'd thought that his concession to let me work with Kenly had been his usual indulgence of my unorthodox requests - but maybe, just maybe, he respected my opinion enough to stand behind my decision.

"Of course, Director." Captain Alvarez smiled. "I'm sure that she'll have some great insights."

For the rest of the afternoon I followed Mac around with my communicator answering questions on each and every student present. I noted the kids that he wanted to pay extra attention to – those whose Talents appeared stronger than reported in their files. For my own personal interest, I also made notes on those with weaker-than-reported Talents.

In accordance with the *Mandatory Testing Act*, every child was tested at the age of five for the presence of paranormal abilities. Each child testing positive was given an initial Talent ranking: High, Medium, or Low. During Placement Exams each student would receive a more precise Talent ranking: Elite, Extremely High, High, Medium, Medium-Low, Low, or Extremely-Low.

Admittedly, the initial rankings were extremely broad. I was perplexed by the number of students whose powers were weak when their initial ranking had been High. The ones who were initially ranked Low or Medium but now exhibited higher levels of abilities seemed more normal to me. After eleven years of training and honing their Talents, it made sense that they would be stronger than the Agency initially thought.

Mac already knew some of the student bios by heart, the ones with particularly strong Talents. He also seemed to know many of them personally, making small talk while we made our rounds. When it came time to observe Kenly, I held my breath. She wasn't the worst combatant, but she appeared slow and uncoordinated compared to the others.

"You sure have your work cut out for you, Natalia," Mac commented after she'd completed several of the obstacles. I smiled thinly in return; I didn't want to press my luck and say something that might make Mac change his mind about allowing me to work with her.

"Thank you all for coming," Captain Alvarez's voice boomed throughout the Arena. "I hope that the past few days have been as helpful for all you students as they have been for us. I look forward to seeing all of you during Placement Exams at the end of the year." With that, Captain Alvarez dismissed the kids from the day's demonstration.

"I'll see you later, Mac," I called over my shoulder as I hurried to catch up with the departing crowd.

I'd only made it a couple of feet when long fingers closed around my wrist. Startled, I swiveled around to face Erik.

"Hey," he began uneasily.

"Hey," I responded, glancing around nervously. I wasn't sure what to say to Erik after everything that had happened with Donavon the previous night.

"I'm leaving tonight ...I was hoping that we could talk before I go?" Erik's thoughts were unguarded, and his longing to spend time with me made my chest ache and butterflies swarm in my stomach.

"I can't, Erik," I said, yanking my wrist free from his grasp. "I'm sorry." I wanted to spend time with him too, and I wanted to touch him so badly that my hands twitched at the thought of feeling his skin underneath my fingertips. But Erik had called me his "friend"; and also, after my reaction to Donavon's admission about Kandice, I knew that I wasn't over him.

I didn't know what I wanted, but I did know that Erik was leaving to go back to Headquarters. He was going back to his real life, and he couldn't be there for me in the way that I needed right now – the way that Donavon could, the way that he had been last night. Erik was patently immature and sarcastic; and even if he took back his claim that we were just friends, I doubted that he'd want me if he witnessed one of my seizures. Not that I blamed him - I wouldn't either.

I shoved my longing aside, willed my pulse to slow, and bit my lip to keep the tears back. Slowly, I turned and walked away from Erik, who let me leave without so much as a word of protest, though his eyes bored through my back and pierced my heart.

Once I was safely outside the Arena, away from Erik, I searched the throng of congregated students for Kenly. Thankfully, her height made her easy to spot in the crowd; she was standing with a group of girls huddled off to one side.

"Kenly," I called as I approached.

She turned her head to locate the person calling her name. When her eyes landed on me, she smiled.

"Hey, Ms. Lyons," she called back, raising one thin arm in a friendly wave.

"It's Talia, and could I talk to you for a minute?"

"Um, sure." She glanced around at the gaggle of girls and nodded, indicating that they should leave.

"So, you want to try out for the Hunters?" I began once her friends were a safe distance away.

"Yeah. I know that it's a long shot, but I really want to be a Hunter, like my father," she answered, bobbing her head so vigorously that her brown locks bounced up and down on her shoulders.

"Placement Exams are coming up pretty soon and you would need a lot of work to be ready," I prompted, attempting to gauge her level of commitment. I knew from watching her that she had heart; but if she were going to be a real contender, she needed focus and determination as well.

"I know. I've been practicing after school."

"How would you like some help? I've asked the Director for permission to help you train." Kenly's brown eyes lit up like a Festivis Day firework.

"Really? You would do that for me?" She seemed shocked that I was taking such an interest in her future.

"Well, yeah. If you want," I added.

192

"Why?" she whispered.

"Why, what?"

"Why would you want to help me? I'm not that good, and the chances that I'll actually make the Hunters are low."

Why *did* I want to help Kenly? She was right; her placing high enough for the committee to select her for the Hunters was against the odds. And it wasn't like I didn't have enough to worry about without the added pressure of someone else's career on my shoulders.

"Because you remind me of someone," I finally answered.

"Who?"

"Me."

Kenly beamed. "I would love for you to help me."

We made plans to start our sessions after school the next day. Now I just needed to figure out exactly how I was going to accomplish this monumental task, how I was going to teach Kenly everything that I'd learned over the course of six years in just three months.

Chapter Nineteen

That evening, I arrived at Donavon's room with dinner in hand. He opened the door just as I raised my hand to knock. He was wearing only black pants and a black belt, his chest bare and his shaggy hair still a little damp. I swallowed the lump in my throat.

"Hi," I stammered.

"I didn't know that we were picnicking for dinner," he gestured to the bag that I held.

"I thought that it would be more fun if it was just us." He gave me a skeptical look. "Besides I hate the cafeteria," I said quickly. Truthfully, I was avoiding Erik.

Donavon opened the door wider, and I brushed past him into the room. He caught my arm, and I turned to meet his clear blue eyes. He leaned down just as I rose to stand on my tiptoes, and our lips met in the middle. Dropping the paper bag holding our dinner, I wrapped both of my arms around his neck. I willed the door shut and heard it slam in response.

The air seemed to rush out of the room with the closing of the door. Penny's voice filled my head, and I inwardly sighed. What was I doing? I pushed lightly on Donavon's shirtless chest.

"Sorry," he said, not sounding sorry at all.

"I just don't know what's really going on between us," I started to ramble.

"You don't need to say anything, Tal." He gave me a genuine smile. "Let's eat. I'm starving." I picked up the paper bag and withdrew two sandwiches, each with thick slabs of turkey, smothered in a creamy cranberry mayo on cornbread. I spread out napkins on the floor while Donavon watched hungrily.

"Please put on a shirt," I mumbled.

"Am I distracting you?" he teased.

"No, it's unhygienic to eat without clothes on," I shot back. Even to my own ears, my voice sounded unconvincing. The look he gave he me told me that he didn't believe me either, but he turned and began rummaging through his closet in search of a shirt.

"There are drinks in that mini cooler under the night table behind you," he said, his back to me. I turned around, opened the cooler, and fished out two bottles of water.

"Any chance you have salt? I forgot to pick some up," I said, sheepishly.

"Um, yeah. In my desk drawer there are probably some packets," he called over his shoulder.

I slid open his desk drawer and began searching for salt. I found several packets mingled with the loose papers and pencils clogging the interior. I fumbled to retrieve all of the loose packets, and my fingers brushed over a glossy surface – a picture. I pulled the photograph free from the mess; it was of a child, maybe a year old with shaggy blonde hair and oversized sunglasses, sitting on a lawn.

"Aww, you're so cute in this picture!" I exclaimed. Smiling, I turned to show Donavon the photograph in my hand. My grin faded when I took in Donavon's tense expression. A trickle of fear leaked from his mind before he sent up his mental barricades.

"Um, yeah, thanks," he replied tightly.

I started to say something else, but Donavon's eyes had gone dark and icy in a Mac-worthy glare. His expression unnerved me. *Weird*, I thought, quickly snapping my mouth shut. He turned back to his closet, making a show of noisily searching through the handful of shirts that hung there.

Not wanting to upset him further, I quickly replaced the picture in the desk drawer where I'd found it. When I tried to push the drawer back into place, something prevented it from closing completely. I wiggled it, attempting to free the hindrance, but the drawer still wouldn't shut. I pulled it back out on the runners and felt around in the back to locate the impediment. My fingers closed around a tightly folded wad of paper, and I yanked it free.

When I withdrew my arm and opened my palm, my blood froze in my veins. My next breath hitched in my throat, and my stomach twisted with terror.

My mind flashed to Henri placing a tightly folded piece of paper in my hand and folding my fingers around the edges ...the same piece of paper that I now held. I had to bite my lip to keep from crying out when I saw the dark stains obscuring my own neatly printed name. The blood, my blood, flaked off of the page and into my palm. A thousand thoughts raced through my head. Why did Donavon have Erik's letter? Why was he keeping it stuffed in the back of his desk? How did he get it in the first place?

"Did you find salt?" Donavon asked, pulling a white t-shirt over his head.

My mind swam with warring thoughts. Should I confront him? I quickly decided not to; I needed more time to process the situation. I shoved the wad into the back pocket of my jeans.

"Salt? Yeah, I did," I said, trying to keep my voice even. Hastily, I slammed the drawer shut with my mind. Donavon turned around to face me once again, and his eyes had returned to the warm blue of a clear sky, all traces of his earlier annoyance gone.

Managing a weak smile, I held one of the sandwiches out to Donavon. He accepted it and quickly began eating. I slowly chewed the first few bites of turkey and bread, not really tasting the contents, but managing to swallow them all the same. Thankfully, Donavon seemed so distracted that he didn't notice my own mental wandering.

Trying to dispel the awkwardness in the room, I began making small talk about the various students from the demonstration, and watched as the tension visibly dissipated from Donavon. Once he seemed relaxed, I took a chance and reached out to his mind, but his thoughts were all on what we were talking about. Well, not ALL of them, but the ones that weren't made me blush, so I quickly retreated into my own head.

After we ate, I cleaned up our little picnic and hugged Donavon goodbye. When he bent to kiss me, I turned my head and his lips brushed my cheek instead. He barely hid his disappointment over my rebuff. Right then, I didn't care about Donavon's feelings. The only thing that mattered was the letter currently burning a hole in the pocket of my jeans – a desperate reminder that I had to see Erik before he left.

The words on those pages verged on treason. The accusations that he'd made would guarantee him a horrible fate, particularly if they were true. And somehow, I'd let them fall into the hands of the Director's son. If Erik got in trouble, it would be my fault; any further bloodshed would be on my hands.

Panic, bordering on hysteria, gripped my lungs as I ran across campus to the hover hangar. Erik and Henri were loading bags onto a TOXIC jet when I breathlessly crossed the threshold. Erik looked up as I approached and waved. Despite the dire reason I'd come, I felt my heart skip a beat and my stomach flutter. The smile that lit up his face fell when he picked up on my emotional state.

"I thought you might not come," he called, crossing the cement floor to where I stood.

"Erik, I need to talk to you," I panted, disregarding his greeting.

Henri had followed Erik over and now stood next to him. "I'll leave you two to say goodbye," he offered, looking awkwardly between my red, sweaty face and Erik's distraught expression. Henri gave me a quick hug and peck on the cheek before retreating.

Erik rested his hands on my shoulders, and I could feel the heat of his skin through my sweater. His turquoise eyes sparkled sadly, and I knew that he'd read my thoughts.

"I'm so sorry, Erik," I whispered.

"I always knew that you would never get over him," he said regretfully, as if I hadn't spoken. "I suppose it's hard to say no to a guy who nearly died for you," Erik continued.

I was so confused that I momentarily forgot the reason that I'd nearly torn a hamstring in my haste to get to the hangar.

"I don't think that willingly risking his life for me and me nearly killing him because I lost control are the same thing," I said slowly, still trying to figure out what the hell Erik was talking about.

"Huh?" Erik sounded confused now. "What are you talking about?"

"What are *you* talking about?" I countered.

"Nevada," he said slowly.

I stared at him blankly, my brain apparently too slow to fit the pieces of the puzzle together. What did Donavon, Nevada, and me nearly dying have in common?

"When the extraction team found you in Nevada, you'd lost so much blood that they didn't think you were going to make it," Erik started to explain. I mentally urged him to continue. I knew all of this, but had no idea what it had to do with Donavon. "Well, there was only so much blood on the plane, and the Medics were unable to stop your bleeding." He seemed hesitant to continue; his words were halted.

"Okay ...and what does this have to do with Donavon?" I demanded.

"Donavon was part of the extraction team," he said, eyeing me cautiously. "You didn't know that?" he guessed.

"No," I whispered. "I didn't." Mac had left that detail out when he'd filled in my memory gaps. And apparently, when Donavon said that he'd never lie to me again and that I could trust him, he'd conveniently forgotten about this.

"Get to the part about Donavon nearly dying," I hissed through clenched teeth.

Erik grimaced, and I almost felt bad since my anger wasn't directed at him.

"Well, when the Medics used all of the blood on the craft and you still needed more, Donavon insisted on giving you his. So, the Medics gave you a direct transfusion. Donavon gave you so much blood that he had to be carried off of the plane when it finally landed in Kansas." Erik looked miserable, like it physically pained him to admit that Donavon had done something so noble.

"How do you know this?" I asked, fighting the hysteria rising in my chest. Why had no one told me? Why had Donavon not told me?

"I arrived in Kansas a couple of hours after you did. The Director was screaming at Donavon, saying that he shouldn't have done it. He kept telling Donavon that he screwed up and that you would have made it to Kansas, where there was more blood, already filtered and cleaned, to give you."

"Why was it such a big deal? Why was Mac so mad?" I asked, more to myself than to Erik. All Operatives were routinely checked for diseases and illnesses; Donavon would've known if he was sick. Surely he wouldn't have given me his blood if he knew that it was tainted.

"Well, it's against protocol; but in extreme circumstances, I'm sure that it's happened before," Erik said. "All I know is the Director was so furious that he made Donavon leave immediately. Donavon said he wanted to make sure that you were okay, but the Director told him he'd already done enough."

"Why wouldn't Donavon tell me?" I asked, voicing the million dollar question.

"I don't know, Tal. I'm sorry that I told you. I figured you already knew."

I shook my head, no longer trusting myself to speak.

"Erik, we need to go," Henri called from inside the craft.

"Tal, I'm so sorry. I wouldn't have said anything if I knew that you didn't know." He wiped his thumb under my left eye and across my left cheek, smearing the tear that had spilled over. He bent down and kissed my cheek, his lips warm against my cool, damp skin.

"I'll see you soon, Tal," he whispered, his breath tickling my ear. He turned and started to walk toward the open plane door.

I shoved my hands in my back pockets to still the shaking, and my fingers closed around Erik's letter. I called out to him, "Erik! Wait!"

He turned slowly, hope filling his features. I hated that what I was about to say would once again wipe that expression off his face.

"Donavon had your letter."

"What?" he demanded, closing the space between us faster than I'd have thought possible. He grabbed my upper arms, his fingers digging painfully into my flesh. "What did you say?" His crazed expression terrified me; I'd seen that look before, and nothing good could come of it.

"I-I-I was in his room, looking for salt; and I found it, stuffed in the back of his desk," I whimpered.

"When?" Erik demanded.

"Just now before I came here," I whispered. Erik's grip on me tightened and I cried out, sure that my arms would be tie-dyed black and blue tomorrow. "I'm so sorry," I sobbed. "I didn't mean for him – for anybody to find it. I was reading it in Nevada when I thought I was dying."

"So he's had it for what, ten months now?" Erik asked, more to himself than me.

"I don't know. The last time I saw it before tonight was right before I passed out. When it wasn't listed with my personal effects, I assumed that it had been burned when the extraction team sanitized the woods where they found me," I explained.

Finally, Erik released me; I swayed unsteadily without him
holding me up. He reached for me again, but this time he wrapped
his arms around me and crushed my body to his. I relaxed into his
embrace, circling my own arms around his waist.

"Shit, Tal, I'm sorry. I didn't mean to hurt you," he murmured
into my hair. "I'm not mad at you; it's not your fault," he
promised.

"Erik! We really need to go," Henri called. "I'm sorry, Tal,"
he added.

"I'll call you when I get back," he promised. "We'll talk about
it then."

Nodding, I reluctantly disentangled myself from his arms. But
we both knew that we wouldn't actually be able to talk about it
over the communicators; the Agency monitored them too closely.

"I'm so sorry," I croaked again. Erik reached for my hand and
gave it a gentle squeeze, then quickly brushed his mouth against
mine. When he tried to pull away, I instinctively grabbed the back
of his neck and kissed him deeper. Erik's lips quirked into a grin as
his hands closed around my waist. Even though Erik had kissed me
numerous times before, the thrill that I felt now was just as intense
as it had been the first time.

The feel of his mouth against mine was familiar and
intoxicating, causing my head to spin. I lost awareness of the
surrounding hangar. He crushed my hips against his, and I tangled
my fingers in his thick hair.

When Erik broke the connection, I physically ached at the
absence of his touch. He beamed, warmth and passion radiating
from his every pore. His fingertips brushed the hollow of my throat
in an oddly intimate gesture that nearly sent me melting to the
concrete. Then with a tremendous amount of effort, Erik turned
and jogged to the open plane door.

I stood rooted in my place until the electric engines of the craft
came to life. I turned and walked slowly from the hangar. The
night air was cool and I hugged myself, fighting off the cold air

and the confusion at the same time. Why wouldn't Donavon have told me? Why was it such a big deal? Why hadn't Mac told me? Why had Mac reacted like that? I felt like I'd somehow been lied to, betrayed. Was an omission really a lie?

Opening my mind as wide as I could, I searched for Donavon. I focused all of my energy on pinpointing his location; he was at his parents' house. I contemplated going up there, but then decided it against it. Confronting Donavon was one thing, but confronting Mac was another. Instead, I walked to the Crypto Bank to find Penny; maybe she could make sense out of all of this.

Chapter Twenty

When I arrived, Penny and Gemma were in their usual positions. Penny's smile froze when she saw me.

"Talia! What's wrong?" she cried.

"Can you access medical records?" I asked quietly.

"Whose medical records?" she asked, looking confused.

"Donavon's," I answered firmly. There must be something wrong with Donavon, something wrong with his blood, something that he'd passed on to me. It was the only reason that Mac would've been so mad.

"No," Penny said slowly. "I can't. I'm sorry, Tal." Penny glanced to where Gemma sat, headphones covering her ears, and looked relieved that she couldn't hear my demands.

"Well, then, how about mine?" I pressed.

"Talia, I can't access anyone's medical records. They're not kept in the same e-files as the rest of your information. Those records are kept in the Medical facility. My clearance isn't that high. What's this about?"

"Did you know that the Medics who rescued me gave me Donavon's unfiltered blood?" I asked bluntly.

"No. Who told you that?" she demanded.

"Erik. He said that when he arrived in Kansas, Mac and Donavon were fighting about it. Mac said that he shouldn't have done it, that it was dangerous. Did I catch something from

Donavon? Is that what's really wrong with me?" I pleaded.

"Oh, Tal," she whispered. "I don't know."

"There isn't anything that you can tell from our records?"
She'd already told me that she couldn't, but I somehow hoped that
if I asked again, her answer would be different.

"I'm sorry, Talia. I really am, but there's nothing in
Donavon's regular file that would tell me that about his medical
history."

"I think I need to go lie down," I said numbly, turning to
leave.

"Tal?" she called after me.

"Yeah?"

"You should probably keep your distance from Donavon until
we figure this out."

I nodded in agreement.

I walked back to my room in a state of shock. I undressed and
crawled into bed in nothing but a tank top and my underwear,
clenching Erik's letter, smeared with my dried blood, in my hand.
The light on my communicator was blinking furiously, but I
ignored it. Carefully, I unfolded the well-worn pages, and reread
the words that I knew by heart.

Natalia,

*A couple nights ago you asked about the circumstances
leading to me going to the McDonough School when I was
fourteen. I know that you were hurt I wouldn't share my story with
you, but I've never shared it with anybody. I've never trusted
someone enough with my secret; I've never wanted to let anybody
get that close to me.*

*I'm so sorry about what happened last night. I'm sorry that I
let things go so far with you when I've known all along that you're
still upset over Donavon. But you're right - I do know how you feel
about me. I've known for a long time how you feel, maybe even
before you knew it yourself. I feel the same way. You've captivated
me since the first time we met, during your placement exams. I*

thought that it was just a crush, an odd fascination with a girl who managed to surprise me. But the more time I spent with you, the more I began to realize that what I'm feeling is so much more than a crush. I'd known about Donavon and the girl – her name is Kandice – for a while. I really wanted to tell you, but Henri persuaded me not to. He thought my feelings for you were clouding my judgment, and he was afraid that if I was the one to tell you, you might not have believed me. He sensed that you were starting to realize I am falling for you. I stand by my decision. I wish that you hadn't found out the way you did, but I'm glad that you found out on your own. Honestly, I'm not sure you would have believed it otherwise.

I can't put into words how much it pained me to see you hurting so much, but slowly you bounced back just like I knew you would. You're a fighter. When you finally started to understand that what you're feeling for me is real, I was elated. I tried to hold back, tried to give you more time to grieve, but I was selfish. I want you, so I started something even though I know that you aren't really ready. I was jealous again when I realized that you still think about him when we're together. I want all of you for myself, and when you thought about him last night, my temper got the best of me. I said things that I can't take back, but hope you forgive me. If time is what you need, that's what I'll give you.

You wanted to give me something that you've never shared with anyone, and I want you to know that I don't take that lightly. I also want to share something with you that I've never shared with anyone. Just know that once you've read what I have to say, you might not like it – or me. That's a risk I'm willing to take; I honestly think that you, of all people, deserve to know. So here it goes:

My parents are firm supporters of the movement to repeal the Talent Testing Act. Both my brothers and I were born at home instead of in a hospital because both of my parents are Talents. They were confident that at least one of us would be born Talented, and they didn't want our births on record. I'm the oldest. When I was three, my parents noticed that I was able to replicate both of their abilities. It unnerved them because Mimics are so rare. They knew that the Agency would come for me if they ever found out. Both of my younger brothers also exhibited Talent at a young age, although neither is very strong. My middle brother is a mono-morph, and my youngest brother is a low-level Brain.

We moved around a lot, staying off of TOXIC's radar. We lived mostly in rural areas and kept to ourselves. I grew up fearing the Agency and what they stood for, but as I got older, I began to think that maybe my parents were paranoid. I met a girl on one of my grocery runs when we were living in North Carolina. We became close and I got cocky. I told her all about my abilities, trying to impress her. She in turn told her parents. Days later, Agency Operatives raided our home. Ordinarily, the penalty for refusing to submit children for testing is jail time and a heavy fine. But my parents were proud and fought. My mother was killed in the raid. My father and brothers probably would've been, too, but I knew that TOXIC hadn't come for them; they'd come for me. The man in charge of the mission told me that I was in no position to bargain, but I could tell he was lying. I surrendered myself in exchange for the lives of my father and my brothers.

Mimics are so rare and I could tell how badly he wanted me, so I called his bluff. I threatened to take my own life if he didn't agree to the terms of my deal. In the end, he agreed. I offered to go willingly to the School and take my "rightful" place within the Agency. In return my brothers would be free to attend regular school and live normal lives, and my father wouldn't be penalized. My father and brothers now live in Raleigh and are closely monitored by Agency personnel. Under the terms of my agreement, I'm not allowed to speak about what happened, visit my family, or step out of line. They'll all be executed if I violate any of these conditions.

I've been closely watched since my first day at School.

Truthfully, I'm shocked that the Agency allowed me to become a Hunter. However, my willing sacrifice – and the constant vigilance of those in charge – has proven me to be a loyal Operative. I don't agree with the Mandatory Testing laws and I don't really care about the Coalition and their rebellion, but I do care about my family's well-being. If that means I have to fall in line and play my part, I will – and I do.

I told you that I'd tell you all of this when you were ready to hear it. I don't really know if you are ready now, but I wanted to share something with you. I also want you to understand that the Agency isn't all that you believe it to be. There are many within it that are corrupt, and the system in general is incredibly flawed.

You had a choice about whether to join this organization. I know that you see it as a chance to right the wrongs in your past, but just remember that the rest of us weren't given the same option. The Agency is responsible for the wrongs in my past.

I feel the deeply buried doubt that you keep bottled up inside of you. I'm not saying that you should leave the Agency or anything like that. I just want you to keep your eyes open, and hang on to that doubt. It's unlikely that Donavon is the only one who's lied to you.

I gave this to Henri because I trust him for reasons he'll have to explain to you some day. I gave it to you now because I wanted you to have a chance to read it away from the ever-watchful electronic presence of TOXIC's prying eyes. I that know you're too curious to not read this before you return, so we can talk about it when you get back if you want to. If you don't, well, that's fine too. I hope that you'll understand how much trust it took for me to write this - and even if you believe nothing I say, I hope that you won't share its contents with anybody.

E.

Crawling out of bed, I made my way to the bathroom. Holding Erik's words under the sink faucet, I turned the knob. Water soaked the pages, and my blood stained the clear liquid red as it swirled down the drain. After several long moments, all that remained in my fingers was a soggy mess of pulp. I wrapped the remnants in toilet paper, and flushed the bits of incriminating evidence. As I walked back to my bed, I caught sight of my reflection in the mirror over my sink. My cheeks were sunken in, the hollows under my eyes so purple they seemed to be reflecting the color of my irises.

I'd thought about Erik's letter frequently over the past several months, but actually reading his accusations in black and white once more drove home the words on those pages. I didn't know how much of what he wrote was true, but if nothing else, I was certain that Erik believed that every word he wrote was gospel. It pained me that Mac might allow such atrocities to go unchecked on his watch. I doubted that the Agency would really kill Erik's family if he slipped up ...or did I? *You have no idea what your Agency does to innocent people.*

Removed from the situation, I was confident that even if Donavon had read the letter – and I assumed that he had – he hadn't shared it with his father. If there was even an iota of truth to Erik's words, he would already know if Donavon had indeed reported the note to Mac. At the very least, Erik would have been sanctioned for his bold statements. Donavon and Erik's dislike for one another ran deep, and I would've thought that Donavon would jump at the chance to get Erik in trouble. The fact that he didn't take the opportunity was telling; I was just unsure what exactly I was being told.

Snug under my covers once again, I closed my eyes and opened my mind. I found Donavon back in his room. Then I heard his mental voice in my head.

"You're back early. Want me to come over?"

I didn't answer him. I had no idea what I wanted. The intense physical reaction to Erik's kiss was an indication that my feelings for him were stronger than ever. His touch unlocked a part of me that only he could reach, and the way that I felt about Donavon would never compare.

Penny was right; I should stay away from Donavon. I'd told Penny that I would. But I thought that if I asked Donavon directly about the blood transfusion, he wouldn't lie to my face.

Sure, he'd omitted the fact that he was sleeping with Kandice; but he'd never bold-faced lied to me, mostly because he couldn't. The connection that we'd forged made it impossible for him to keep me out of his mind if I wanted in.

"Talia?" Donavon's mental voice interrupted my thoughts. I still refused to answer him. *"Talia, I'm coming over."*

Several minutes later I felt him approach, and I unlocked the door to my room. He pushed the door open and walked into my darkened space. I could make out his silhouette as he made his way towards me, but all of his features were no more than shadows. He knelt down beside the bed.

"Talia?" he said tentatively.

"Why didn't you tell me that you were there in Nevada?" I blurted out. After everything that I'd already been through tonight, tact was low on my list of priorities. He heaved a big sigh, and for a second I thought that he might not answer.

"I didn't know what to say to you. My father wouldn't let anyone near you when you first got back. Then when you came down here, you wouldn't speak to me. And when you finally did start coming around, I wasn't really sure how to bring it up." His voice was tight, but he sounded like he was telling the truth. I scanned his mind, and found the same ribbons of panic that I sensed earlier. I contemplated pushing through his barricade, but I lacked the strength.

"Why didn't you tell me that they gave me your blood?" I demanded.

"I didn't want you to think that you owed me something." He placed his hand on my back. "I'm sorry, Tal. If I'd known that it would upset you so much, I'd have told you myself."

"Why was your father so mad at you for doing it?" I felt

Donavon's hand tense, and he gripped a handful of my tank top. The trickles of panic leaking through turned to gaping holes, and he desperately tried to patch the damage. Donavon was afraid of his father, terrified that if Mac found out that I knew about the blood transfusion he would be furious. I'd already surmised that Mac didn't want me to know, but Donavon's distress seemed extreme.

"Well, for starters, it's against protocol. Direct blood transfusions are extremely dangerous, and we had no idea what had been done to you. Your body might have rejected the transfusion. I should've known better, but ...well, I was scared. The Medics said that you might die. I wasn't thinking straight. And honestly, I didn't care about protocol or the consequences of my actions, or anything else. I couldn't just sit there and let you die."

"I don't understand why it's such a big deal. You probably saved my life. Are you sick or something?"

"I'm not sick. It's just extremely dangerous to give anyone unfiltered blood. You know that. Dad said that it was even more dangerous because we had no way of knowing what else was in your bloodstream and how it would react. We have no idea what kind of technologies the rebel coalition has."

I turned to face him. "Is the transfusion really why you aren't a Hunter anymore?" I asked softly.

Donavon exhaled loudly. "Yes, it is. Captain Alvarez said that he would excuse the breach of protocol, but my father wasn't as lenient. He said that I was on suspension until I learned to follow orders. Dad probably would have let me go back once he calmed down, but when you gave your report and he realized that we had a spy, he decided to keep me here to help him investigate.

"Wow, Mac was really that angry?" I knew that Mac's tolerance for rule breaking was low, but usually Donavon and I were granted exceptions. Some might even argue that I broke the rules more than I followed them.

"Yeah. He was, but he's over it now," Donavon promised with

a small smile. Once again I knew that he was lying. The fear rolling off of Donavon was palpable; Mac was definitely not over it.

"The other night after I had the seizure, Mac told you not to do something ...what was it?" I held my breath as I waited for his answer. I'd just assumed that Mac had told him not to get me excited again, but now I wondered if Mac had been reminding him not to tell me about the transfusion.

Donavon sank back on his heels and looked absently at the wall. He chewed his lip, debating whether to lie.

"You said that I could trust you. Tell me the truth, Donavon," I begged him. I felt like the future of our friendship hinged on his answer right now. If he lied to me again, I would never trust him.

I was certain that Donavon knew how crucial his next words were. It was as if, in this moment, I was asking him to choose between me and his father. If he told me the truth, he would be betraying a promise that he'd made to Mac. If he lied, he would lose me forever.

I thought about letting him off the hook. After all, I didn't really need his verbal confirmation – his hesitancy to answer was enough. And even if he told me the truth, it was too late. Trust or no trust, I didn't love him like that anymore.

"Never mind about the other night," I said finally. "But I do wish that you'd told me about the transfusion."

Donavon turned his head to look at me again. "I do, too. I should have told you that I was your knight in shining armor," he joked, trying to lighten the mood. He tentatively reached for me, and when I didn't pull away, he stroked my cheek with the back of one finger. "I am really sorry, Tal. Dr. Thistler and the Medical team working on the equalizer know about the transfusion. If there are any repercussions, they're already being factored into your treatment."

Of course, Dr. Thistler knew. I was always the last to find out.

Donavon's words hung in the minute space between us.

I stared into his blue eyes and wondered what other secrets he was keeping from me. Donavon looked miserable, and part of me felt badly for him. I'd been trapped in Mac's house for nine months while I recovered from my physical injuries, but he would always be trapped in his father's shadow. Mac's control over me was strong, but his hold on his son was absolute.

"Were you the one who found me?" I asked quietly as Donavon leaned his head against my mattress, his hair tickling my face. I already knew that he was; it was the only explanation for his having had Erik's letter.

"Yes," he whispered. "I was."

"So, you found my letter?" I wanted him to admit it, to tell me the truth about something.

Donavon tensed. "Yes," he mumbled. "I did."

I scrambled to get the next question out before I lost my nerve. "Did you read it?"

"No."

With that one word, my mental tally of Donavon's lies had another hash mark.

Chapter Twenty-One

The next morning, I felt Donavon stir, well before sunrise. I peered up at him through narrow slits and mumbled a nearly incomprehensible goodbye. Letting him sleep in my bed after everything that happened seemed wrong, but he'd been so upset after our conversation that I'd been unable to turn him away.

Just as I'd been sure that Donavon had read the letter, I was sure that he hadn't told his father. He'd practically shut down after I'd mentioned it. His thoughts had become troubled and darkness had enveloped him, shrouding him in an impenetrable cloak of sadness that was so bleak I'd been scared about what lay beneath the folds. Even after he'd fallen asleep, he'd been restless, tossing and turning fretfully throughout the night.

"Sleep, Talia," he whispered in my ear as he kissed my cheek.

I nodded and returned my lids to their closed position. I didn't open them again until my alarm went off. The sun was just coming up over the horizon, casting a pink tint on my beige carpet. How early had Donavon left? Rolling over, my face made contact with the pillow that he'd slept on, and the smell of his cologne filled my nose. The familiar scent was comforting and unsettling all at once. Being around Donavon was like having a security blanket; despite all of the lies and secrets, he always relaxed me.

Even after he'd admitted everything about the transfusion and what happened in Nevada, he'd still kept Mac's real reason for keeping it from me. I could've pushed, but I wasn't sure that I really wanted to know why. There was no explanation that Donavon could give that would make Mac's omission okay in my eyes. I could understand why Donavon hadn't told me; I didn't like it, but I understood. Mac, on the other hand, had spent countless hours with me during my recovery and had plenty of opportunities, yet he'd conveniently left out both Donavon's presence and the blood transfusion.

After I was fully dressed and had succeeded in making my curly hair stick-straight, I checked all of the messages from the night before. One was from Donavon before he'd come to see me. One was from Penny, checking to make sure that I was okay after my near-breakdown in the Crypto Bank. And one was from Erik. It came in after Donavon and I had fallen asleep. All the message said was that he was back at headquarters, and to call him when I got the chance.

My heart fluttered in my chest, and a tingly sensation warmed me from the inside out at the sound of his voice. My fingers automatically flew to the reply button before I remembered that there was nothing I could say to him that the omnipresent ears of the Agency wouldn't flag. If that happened, we'd both be hauled in for unpleasant questioning. Instead, I busied myself by tidying up my bedroom and bathroom, and thought about a way to communicate with him without being monitored. I came up empty.

Realizing that if I didn't leave soon I would be late for my standing appointment with Dr. Thistler, I headed for Medical. As I sat on the crinkly white paper that covered the examination table, waiting for Dr. Thistler to administer my injection, I contemplated asking her about Donavon's blood transfusion. If his blood really was clean, then she should be able to put my fears to rest. But when I remembered the terror that Donavon had felt as he worried about his father finding out that I knew, I decided against coming out and asking her directly.

"Dr. Thistler?" I asked, drawing her attention away from the entries that she was making on her electronic pad.

"Yes, dear?" she replied, fixing me with a cold, gray stare.

"Is it possible that whatever is causing my seizures is a result of the blood transfusions that I received on the plane, or in Kansas?" I carefully observed her reaction, but her face and her thoughts remained neutral.

"No, dear, it's not," she answered flatly.

"Are you sure? I mean, isn't it possible that some of the blood was ...I don't know, contaminated?"

"All of the blood used for transfusions is filtered and scrubbed clean," she insisted, plastering a slightly manic smile across her worn face. Donavon had said that Medical knew about his blood, which meant that Dr. Thistler knew; but she wasn't about to admit to it for some reason.

"I really need to see some other patients, dear. Your levels look good today. I'll see you tomorrow." With that, she practically ran from the room before I had the chance to ask any more questions. Great. Now my only option was to ask Mac, and I still wasn't ready for that.

Ten contemplative minutes later, I arrived at the Crypto Bank.

"Ready for another exciting day of sifting through personnel files?" Penny greeted me with mock cheeriness.

"I can hardly contain my excitement," I replied sarcastically.

The smile dropped from Penny's face, and was quickly replaced by a nervous expression.

"Did you see Donavon last night?" she asked, accusingly.

"If I didn't know better, I'd think that you were the mind reader," I joked half-heartedly.

"What happened?" she demanded.

So I told Penny the story, the same way that Donavon had told me. When I finished, I waited anxiously for her to say something, anything. She didn't. Instead, Penny turned to face her computers.

"Why do you think Mac doesn't want me to know?" I asked, talking now to the back of her head.

Penny sat unmoving, her thin shoulders vibrating with tension, seemingly weighing her next words carefully.

"I honestly don't know," she said softly.

When she turned back around, her expression was neutral. Her posture was rigid, and her normally bright eyes were dark and troubled.

"Tal, when you have these seizures, what happens exactly?" she asked quietly, glancing at Gemma to ensure the other girl was preoccupied. As usual, Gemma was so engrossed in her work that she barely acknowledged our presence.

"Um, well, I start shaking, kind of lose control of my body, and then I usually pass out," I said uneasily. The episodes were so embarrassing, I hated talking about them.

"Usually pass out? Have you ever stayed conscious through one?"

"Once," I admitted. I hadn't told Penny about the seizure in my bedroom during Career Fair; I'd been worried that she would agree with Dr. Thistler, and insist that I refrain from physical activity. Not that I would have listened to her any more than I'd listened to the doctor, but still.

"Did anything else happen, besides the shaking?" Penny studied me with concern and something bordering on horror. If she thought that the convulsing was bad, how would she react if I told her that I'd clawed Donavon's neck and torn his shirt? She'd think that I was nuts and that I belonged next to Ernest in the Psychiatric Ward, and I couldn't have that.

"No," I lied to my best friend for the first time ever. "I mean, I couldn't speak or even communicate with my mind, but that always happens."

Penny's shoulders sagged ...with relief? I was glad that I hadn't told her the truth; she obviously couldn't handle it.

"Tal," she began slowly. "Please promise me that you will be cautious with Donavon, and maybe even with the Director. Maybe this isn't a big deal, but they did lie to you. What other secrets are they keeping?"

Weren't those the same ideas that I'd been contemplating myself? Penny was right. Maybe this wasn't a big deal - but then again, maybe it was.

"I'll try, Penny," I promised.

I looked over at Gemma again; she still wasn't paying attention to us. Talking about such a sensitive topic in the Crypto Bank was a bad idea. This room, like every TOXIC facility, was monitored by security cameras and listening devices, and a conversation where I accused the Director of TOXIC of lying would definitely be flagged. If Gemma were a loyal Operative and she overhead us, she would report it. Penny seemed to realize my concern.

"You know what, Tals? You're right. I'm sure that it's not a big deal. Once we find the spy, that person will be able to tell us what you were injected with. Then Dr. Thistler will find a cure, and all of this nonsense about Donavon's blood won't matter anyway." With a great deal of effort, Penny offered me a big grin, but her hands gripped the arms of her swivel chair so tightly that her knuckles cracked from the effort.

"And on that note, let's get to work finding that person so we have something to report at our status meeting," I suggested with an exaggerated eye roll. Our status meetings were unproductive, at best. Mac always gave the same tired speech about the importance of finding the spy, as if we weren't all aware that we weren't making any progress and didn't appreciate the danger of having such an infiltrator. I was living proof that the person was dangerous.

We worked for the next hour in relative silence. A couple of times, I contemplated breaking my resolution to never read Penny's mind and just take a quick swipe. Penny might have said that she didn't know why Mac was lying, but her reaction and her questions about the seizures told me that she at least had some theories. Still, every time I thought about it, I quickly rejected the idea.

After what seemed like all day, I sighed in exasperation. Penny removed her headphones and smiled at me. "I know that it's slow going."

"I feel like I've been through every single Operative's file," I whined.

"Not hardly!" She laughed. "You've only just started on the Operatives not living here on campus."

I groaned, cursing the vast size of the organization. "I have to go to class now, so this will have to wait until later," I said, rubbing my temples as I did. Staring at that computer screen was giving me a horrible headache.

"Have fun. Catch us a spy," Penny quipped as I headed for the door.

I spent the next ninety minutes grading Annalise's latest homework assignment while she rambled about verb conjugation in Spanish. Then I endured an hour and a half where Cadence alternated between ignoring my presence and barking orders at me. Since Ernest was still unaware of who he was, I returned to the Crypto Bank to spend the lunch hour with Penny and Gemma. After lunch, I joined Thad at the front of his classroom and observed the students taking a pop quiz.

"So, exactly how did you end up as an assistant Instructor?" Thad whispered, giving me the opening that I needed for a more in-depth exploration of his mind.

"I failed my solo mission for the Hunters," I admitted, staring at my tightly clasped hands in my lap.

"Really? I saw you in the demonstrations the other day, and you seemed to know what you were doing."

"Yeah, but being in the field is so different. I was sloppy, and it got me captured." I glanced up to gauge his reaction. The fact that I'd failed my qualifying assignment was common knowledge, but being captured wasn't.

"A Hunter's worst fear." He nodded knowingly and gave an

involuntary shudder.

"Were you ever captured?" I asked, diving into his thoughts. Images of close calls and near misses floated through his mind.

"Thank goodness, no." He sighed. He was telling the truth. "There were a couple of times that I thought for sure my team wouldn't make it out, but we were never taken."

"Mr. Wietz, I'm finished," a curly-haired boy proclaimed, setting his quiz paper in front of Thad.

"Great, Justin. You're excused for the day," Thad responded.

After that, students began to stream to Thad's desk to turn in their quizzes. My chance to engage him in any more reminiscing was gone, but it didn't matter. It wasn't necessary; Thad wasn't our spy. I decided to ask Mac to let me out of my obligation to assist in the history class.

As usual, Griffin's class was the highlight of my day. I loved watching his students improve from one day to the next. After their initial hesitancy about my abilities, many of them had come to regard me with a certain amount of reverence, especially after watching me in the Hunters' demonstrations. The students were actually interested in my help, and they took my advice to heart.

I was in a good mood when I arrived at Ursula's class, but unfortunately it didn't last long.

"I hear you offered to train Kenly Baker." Ursula smirked as we stood side by side, watching the students attempt to throw one another across the mats using their minds.

"Yup," I confirmed.

"She's a lost cause, Talia," Ursula insisted, placing her hands on her ample hips.

"Eh, I wouldn't count her out just yet. She just needs more training." Even as I was singing Kenly's praises, she failed to make her partner so much as stumble when she concentrated her energy on the girl. Ursula gave me an "I told you so" glance. I just shrugged, trying to appear unfazed by her poor showing.

"You aren't focusing, Baker," she shouted at Kenly, causing

the girl's face to flush and her feet to became entangled in each other.

"It's okay, Kenly," I called reassuringly. "Just concentrate and envision your ultimate goal."

Ursula laughed. "Good luck with that one."

The way that Ursula mocked Kenly angered me. I knew that I shouldn't, but I couldn't stop myself from sending her partner flying through the air on Kenly's next attempt.

"Nice!" I yelled to Kenly, who looked shocked as her partner lay on the mats gasping for breath.

Ursula looked irritated that Kenly had proven her wrong, and she decided to take her frustration out on me.

"So, how do you know Erik?" she asked, a devilish grin on her pouty lips.

"From the Hunters," I said slowly, turning my attention to her. "How do you know Erik?"

"Mutual friends. We all go way back," she replied evasively.

"Like who?" I pressed, hoping she would dispel my fear that she knew him on an intimate level.

Ursula sized me up, the gleam in her eyes giving away how much she enjoyed making me squirm. "Erik......dated my best friend for years," she finally answered.

"When?" I hissed through tightly clenched teeth, hating myself for playing right into her trap.

"Oh, it was ages ago, before he got hung up on some chick that he met last year and stopped being fun," she rolled her eyes skyward. "You might as well give up any fantasy of catching that boy. It's as much a lost cause as you making Baker a Hunter."

"Who said that I wanted to 'catch' him?" I demanded.

Ursula gave me a sympathetic look, like I was a child and she was about to tell me that unicorns weren't real.

"I saw the way that you look at him. You've got it bad. I'm telling you, he's not exactly a one-girl kind of guy. After the way he's been acting since that chick broke his heart, you don't stand a chance."

Broke his heart? Had I broken his heart? He was the one who'd stormed out of my room! He was the one who hadn't called. Well, okay, maybe neither of us had called; but where was he when I needed him? Where was he while I was learning to walk again? Sure, he claimed that he'd missed me and the kiss in the hangar made it feel as if nothing had changed between us, but still.

"Don't look so depressed, Talia," Ursula continued. "The way I hear it, you've got the Director's son wrapped around your little finger." She held up her pinkie for emphasis.

"It's not like that," I insisted.

Ursula didn't look convinced. "If that's the case, turn him loose so that the rest of us can have a shot. He's the only good-looking guy with all of his hair at this school, unless you count the students." Ursula shrugged, surveying her class of teenagers like she was selecting her next meal. I gaped at her, shocked and disgusted. The oldest students at the School were two years younger than I was, and like six years younger than Ursula.

"Alright, class dismissed. Good job today, guys," she yelled, cupping her hands around her mouth to amplify her voice.

I turned and left without another word, feeling slightly dirty after watching her ogle her male students. It was unlikely that Ursula Bane was a traitor, but she was most certainly a cradle robber.

I caught up with Kenly, and we walked together to the indoor arena for our first nightly training session. After her less-than-stellar performance in Ursula's class, I decided to start with the basics.

Since Kenly's Higher Reasoning Talent was more developed than her Telekinesis, she hadn't taken advanced combat and weapons training. I'd hoped that Kenly's poor performance during the Career Fair was nerves. Unfortunately, the more that I watched her, the less optimistic I was; Kenly wasn't a particularly good fighter.

We worked on basic maneuvers into the night, but she never once complained. Every time that she fell, she got right back up. She took every correction that I made to heart, and tried to implement them immediately – emphasis on *tried*. By the end of the evening she'd made no discernible improvement, yet I still left the Arena feeling confident in my decision.

"It takes time," I assured her as we crossed the campus grounds.

Kenly pulled absently at a loose thread on the hem of her workout tee. "I know, but it feels like all the practice in the world couldn't prepare me for my exams," she replied.

"You'll be ready," I promised, willing her doubts away.

"I'll see you tomorrow, Ms. Ly – I mean, Talia," she said, turning to veer right on the path leading to her dorm.

"'Night, Kenly," I called after her.

When I returned to my room, I had several comms waiting for me. One was from Erik, one from Donavon, and one from Mac. Mac wanted to know how my training session with Kenly had gone. I wasn't eager to inform him that she was even worse than he'd originally thought, so I decided against calling him back. Donavon wanted to know if he could come over; I knew that was a bad idea, so I didn't respond to him either. Erik's message reminded me of something that I'd forgotten about: Festivis Day.

I hit the reply button immediately, and Erik answered on the second ring.

"Hey," his voice filled my room.

"Hey ...how are you?"

"Better now that you decided to call me back," he teased. I heard the bedsprings squeak and I imagined him flopping carelessly on to his bed, hopefully shirtless.

"Sorry, I've been busy," I said lamely.

"Yeah, I kinda figured. So ...how about meeting me in the city for Festivis?" Erik asked tentatively.

"I have to ask Mac. I'm not really clear on whether I'm

allowed to leave campus," I said apologetically. I wanted to go - I wanted to see him. Hearing his voice wasn't enough; I needed to touch him.

"Why don't you suggest that you deserve some time off?" he said, emphasizing "suggest." I caught his meaning; he wanted me to manipulate Mac into letting me go. A thrill ran through me; I wasn't the only one missing the physical closeness.

"I'll ask," I promised, not bothering to hide the smile creeping into my voice.

"Good. Call me as soon as you know?"

"I'll talk to him tomorrow," I swore.

There was a long pause, neither of us speaking. Erik's breathing became heavier, and my thoughts of him half-naked in his bed ran wild.

"I miss you, Tals," he finally whispered.

"I miss you, too," I breathed, getting a little choked up. I swallowed over the lump forming in my throat. "I'll talk to you soon." I disconnected before Erik could realize how emotional I was.

I considered calling Mac right then, but I wasn't sure if he was on campus. If I was going to "suggest" that he let me go to the city for Festivis, I needed to see him in person. Resolving to hunt Mac down the following day, I crawled into bed feeling a little happier. I wasn't sure that I'd be able to convince Mac, but the prospect of seeing Erik again so soon was too enticing to not at least try.

Chapter Twenty-Two

"So, what would it take for you to help me with Kenly?" I asked Donavon the next morning over runny scrambled eggs and burnt bacon in the cafeteria.

"Wow, admitting that you can't do this already? She must be really awful," he teased.

"No, no, I'm not admitting anything. I'm just asking for a little help. After all, you're a teacher, aren't you? Maybe you could just give me some ideas."

"Tal, you've been training to be a Hunter for years. Why don't you just do the same things that we were taught?" he asked, shoveling a huge spoonful of egg in his mouth.

"Right, and Kenly doesn't have years. I'm looking for more of a crash course in becoming a Hunter."

"Exactly. That's why this is a lost cause – there's no such thing as a 'crash course' in becoming a Hunter." He grinned and bit into a heavily buttered piece of cranberry bread. I rolled my eyes.

"Donavon, look at me," I demanded. "I really need your help."

"Don't you dare use your manipulation on me, Tal," he warned.

"Pretty please," I begged, switching tactics.

"You're pathetic," he declared. "But I'll make you a deal. Tell me why you didn't return my message last night, and I'll help you."

"I told you. I didn't see your comm before I went to bed." The lie came easily to my lips. Part of me had really wanted to see him, but part of me felt guilty about doing so after I'd promised Erik that I would try to meet him in D.C. If I'd agreed to let Donavon come over, I would have only been using him for the comfort that he provided. That wasn't fair to either of us, or to Erik. I wasn't ready to distance myself completely from Donavon, evidenced by the fact we were currently having breakfast together, but I knew that I needed to put a stop to any alone time.

"You're lying," Donavon accused.

"How dare you make such an accusation!" I feigned outrage.

"Talia, I know you better than you know yourself. I know that you're lying."

"You're right," I admitted, hoping that honesty would win me some brownie points. "Look, Donavon. I just need some time to think. I'm really confused right now."

"About us?" he asked.

"Well, yeah - us, the spy, my health, everything," I rambled. I knew that I didn't want to get back together with Donavon, but I also wasn't ready to lose him completely. If I told him about Erik, that we'd kissed and I'd nearly fainted, it would be the end of our friendship. *Now who was the one lying and omitting important details*, I thought.

He put down his fork, reached across the table, and took my hand. "Take all the time you need, Tal. If you want help with Kenly, then I will help you. And if you don't want me to come over at night, I understand."

"Thanks," I whispered. "I just need some time to think."

By the end of the school day, I was in a horrendous mood. My extra time in the Crypto Bank wasn't yielding any results, I wasn't getting anywhere with my remaining suspects, and I hadn't managed to locate Mac. I felt dejected and hopeless. If we didn't find the spy, would I ever get better? The Instructors that Mac assigned me to had raised red flags initially, but they couldn't be the only ones. I understood that they were just a starting point since they were here, but was Mac planning to send me undercover everywhere that he found a suspect? That would take years. I didn't have that much time; Ian Crane was still out there, killing innocent people ...or was he? *You have no idea what your Agency does to innocent people.*

At the very least, I needed to talk to Crane again. I needed for him to answer my questions, and I needed to know why he'd sent his men to kill my parents. I needed to know what he meant by those words, the ones that played in my mind like a mantra – *You have no idea what your Agency does to innocent people.*

That afternoon, Donavon showed up to help with Kenly as promised. Every time that he got close to her to guide her through the moves, she blushed. I began to worry that maybe his presence was going to be more of a distraction than an asset. By the end of our second practice, I felt significantly less confident about my decision.

"Do you think she'll ever get it?" I asked Donavon after we'd parted ways with Kenly.

"Hard to say, but doubtful, given the time constraints," he responded, cupping the back of my neck and massaging the knots of tension away. I let his hand linger for several seconds before shrugging out of his grip. Donavon sighed heavily, but refrained from touching me again. We said goodnight in the lobby of the dorm. He didn't ask if I wanted him to come to my room, saving me the unpleasantness of saying no.

Back in my room, I sank down on my bed, exhausted. Both Erik and Mac had left me comms. My first instinct was to call Erik back first, but I had nothing to report and decided I would wait, despite my desire to hear his voice. Instead, I dialed Mac's number.

"Natalia," he greeted me after the first ring.

"Hey, Mac," I responded.

"How is the training with Ms. Baker?" he asked, sounding distracted, and as if he didn't really care.

"Um, you know, pretty good. She'll get the hang of it," I mumbled, hoping that vague answers would suffice. "So, where are you? Are you on campus?" I asked.

"I just got back a couple of hours ago. I am in my office. Why?" Mac responded, finally sounding like he was giving me his undivided attention.

"I kinda wanted to talk to you about something. Can I come over?" I crossed my fingers and said a silent prayer.

"Are you okay? Did something happen?" Mac sounded alarmed, and I could imagine his gray eyes narrowing in concentration.

"Oh, I'm fine. It's nothing like that. I just wanted to ask you a question and thought that it might be better if we talked in person," I hedged, cringing a little at how obvious I must sound.

Mac sighed. "It's late, Natalia. What is it that you want now?" He wasn't going to agree to an in-person meeting – crap.

I debated for several seconds. If I asked him over the communicator and he said no, then I would've blown my chance; but if I waited until tomorrow, he'd likely be prepared for my suggestive question. I decided to just go for it.

"Can I go into the city for Festivis next week?" I held my breath, willing him through the phone to agree.

"I don't know......" he began.

Since it wasn't an immediate no, I jumped at the opportunity to plead my case.

"Mac, please," I begged. "No one will really be on campus anyway, and I haven't been off this compound since you brought me here ten months ago."

Mac didn't answer right away, and I started to lose hope. Then he gave another tired sigh and cleared his throat.

"How are you planning to get down there? You cannot drive yourself, and I am sending Donavon to Atlanta to take part in a

Festivis Day ceremony there."

Atlanta? Why hadn't Donavon mentioned that? Even as I felt a slight pang of bitterness, I realized that if Donavon were preoccupied I wouldn't have to tell him that I was going to meet Erik. I knew that I should tell him, but I didn't want to upset him.

"I thought that Penny could drive. She has her hover license and, unless I'm mistaken, she isn't under the same restrictions that I am. She's free to leave whenever she likes, right?"

Mac grew quiet again, and I heard the shuffling of papers across his desk and his fingers chirping on computer keys. "You may go," he finally decided.

I let out the breath that I'd been holding and smiled from ear to ear. He'd actually agreed, and I didn't even have to manipulate him.

"Thank you so much, Mac!" I exclaimed, wishing that I'd talked to him in person so I could hug him right then.

"Hold on - don't get too excited just yet. You may go, but there are a couple of conditions," he warned, backpedaling slightly. Conditions? I didn't like the sound of that.

"Okay, sure. What conditions?" I asked hesitantly.

"No drinking, and I want you back at a decent hour," Mac insisted. No drinking? That was fine; it wasn't like I wanted to go just to get drunk. And a decent hour just meant that I couldn't stay out all night. No big deal; most of the celebrations took place during the day anyway.

"No problem!" I agreed, audible excitement evident in my voice. "Thanks, Mac, I really appreciate it."

"Gretchen and I will be in New York for the holiday. We have a banquet to attend, but Janet will be here if you need anything. I want you to report to her when you return, so that she knows you are okay," Mac continued.

"I can do that!" Janet was much more lenient than Mac. As long as I didn't have a seizure, she'd let me do whatever I wanted. Now I just had to convince Penny, and I doubted that she would need much encouragement; Penny loved getting dressed up.

I felt a hundred times better as I brushed my teeth and got ready for bed. While I was mostly excited about seeing Erik, I was also happy to finally leave the grounds. Even with my newly-acquired freedom, the campus still felt like a prison.

After donning my pajamas, I dialed Erik and rested my head on the pillow while I waited for him to answer.

"Hello?" he said groggily.

"Guess what?" I practically squealed.

"Hey, Tals," he replied, sounding more awake now that he knew it was me. "I'm guessing by how excited you sound that you talked to the Director?"

"I did," I confirmed. "And, he said I can go!"

"Good," Erik sounded relieved, but not nearly as enthusiastic as I'd hoped.

"You still want to meet me, right?" I asked, a little worried that he'd changed his mind.

"Of course. I'm sorry, I'm just really tired. It's late, and Henri and I are leaving in the morning for a mission," he said, trying to muster a happier tone for my benefit.

"Oh, I'm sorry, I didn't know......" I felt just the tiniest bit guilty now. I should've checked the time, but in my haste to hear his voice, I hadn't bothered.

"It's okay. I can't wait to see you," he added.

"Yeah, me too. 'Night, Erik. Be safe tomorrow." I smiled, wishing that I'd chosen the holograph option when I called, so that I could see his face.

"'Night, Tals. I'll call you when I get back." With that he disconnected and I pulled the covers tighter around me, wishing that they were his arms.

Chapter Twenty-Three

The days quickly began to run together. Every morning I woke and met Donavon in the Instructor cafeteria for breakfast. After that was my routine visit to the Medical building for a daily dose of Dr. Thistler and her not-so-miracle equalizing drug. Some mornings I would sneak down to the Psych wing and visit Ernest after I met with her. Most days I just sat in his room and watched him stare off into space. Other days I brought books and read random chapters to him, hoping to elicit a reaction. Someday I hoped to have the courage to try restoring some of the memories that I'd stolen, but as of yet I was too scared.

After my visit with Ernest, I'd make my way over to the Crypto Bank. I spent the following hours searching through personnel files while Penny and Gemma did whatever it was that Crypto workers actually did on a day-to-day basis. I spent my lunch hour training with Kenly since her skills were more remedial than I'd first thought.

I also attended the classes that Mac still wanted me to assist in. Annalise kept me busy grading papers, and I continued to engage her in small talk at every opportunity. Cadence continued to dislike me, and I continued to reciprocate her feelings. Mac grudgingly agreed to release me from my obligation to assist Thad, so that was another hour that I spent back in the Crypto Bank. I took out my aggression by sparring with Griffin's students; some days my feelings were so out of control that he had to remind me to go easy on them. Ursula's class gave me more time to work with Kenly, and I didn't waste it. I routinely spent the hour focused on helping her develop her abilities, and avoided talking to Ursula about Erik.

Ursula's comment about the "chick" that had broken his heart weighed heavily on my mind. Was I really that "chick"? I was almost certain that I was.

Thoughts of Erik consumed my dreams and distracted me from my daily tasks. I played his messages over and over again just to hear his voice. It didn't compare to actually talking to him, but I didn't really have another option since he was away on his mission.

When I asked Penny about going into the city for Festivis, she readily agreed, just like I'd known she would. We spent the week planning our outfits and deciding what bars we wanted to try. It felt like old times; and for the millionth time since meeting her, I was thankful that I had a friend like Penny.

She'd talked to Harris, and he'd agreed to come with Erik. The way Penny smiled when she talked about him made me think that whatever had started between the two the previous year definitely wasn't over. I hadn't seen her so happy in a long time, and I liked it. Investigating the spy was taking its toll on her - she often looked tired and stressed - but the prospect of seeing Harris had revitalized her.

"Do you think that we will ever find the spy?" I asked Penny the morning before our Festivis holiday began. Despite my mounting enthusiasm for the celebration, my lack of progress and Mac's continuous reminders of that fact were dampening my mood. Penny tore her attention away from the monitors and gave me a wary smile.

"I don't know, Tal. I mean, I know the Director thinks that a spy is the only way that Crane could have known who you were and all; but have you thought that maybe he just recognized you?"

Recognized me? I actually hadn't considered that - but Crane hadn't known what I looked like, had he?

"Think about it, Tal. We have workups on all of the major players in the Coalition, right? You knew what Crane looked like because we had pictures of him. Don't you think that they probably have the same information on us? I mean, you said yourself that they have better technology than we do. If that's true, then I'm sure they have facial recognition software and all that," she continued, barely pausing to take a breath.

"I guess you could be right," I said weakly. If she was, then I really was chasing a ghost. This whole assignment could be a complete waste of time. "But then, why would Mac have pulled you from your work at Elite? And why would he have Donavon undercover here? And Janet and the Assistant Director and the Captain are all investigating this, too," I pointed out.

"He obviously really believes that there's a spy. Seriously, Tal —even though we've been combing these files for weeks and the Director has been investigating this for months, no one has found anything. I just think that it's time we considered the possibility that Crane just knew who you were." Penny sighed, sitting back in the chair like her speech had exhausted her.

Scrutinizing Penny's drawn features and bloodshot eyes, I realized that she looked horrible. Her appearance was becoming increasingly more haggard and run-down. I wondered how much time she'd spent digitally hunting the traitor when I wasn't around. Penny was always at her desk when I got there in the mornings, and she often stayed until well past midnight; she must be sleeping even less than I was. I'd been so distracted by my seizures and my personal life that her extreme efforts hadn't registered.

"Well, Penny," I began, giving her a pointed look. "I'll let you be the one to break that news to Mac."

Penny laughed. "Um, I'm not stupid, Tal. I think that I'll wait for him to reach that conclusion on his own."

"Probably for the best," I agreed. She was right; Mac wouldn't like her assertions even if they were right. Particularly if they were right. The fact that the Coalition's technology surpassed our own was a sore spot for him; he would really hate being reminding of it.

That evening, Donavon and I tried a number of sensory deprivation techniques with Kenly to no avail. I decided that we should move on to weapons training since she was seriously lacking in that department as well. The fact that nobody was injured badly enough to warrant stitches was the most positive thing that came out of the night's practice.

"Have you thought about trying to mentally walk her through the exercises?" Donavon suggested as he walked me back to my room.

"You mean control her, so I can will her to do the moves?" I asked, amazed that I hadn't thought of the idea sooner.

"Yeah, at least then she would know what it feels like to actually do the moves correctly," he shrugged. "Just a thought."

"You're a genius!" I exclaimed. The idea really was great. If Kenly got the feel for the movements, she might start doing them correctly on her own.

When we reached the door to our building, I hugged Donavon goodbye and reached for the door. I was in a much lighter mood, now that I had a plan that I genuinely believed might work.

"Tal?" Donavon's mental voice called after me tentatively.

"Yeah," I replied.

"I'm going to Atlanta for Festivis Day. Dad wants me to preside over the celebrations down there. I'm leaving in the morning, and won't be back for a couple of days. I know you said that you need time to think, but maybe we could talk when I get back?"

Donavon reached out and grabbed my arm, pulling me around to face him. I tensed. Conflicting emotions warred in my mind. I recoiled even as a small part of me hoped that he would kiss me. What was wrong with me? I was going to meet Erik in the morning. I'd been looking forward to seeing him again since the moment he'd left campus. But now that I was standing so close to

Donavon, his breath warm on my face, I longed to feel his lips on mine.

Donavon brushed his mouth across my forehead.

"Goodnight, Talia," he said aloud. "Have fun at Festivis," he added.

"Yeah, thanks." I still hadn't told him that I was going to meet Erik, but I think he knew.

"Goodnight, Donavon."

Turning, I quickly fled into my building. I needed to tell him the truth, and soon; our relationship couldn't remain in this emotional limbo any longer.

Lying in my bed, I mentally reviewed all of the unsettling information that I'd acquired in the past week. Nothing made sense anymore. Why hadn't Mac told me about the transfusion? Why had Dr. Thistler freaked out when I'd brought it up? Why was Donavon so scared for his father to find out that I knew? What had Mac reminded Donavon not to tell me after my last seizure? Was Penny right? Was there no spy? Did Crane know who I was because the Coalition had a file on me? That scenario didn't really add up for me, though; I'd been a Pledge when I went to Nevada. Sure, I'd buy that they had a file on Mac and Janet and anyone like that, but not on me. They probably did now since I'd actively tried to kill Crane. But before my mission, I'd been no one to the Coalition - just another Talented cog turned out by the School's assembly line. Or had I?

Your father, Crane had said to me when I asked how he knew so much about Mind Manipulation. If Crane had known my father well enough for that to be true, then maybe he did know who I was and what I looked like. Maybe he'd been expecting me to come for him one day.

The encounter that I'd just had with Donavon added to the questions churning in my head, and made it impossible to sleep. I didn't want to be with Donavon, but why couldn't I give him up? Why couldn't I just tell him about Erik? Why, after all the lies and secrcts, was I so eager to keep him in my life?

Because you're selfish; you need his support. Erik isn't reliable, and Erik won't want you after he realizes how bad your condition really is, I thought.

Would Erik run the first time that my temper flared out of control and I started convulsing? Would Erik sit on my bedroom floor while I slept just to be there in case I had another seizure? Would Erik forgive me if I went crazy and slapped him, then tore his shirt and clawed at his face?

Erik didn't cheat on you, I reminded myself, remembering Penny's statement at Captain Alvarez's dinner. She was right. I trusted Erik. But did I trust him enough to let him see me at my worst?

Chapter Twenty-Four

Despite not setting my alarm, I woke before the sun. I stretched, and a ripple of excitement ran through me when I remembered that today was the start of Festivis. Today I would get to see Erik! All of my misgivings from the previous night were gone. I didn't care if he was irresponsible or if he would be there for me when I needed him. I concentrated instead on the feeling of pure elation that just the thought of him brought about. I thought about being close to him and how, even when we were surrounded by a group of people, we still managed to create our own world. I thought about the kiss in the hangar, and how I'd soon be reliving it for real and not in a dream.

There was a slight bounce in my step as I took a very cold shower. Selecting an outfit from the ones that Gretchen sent, I bypassed the boring black cocktail dress and the floral-print shift, and finally decided on a ballerina-length royal blue sheath. The dress was one-shouldered and belted at the waist with a tightly knotted gold rope.

By the time Penny knocked on my door, I was standing in front of my bathroom mirror, applying gold eye shadow.

"Come in, Penny," I called. The pounding came again, a little more insistently this time. "It's open, Penny," I yelled a little louder, hoping that she heard me. When she still didn't open the door, I trudged from the closet-sized bathroom to the door, tightening the belt on my bathrobe.

"Sorry, I thought you'd be able to......" I let my voice trail off when I opened the door and realized that it wasn't Penny.

"Hey, Talia," Ursula greeted me brightly, her plump lips curving up at the corners in a tentative smile.

"Oh, hey. Sorry, I was expecting Penny," I said awkwardly. What on earth was Ursula doing here? She'd never dropped by my room before; it wasn't like we were exactly friends.

"Yeah, I kinda figured that when I heard you calling her name," Ursula smirked. "So, you two are going into D.C. for the celebrations?"

I shifted uncomfortably from one foot to the other. Ursula's body-hugging mini-skirt and halter top made me feel skinny and unattractive in my too-big bathrobe. "Um, yeah, we are. I've been cooped up on campus for months, so it should be nice to get out and have a little fun." I wasn't sure why I felt the need to explain myself to her, but for some reason I did.

"Awesome. Mind if I tag along? My friends bailed, so I called Erik and he said that he was meeting you......" Ursula let the question hang in the air between us. The way that her eyes twinkled, coupled with the open curiosity on her dramatic features, told me that she was fishing for information. She wanted to know just how well Erik and I knew each other. I wasn't about to feed into her nosiness, but I also wanted her to know that I was the "chick" that Erik was hung up on.

"Yeah, of course, you're welcome to join us. I mean, I don't know if you'll find us as exciting as your friends, but we had a good time last year." I smiled, giving her just enough information to leave her salivating for more.

Her hazel eyes widened when I insinuated that I'd spent last Festivis with Erik, too. In truth, I had; and we'd had a good time, a really good time. The night after Festivis was the first time that Erik had kissed me.

"Awesome. What time are we leaving?" she asked, placing her

hands on her hips and trying to affect a nonchalant air.

"Um, I guess whenever I'm ready. Want me to send you a comm?" I was hoping that she didn't intend to sit in my room while I got dressed. Sure, I could use the time to pick her brain a little, but I was fairly confident that she wasn't the spy and therefore didn't welcome the intrusion. Penny and I had spent so little quality time together since my arrival – we were always too busy working – and I was really looking forward to our time-honored tradition of getting ready together.

"Oh, sure - that would be great," Ursula looked a little put off by my dismissal, and I felt the tiniest bit bad, but not enough to invite her in. She recovered quickly, giving me a small wave over her shoulder as she turned to leave. "Talk to you soon!"

"Right," I mumbled. I would definitely have to thank Erik for telling her about our rendezvous.

Before I got the chance to retreat into the safety of my bedroom, bright-red hair rounded the corner and big lime-green eyes greeted me.

"Hey, Tal!" Penny waved with her free hand. She clutched a garment bag in the other one that I assumed held her chosen outfit.

"Hey, Penny," I said, relieved that she was here.

"Was that Ursula I saw leaving?" she asked, squeezing past me into the tiny room. Penny tossed her belongings on my bed and settled into the desk chair.

"Um, yeah. She wants to come with us." I laughed nervously. I didn't think that Penny would mind the company, but I knew that she'd been looking forward to relaxing and letting loose. Ursula's presence might not make that possible.

"How do you feel about that?" Penny snorted, obviously remembering my insane jealousy when I saw Ursula flirting with Erik.

"Eh, whatever. She seems a little lonely. So if she wants to tag along, that's fine, I guess." I closed the door and crossed back to the bathroom to finish my makeup.

"She'd just better keep her hands off of Harris," Penny called as I heard her rummaging through her own impressive makeup bag.

"I thought you two broke up?"

"Oh, we did," Penny answered quickly. The hasty tone of her voice let me know that if I could see her face, it would match her hair. Maybe when Penny said that there were too many cute boys to be tied down to one, she was lying? "But he's been calling a lot, and you know, I just don't want to see him with someone else." I had to admit that I knew how she felt. I'd been ready to draw blood when I saw Ursula touching Erik, and it wasn't like I had any claim to him.

While we finished getting ready, Penny filled the conversation with trivial topics. I was glad; it was the first day in recent history that no one asked me how I was feeling or how I'd slept or talked about the spy. It felt good, normal; and despite our added tagalong, I was determined to have a fantastic day.

After we were dressed, primped, and gossiped out, I called Ursula and told her to meet us at the hover hangar in twenty minutes. Unfortunately, I still had to run by Medical before the fun could commence.

Penny waited in the reception area while I received my daily dose of Dr. Thistler and her asinine questions. She reiterated Mac's insistence that I refrain from drinking and added that I should "take it easy." I promised that I would, and she released me to start my day.

"Ready?" I called to Penny as I exited the swinging doors. I rubbed the crook of my elbow absently, hoping that the needle marks would fade quickly; they didn't really go with my outfit.

"Let's get the party started!" Penny whooped, jumping to her feet.

At the hangar, Penny signed out a hover plane while I waited outside for Ursula. I shifted uncomfortably in my gold flip-flops, wishing that she'd hurry. I was eager to get going and get to Erik.

Finally, Ursula's bushy hair came into view. She'd changed into an equally curve-hugging red dress, and I hated to admit that she looked good. I glanced to where Penny was still talking to the hover guard and prayed, for her sake, that Harris wasn't interested in the older girl. When I looked back at Ursula, my stomach and mood plummeted – she wasn't alone. Cadence was with her.

"Hey, Talia!" Ursula called, giving me an overly enthusiastic wave. Cadence kept her beady eyes trained on the grass. Her shoulders were hunched over, and the black dress that she wore hung shapelessly on her angular body.

"Hey, Ursula," I said tersely as they neared. Turning to Cadence, I said, "Hey, I didn't know you'd be joining us." Cadence finally tore her gaze from the ground, but looked at the hangar behind me instead of meeting my eyes when she spoke.

"Ursula practically begged me to come," she replied, rolling her eyes to emphasize how little she looked forward to a day with me.

"Well, the more the merrier," I shrugged, trying to sound like I was pleased by her unexpected appearance.

Cadence mumbled something that sounded like "whatever."

I turned to join Penny, and the two Instructors followed several paces behind. Penny's eyebrows shot skyward when her gaze landed on Cadence, but when she looked to me for answers, I just shrugged. I was also dreading spending the day with Cadence; but at least I could use the time to form a stronger connection with her, delve further into her mind, and maybe find out something useful.

Ursula dominated the conversation on the ride to the city. She talked about all of the bars that we "just had to go to" and which food vendors were "to die for." I listened without comment. While Penny and I had already made a mental list of the places we planned to visit, I really didn't care where we went, so long as I was able to spend the day with Erik.

He was waiting, along with Harris and Henri, when we landed

at TOXIC's parking garage in Southwest D.C.

"Erik!" Ursula exclaimed, running to greet him, her movements restricted by the constricting fabric she'd squeezed herself into.

"Hey, Ursula," he smiled, returning her hug half-heartedly. I gritted my teeth and swallowed my agitation.

"Sorry," he sent. The dazzling smile that lit up his features extinguished my irritation before I could act on it. Once he disentangled himself from Ursula, he walked swiftly over to where I stood. Erik leaned down and planted a kiss on my cheek. "You look nice," he whispered.

"Thanks." I beamed. And just like that, I forgot about Ursula and Cadence and the potentially ruined day because being close to him reminded me of why I'd begged Mac to let me come in the first place.

"You'll have plenty of time to fondle each other later," Henri interrupted, nudging Erik aside to wrap me in his long arms. "It's good to see you again, Tal."

"You, too," I agreed, returning his embrace. "Where's Frederick?" I inquired, glancing around to make sure that I hadn't missed him. Harris and Penny stood off to one side talking. She giggled as he tucked a loose strand of her hair behind one ear. Ursula had her hands propped on her hips, her eyes darting between me and Erik, deciphering our body language. Cadence stood off to the side, looking uncomfortable and out of place. I felt a pang of sympathy for her. I knew what it was like to be the outsider; that was what I'd always been with Donavon and his friends.

"He's meeting us downtown. He went ahead to The Rooftop to get a table, so we can watch the parade from there," Henri answered.

"Oh, I love The Rooftop!" Ursula squealed, clapping her hands like a child who'd just been told that she was getting a new puppy.

"Well, let's go then," Erik declared. He held his hand out to me, and I debated whether to take it. With Ursula and Cadence around, Donavon would be sure to hear a blow-by-blow account of our interactions. But we weren't dating, so it wasn't like I should feel badly about holding Erik's hand, right?

Sensing my hesitancy, Erik let his hand drop; but I caught the flicker of hurt that crossed his features before he turned to start walking. Throwing caution to the wind, I grabbed his fingers and laced them with mine. I'd deal with Donavon later.

The Rooftop was a bar on top of the Woffard Hotel in the center of D.C. The sidewalk out front was lined with people eagerly waiting for their turn to ride the elevators to the twenty-first floor. Instead of leading us to the back of the crowd, Henri walked to the large man guarding the velvet-roped entrance. They exchanged several brief words, and then the man unhooked the rope and waved our party through. We boarded the glass elevator, and I watched as the city streets and their inhabitants grew smaller the higher we ascended.

When we exited the car, a perky blonde with wide magenta eyes greeted us.

"Name of your party?" she asked pleasantly, already glancing down at her electronic clipboard while she waited for Henri to reply.

"Should be under Reich, but I think my boyfriend is already here?" Henri answered.

The hostess ran a finger down the tablet until she found Henri's name and then nodded, confirming that we were on the list.

"Yes, he is. Follow me," she gestured, turning to lead us through a throng of well-dressed partygoers.

The space was open, and a light wind ruffled my hair as I clung to Erik so that we wouldn't get separated in the crowd. A ring of black leather booths decorated the perimeter of the bar, and she led us to one overlooking 15th Street below. A beautiful blonde man with delicate features and warm brown eyes sat in the center of the rounded bench, sipping from a glass of wine.

"Frederick!" I exclaimed, breaking free from Erik to greet Henri's boyfriend.

"Hi, sweetheart," he kissed my cheek when I slid around the semicircle to sit next to him. "How are you feeling?"

"Good," I assured him, giving his hand a small squeeze. "It's so good to see you," I added. I'd forgotten how much I enjoyed hanging out with him. Frederick was a gentle, easygoing guy and had a way of putting everyone around him at ease. He was the perfect complement to Henri's more rigid and controlled demeanor.

"Thanks for getting the table," Henri said, sliding around to Frederick's other side.

"Sure." Frederick gave his boyfriend an affectionate smile, and I felt the need to look away from the personal exchange.

The others filled in the empty spaces, Erik sitting next to me with Penny and Harris on his other side. Ursula plopped down next to Henri, while Cadence sat awkwardly on the end, looking unsure why she was here. I shared her sentiments; why had she come?

"Cadence, this is Frederick." Henri gestured, introducing the two. Frederick extended his hand and Cadence tentatively shook it. "You know everyone else, right?" Henri asked his boyfriend. When Frederick agreed that he did, Henri flagged down a waitress and ordered several bottles of the featured Festivis Day wine and several appetizers for us all to share.

Despite Mac's warning, I sipped my wine while everyone talked around me. I promised myself that one or two glasses would be fine, and I'd need it if I was going to put up with Ursula's flamboyant attitude and Cadence's not-so-subtle death glares.

My friends began a lively debate about the floats that would be in the parade. It surprised me that Ursula and Frederick seemed to know each pretty well; their teasing and easy banter suggested that they'd known one another for some time. They were about the same age, I reasoned. Maybe they'd been in school together?

"So, how are you really feeling?" Erik asked once everyone else was preoccupied.

"I'm okay; no more seizures or anything like that," I assured him.

"Good......did you talk to Donavon about what happened in Nevada?" Erik's turquoise irises shone with concern.

"Yeah. I asked him about the transfusion, and he said that he didn't want to tell me because he didn't want me to feel like I owed him anything." I looked uncomfortably at my hands clasped in my lap. Erik pried one hand free and began tracing the lines of my palm.

"And do you, you know, feel like you owe him?" Erik's tone was tense, like our relationship hinged on my answer.

"No, of course not. He did save my life, but it's not like that," I quickly assured him. I didn't feel like I owed Donavon anything, except maybe the truth about Erik.

"You didn't tell him about us?" Erik guessed, reading my thoughts.

"No. I was going to, but I don't know, Erik. Things are so complicated right now."

"I see. You're having second thoughts about us." He pulled his hand back and stared off across the bar at the crowd of people on the dance floor. Equal parts frustration and hurt radiated from his body.

"NO! That's not what I mean. I want to be with you, but I want to be friends with him, too. He's been helping me so much, and we're working together." I touched his forearm tentatively and willed him to look at me.

"So, are we friends, Tal? Is that what you want?" he demanded, refusing to turn to face me.

"Erik, please - that's not what I meant! I like you as more than a friend. I just need some time to tell Donavon," I begged him. Why was nothing coming out right? It was like my thoughts

were jumbled and I couldn't form the right words.

Erik sighed and then finally turned to face me. But whatever he was about to say was interrupted by Harris.

"Would you two quit being so serious? The parade's about to start," he declared, climbing over me and Erik to get a better view of the street.

Sure enough, the entire crowd at The Rooftop was making their way to the railing, all clamoring to see the spectacle.

I turned around and leaned over the back of our booth as elaborate floats and fire baton twirlers marched down 15th Street. Speakers began blasting the National Anthem, and off-key singers added their own accompaniment.

"I'm sorry, Tal. I don't want to push you into something that you're not ready for," Erik sent, lightly running his palm up my spine. I shivered, goosebumps erupting all over my skin when he touched me.

"You're not. I do want this. I just think that Donavon should hear about it from me, and not someone else." I wiggled around to face him, turning my back to the sword jugglers and waving politicians now delighting the crowd. Pinned against the booth, underneath Erik, I blushed at the intensity of his gaze. He wasn't watching the parade either. He slowly leaned down and kissed me softly. Not caring whether anyone was watching, I kissed him back, wrapping my arms around his neck.

"Get a room," Ursula called, playfully throwing a cheesy French fry that bounced off of Erik's back. Startled, Erik pulled away, but he didn't look the least bit embarrassed.

"Sorry," I mumbled, mortified that she'd called us out. I smoothed the silk of my dress back in place and sat back on the bench. I could feel her eyes on me, and I chanced a look in her direction. Her expression was unreadable, but she was projecting a sadness that I didn't understand. When she said that her friend had dated Erik, had she really been talking about herself? Surely not; I quickly dismissed the thought.

The others settled back into their seats once the parade ended and resumed drinking from their wine glasses. Erik rested his arm over my shoulders, his fingers skimming my bare skin, and I found it hard to concentrate on the conversation. I, too sipped from my wine glass, but was careful not to overindulge. When Ursula ordered shots of bright red and blue layered liquors, I politely declined. To my surprise, Erik did, too. I glanced down at his barely touched wine and realized that he hadn't really been drinking at all. It was unusual for him since he was normally the one leading the drunken charge.

After three rounds of the spirited shots, everyone, except Erik and me, was drunk. The conversation turned to gossip of mutual friends and people I didn't know, so I leaned against Erik and played the role of observer. It was nice to be away from school, Mac, and Donavon. As I listened to my friends, I forgot about my own problems. I found myself smiling as they recounted drunken tales from past nights out, and embarrassing school memories. I was reminded that there was life outside of TOXIC; a whole world existed beyond the perimeter of the campus that I'd been confined to for the better part of a year.

When Penny got up to use the bathroom, Ursula managed to finagle her way next to Harris and talked him into yet another shot. She trailed her perfectly painted nails – today the same bright red as her dress – up his arm when she spoke, and I had an urge to kick her. Watching her flirt with Harris was almost as infuriating as watching her flirt with Erik.

As Penny returned to the table, she stopped short when she saw the way the two were canoodling, narrowing her eyes at Harris. Pain and regret contorted her features into an ugly grimace as she took a seat next to Cadence. Incensed on Penny's behalf, I waited for Ursula to take a drink, then forced the glass to tip until the contents poured down the front of her dress.

"Oh, my God!" she exclaimed, jumping from the booth.

I met Penny's eyes across the table, letting her know that it had been mc. Her hand flew to her mouth as she tried to suppress a fit of drunken giggles.

"Tal!" Erik exclaimed in my head. *"I can't believe you did that!"*

"Sorry," I said sheepishly, though I wasn't sorry at all. Sure, it had been a mean thing to do, but Penny was upset and I didn't like it. And maybe I was still a little miffed about the way she'd taunted Kenly, and about her hand on Erik's arm at the dinner.

Despite Erik's comment, he was also trying to hide his amusement as Ursula blotted uselessly at the front of her ruined dress. The only other person who seemed to realize what I'd done was Cadence. She eyed me suspiciously across the table. I met her beady gaze boldly, daring her to say something. Cadence pursed her lips and kept her mouth shut.

Ursula excused herself to tend to her dress. Penny glared at Harris, but he was too drunk to notice that she was upset. Well, this was shaping up to be a super fun day.

"Tal, she's a really nice girl. Give her a chance," Erik chided. *"She's just a flirt; that's who she is."*

"Sorry," I sent back. This time I really did feel bad; the trick had been petty. Impulse control was definitely something that I needed to work on.

"Do you guys want to go somewhere else?" Frederick asked, picking up the last bottle of wine and emptying the contents into his glass.

"Yeah, let's go get some real dinner somewhere. I think we need to soak up some of the alcohol," Henri agreed, glancing at the pile of crumpled napkins that Ursula had used to sop up the spilled wine.

Once Ursula returned, we made our way through the thinning crowd and descended back to street level. Frederick navigated our way through the pedestrians on the sidewalk, ducking into a place called the Old Crow several blocks away. The restaurant was packed, but most of the people were dancing, so we were able to get a table and order dinner.

Ursula wiggled her way next to Harris, but when she went to sit in the chair next to him, she missed and fell to the dirty floor in an ungraceful heap. The one glass of wine had gone straight to my head, and I had to bite my lip to keep from laughing out loud as I stared at her sprawled on the ground.

"Damn, Ursula. Are you okay?" Erik rushed to her side since Harris was oblivious to the fact that she'd fallen. Erik grabbed her upper arm and hauled to her feet. Then his eyes narrowed on me.

"Come on, Tal. The first time was funny, but that was just mean." He gave me a pointed look.

"Erik, I swear that wasn't me!" I sent. It really hadn't been. The chair had seemed to disappear beneath her, causing her to misjudge its position. I hadn't used telekinesis to move it. Wait, disappear and reappear? That was light manipulation, Cadence's specialty. I looked in her direction, but the blank expression on her scrunched features gave no indication as to whether she was the one to play the nasty trick.

"Ursula is just drunk," I added silently to Erik. He didn't look completely convinced of my innocence, but he couldn't argue with my statement. Ursula was clearly drunk, and she was laughing hysterically now that the initial shock had worn off. Erik helped her into the fully visible chair, then made his way around the table to sit next to me. Clearly irritated, he refused to look at me. Feeling guilty for something that I didn't do, I silently flipped through my menu.

The rest of dinner was uneventful. Erik's annoyance with me didn't last through our drink orders, so I quickly forgot that Ursula had managed to fall off a chair that hadn't been there. Penny and Harris were once again chatting comfortably, and I figured that she must be drunk enough to forget her earlier irritation.

Since Cadence had consumed enough alcohol to drown a cat, I figured that her guard would be down. I tried to read her mind, but - amazingly - her walls were still firmly in place. Despite that, her feelings apparently couldn't be contained; and all of a sudden I was overcome by a fierce hatred. Cadence's loathing burned deep inside of her. No concrete images leaked through, only a collage of colorful emotions: white fury, red rage, and black guilt. Normally she was able to smother the flames, but the alcohol seemed to weaken her resistance. I started coughing, hastily reached for my water glass, and brought it to my lips. The cold liquid was like a shock to my system, severing the tenuous connection to Cadence.

"Tal? You okay?" Erik asked, concern lacing his every word.

"Huh? Yeah, fine," I mumbled, between gulps of water. Maybe I'd been a little quick to discount Cadence. She'd made it obvious from day one that we weren't friends. I'd written off her dislike since it seemed to stem from jealousy, but now I wasn't so sure. While I couldn't be positive that her hatred was directed at me, the intensity and depth of it were alarming nonetheless. I needed to have a closer look at both her and her brother's files.

Erik continued to watch me through dinner. He knew that something had upset me, but he didn't pry. I made weak attempts to reassure him that I was okay. And I really was as long as I stayed in my own head.

I stole glances at Cadence, but didn't open my mind back up to hers. I'd seen her in class and in training on her own, so I knew that she was incredibly focused and calculated. Watching her now, I realized that she carried those traits through to every task. When she cut the meat on her plate, she did so with surgeon-like precision. She chewed every piece of food exactly the same number of times as the one before it. Every third bite she took a drink from her wineglass. Each move that she made was perfectly timed and deliberate.

I tried to envision her as a traitor. I conjured up images of Cadence skulking in darkened alleys and having clandestine meetings with men in trench coats. I envisioned her hiding in a broom closet in the Crypto Bank, waiting for an opportunity to tiptoe into an empty computer lab and hack into the system.

Admittedly, my imagination was running a little wild, but her brother was currently imprisoned for aiding the escape of a Coalition Operative. Maybe she shared his ideals? Maybe he'd gotten her involved with Ian Crane? I definitely needed to take a second, much closer, look at Randy and Cadence Choi.

After dinner Frederick suggested that we all stay at his house since Penny was no longer fit to drive.

"I really can't. Mac made me promise that I would be back at a decent time. I can drive," I added, noting the way that Penny was leaning on Harris for support.

"Are you sure that's a good idea?" Erik asked hesitantly. "I mean, you aren't really allowed to drive……"

"I know, but I think that Mac would be less upset if I drove than if I stayed in the city," I pointed out. I wasn't entirely sure that was true; he would probably have preferred that I'd been responsible enough to demand one of my friends stay sober.

"How about this: I'll take Talia back and you guys can stay at Frederick's. Henri, I'll come get you tomorrow?" Erik offered.

"You don't have to do that. I don't want to cause you any trouble," I muttered, although I secretly liked the idea of spending the ride alone with Erik.

"It's no trouble, and I've barely had anything to drink, so I'm good," he promised me. "That cool with everyone?"

Only Cadence looked like she wanted to protest, but Ursula didn't give her the chance.

"Totally," she declared, "let's pick up some more wine on the way back!"

After I made sure that Penny would be okay if I left her, as if the puppy-dog-eyes she was making at Harris weren't enough of an indication, Erik and I said our goodbyes. Then he took my hand and led me back to the hover garage. The streets were still filled with people, and I wished that Mac hadn't placed such strict rules on my outing. Yet even as I thought it, I realized that I was exhausted. It was late, and we'd been partying all day. My bed sounded more appealing by the minute.

Chapter Twenty-Five

"Did you have fun?" Erik asked once we were airborne.

"Yeah, I did." I smiled at him across the darkness. The muscles in his forearms twisted as he maneuvered the vehicle through the air, and a lock of dark hair curled over his forehead. I wound my fingers together in my lap to keep from reaching over to push the strands back.

"What?" he asked, tearing his eyes away from the sky when he felt me staring.

"Nothing," I said hastily, feeling my face color with embarrassment.

"Admiring the view?" he teased.

"Something like that," I mumbled.

Erik laughed, and reached one hand over to rub my bare shoulder.

"Yeah. Me, too."

His thumb stroked the hollow of my collarbone and I leaned into his touch, nuzzling the back of his hand with my cheek. Erik let his fingers dip a little lower toying with the neckline of my dress. I inhaled sharply and Erik swerved.

"You should keep your hands on the wheel," I choked out.

"Nervous, Tals?" he chided me. I knew that he wasn't referencing his driving abilities.

Erik laughed again, trailing his fingers down my bare arm on the way to my hand. "Don't worry, I won't crash," he promised, raising our hands to his lips. He kissed the inside of my wrist, his lips lingering on my jumping pulse. I melted like hot candle wax. Just then, I didn't care if we did crash.

Despite his taunting and teasing on the ride, Erik made no move to get out of the vehicle when we landed. He left the engine idling when he turned to kiss me goodbye.

"Want to stay for a little?" I asked, not wanting our time together to end so soon. "I know that it's late, so I understand if you'd rather just go back to headquarters," I rushed on when he didn't answer right away.

"You sure?" he asked, searching my face for the answer. Apparently his games were just that – games. He might toy with me, but he wasn't going to let it go any further until I told him that it was okay.

"Of course, I just need to tell Janet I'm back so that she won't worry," I confirmed.

Erik turned off the engine and we set off for my room. Once inside, I called Janet and let her know that I was safe and in for the evening. I didn't bother to tell her about my guest; Mac hadn't specifically forbidden visitors, but I doubted that he'd approve.

Erik suggested that I change into jeans and a t-shirt, so that we could go for a walk around the grounds. I'd been hoping for something more along the lines of lying in my bed, but he was insistent, so I complied.

Once we were out of the dorms, Erik took my hand and led me through a wooded area that I was pretty sure was off limits.

"Where are we going?" I asked suspiciously.

"You'll see. It's one of my favorite places," he added, tugging my hand to make sure that I'd follow.

After several more minutes of traipsing through heavy underbrush, we emerged at a gate. Erik released his grip on my hand and began peeling back the metal fencing from its post. When the hole was wide enough for us to fit through, he took my hand again and pulled me to the other side. There was only about ten feet of solid ground, then the rocky ledge dropped off.

Erik pulled me to the edge and sat, letting his feet dangle over the side. I tentatively sank down beside him, peering into the abyss below.

"You can see over three states from right here," he said wistfully, pointing to the lights littering the landscape. "That's Virginia," he pointed to the south. "That's West Virginia," he added pointing slightly to the north, "and, of course, we're in Maryland."

"It's beautiful," I breathed. It was. From our vantage point, I could see for miles. In the distance, the lights from small towns still glowed brightly. The stars seemed closer here, exceptionally lovely against the black backdrop.

"Sure is," he agreed, but Erik wasn't looking at the scenery anymore.

I blushed, thankful that there wasn't enough light for him to see the color in my cheeks.

Erik wrapped his arm around my waist and pulled me closer. I rested my head against his shoulder and closed my eyes, absorbing the calm that had settled over him. He trailed his fingers up my side above my t-shirt, making slow, lazy lines up and down my ribcage. His heart pounded, and I knew that he wanted to explore more than the cotton.

I stretched to kiss just underneath his chin. Erik sighed happily.

"I don't want to pressure you, Tal," he mumbled softly toying with the hem of my tee.

"You're not," I promised, twisting my body closer to his.

Erik dipped his head so that our lips met and slid his hand underneath my shirt, resting it on the waistband of my jeans. He kissed me softly, chastely at first, but when I opened my mouth, he didn't hold back. His fingers crept over the bullet scars and, though I could tell that marred flesh unnerved him, he didn't shy away.

The fingers of Erik's other hand found their way up to the back of my neck and he began massaging the tension away. I moaned against his mouth. I felt like I should've been embarrassed by my audible reaction, but it seemed to encourage him more. He lay back on the dirt ledge and pulled me down, so that I was leaning over him. I planted my hands on his biceps, and his mouth left mine to trail kisses down my throat.

Being with Erik, touching him and having him touch me, I felt alive and sane and normal for the first time in months. I didn't want him to stop. I wanted to live in this moment forever. He wasn't treating me as though I might break; he didn't care that I was scarred. His mind was open, his feelings on full display. I didn't worry that he was keeping secrets or was lying to me; I knew what he wanted and I wanted it, too.

When his fingers found my bra clasp, I started to tremble, and Erik hesitated.

"It's okay, Erik," I promised.

"You're shaking, Tals," he sent back, sounding more than a little worried.

"I'm just cold," I insisted. But even as I thought it, the trembling began to increase and I collapsed onto Erik's chest, tremors running through my entire body.

"Tal? Tal, are you okay?" His hands flew to my face and cupped my cheeks, forcing my face up so that he could look at me.

"I don't know," I chattered, my teeth painfully clanging together.

Erik scurried to a sitting position and gathered me into his lap. He stroked my hair and made soft, soothing noises. When the trembling didn't subside, Erik sent me waves of calming thoughts, and I clung to them. Desperately, I willed myself to not have a seizure. This couldn't be happening; I didn't want him to see me like this. He was the only person who didn't think that I was on the edge, but once he realized how sick I was, he would run.

"I'm here, Tal; you're okay," he whispered, rocking me back

and forth.

I relaxed. He was here, and he wasn't running away screaming. Erik was slowly taking control of my mind, reading my every thought and dispelling every panicked belief.

"Just let go, Tal. Let me do this," he urged, his voice was calm, strong, and determined. He wasn't scared; he wasn't afraid that I might hurt him. I released the small amount of control over my mind that I had left.

"Good. Now breathe, slowly in and out," he ordered gently.

Erik's manipulation slowly started to work. My teeth stopped chattering first, and my jaw muscles unclenched.

"You're doing good. Keep breathing," he said, running his palm up and down my back.

Every muscle that he touched relaxed under his hand. Soon the tremors died down until only my hands shook with small aftershocks. Erik still didn't let go; he held me tighter, and continued to control my thoughts. He didn't release my mind until my body went still.

"I think I'm okay now," I mumbled, completely mortified now that I was in control. What guy wanted to make out with a girl who convulsed every time he touched her?

"It's okay, Tal. I shouldn't have pushed you," he whispered, still rocking me gently. "But I'm going to need a lot of cold showers if this happens every time," he teased.

I smiled in spite of myself, but it quickly faded.

"Aren't you turned off by me?" I whispered.

"Turned off? Why would I be?" He seemed offended that I would even ask.

"Because I'm sick, Erik. I'm diseased. These seizures aren't stopping, and they're no closer to finding a cure!" I exclaimed, trying to wiggle out of his arms.

Erik let me struggle, but he was so much stronger that my efforts didn't get me far.

"Stop, Tal," he said when my attempts became weaker, more

pathetic. "I don't care about the seizures, and I'm not going anywhere. I'm in this for as long as you want me, do you understand?" Erik chanced freeing one of his arms from my waist and tipped my chin up, forcing me to look him in the face. His voice was firm, almost angry, and his eyes blazed with a bluish fire.

I nodded slowly. I hated that he knew how worried I'd been about him leaving because he'd read it in my mind. Erik's expression softened when he stared into my eyes.

"So is this going to happen every time I touch you, or should I just avoid certain areas?" he smiled mischievously. Without giving me time to answer, he planted his lips firmly on mine, holding my chin in place so that I couldn't pull away. Not that I wanted to pull away. When the episode started, I thought for sure that this would be the end. Now I knew that I could count on him, trust him, and he would be there if I needed him. But he also wasn't going to walk on eggshells with me; the way his mouth was moving across my jaw and down my throat let me know that he was still reckless, and would deal with the consequences if they came.

"Is this okay?" he teased, nudging the neckline of my shirt aside and kissing my collarbone. He moved his mouth across my shoulder and nipped softly before looking up at me. He still wanted me, I could see that, but he was just teasing me now. He had no intention of actually trying anything more tonight, but his point came across loud and clear.

"I don't know. Dr. Thistler told me that overstimulation triggers the seizures," I said, wishing that he wouldn't stop but knowing that it was probably for the best.

Erik actually laughed.

"So, you're saying that I overstimulate you?" he joked, pushing my hair back to kiss my cheek. My face flamed. That was what I meant, just not what I meant to say aloud. I couldn't formulate words to answer his chiding. Erik laughed again.

"Don't be embarrassed. I want to overstimulate you."

"Thanks, Erik," I whispered, kissing the corner of his mouth.

Erik swallowed hard. "I'm here for you, always," he promised. "Why don't I walk you back? I think you've had enough for tonight."

"Just a couple more minutes," I urged. "I don't want to be alone yet."

"Only if you promise that you won't get overstimulated again," he teased.

"Just tonight, or in general?" I said back, playing along.

"Just tonight. We'll figure something out after that."

I stayed in Erik's arms for another hour, talking while he rubbed my back. We talked about his letter, and he told me about his mother's death. When the fury and anguish began to build as he recalled the memories, I returned his earlier favor and dulled the emotions. He told me about his father and his brothers, Edmund and Evan. I felt his comfort when he thought that at least his sacrifice had been worth it.

"You're really sure that Donavon hasn't told anyone about the letter?"

"Yeah, positive," I said. I hesitated before adding, "he did read it though."

"Can't blame him for that. I would have, too." Erik sighed. "What's he doing here, anyway?"

Mac didn't want me talking to very many people about the whole spy thing, but I knew that I could trust Erik; I'd trusted him since the moment I met him. So I told him about the spy and my unofficial assignment to find him.

"Mac thinks that my whole mission to Nevada was a trap. He thinks that we have a spy, a traitor in the Agency."

"Of course, we do," he scoffed.

"You knew that we had a spy?" I asked, shocked.

"We probably have a ton of them. It only makes sense. We have a number of spies inside the Coalition. Why wouldn't Crane have spies placed here? If McDonough thinks otherwise, he's deluded. What makes him think that your mission was a trap?"

I hadn't even considered that. Of course, Ian Crane would have infiltrated our ranks. How else did he stay so well hidden?

"Crane knew that I was coming; he was waiting for me. He knew who I was," I rambled.

"Have you found anything?" Erik asked.

"No; it's so frustrating. Sometimes I feel like I have no suspects, and sometimes I feel as if I have too many. And then Penny seems to think that maybe Crane just recognized me and that we don't have a spy at all!" I shook my head, agitated; just thinking about the fruitless endeavor got me worked up.

"Well, we definitely have spies. Whether that is how Crane knew who you were, I can't say," Erik shrugged against my back. "Wish I could be more helpful."

"It's just nice to be able to talk to someone who doesn't overthink everything I say," I said.

We talked about the blood transfusion for a while, and Erik couldn't fathom a reason for Mac to keep it a secret either. Just like with the spy business, it was nice to speak freely without worrying that I might get in trouble for my doubts and beliefs.

When he finally deposited me in my room, I didn't want to let him go. But the sky was already fading from black to vibrant pinks and oranges, and I knew that he should leave – Mac was not going to like his all-night visit. When I put my arms around him to hug him goodbye, he pushed me against the door, not concerned whether I became overstimulated, and crushed his mouth to mine. I didn't care either. I kissed him back, letting him into my heart and my mind.

My unchaste thoughts got Erik very worked up and he pulled back, holding me at arm's length pressed against the door.

"You'd better go to bed, Tals," he panted, his eyes deep intense pools of turquoise liquid.

"When will I see you again?" I whispered.

"Soon," he promised. "If the Director let you go to Festivis, then I bet he'll let you come into the city again. We'll work it out."

Chapter Twenty-Six

There was still another day left of Festivis break, so I didn't have any classes to attend. After just two hours of sleep, I made a brief stop at Medical. Dr. Thistler took one look at my puffy eyes and promptly launched into a long lecture about the merits of getting enough sleep. I listened politely and assured her that I would be sure to remember that for the future.

Penny was already waiting for me when I arrived at the Crypto Bank, and she looked awful. She was wearing torn jeans and a rumpled white t-shirt that sported several coffee stains. Her hair was piled in a messy knot on the top of her head, and red cobwebs spiked around her lime-green irises.

"Hey," she called, rubbing her temples.

"Hey, how are you feeling?" I asked, mirroring Penny's wince at the sound of my voice.

"Promise me that next time someone offers me a shot, you'll say no," Penny moaned, then took a long swallow from her steaming mug.

"I'll try," I promised, positive that once Penny was feeling better, she'd conveniently forget this conversation. It wasn't as though this was the first hangover that I'd watched her nurse.

Taking a seat in my chair, I hit the power button on the keyboard. The monitors sprang to life before my eyes. I typed my passwords into the white boxes and waited while the Operatives' files loaded.

"Where's Gemma?" I asked, nodding to the chair that the girl normally occupied.

"Um, she went home for the holiday. Hopefully she'll be back tomorrow – I haven't accomplished anything without her."

I glanced over at Penny. She stared blankly at the scrolling gibberish of numbers and letters running down the screen in front of her. My heart went out to her. Sure, getting drunk was her own fault, but I hated how miserable she seemed.

"Did you at least have fun while it lasted?" I joked.

Penny managed something between a smile and a grimace.

"Yeah, I had a great time last night. It wasn't until this morning that I started hating life."

"So you and Harris kissed and made up?" I teased.

"The end of the night is a little fuzzy, but yeah, I think that we did." She giggled, then immediately seemed to regret it. She massaged the crown of her head.

"How about you? I noticed that Erik didn't leave until this morning..." Penny tried to shoot me a sly smile, but it appeared to hurt her face too much.

"We just talked," I mumbled, blushing as I recalled what happened on the ledge. "How did you know when he left?" I added suspiciously. I didn't mind Penny knowing about my overnight tryst; I would've told her anyway. Maybe not all of it, but I didn't think that she'd have much interest in the touchy-feely heart-to-heart moments anyway.

"Hover records." Penny shrugged, looking only the tiniest bit guilty about checking up on us. "When I signed in this morning, I saw that he'd just signed out."

Hover records; I hadn't even thought about that. If Penny noticed, then someone else – say, Mac – might, too.

"Anything you want to tell me?" she teased, using a great deal of effort to widen her eyes suggestively.

"No, nosey, there isn't. Like I said, we mostly just talked." I rolled my eyes, but the blush returned to my cheeks. If we didn't change topics soon, I might get overstimulated just sitting here.

"Uh huh, sure......"

"You'll be the first to know," I promised her.

"I'd better be." She gave me her best impression of a stern look. "Alright, enough gossip. Where do you want to start today?"

"I want to take a closer look at Cadence's brother," I began. While I'd pretty much ruled her out as the spy, I didn't have any better leads, and I figured that covering all of my bases couldn't hurt. Even now, the memory of her intense emotions caused me to shiver uncomfortably.

"Okay, what's his name?" Penny asked.

"Randy Choi. He's imprisoned at Tramblewood."

Penny paled to match her tee.

"Oh, yeah. He's the guy who helped that Coalition woman escape. Let me see if I can find the incident report." Penny's fingers flew across the keys, entering search terms into boxes that popped up on her screen. "Here, sending it now."

"Thanks."

My monitor instantly went black and then a report filled the screen. I began to read. Six years ago, Randy Choi was arrested for helping Ellen Larson escape from Tramblewood Correctional Facility. Larson had been imprisoned after she was caught breaking onto school grounds. Using psychic interrogation, Dr. Wythe had determined that she was a member of the Coalition. The mention of Dr. Wythe gave me unpleasant reminders of my time in his office; his probing questions and suggestive counseling techniques were not something that I wished on anyone.

I knew from Cadence's file that Larson was Crane's sister, but seeing the relationship now was still unsettling. When I thought about Crane, I never really considered the fact that he had a family. To me, he was this monster, a beast that had no regard for the pain that his actions inflicted. To me, he was my parents' murderer. But to Ellen, he'd been a brother, a friend. Maybe to someone else, he was a father, a son, a husband. I didn't like to think of him that way; it made him too human.

Dr. Wythe had diagnosed Ellen as "crazy" and "delusional" based on her "outrageous claims," but there was no mention of what her actual claims were. I scanned through the rest of the twenty-page report, but couldn't find anything useful.

"Is there anything else about this?" I asked Penny.

She didn't answer right away. When I looked in her direction, her head was resting on top of her crossed arms on the desk.

"Penny?" I shook her shoulder gently, prodding her awake.

"Hmmm," she mumbled, wiping the back of her hand across her mouth.

"Sorry," I apologized, hating to disturb her. "I was just wondering if there is anything else about Randy's interrogation or this woman, Ellen Larson."

"Crap, did I fall asleep?"

"Yeah, kinda."

"I'll check; gimme a minute." Drowsily, Penny returned her attention to the computer and searched for Randy Choi and Ellen Larson. "Um, his official interrogation report is sealed, but I can call the Director tomorrow and have it unlocked if you want. There is one other report that mentions Ellen Larson – looks like after she escaped from Tramblewood she was caught just before she could cross the border into the Coalition's territory, and was killed." Penny's voice wavered slightly when she said the last part, and I gave her a worried look. "I'll send it to your computer."

"Thanks," I said. I tried to get a better handle on her emotions, but her face was now composed, and I wondered if maybe I'd imagined her reaction.

When the report appeared on my screen, I started reading. Ellen had refused to surrender when TOXIC's guards had caught up with her, and she'd lost her life as a result. I understood Penny's pain when I saw the photographs of the woman's mangled body. She hadn't just been shot; she'd been torn apart. The automatic weapons the Operatives had used destroyed Ellen's features, making her virtually unrecognizable. Disgusted, I quickly clicked through the pictures to the end of the report. I shuddered. What an awful way to die.

You have no idea what your Agency does to innocent people.

But Ellen Larson wasn't an innocent person; she'd been one of them. Why had she been trying to break into the School? Of all the TOXIC facilities, it seemed like the place that would be of least interest to the Coalition. What had she been looking for?

"Do you want me to have Randy's file unsealed?" Penny asked beside me.

Tearing my eyes away from the screen, I nodded. "Yeah, thanks."

"Approval has to come from the Director, I think, but I can try Janet if you want to see it today."

"Um, yeah, call Janet," I decided. I wasn't sure how important the file would prove to be, but it was the most solid lead that I had.

Penny picked up the communicator on the desk and dialed. When Janet answered, she agreed to unseal the record and have it sent to my computer. As promised, several minutes later I had an incoming message.

I opened the email and began quickly scanning the contents.

Just like with Ellen, Dr. Wythe concluded that Randy was "delusional" and his claims were "unsubstantiated." And just like with Ellen, there was no indication of what that actually meant. I wondered whether the report had been redacted or was purposely left vague. I resolved to ask Mac when he returned.

After leaving Penny for the day, I headed back to my room. The campus was eerily quiet since the students and Instructors that went home for the holiday wouldn't return until the following day.

When I passed Medical, I detoured, deciding to visit Ernest. I hadn't seen him in a couple of days, and while I doubted that his condition had improved, I wanted to check on him.

I wound through the long corridors of the facility until I

reached the Psychiatric Ward. Today, Ernest was propped up in a large recliner in the corner of his room. His hazel eyes darted in my direction when I entered, but they remained unfocused, and I knew that he didn't actually see me.

Feeling a rush of sadness, I pulled a chair next to his and sat. Dr. Thistler had said that a memory implantation was too risky, but the emptiness inside of his mind broke my heart.

I took one of his limp hands in mine, closed my eyes, and concentrated on the images that I'd pulled from his head. Selecting his childhood memories first, I projected the scenes toward him. At first nothing happened; the same hollowness remained. I focused harder, and then slowly a faint smile graced his lips. It was all the encouragement that I needed, and I pushed more and more of his memories at him.

The effort proved to be too much for both of us. Ernest's smile was quickly replaced with a grimace, and he started to shake. He wasn't the only one; my hands trembled and my peripheral vision darkened. Pulling back before I lost consciousness, I slumped against the back of my chair, panting. My head felt two sizes too big, and sweat trickled down the sides of my face. Dr. Thistler was right: Memory re-implantation was not easy.

When I looked at Ernest, his eyes held a spark of life and wisps of thought floated through his head like smoke. I knew then that the physical toll the effort had taken on me was worth it. I wouldn't be able to restore him completely, at least not in one session, but I felt confident that in time I'd be able to give him back the life that I'd stolen.

Completely exhausted, I stumbled back to Instructor housing. A comm from Erik waited for me, and I grinned stupidly as I hit reply and flopped onto my bed. He didn't answer, so I left him a message, sad that I couldn't at least hear his voice after what I'd just done.

I didn't have the energy to pull myself out of bed to brush my teeth and wash my face; instead, I just closed my eyes and fell into a dreamless sleep.

The next morning, it was back to business as usual. Donavon hadn't called me once over the holiday and didn't meet me for breakfast in the cafeteria. I sat alone in a corner, picking at my food until the cleaning staff began to wipe down the tables. I contemplated reaching out to him mentally, but I was afraid that he would block my attempts. Numbly, I moved through the rest of my day.

I spent more time than usual reading to Ernest. The Medicals assigned to his unit no longer questioned my presence; Dr. Thistler had told them that as long as Ernest didn't become agitated, I could sit with him for as long as I liked. Secretly, I figured that Mac had been the one to give the go-ahead since nothing around here happened without Mac's say-so.

That train of thought brought me back to Erik's letter and what he'd told me on the ledge. Had Mac known about the raid? Had he approved the exchange of Erik's service for the lives of his remaining family members? Worst of all, had Mac been the one to broker the deal? Erik hadn't named the devil he'd sold his soul to, and I now wondered if that had been intentional. He'd wanted me to believe him, and accusing Mac of something so heinous wouldn't have helped in that department. Originally I tried not to give too much thought to Mac's potential involvement, but now I really needed to know.

I considered looking up the report on the raid of Erik's family and his subsequent collection. The names of the TOXIC men involved would be listed. However, as much as I wanted to know, I also wasn't eager to verify that Mac was keeping another secret from me.

When I arrived at the Crypto Bank, Penny and Gemma were in their usual positions. They both smiled when I entered. Since I'd spent more time than I usually did with Ernest, I set right to work on my never-ending task of analyzing Operatives' files.

"What are you doing this afternoon?" I asked Penny, gathering my belongings in preparation to leave for Annalise's class.

"You're looking at it." She gestured to the scrolling lines of text on her monitors.

"Any interest in helping with Kenly?"

"I thought that Donavon was helping?"

"He kinda gave up," I mumbled.

Penny shot me a relieved smile. I knew that the less time I spent with Donavon, the happier she was.

"Sure, I'll help. I mean, I doubt that I'll really be any help; but if you want company, I'm game," she said.

"Thanks, Penny. Meet us at the practice arena at the end of the school day?"

"I'll be there." She smiled.

During lunch, I tracked down Cadence. Her brother's file had been too sparse to get any useful information; if I wanted answers about Randy Choi, I'd have to ask his sister directly.

Cadence sat alone in the corner of the cafeteria, angrily stabbing carrots into a blob of ranch dressing.

"May I sit?" I asked, approaching from her right side.

Cadence glared at me through long, black lashes. "If you must."

Taking that as an invitation, I sank into the seat beside her. I started in on my own lunch of meat loaf and sweet corn, watching her out of the corner of one eye.

"What do you want, Talia?" she asked after I'd taken several bites.

I swallowed, debating whether I should gradually lead up to my ultimate question or just go for it. I had a sneaking suspicion that Cadence might not sit here long enough for me to beat around the bush. Unless I wanted to actively control her in a room full of other people, there was nothing I could do to make her stay. I dove right in.

"I want to know about your brother, Randy," I said evenly.

Cadence's expression went blank and she just stared at me; it was a little unnerving.

"He's a traitor. He can rot in jail for all I care," she replied calmly.

Her words held the same amount of emotion that someone would use when talking about the weather. The inflection was flat, like she'd repeated the phrase so many times that the words had ceased to hold meaning. I felt the same hatred that I'd felt at the Old Crow trickling from her mind. It wasn't gushing like a burst pipe, the way that it had been that day, but it was definitely still there. I wasn't sure then whether the feelings were towards me, and now I still couldn't tell. If I didn't know better, I might have thought that feelings were directed inward.

"If you'll excuse me, I have somewhere I have to be," she said, rising from the table without giving me the chance to answer.

That went well, I thought to myself sarcastically.

Cadence walked quickly across the cafeteria, deposited her tray on the conveyor belt, and then dashed for the exit. I was pretty sure that the "somewhere" she had to be was anywhere I wasn't.

That evening, my training with Kenly went as well as could be expected. Using my manipulation, I walked her through the same moves that we'd been working on before Festivis. Her coordination improved with every repetition. Toward the end of our session, I released her mind and let her use me as a practice dummy. A couple of her hits landed hard enough that I thought my arms and torso might sport faint bruises in the morning; I couldn't have been prouder.

True to her word, Penny wasn't actually of any use, but she was a great cheerleader.

"You did really well tonight," I praised Kenly as we cleaned up the practice area.

"Thanks," she said shyly. "I've been practicing in my room." Her big brown eyes were shining with the same determination that had originally made me want to work with her. I hated to say what I said next, but I felt that she deserved the truth.

"Kenly, I am going to do everything I can to help you get ready for your placement exams," I began.

"Oh, I know. I appreciate it so much," she nodded earnestly.

"I know you do. But I feel like I should warn you that it might not be enough. A lot of the students that are chosen to pledge the Hunters have been training for years, and they have natural abilities that you don't." I met her eyes, afraid of the disappointment that my words were likely to invoke.

"I know," she replied in a clear voice. "I know that it's a long shot. I'm planning to take exams for the Crypto and Interrogation Divisions as well. I just really want to be a Hunter. I'm from D.C., so when I'm home on holidays I see the Hunters come into the city, and I've always wanted to be part of a team like they are. I think that it would really make my mom proud. My father was a Hunter and was killed in a mission when I was eight. Mom always talks about what great things he did to stop the Coalition. I just want to do that, too."

I smiled. I knew her story already; I'd done a very thorough background search on her family after I'd convinced Mac to let me train her. Her father had been part of a special team, sent to arrest two known Coalition supporters who were actively working to start a rebellion. Unfortunately, the mission hadn't gone well, and most of the Operatives died.

"I'm sure she'll be proud of you, no matter what," I promised. "Cryptos and Interrogators do very important work for the Agency, too. But I'll do everything I can to help you get ready."

I was so focused on Kenly that I didn't notice the baton until I stepped on it. One of my ankles twisted painfully as my other leg flew out from underneath me. Before I could come crashing to the ground at the awkward angle, Kenly grabbed my arm to steady me. Gravity still should have pulled me down, but Kenly also used her Telekinesis to halt my fall. I was now teetering precariously on the outside edge of my twisted foot, while the other foot was still thrust in front of me.

"OMIGOD, Tal!" Penny exclaimed running, over to grab my other arm so I could get both feet firmly back on the ground. "Are you okay?"

"Um ...yeah, of course," I answered, wiggling my wrenched ankle to make sure it wasn't sprained. The joint popped, but otherwise seemed unharmed. "Thank goodness you were here, Kenly," I said turning to the younger girl. "That was a really awesome use of your abilities. I think that you just might be ready for those Placements after all."

Kenly still clung to my arm, shock and disbelief creating creases in her forehead.

"I-I-I-I ...it was nothing," she replied, staring down at my feet like they might take flight again.

"That was really amazing, the way that you stopped Tal from breaking her ankle," Penny said, placing her hand on Kenly's free arm to steady the slightly shaken girl.

"Yeah, right ...thanks," Kenly said, still looking confused by her rare display of adept talent.

Penny and I walked Kenly back to her dorm before heading to the Crypto Bank, where our dinner from Gretchen was waiting.

"I think that you might really have a shot with Kenly after all," Penny declared, digging into a plate of noodles smothered in cheese sauce.

"I hope so. She is so determined," I replied, twirling long strands of spaghetti around the prongs of my fork.

"That little trick to keep your clumsy butt from falling was awesome," Penny continued, through a mouthful of pasta.

"I know, right?! She seemed amazed that she had actually been able to pull it off," I agreed.

"You must be an awesome teacher for her to have improved so much in a week," Penny smiled.

"Thanks, Penny that means a lot."

The next few days passed with much the same routine. My stubborn nature – and Penny's nagging voice in the back of my mind – kept me from actively seeking out Donavon. I wasn't positive that I knew why he was ignoring me, but I had a pretty good guess: Someone must have told him about Erik.

I wanted to go to him, but nothing I'd say would make the situation better. Telling him that I needed more time to sort out my feelings was pointless, redundant, and untrue; I knew that I wanted to be with Erik. Now I just needed to pluck up the courage to tell Donavon. Since he was already avoiding me, the truth couldn't make the situation much worse – I'd already lost him.

My sessions with Kenly weren't evolving like I'd hoped. She was improving, but I'd imagined that she would be much further along by now. The glimmer of hope that I'd felt after using manipulation to help her feel the movements had petered out. Penny researched dual Talents and concluded that Mac was right; Kenly would never be strong in both areas.

For his part, Mac kept telling me that I couldn't expect miracles, reminding me that I was attempting to teach Kenly skills in just a short amount of time that had taken me years to master. Again, my stubborn nature didn't allow me to concede to either point of view. The more that they both protested, the more determined I was to make her a Hunter.

It had been nearly two weeks since Donavon had last spoken to me. I was running late, so naturally I literally ran into him when leaving my building.

"Hey," I said awkwardly.

"Natalia," he responded tersely.

We stood there momentarily in uneasy silence.

"I'm late," I blurted out when I couldn't find another means of escape.

"Well, then, I guess you better go," he answered evenly.

Nodding, I started to walk away. I made it only several paces before I turned. He was still standing in the same place, watching me regretfully.

"Donavon," I began.

"Tal, don't," he interrupted.

"You don't even know what I'm going to say," I argued.

"It doesn't matter, Talia. I know that you spent Festivis with Erik. I know that he came back with you, and didn't leave until seven o'clock the next morning. I know that you offered yourself to him after a week, but barely let me touch you in six years!" By the end of his tirade, Donavon was shouting loudly enough for the whole campus to hear.

My mouth gaped stupidly. I had no idea what to say. At first, I was so stunned that I couldn't even process his words. Then as the meaning sunk in, my blood began to boil. I fisted my hands at my sides and tried to swallow the blinding rage. In the same breath, Donavon had basically called me a slut and a tease.

"Sucks to be lied to, doesn't it?" I snapped, rooted in place. If I moved, my feet would propel me at him, and I'd likely punch the horrified expression right off of his face.

Donavon paled and looked around nervously. "That's different and you know it," he hissed.

"Yeah, it's worse! I don't owe you anything, Donavon. Isn't that what you said? You didn't want me to feel like I owed you? Or was that a lie, too? Because I think that we both know the real reason that you didn't tell me – you're too scared of your father!" I screamed.

Donavon closed the distance between us, and I thought for a brief moment that he was going to strike me, but I refused to give him the satisfaction of flinching. I steeled myself for the blow, but it never came. Donavon clamped one hand over my mouth and backed me against the wall of the dorm. My eyes popped wide with disbelief; I'd have been less shocked had he actually hit me.

"You don't know what you're talking about," he growled. His irises went black, his eye sockets elongated, and he sounded more animal than human.

My own primal urges took over, and I sank my teeth into his fleshy palm. My incisors sliced through the skin and his blood trickled into my mouth. Disgusted, I jerked away and gagged, spitting red liquid on the perfectly manicured grass. The coppery scent made my stomach roll, and I bent over and dry heaved painfully. When I was certain that nothing more would come out, I scrubbed my tongue with my shirt sleeve to rid my mouth of the taste.

Donavon stared at me, shocked and scared as bloody rivers weaved down his forearm to meet at his elbow. Two puncture wounds showed on the heel of his hand. He opened and closed his mouth several times in a good imitation of a trout fish. Then without another word, he turned and stalked off, leaving me confused and terrified in his wake.

What just happened? Had I really bitten him? I'd felt like a cornered dog when he'd put his hand over my mouth to silence my spiteful words, but the faint smears of blood on my sleeve shamed me. I'd definitely overreacted. Donavon would never physically hurt me. How could I have bitten him?

The part of me that was still fuming over his accusations wanted to run after him, demand that he apologize. But he really didn't have anything to be sorry for; everything he'd said was true. I had done all those things, and I was wrong when I said that I didn't owe him anything. At the very least, I'd owed him the truth about Erik.

Chapter Twenty-Seven

After the shortest trip to Medical on record, I rushed to the Crypto Bank. I needed to vent my frustration and embarrassment over the encounter with Donavon to Penny before I exploded. I knew that I was in store for a big "I told you so," but I really didn't care. Honestly, I deserved it. She'd been right about him and about us. Donavon and I were no good together; our story was a doomed broken record, repeating the same painful chorus over and over again: lies, secrets, lies, secrets.

When I made it to the glass doors, the absence of bright red-orange was immediately apparent.

"Where's Penny?" I demanded as soon as the doors opened.

"She was called away," Gemma responded distractedly, removing her headphones. "No worries though. I have you all set up. This is Andel," she added, pointing to the bespectacled boy sitting next to her.

"Hi." I waved dismissively in his direction.

"Natalia." He smiled nervously and replaced his headphones, returning to his computers.

Reluctantly, I took my seat and began my daily grind. My brain warred between thoughts of Donavon and the task at hand.

I'd barely made it through three files when the shrill sound of an alarm broke my concentration. Yanking my headphones off, I watched as Gemma hit a red button on her console.

"Operative Reins," she answered. She paused while the person on the other end of the line spoke. "Right away, Captain Anderson." Pause. "I see the file now, sir." Pause. "Affirmative, sir." Pause. "Understood." She hit the red button again.

"What just happened?" I asked.

"Emergency intelligence that needs verification," she answered in an off-handed manner.

"What does that mean?" I'd been sitting in this room for weeks, and had never seen something like this happen.

"A Crypto unit at Headquarters came across information regarding the Coalition President that we need to act on ASAP," Gemma explained, her fingers a blur as they flew over her keyboard.

"Um, okay." I was confused. "I still don't understand."

"Protocol dictates that high priority intel needs independent verification to ensure that it's legit," she said patiently, her eyes never leaving her screen.

"What constitutes high priority intel?" I asked.

"Anything involving significant members of the Coalition and their movements."

"Like what?" I pressed. Gemma hesitated. "Like what?" I repeated. She didn't answer. "Like when I was sent to Nevada?"

"Yeah, like that," she finally answered.

"When the intelligence came in that Crane was in Nevada, what would have been the protocol?" I asked in a low voice. I was already on edge from my fight with Donavon, and it was hard to maintain control.

"Given the nature of the information, the intel would've been sent to a second Crypto unit to be verified," she answered.

"Why?" I asked, struggling to sound calm.

"To make sure that the Operative receiving the information wasn't compromised that he or she isn't a spy. Plus then there's always the possibility that whoever intercepted the intel decoded it incorrectly."

"Does that happen a lot? The decoding incorrectly thing, I mean?" I already knew that we didn't uncover spies on a daily basis.

"On occasion." Gemma shrugged. "Usually everything checks out and it's not a big deal, but every so often the verification team finds a mistake."

I sat back in my chair, tapping my fingers thoughtfully on the desk. This was important, very important. Mac said that all of the Operatives on Penny's team had been investigated, but what about the verification team? Mac was thorough – no stone unturned and all that. Yet, I had a nagging, uneasy feeling about the whole situation. Could it really be that simple? Had one of the teams made a mistake? One team, I'd buy - but both teams seemed unlikely. I needed to speak with Mac.

Saying a hasty goodbye to Gemma and Andel, I set off for Mac's office, praying that he was there. Thankfully he was, and his secretary waved me back immediately.

"Who received the intel about Las Vegas?" I asked, barely through his door.

Mac looked up surprised, but recovered quickly. "Penelope's team at Headquarters," he answered. "You know that."

"Who verified the data?" I continued.

"A Crypto unit here at School. Why?" Mac seemed impervious to my brash manner.

"I want to speak with the person who originally found the intel."

Mac gave me an exaggerated sigh and rubbed his temples, like I was giving him a headache. "Cal Simmons and his team have been questioned extensively. I am confident that they are not spies."

"Not by me," I pointed out.

"Natalia, the intel that we received regarding Crane's presence in Las Vegas was real," he said it slowly as if I were stupid or hard of hearing. "I explained this all to you already. I have you going through personnel files to find someone with the skills to infiltrate our system because we are certain that the intel was not planted. I do believe that we have a spy. I believe that someone gained access to your mission file and tipped off Crane."

"Mac, please," I insisted. "You said that you wanted results. You said that I should be questioning everyone who could possibly have accessed the information regarding my mission. So, please, let me talk to Cal Simmons." I thought about willing Mac to let me go, but decided against it at the last minute. Mac *really* hated it when I did that.

"What exactly do you hope to learn from Mr. Simmons and his team?"

"I don't know," I replied, frustrated. Was I hoping that they'd made a mistake? Even if they had, did it matter?

"Going to speak with Operative Simmons is a waste of your time, and time is something that we are running out of. His entire team has been vetted by me." Mac didn't raise his voice, but the way he clipped each word put my teeth on edge.

"You said that the investigation was cursory, at best," I nearly shouted, losing my temper. "You said that it was best not to alarm people. I can question people more comprehensively, and they won't even know!" The sense of urgency that I'd been feeling ever since Gemma took that call grew with each passing moment. I took a deep breath. "Mac, I'm asking you to trust me. I know that I need to talk to Cal Simmons. I can feel it. Please," I urged, careful to keep the nasally whine to a minimum.

Mac studied me for several long seconds. "I'll arrange it. Be ready to go around dinnertime."

I gave him a curt nod and turned to leave.

"Do you want to talk to Operative Eisenhower as well?" Mac called after me.

"Huh?"

"Jennifer Eisenhower was also in the room when Simmons came across the information."

I turned slowly back around. "Anyone else?" I asked tersely.

"If you'd been paying more attention in our first status meeting, you would know," he gave me a pointed look. Admittedly, I hadn't been paying much attention in that meeting; I'd been busy thinking ill thoughts towards Donavon.

"Penelope was also there, of course," he continued.

I nodded. I already knew that – it was the only reason Penny had been privy to the specifics of my mission.

"While you are at it, you might as well speak with the verification team – Grace Howard and Rider Trindel. They worked with Latimore, Simmons, and Eisenhower to compile the intel packet that you were given."

"Right, of course," I stammered. I couldn't fathom why Mac didn't have me question all these people before. Sure, some other mind reader had probably questioned them, but I was an Elite-level Talent; I'd know if they were lying.

"You have two days, Natalia. I firmly believe that this is a waste of time, and I will not have you chasing theories on a whim. I want results, and I want them now."

If I didn't know better, I'd have thought that he was threatening me. Did he think that I didn't want results? Did he think that I didn't want to catch this spy, a hundred times more than he did? He wasn't the one who'd been strapped to a bed. He wasn't the one who nearly bled to death. He wasn't the one who was injected with a cocktail of chemicals that our entire Medical staff couldn't seem to cure. I wanted to scream at him, make him understand how badly I wanted to find the person responsible for all of those things.

Instead, I held my tongue and tightly replied, "I understand."

"Howard and Trindel work at the Crypto Bank here. I will have my secretary locate them for you."

"Thank you," I replied, stiffly. I vaguely recognized their names from my months of sifting through files, but I didn't recall either of them raising red flags. "Can I get access to the initial interrogation reports and their classified files?" I wanted to review the reports the initial interrogator made after he'd questioned them. I also wanted a look at any additional information the Agency had that might have been termed classified. I wasn't sure what all was considered classified, but I figured it couldn't hurt to see it.

"I will have all of that information sent to your communicator," he agreed.

"Thanks, Mac." I smiled.

"I do trust your instincts, Natalia," Mac said, his voice softening. "I just do not want to waste time on theories that have already been pursued. That being said, report any useful findings to me immediately. Call my communicator the minute you find something."

"I will," I readily agreed. He might not be happy about my request, but at least he trusted me enough to let me pursue it.

I'd already missed Annalise's class and lunch, so I decided to just skip the rest of my classes, too. I wanted to question Grace and Rider as soon as Mac's secretary located them before I left for Headquarters.

I hurried back to my room, packed a bag, and waited impatiently for the files that Mac promised me. Cal Simmons and Jennifer Eisenhower were at Elite Headquarters, which was only a short flight away, but I figured I would be spending the night if I left around dinnertime. I had no idea how long the interrogation sessions would take; but if Ernest's was any indication, it would be hours.

Kenly was still in class, so I left her a message with a detailed workout plan for the evening. I felt marginally bad about abandoning my protégé, but this was way more important. Next, I called Erik; another advantage of the trip to Headquarters would be seeing him again. He didn't answer, so I left him a comm saying that I would be there tonight and asking if he knew Cal or Jennifer. Finally, I called Penny and told her that I would be away for a day or so and that I'd explain when I saw her next.

By the time I finished leaving all of my messages, I had two comms from Mac's secretary. She'd located Grace and Rider; they were both working the two-to-two shift at the School's Crypto Bank. I checked the time on my communicator: 2:40, perfect timing.

Grace and Rider proved very easy to find; they were working together in one of the smaller rooms on the main level of the Crypto Bank. I glanced through the glass panel to the right of the door before knocking, and neither Operative was paying much attention to their monitors. All I could see was a pale, bony hand buried in a frizzy mass of blonde hair as the owner of the head and the owner of the hand tried to devour each other's face while still sitting in their respective computer chairs.

Stifling my laughter, I raised my hand to knock on the metal door. I banged three times as loudly as I could. The squeak of plastic on plastic assaulted my ears when Grace and Rider jerked their chairs apart. The soft tapping of Grace's rubber-soled shoes on the marble sounded through the closed door.

Grace poked her blonde head through. She was several inches taller than me, and her dark eyes narrowed in impatient glare at my unwelcome intrusion.

"Can I help you?" she asked, sounding a little flustered.

Oh, my God, get a room, I thought, irritated.

"Actually, you can. Are you Grace Howard?"

"I am," she replied, cautiously.

"And your make-out buddy is Rider Trindel?" I hadn't intended to call her out on what I'd witnessed, but her flippant attitude irritated me.

"Um, yeah." She paled further.

"I'm Talia Lyons." I saw a spark of recognition cross her expression. "I need to ask you a few questions about the night you verified some intel from Elite Headquarters."

"You'll have to be more specific. We verify intel all the time," Grace replied glibly.

"The intel regarding Ian Crane being in Las Vegas, Nevada, about ten months ago." Grace swallowed thickly, and I knew that she remembered the mission I was talking about.

"We already gave full reports," she snapped, defensively.

I locked her in a penetrating stare. Her right eye twitched nervously, and I invaded her consciousness.

"You did give reports," I started, slowly. "But not to me. You want to sit down for me now, and you want to tell me every excruciating detail about the intel that you verified about Ian Crane in Las Vegas," I coaxed.

"Of course," she said, her features going slack under my control.

Grace opened the door wider, gesturing me inside. The room was much smaller than the one that I used with Penny. There were only two large computer screens hanging on the wall opposite the door with the now-all-too-familiar scrolling lines of gibberish. Two high-backed, black computer chairs sat facing the monitors. The owner of the white hand – Rider, I assumed – was craning to look at me as I entered.

"Rider Trindel?" I asked.

"Yes," he said in a small voice.

I shifted my concentration to him.

"My name is Talia Lyons. You know who I am, right?" Rider nodded, jerkily.

"Good. I need you to tell me about the intel you verified regarding my assignment in Las Vegas ten months ago. Do you remember it?" I didn't have the patience to establish a connection with each Brain so that I could read their thoughts. Actively controlling them would make me tired, but I didn't care just then.

Rider nodded again.

"I remember," he said slowly.

"Good. Grace, why don't you start? Walk me through everything from the beginning." I used the most soothing, patient voice that I could manage.

Grace launched into her version of the events, speaking so quickly that I could barely keep up. She explained that she and Rider were working the eleven-to-eleven shift in the main Crypto room that night, and Captain Anderson had called not long after they'd started. He'd told her that Cal Simmons' unit received intel that needed verification. He sent over the request, and Grace and Rider decrypted the data and analyzed the results; they determined that the intel consisted of partial plans for Coalition President Ian Crane's stay in Las Vegas, Nevada. Grace had then called Headquarters and reported the findings.

The next day, both Grace and Rider were ordered to abandon their normal assignments and focus solely on combing all electronic communications for information regarding Ian Crane and Las Vegas. The duo spent the entire week gathering intel on both subjects. They also continued to verify the data found by Cal's team.

While I was fairly confident that Grace was telling me the truth since I was compelling her to do so, I also searched her mind for any traces of fabrication. I could tell that there was something she was holding back, but decided not to dig too deeply just yet; I wanted to see inside Rider's head first.

Rider's version of events matched Grace's to the tee. Still, I could feel that he also wasn't telling me something. His guilt was stronger than hers, so I dug into his mind first.

"Rider, do you know Ian Crane?" I asked bluntly.

"No," he stammered. "I've never met him. I just know about him." Rider's blue eyes were wide and innocent looking. I scoured his brain for any signs that he'd met Ian Crane. Finally, seeing nothing, I continued with my questions.

"Are you a spy for the Coalition?" I demanded. I didn't see a point in beating around the bush. Grace gasped behind me.

"What?!" Rider exclaimed, his eyes lighting up with shock. "Of course not!" His tone was indignant, but the images in his mind were scared.

Rider imagined himself being dragged by two large, faceless men to stand before a judge while she declared him a traitor. Then his mind jumped to scenes of himself strapped to a gurney while an executioner in a black hood injected a dark liquid into his arm.

I sighed. I could take his morbid images as a sign of guilt, but I had a feeling that he just had an overactive imagination. "Rider, what aren't you telling me?"

He hesitated. I was tempted to regain control of his mind and force him to answer me, but images of Ernest in his hospital bed clouded my vision. I needed to be careful; I couldn't handle it if I turned another innocent person into a vegetable. Gently, I probed Rider's brain. At last I saw what he was hiding take shape in his mind.

"What about the encryption seemed off?" I demanded before he could decide whether or not to tell me the truth. My throat felt tight; I *knew* that this was going to lead me somewhere.

Grace gave a strangled little yelp behind me, but I didn't break my focus on Rider.

"Tell me, Rider," I ordered. I took control of his mind, not caring about the consequences anymore.

Rider was weak-willed, thank God, and he relented quickly.

"The encryption was kinda low-level for that type of information," he answered.

"What do you mean low-level?" I pressed, narrowing my eyes in concentration.

"Well, I'm a pretty strong Higher Reasoning Talent." His blue eyes shifted over my shoulder to where Grace sat. "I mean, I *am* an Elite, so I can basically crack any code."

"I know what it means to be an Elite," I snapped. I could feel the adrenaline starting to pump in my veins, urging me into some kind of action.

"Well, Grace isn't," he said softly. "She's actually an Extremely Low-Level Talent." He gave her a miserable, apologetic smile, like he couldn't believe what he was saying. Suddenly, I got it. The whole scenario flooded to the front of his consciousness.

Rider helped Grace cheat on her Placement Exams, so that she'd be assigned to the Cryptos and they could be together – they were in love. They'd requested to work together, and volunteered for less-desirable assignments so that Rider could manage most of the workload. All they wanted was to be together, and they'd known that Grace would have been assigned to a remedial position if she ranked poorly on her Placement Exams. Both Grace and Rider knew that the encryption wasn't very advanced because Grace had easily decoded the transmission.

Earlier, I'd misread Rider's images of being branded a traitor; he *was* feeling guilty. He knew that if anyone ever found out he'd helped Grace cheat, there would be repercussions. Rider felt horrible because he'd chosen to keep their secret instead of admitting that there was something amiss with the encryption. The guilt was eating him up inside; he thought if they had said something then I might not have been sent to Nevada, and I might not have been hurt. He'd never imagined that his omission would have such grave consequences.

I closed my eyes and gritted my teeth. The desire to lash out at both of them was so strong that I wasn't sure how much longer I could suppress it. I wanted to scream obscenities, let them know just how much their love affair had cost me. Did they really think that keeping their secret was worth risking my life?

Taking control, I tried to swallow my anger. I needed to stay focused right now. Screaming at them wasn't going to help. I didn't know what the punishment for cheating on your placement exams was; but if I had to guess, it was probably a stiff reprimand and reassignment to a more fitting division. Neither penalty was sufficient in my opinion.

When I looked from Grace to Rider, I saw unbridled fear. The terror emanating from them was palpable. While the prospect of being separated worried them, it was the fear over the punishment that terrified them. Although I was confident that they wouldn't be declared traitors to the government and executed, I had to wonder if maybe the consequences were more severe than reassignment.

"I promise I won't tell." The words were out of my mouth before I could stop them. Was that really a promise that I was prepared to make? Their lie had cost me my future with the Hunters, and nearly cost me my life. If I hadn't gone to Nevada, I wouldn't have been injected and I wouldn't be plagued by seizures now; I didn't want something like that to happen to someone else.

When I saw the grateful looks that they gave me – and the lovey-dovey eyes they made at one another, the fear hovering right below the surface – I knew that I couldn't expose their secret. I would figure out a way to ensure that they weren't assigned any more high-profile cases, but I wouldn't tell. Briefly, I considered willing them to forget my interrogation, but I decided against it; I wanted them to remember how scared they were, how close they'd come to being discovered. I wanted them to know better next time.

Heading back to my room, I pondered the level of encryption. I couldn't explain how I knew that it mattered, yet I was certain that it did.

I'd just finished gathering my belongings to leave for the hover hangar when I heard a knock on my door. I opened my mind – Penny.

"Hey," I called brightly. "You're just in time to walk me to the hangar."

"I got your message. Where are you going?" she asked curiously.

"Headquarters," I answered. "I'm going to interview the other two people who were working the night that the intel came in about Crane."

Penny's face fell. "Why? Haven't they already been interviewed? Submitted full reports?" She seemed a little jittery.

"Well, yeah, but not by me. I want to dig around a little bit, see what I can find." I smiled at her.

Penny frowned.

"Tal, look. I know that you're really trying to figure this out, but the Director brought me here to go through the personnel files and look for a hack in the network because all of the intel checked out. It was legit. Ian Crane was in Nevada just like we thought he'd be. Nothing at all was unusual about the intel."

Her voice was firm, and I suddenly felt silly for getting so excited about the low-level encryption. Her features softened when she saw the dejected look on my face.

"Tal, you know that I want to find this person just as much as you do. I want them to pay for what happened to you, but I just don't really think that this is productive." Her green eyes shone with unshed tears.

I was so touched by her concern that I almost told her that she was right, that I wouldn't go chasing wild theories. But I couldn't; I *knew* that the encryption was important. I felt it with every fiber of my being. I just needed to connect the dots.

My brain was murky, but I had this feeling that something important hid beneath the surface. Something good? Something bad? I didn't know. I just knew there was something.

"I really value your opinion, but I know that this is going to lead somewhere. I can feel it." A thought struck me. "Penny ...you didn't tell Harris about my mission, did you?"

Penny fixed me with a steady gaze, full of hurt that I would even ask. Shame clouded my brain.

"I would never have done that!" Penny exclaimed, sounding truly wounded by my inquiry.

"No, of course, you didn't. I just wanted to cover all my bases," I replied lamely before letting the subject drop. I was relieved that she hadn't. Harris had been a good friend to Donavon and Erik for years, and I hated the thought of having to question him.

"Why don't you at least let me fly you out there?" Penny asked hopefully.

"Thanks, but Mac already arranged someone."

When we got to the hangar, I instantly regretted not taking her up on the offer. A small two-seater hover car was pulled out of one of the hangar bays, and a tan, broad-shouldered guy with shaggy blonde hair stood next to the opened driver's side. He was dressed casually in dark jeans and a white t-shirt tossing the keys lazily in the air. Crap. Donavon.

"Tal," he greeted me coolly, but gave Penny a dazzling smile. I wanted to kick him.

"Donavon," I matched his icy tone.

Penny gave me a quick hug, which I returned without taking my eyes off of Donavon's. "Call me if you need anything," she whispered.

"Thanks," I whispered back.

Penny moved away from the plane, but didn't leave. She watched as I slowly walked over to my side of the vehicle and hoisted my bag, then myself into the passenger seat. I gave her a small wave while Donavon made a great show of clamoring noisily into the driver's seat. Once he was settled, I risked stealing a sidelong look at his face. His jaw was clenched, the muscles in the back moving almost imperceptibly as he ground his teeth together. A white, gauze bandage was wrapped around his right hand. As soon as I noticed it, the earlier shame and humiliation returned. I had bitten him. What was wrong with me?

He turned the key in the ignition with way more force than was necessary. The engine gave a loud, screeching whine in protest of the display of strength. He jammed his right foot down so hard that the vehicle shot forward, sending me flying back against my seat. I grumbled audibly. Donavon didn't acknowledge my presence, let alone say he was sorry. This was going to be a *very* long ride.

Chapter Twenty-Eight

No matter how angry Donavon seemed, I knew that his hurt feelings were the root of his animosity. He'd thought that we were working out our issue, then Erik just showed up. He blamed Erik for telling me about the blood transfusion, but I wanted him to know that it wasn't Erik's fault; Donavon had no one to blame but himself. And it wasn't just the transfusion - he'd lied about so many things that I didn't know how he could expect me to forgive him.

I busied myself reviewing the old interview reports for Grace, Rider, Jennifer, Cal, and even Penny. Grace's and Rider's reports were exactly as I'd expected. They were both interrogated by a Mid-level Telepath named Sandi Yardly, and the reports included a narrative almost identical to the one that both Cryptos had given me. Sandi concluded that both were telling the truth, but noted that low levels of deception were present in each interviewee. She'd indicated that their dishonesty was a result of the relationship of a "sexual nature" between the two. She made it sound so clinical.

I wondered if the official reports on my destruction of Donavon's cabin alleged that my actions were the result of a relationship of a "sexual nature" between us. I shuddered; I really hoped not – how humiliating to have that on record.

Moving on, I saw that Cal, Jennifer, and Penny's reports were consistent with what I already knew. Penny had helped me prepare for the mission, so I was pretty well acquainted with what had transpired on their end that week. Mac and Captain Alvarez had personally interviewed all three while Sandi watched through the two-way mirror. She concluded that none of the three was hiding "anything remarkable." She believed that each gave the best version of events "as they knew it to be true" – whatever that meant.

None of the Cryptos had commented on the encryption being unsophisticated. I wasn't surprised to learn that; if they'd said something, it would've been investigated. I was pretty sure that the only reason Rider admitted it was because the person who'd been harmed by his omission asked him directly. Also, I hadn't simply read his mind like Sandi; I'd been controlling it, digging through his memories. He really hadn't had a choice.

Mac annotated Penny's evaluation to explain that "Operative Latimore's feelings of dishonesty are related to the unauthorized assistance that she provided for Hunters' Pledge, Natalia Lyons." Oopsy. Now if I was ever cured, not only would I have to answer to the Placement Committee for totally screwing up my solo mission, but also for accepting outside help – Pledges were supposed to plan and research their solo assignments alone.

"Everyone cheats. The committee won't deny your appointment just because you had help on your solo assignment."

Donavon's voice startled me so much that I jumped slightly in my seat. I'd connected my communicator to the small computer in the passenger-side dash since the screen was larger. Apparently, Donavon was reading them, too.

"I wasn't worried about that," I shot back, haughtily. Obviously I'd just been contemplating that very notion, but I hated the way that Donavon sounded all-knowing.

"Whatever, Tal."

The tension in the cramped space increased exponentially. This ride needed to end now.

Thankfully, we were almost to Headquarters. When we did

finally touch down, fifteen minutes later, I grabbed my bag and jumped out of the vehicle as quickly as I could mentally pop the door lock.

Captain Alvarez was waiting for us outside the hangar.

"Lyons, McDonough, how are you?" he asked as Donavon exited the car, slowly and much more gracefully than I had.

"Good, thank you, sir," I responded with a tight smile.

"Glad to be back on my old stomping grounds, sir," Donavon answered cheerfully. Apparently his surly mood was reserved exclusively for me.

"Good. I have rooms in the guest tower for both of you. Natalia, it's my understanding that you want to speak with two Crypto Operatives?"

"Yes sir, as soon as possible," I replied quickly.

"Director McDonough called ahead and asked me to track them down. They're both waiting for you in an interrogation room in the main administrative building."

"Thank you." I smiled.

"Follow me," he said before turning to Donavon. "McDonough, I trust I'll see you again before you head back to school?"

"Of course, sir." Donavon inclined his head slightly in a show of respect.

"Find me whenever you're done with this fishing expedition," Donavon sent me in a tone that displayed anything but respect.

"Whatever," I sent back.

Following Captain Alvarez across the lush Headquarters grounds, I inhaled the earthy scent of the dirt and trees and the sweet smell of the tiny flowers that grew along the stone pathways. A sense of longing filled me; I really missed being here.

The Captain led me into a small building, and then down a short hallway to the right. He held the door to the main room open to let me pass through. Cal and Jennifer were seated in separate interrogations rooms. Both were visible through the two-way mirror in the larger exterior room, but a thick, soundproof wall divided the interior rooms. I watched both Brains through the glass for several long minutes.

Cal was in the room to the left. He sat hunched over, his shaved head resting in large hands. I was surprised to find that I didn't recognize his coffee-colored face and dark brown eyes when he finally withdrew his head from his palms. I just assumed that I would've seen him with Penny at some point. While his skin was smooth, untouched by age, I knew from his file that he was thirty-five. He was well built, like a Hunter, and tall; even sitting down, I could tell that he was at least Donavon's height.

As I studied his body language, his eyes darted nervously around the room. His mind buzzed steadily, indicating a great deal of brain activity, which was actually typical of most Brains that I encountered. Their minds were always churning, constantly working, analyzing every detail of a given situation.

When I was done analyzing Cal, I turned my attention to Jennifer. She was younger than Cal – twenty-eight according to her file. Stringy black hair hung limply around an extremely pale face with deep-set, dark eyes, and she hugged her bony arms around a boyishly skinny frame. I'd seen her several times with Penny when I was a Pledge, but couldn't recall having ever exchanged more than pleasantries with the girl.

Since Cal was the one who'd actually found the data originally, I decided to start with him.

Captain Alvarez took a seat in one of the comfortable chairs on the exterior side of the mirror as I made my way into the room on the left.

"Cal Simmons?" I asked when I entered.

"Yes ma'am," he replied in a deep southern drawl.

"I'm Talia –," I started to say, but he cut me off.

"I know who you are."

"Then you probably know why I'm here?" I continued.

"You want to know about the Nevada Crane intel?" he

guessed. He didn't look nervous, but vibrations of uneasy energy tickled my skin.

"I do."

The exchange was enough for me to latch on to his brain patterns. I knew that Sandi had already gone the telepathic route, but I was a much stronger Talent, and I didn't want to compel the answers out of him unless I was sure that it was necessary. Besides not wanting to irreparably damage his mind, I hadn't been exercising my mental muscles since being away from the Hunters and had yet to recover the energy that I'd expended questioning Grace and Rider.

"Was there anything strange about the intel?" I asked.

When Sandi questioned Rider, he hadn't mentioned the encryption, so Mac hadn't known to ask Cal and his team about it. Whether it was the mounting guilt that the lovesick Brains now felt, or because I really was that much better than Sandi, I couldn't say. Since I knew what questions to ask, I felt that there was no reason to play coy.

"Strange?" he shifted his eyes to the floor. He knew exactly what I was talking about.

"The data - did you think that the encryption was too simple, considering it was about where Ian Crane would be staying?" I demanded.

Yes, flashed through his mind, but he hesitated before saying, "Not really."

"You didn't think that the code was ridiculously easy to crack?" I pressed, placing my palms firmly on the edge of the small table.

Yes! His mind screamed so loudly that I was certain I couldn't be the only one who heard it.

"It was crude encryption," he answered, tentatively.

"Does data involving Ian Crane's whereabouts normally have crude encryption?" I fired back.

Anger and annoyance were starting to control me. Why was

everybody lying about the encryption? Why was this so important? Why couldn't anyone just admit that there'd been something strange going on? Why did none of these imbeciles realize how much damage could be caused by omitting a detail like that?

"No, not normally," Cal admitted.

"Why didn't you say anything at the time? Didn't you think that it was odd enough to warrant saying something?" I hissed through clenched teeth. I was now leaning over the desk, my face inches from Cal's ear. His face was still turned down, looking at some non-existent spot on the table.

"The information was important. Teams had been searching for this type of intel, praying to intercept communications about Ian Crane's whereabouts. And I did. I found out where he was going to be; I cracked the codes that led to us finding Crane in Nevada." He met my eyes for the first time, urging me to understand.

I did. He was proud of what he'd done. He felt triumphant that he'd been the one to intercept such an important communication. He hadn't been able to contain his delight when he called in the find. He'd thought that he would be promoted. I understood completely. He'd risked the safety of another Operative for his own advancement; he'd risked *my* safety for his own advancement. I snapped.

"You cracked the codes that led *me* to Nevada! You cracked the codes that led me into a *trap!*" I screamed, not caring that I was going completely off the rails with Captain Alvarez watching from the other side of the mirror.

"I didn't know," he stammered. "I didn't think ...I didn't know. I'm sorry." Tears welled up in his dark eyes.

"Obviously you didn't think!" I shrieked, unable to control my emotions.

I wanted to hurt him, wanted to reach across the inches that separated us and strangle him. Instead, I bore into his mind. Digging out the memories from that week, I searched for anything that would connect him to the Coalition. I didn't find even a scrap of evidence supporting the notion that he was either in league with the Coalition directly, or a supporter of Crane's objectives. I dug deeper. I knew it was risky. I didn't care.

Cal's mind told the tale of a small boy who'd come to McDonough School when he was five. He'd proudly left his home in Florence, South Carolina, on Collection Day when government officials collect all of the children who tested positive for Talents and take them to the School.

Like me, Cal spent his whole childhood training to become a Hunter. He'd, of course, known that he was a Higher Reasoning Talent since his testing results, but he'd never thought that meant he couldn't become a Hunter.

After his junior year in school, he'd taken the examinations to become a Hunter. He hadn't even bothered to take the Crypto test. His arrogance at choosing only the Hunters made me squirm; I'd also put all my eggs in the proverbial Hunters' basket.

Surprisingly, he'd been chosen to Pledge. However, Cal's team captain hadn't reported favorably on his performances during the several missions he'd been a part of. He wasn't recommended for permanent appointment to the Hunters. Cal never even got to go on his solo mission; he'd been dropped as a Pledge weeks before then.

Luckily for Cal, he was an Elite-level Higher Reasoning Talent. When Cal was dropped from the Hunters' Pledge class, the head of the Crypto unit offered for him to complete his Pledge year with them. He'd accepted, and even managed high marks from his mentor. Cal received an official appointment to the Crypto Division after graduation and eagerly accepted it. Still, his failure with the Hunters nagged at him; he was desperate to prove himself. So desperate, in fact, that he was willing to overlook a glaring, almost fatal inconsistency in the data.

Disgusted, I drew back out of his mind. I felt dirty after witnessing such raw ambition. He was pathetic. Suddenly, I found it difficult to be in the same room with him. I stared straight into his slightly dazed, wholly terrified eyes. I might not have robbed him of memories, didn't thoroughly demolish his subconscious the way I'd unintentionally destroyed Ernest's, but I knew that my interrogation hadn't been painless. I hadn't meant for it to be.

I could gently sift through a person's mind without them knowing that I was there. Digging deeper without their knowledge was a little harder, but not impossible. But from the moment I knew that Cal was lying to me, I'd wanted him to know how powerful I was. I wanted him to know that no matter how good he thought he was, I was better.

Part of me knew that I was being just as egotistical as he had been, wanting to prove my worth to him like he'd wanted to prove his to Mac. It was silly; our Talents weren't even similar, not comparable at all – mine were much cooler.

"You make me sick," I whispered in a low, threatening voice. I was so close to him that I swore I could feel a tiny whoosh as the dark hairs on his arms stood at attention. Pushing back from the table, I turned and walked through the door to the observation room, clenching my hands into fists to stop them from twitching.

"Are you alright?" Captain Alvarez asked when he saw me enter the observation room.

"I will be," I replied tightly.

His dark forehead was creased with worry, and his nearly black eyes shone with an unreadable expression.

"You have every right to be mad," he said quietly.

"Did you know him? When he was a Pledge?" I inquired. I hadn't intended to ask, but suddenly I wanted to know.

"I did. I'd been hesitant to take him. His physical abilities were decent – he did well on his combat examination, wasn't too bad with weapons either. But I didn't really see the point in wasting his God-given gifts. The Talent evaluation showed that he had an off-the-charts level of Higher Reasoning. I've only ever seen one other person test so high," he mused.

I didn't need to read his mind to know that he was talking about me. I'd felt Cal's strength the moment I walked into the room. It was partially what made me so desperate to display my own; the parallels made me uneasy.

"I'd like to speak with Jennifer now," I said, chewing nervously on my lower lip.

"You can take a couple of minutes if you like. She isn't going anywhere," Captain Alvarez replied gently.

I gave him a tight smile. "I want to get this over with."

Jennifer had been staring nervously at the door, and when I walked in, her small eyes immediately lit up with recognition and her posture relaxed slightly.

"Hey, Jennifer." I tried to sound pleasant.

"T-t-Talia," she stuttered.

"Did they tell you why you were asked to come here?" I didn't waste any time with her either.

"Captain Alvarez said that someone from the Interrogation Division needed to talk to me. I didn't know that you'd been reassigned."

"Yeah, me neither," I answered dryly, giving the two-way mirror a snarky look. "I need to ask you some questions about the intel that you intercepted."

"The stuff about Ian Crane?" she guessed, her anxiousness increasing.

The claustrophobic room was making my senses even more acute than usual. I could smell the slightest hint of body odor, could see the tiny beads of perspiration beginning to form along her hairline.

"Yes, the stuff about Ian Crane," I replied, stiffly. Her brain activity was all over the place, her thoughts racing over the week before my ill-fated mission.

"Was there anything off about the intel?"

"I already answered a bunch of questions," she squeaked.

"I know that you did," I soothed, trying to put her at ease.

"I'm just following up on some leads. Was there anything off about the intel?" I repeated, more firmly this time.

She hesitated only briefly before answering, "Kinda."

Her honesty gave me pause; I hadn't expected her to admit anything without more prompting.

"What was strange about it?" I tried to stay calm. I could feel that she wanted to tell me. Jennifer was like an overinflated balloon, ready to pop with the guilt that she'd bottled up inside, so I waited. I was mentally drained. If she wanted to tell me on her own – without me having to pick it out of her head, I would wait all night. Besides, three people had already confirmed that there had indeed been something off with the intel.

"Well, the encryption was crude. It was way too simple, nothing that you'd expect from information about President Crane's whereabouts. Usually, anything having to do with Crane is impossible to decipher. We're normally only able to decrypt like every third word - it never makes any sense, but this information wasn't like that at all. It was easily identifiable," she rambled, her pinched face contorting like she'd eaten something unpleasant.

"Why didn't you say anything?" I demanded.

"I did," she urged. "I told Cal. I told him that we should look into it, that something was off." Tears began to pool in her eyes.

"What did Operative Simmons say when you told him that?" My jaw was so tight, I was surprised that the words slipped through my teeth.

"He said that it wasn't a big deal. He said that someone in Crane's organization must've messed up and that we were lucky to intercept such valuable information. Cal said we'd be promoted," she wailed. The tears started to flow down her cheeks, and I almost felt bad for her. Maybe if I hadn't been shot and poisoned as a result of her mistake, I would have been more sympathetic.

"Did you report it to anyone else?"

"No," she hiccupped. "I wanted to. I really wanted to." She was a fairly strong projector; she showed me exactly how Cal had threatened her when she'd suggested telling. Her inability to take a stand against him, her weakness, nauseated me.

"So you never reported it?" I pressed, the calm in my voice surprising me.

"No," she cried harder. "I'm so sorry. I'm so sorry." She hugged herself with her twig-like arms, her body racked with sobs.

I didn't probe further into her head; there wasn't a need to do so. Her guilt was flooding into my mind, almost suffocating me. I needed to get out of that room, needed to get away from her before I did something that a moral person would later regret. I turned around and yanked the door open, fleeing to the observation room.

I inhaled deeply through my nose, exhaled long huffing breaths through my mouth. My head was spinning so fast. Collapsing into one of the chairs sitting against the far wall, I wedged my head between my knees.

Why hadn't someone said something? Rider had cited love. Cal claimed ambition. Jennifer was just plain weak. I couldn't decide who I wanted to throttle first.

"I know that it probably doesn't change anything, but Cal and his team weren't promoted," Captain Alvarez said gently. "In fact, now we'll launch a full investigation into all three of them."

Three of them? Oh, right - Penny.

"Penny was just a Pledge. If Jennifer couldn't stand up to Cal, there's no way that she could have." I was quick to defend her even though my attempts felt lame, even to me. "Maybe she didn't even realize what was going on." Penny was an Elite Talent; there was no way that she hadn't known. Even if she didn't say something to Cal, why didn't she say something to me? Why hadn't she warned me that I might be walking into a trap?

"The fact that she was a Pledge might be the only thing that saves her from suspension, or worse."

The way he said it sent fingers of fear skittering down my spine; what was the "or worse"?

Chapter Twenty-Nine

Still shaken from the interrogation sessions with Cal and Jennifer, I walked aimlessly in the general direction of guest housing. In the past twelve hours, I'd learned more than I had in all the weeks I'd spent observing the Instructors and sifting through Operatives' files. Unfortunately, I had no idea what any of it meant.

What did Grace cheating on her Placement Exams, Cal's ambition, and Jennifer's spineless nature have in common? Why did four separate people – five if you counted Penny – lie about the same thing? Was that a coincidence?

It was late and I was exhausted, but I knew that sleep would prove impossible. Instead of going to guest housing, I made my way to Erik. While I doubted that he'd be able to shed any light on my findings, at least I wouldn't be alone.

When I reached his door, I leaned my forehead heavily against the wood and knocked. There was no answer, and disappointment darkened my already black mood. I turned to leave.

"Tals?" Erik's melodic voice called when I'd made it halfway back to the elevator.

Calm relief washed over me and a smiled unwittingly tugged at the corners of my mouth. I turned slowly back around. Erik hung out of his doorway, one hand gripping the frame as he leaned into the hall. His plaid pajama bottoms were slung low on his hips and his chest was bare. Despite everything else going on, I wanted to run over and throw my arms around him, feel the warm skin of his chest against my cheek.

"Hey," I called back, my smile becoming a full-on grin when I met his eyes.

"I've been waiting for you," he said, beckoning for me to come closer.

His turquoise irises shone brightly even in the dimly lit corridor, and my heart pounded. Why was it that no matter how many times I saw him, or how much time I spent with him, he always took my breath away?

I ran the short distance and flung myself at him. Erik stumbled, but quickly wrapped his arms around me, pressing his lips on the top of my head. He didn't ask me if I was okay; I think that he knew I wasn't. With one arm still wrapped protectively around my middle, he pulled me into his room.

As soon as I walked through the doorway, I felt at home in the familiar setting. I hadn't spent a lot of time in Erik's room in the brief time I'd lived in the dorms – we usually hung out in mine – yet the plush navy carpeting and plaid papered walls calmed me. There was a small blue plastic table with four blue chairs in the middle of the huge room, and his bed ran the length of a scenery window. He currently had the window set to natural, so I could see the trees and lake that were situated behind the building. The full moon bathed the grounds in an odd silvery glow.

Erik led me over to his bed. He gently guided me to sit on the plaid comforter, and knelt on the floor next to the bed.

"What happened, Tal?" he whispered, running his hands up and down my arms to warm my cold flesh.

"I don't even know where to begin," I said, shaking my head.

Erik leaned closer, resting his forehead against mine. Thoughts of interrogation rooms and lying, cheating, ambitious, lovesick Operatives flew from my mind. I brought my lips to his, keeping my eyes open until the last second so that I could absorb the full impact of his emotions. Once his mouth was on mine, I reached to run my fingers through his hair. Erik caught my wrist and gently guided it, and me, back onto the mattress. Pinning my arm over my head, he hovered over me, his fingers laced with mine.

Slowly, Erik's lips trailed down my chin, nestling in the hollow of my throat. The more he touched me, the more I relaxed. The tension ebbed with every kiss, and it wasn't long before I was a puddle beneath him. He ran his tongue up the side of my neck and nibbled on my earlobe.

"What happened?" he whispered. Erik felt how upset I'd been when I first arrived, and he wanted to know why. Even though I knew that once he saw what I'd been through, he'd stop kissing me, I dropped the barriers. As I'd predicted, Erik pulled away several seconds later. Except instead of looking worried, hysterical laughter burst from his lips.

"You bit him!" he exclaimed. "That's awesome!"

"It's not funny," I retorted defensively. But the more I thought about it, the more hilarious I found it, and soon I was laughing, too. It felt good.

"Man, I wish I'd been there to see the look on his face," Erik sighed, wiping a tear from the corner of his eye.

"I can't believe I reacted like that. I drew blood!"

"You were scared. He cornered you; it was instinctual," he assured me.

"Instinctual? Maybe for a normal person, but I'm a trained fighter. Hitting him, kicking him, even kneeing him in the balls would've been natural. Biting him, though? That was just crazy," I said.

Erik's amused expression turned thoughtful, and he shifted to take his weight off of me. He rested on one elbow, absently twirling one of my curls around his finger as his mind churned over what I'd just said.

"What?" I demanded after he'd been silent for too long. "You think that I'm nuts, don't you?"

"Of course not, Tal," he said calmly, pulling the curls straight and watching, fascinated as they sprang back. I wanted to swat his hand away, but his kid-in-a-candy-store expression held me back.

"Then what is it?"

"Just wishing that you'd bite me," he teased.

This time I did swat his chest, blushing from the roots of the hair that he was playing with to the tips of my sneaker-clad toes. Erik moved so quickly that I didn't realize what he was going to do until his jaws closed on one side of my neck. His teeth only nipped playfully at the skin, and my startled yelp quickly turned to a high-pitched giggle. Erik bit down a little harder before releasing me.

"Let's take a walk," he abruptly suggested.

"A walk? Erik, I'm exhausted," I said, baffled by his ability to flip the switch on his hormones.

"Please, Tal. Let's take a walk to the lake," he sent. His eyes darted around the room, urging me to understand something – and I did. The reason that he'd wanted to talk on the ledge the other night was the same reason that he wanted to go to the lake now.

TOXIC common areas and secure facilities like the Crypto Bank were constantly monitored by security cameras and audio devices. Operatives' private apartments weren't on a live feed, but were randomly screened for inappropriate or illegal activity. To my knowledge, the only inappropriate behavior that took place in the bedrooms was drinking and naked sleepovers. Though neither was against the rules, depending on the circumstances, they might be heavily frowned upon.

"You're right. Fresh air would be good," I finally agreed.

I wasn't sure what Erik wanted to talk about, but I figured he must have a good reason to drag me across campus late at night.

Erik found a shirt and flip-flops, and led me from the warmth of his bed. When we reached Hunters' Village, I felt an immediate sense of longing. Memories flooded back as we passed the cabin where I'd lived with Erik and Henri for most of my time as a

Pledge. Opening my mind, I felt a flurry of activity inside. It was late, past curfew, meaning all the Pledges were safely tucked into their homes.

"You okay?" Erik asked, squeezing my hand affectionately.

"Yeah, nostalgia and all that." I rolled my eyes.

Erik gently tugged me toward the dark path that led to the lake. The only sound was the crunching of rocks and twigs under our feet as we wound our way through the woods. It wasn't long before reached the water. Erik selected a fallen log close to the lake's edge. He sat, pulling me down beside him.

The lake was shimmering black glass under a cloudless sky. The moon hung ominously against the dark night, and the stars twinkled brightly above us. Cold air numbed me from the inside out. Erik seemed impervious to the temperature, but rubbed my back when he noticed me shivering. Under different circumstances, the moment would have been romantic. Long moments of silence stretched between us, Erik tracing the curve of my spine while I stared into the darkness.

"Start at the beginning and tell me everything that happened in Nevada," he finally said.

I turned to meet his insistent turquoise eyes. We were sitting in the shadows of ancient trees and the moon provided little light, but my heightened sense of sight could make out every detail of his smooth features. There were small lines around his clenched jaw, and his eyes scrunched at the corners, scrutinizing my own face. His expression was both tense and concerned.

I heaved a huge sigh before launching into a detailed account of my mission, starting from when I jumped from the hover plane outside of Las Vegas. I told him about meeting Kyle, gaining his confidence, probing him for information, and using him to gain access to the house where Crane was staying. I retraced my journey through Crane's compound – breaking into his office, downloading the information from his computer, the decision to invade the basement, and the odd resistance that I encountered at the door leading into the bowels of the building. I didn't pause when I described being caught and waking up strapped to a bed, hesitating only when I recounted the conversation with Crane when he intimated that he'd known my father.

Throughout all of it, Erik traced small circles at the base of my skull with his thumb, soothing me as I spoke. His fingers went rigid against my skin when I described the bullet hitting my back, and I knew that he felt the pain as acutely as if the memory had been his own. The fingers gripping my neck tightened painfully, and anger radiated off of him. I ended my story at the point when I'd released Crane's mind from the pain that I'd been projecting – my own pain. When I finished, my eyes remained on the pebble that I was kicking back and forth with the toe of my tennis shoe. Erik took deep, calming breaths to quiet his outrage. He wanted to kill the man who'd shot me, and it wasn't just an idle thought; when I'd been injured on our very first Hunting Mission together, Erik hadn't even hesitated before plunging a knife into the throat of the man who stabbed me.

"So Crane recognized you in the pub, you think?" he asked when his breathing was finally under control.

"I don't think he recognized me. It was more like he felt me, like he knew that I was Talented," I said, shuddering at the memory of our eyes briefly locked.

"But he knew your name when you woke up after being caught?"

"Yeah, he called me by it. He called me Talia."

Erik sat looking pensive for several long minutes. He picked up a handful of pebbles with his free hand, skimming them across the lake's surface. Tiny ripples appeared on the otherwise placid water as the stones bumped along before sinking to the bottom.

"Do you believe him about your father?" Erik finally asked.

"I don't know. It was weird. His mind was blocked – it wasn't until after I'd been shot that I broke down his defenses. Even then, I think that maybe he let me, like he wanted to take the pain away."

I hugged myself. I hadn't admitted that to anyone. The connection that I'd formed with Crane had been absolute, our minds woven together like a quilt. I'd been too focused on projecting to read his thoughts, but he would have had access to every memory of mine, every detail of my life. I hoped that the pain had been too intense for him to look.

"Did you see anything in his head, anything at all that could tell us who sold you out?" Erik asked, pulling me closer to him.

"No, but I didn't look either. I just wanted to get out of there. I barely remember anything that happened between getting shot and waking up in the hospital. Mac told me most of what I just told you; he pieced it together from the extraction team's reports."

Erik grew quiet again. He leaned his head against mine and dulled my emotions. While I appreciated his efforts, I didn't want to lose the anger and frustration that I'd been holding on to. I wanted to hate Crane for what he'd done to me; I wanted to hate him for killing my parents. It was the hatred that had gotten me through the years following their deaths, and it was what drove me still.

"You didn't ask Penny about the encryption when you saw her?" The question was rhetorical; Erik already knew that I hadn't, but I felt the need to answer anyway.

"She was agitated; I didn't want to bring it up."

Erik rubbed the space between his eyes with the heel of his palm, but didn't comment.

"She would've told me if she knew, right?" I asked in a small voice. I needed his assurance to quash my own doubt.

"She's your best friend, Tal. I'm sure that if she knew she would have told you," he said. "She probably didn't realize how simplistic the encryption was. She was just a Pledge, and pretty new at decrypting intel." He was giving her the benefit of the doubt, but I could tell that he didn't really believe she was so naïve.

"I've spent every day of the past few weeks with her, and we talked about the mission – I would have known if she wasn't telling me something," I replied confidently, trying to dispel our mutual skepticism.

"You're right," Erik agreed, turning to give me a small, genuine smile.

But it was Mac's words I heard instead. *"Sometimes, those closest to us are the best at deceiving us; you of all people should know that,"* he said. He was talking about Donavon then, but maybe those sentiments applied to Penny now.

No, I thought firmly. She'd cried when she learned what happened to me in Nevada. She'd risked sanctions, and possibly even her appointment to the Crypto Division, when she'd broken protocol to help me prepare for my mission. Besides, she was an orphan; there was no way she had any ties to the Coalition. The only time she ever left Headquarters was with me; I definitely would have known if she was having clandestine meetings with members of the Coalition when we went into the city. I hated myself for even doubting her, and I hated Donavon for creating a mistrust in me that hadn't been present before his infidelity.

"What about the other Cryptos?" I asked. "I know that they all had their reasons for not telling the truth earlier, but I was so caught up in the whole encryption nonsense that I didn't really try to figure out if they had ties to the Coalition."

"Could be," he shrugged. "But cheating on your Placement Exams doesn't exactly make you a criminal mastermind."

"I don't know," I said slowly. "It seems like tricking the examiners into believing that you're Elite would be pretty hard."

"Eh, it could be done. Depends how good the Mimic was that tested her," he replied absently.

"Mimic?" I asked, surprised. I tried to recall my own Talent Ranking session. Mac, a Telepath, and a Manipulator had made up the panel that asked me questions and forced me to display my abilities. The Manipulator had been strong – I'd felt his strength just like I'd felt Cal's. Looking back, that was a little odd; Mac had always told me that I was the only TOXIC member with such strong powers of Manipulation.

"Yeah, all testing panels have a high-ranking Agency member, an Operative with the student's same abilities, and a Mimic. Exceptional Talents, like you, are easy to feel – most people with any extra perception will pick up on it. Even non-Talented people can feel your power; they just don't understand what they're feeling. It's harder, though, with your average Talent, which is why they use us. Mimics are best equipped to get a read on a Talent's strength," he explained.

"I don't remember a Mimic being on my panel," I said, shaking my head.

"Do you remember a Manipulator being there?" he countered.

"Of course. Mac said that a person with my same abilities would sit in to gauge my strength relative to his."

"I bet you that was a Mimic."

"No way. I'd have known," I declared. I would've ...right?

"Did you know what I was when we fought during your trials?" Erik asked, giving me a playful nudge. I smiled at the memory of our first encounter.

In addition to the Talent-ranking portion of my Placement Exam, I'd also had a physical trial. Erik had been one of the combatants that I'd faced, and I'd been sorely unprepared. All of the other fighters had been easy to defeat; I'd been able to control them through manipulation. Not Erik, though. The moment I tried to take over his mind, he'd thrown my abilities right back at me. The match had quickly turned ugly.

"Point taken," I said. "I knew that you weren't a Manipulator. I just didn't know what you were."

"If I'd been better at replicating your powers, you would've thought I was a Manipulator. I bet that the Mimic on your panel was better acquainted with Manipulation than I was."

"I doubt that; you're an Elite," I pointed out.

Erik fidgeted uncomfortably, pulling at the drawstring of his pajama bottoms. He seemed almost embarrassed, and refused to meet my eyes.

"I'm not exactly an Elite, Tal. Mimics don't have rankings," he finally said.

"Are you serious?" I exclaimed. All Talents had rankings. At least, I'd thought they did. But Mimics were rare, and Erik was the only one that I knew personally.

"Yeah. If you're a Mimic, you just ...are. Mimics are only as strong as the Talent they're imitating, and even then it's complicated," he mumbled.

Ahh, so that's why I felt the guy on my panel, I thought. I was actually feeling my own power when he mimicked me. How weird.

"Complicated seems to be the word of the day. Explain it to me," I said.

"Like I said, Mimics are only as strong as the Talent they are mimicking. I can morph into any animal and even other humans when I'm around Henri because he can do all of that. When I'm with you, I can read people's minds, control them just like you do."

"I've noticed," I quipped. Erik frequently read my thoughts now, and even controlled them on occasion.

He smiled, not ashamed at all.

"I only do it to you when you're really upset," he promised.

"Yeah, yeah, yeah - just get to the complicated part." I gave him a scowl even though I wasn't really upset. I knew that he did it because he cared.

"Well, I have to learn how to do those things. That's why it took us so long in the beginning to form the three-way connection between you, me, and Henri. Remember?"

I did remember. At first, it had seemed like we would never pull it off. Henri had been so frustrated sometimes, I'd worried that he regretted offering to take me on as part of his team.

"Higher Reasoning is the same way. I can mimic one, my brain will analyze the data and compute things really quickly and all that, but I don't know what to do with the information once I have it. I doubt that I'd be able to gauge their strength since I don't really understand how their abilities work."

I'd always thought that being a Mimic would be cool, having the ability to possess so many different gifts. But after hearing Erik's description, I wasn't sure. It actually sounded like a lot of work. After spending years learning how to use my own gifts, I couldn't imagine how much effort and dedication it took to learn everyone else's, too.

"If Grace did well on her written exams - like if Rider had given her the answers and coached her through it - and the Mimic on her panel wasn't well versed in how Higher Reasoning works, he might've just thought that his reading was off," he continued.

"So when you're around Penny, for instance, you can't tell she's an Elite?" I asked, oddly fascinated by the revelation.

"No, I can't," he admitted. "I've never tried to mimic her specifically, but I imagine that if I did, I'd be able to replicate her powers, just not implement them."

"What about other Mimics?" I pressed. "What do you feel when you're around them?"

"I feel nothing, unless they're mimicking another Talent. If that's the case, I feel the other Talent's abilities. When they're at rest, it's kind of like being around a normal human ...but not," he finished lamely.

"What do you mean?" My brain was on overload. I couldn't process all of this. I should've brought Penny; her analytical abilities would've come in real handy right about now.

"Their Talent essence is still there. I can feel that there's something that separates them from your average person, but it's blank and undefined."

"Weird," I whispered.

"Yeah, thanks. I know, I'm a freak." He laughed, pulling a lock of my hair to demonstrate how much he appreciated my commentary.

"That's not what I meant! I just never knew any of this. Why didn't you ever tell me?"

Erik shrugged. "It never came up. TOXIC puts such an emphasis on rankings that I don't like to tell people that I don't have one. I am the only Hunter who isn't Elite; it's kind of embarrassing."

I turned and stared directly into his eyes. He looked so vulnerable. It was almost troubling to see Erik this way; he was always so confident, so sure of himself. I leaned in and kissed him softly. The hand on my neck tangled in my hair as his lips parted. I loved the way he tasted and I scooted closer until I was practically on top of him, but Erik gently pushed me back with his free hand.

"Easy, Tals," he whispered. I shrank away from him, humiliated by his admonishment. "Hey, it's not like that," he promised, cupping my chin and stroking my cheek with his thumb. "You've had a long day and it's late. Why don't we go to bed? If you get some sleep, maybe all of this stuff about codes and everything will make more sense in the morning."

Erik stood and offered me his hand, which I took.

"Guest housing? Or my place?" he asked as he led me from the woods.

"Do you even have to ask?" I teased. Of course, I wanted to stay with him.

"My place it is."

When I met his gaze, the intensity lit my skin on fire, and I had to look away. Erik laughed softly and squeezed my hand. Sometimes I thought that making me squirm gave him a thrill.

When we got back to Erik's room he found a pair of workout shorts and an old t-shirt for me to use. In his bathroom, I found an extra toothbrush and set about getting ready for bed.

Erik was already in his bed with the covers folded back when I finished. I crossed the room to join him. Erik covered me with the blankets before drawing my head against his chest. He folded one hand behind his head and slid the other around my waist. I turned my face up, expecting him to kiss me, but his eyes were already closed and he didn't bring his lips to meet mine. I kissed the side of his neck and began working my way to his mouth.

"Tals, don't," he mumbled, his pulse quickening.

"Why?" I demanded. I could tell that he wanted me; why was he being like this?

"Exactly, but you're too vulnerable," Erik said, reading the thoughts straight from my head. "Please don't make this any harder than it already is."

Vulnerable? He thought I was vulnerable?

Erik sighed audibly. "Tal," he began, "I just meant that you've been through a lot today and you're exhausted and on edge. I can feel all of that. I can feel how badly you need to sleep. I don't want you to have another seizure on my account."

"Stay out of my head," I mumbled.

"I'm not in your head. You're projecting." I didn't doubt that he was right; my thoughts were bouncing around my skull, fighting for freedom from their cranial prison.

I turned away from him and scooted to the edge of the bed. Erik let me go and didn't even react when I purposefully removed his hand from my waist. He let me stew, lost in my thoughts. I let the events of the day overtake my bruised ego.

All of the information that I'd learned raced through my mind on separate tracks, like sprinters in their own lanes, all aiming for the same finish line but never crossing paths. The facts seemed like pieces of different puzzles – the lying Operatives, the simplistic encryption, Ian Crane knowing my name, the fact that Mimics didn't have rankings. There had to be a common denominator - I just needed to find it.

I became so lost in thought that I didn't realize Erik was still awake. He didn't say anything when he curled his strong body behind mine, wrapping one arm around my waist. He pulled me tight against his chest, nudged my curls aside with his chin, and buried his face in the back of my neck. His mouth was next to my ear, his lips brushing my skin.

"It's gonna be okay, Tal. We'll figure this out. Please don't cry."

I brought my fingers to my cheeks, surprised to find that hot tears were weaving patterns across my cheekbones and dripping down the sides of my nose. My body began shaking as I started to openly sob. I didn't even know why I was crying. The shaking became so violent that I thought it might be the beginning of a seizure. It just made me cry harder. Erik rolled me over to face him and tightened his hold. I cried harder, balling handfuls of his shirt in my clenched fists. The harder my body convulsed, the tighter Erik held me.

After what seemed like forever, my muscles relaxed and the spasms stopped. My tears gave way to hiccups. Erik gently detangled my fingers from his shirt and laced them through his. He forced my head back, and I looked up at him through swollen eyes. His expression was so gentle. He brought his mouth to mine and kissed me softly, our lips barely touching. I tasted my salty tears.

Erik's mind was open, and his feelings for me clouded all of my other thoughts. The weight that had been bearing down on me since Nevada lifted. I felt light, free. I wanted this feeling to last forever. Suddenly, I was so overcome with the desire to sleep that I couldn't keep my eyes open. My mind seemed to go blank and my thoughts became shadows that I couldn't catch.

"I don't know about forever, but at least long enough so you can get some sleep," Erik whispered, pulling back from the kiss but staying close enough that his lips still brushed mine when he spoke.

The small part of me that wanted to retain control fought against Erik once I understood what he was doing. As much as I enjoyed the unburdening of my consciousness, I hated surrendering my will even to him.

"I just want to help. Don't fight," Erik said gently.

"You've apparently mastered my abilities," I mumbled.

"Do you want me to stop?" he asked, lessening his hold so I could make the decision for myself.

"No," I decided. "I don't."

I really didn't. I felt weak and more than a little pathetic letting him do this for me; but before he'd taken over, I'd felt manic and unstable. Between the two states, I'd rather be the former.

"Sleep, Tals. I'm right here. I'm not going anywhere," he soothed.

"Promise?" I whispered, hoarsely.

"Promise."

Chapter Thirty

That night my dreams were consumed by lines of scrolling text. The letters L, I, A, and R blazed orange as strings of white letters, numbers, and symbols crisscrossed my subconscious. A voice chanted "liar, liar, liar" over and over. Those images gave way to me standing in the center of the School's indoor practice arena, facing my placement panel. *"I know you are, but what am I?"* a man's voice taunted me.

As I stared at him, perplexed by his malicious expression, he transformed into Cal. Suddenly, I was in the claustrophobic interrogation room with Cal's hulking form looming over me. He became a giant tiger before my eyes, and Captain Alvarez's voice boomed through the speakers. "Elite, Elite, Elite," he proclaimed. Then I was with Kenly, helping her train. I advanced on her, preparing to demonstrate some combination of offensive maneuvers when the earth quaked and a deep chasm appeared. I teetered on the edge, my arms flailing as I tried to regain my balance. I called to her for help, but instead of catching me like she did when I slipped on the baton, she let me fall.

I woke with a start, panting heavily and bathed in sweat. *Nightmare, just a nightmare*, I assured myself. I glanced down at Erik's sleeping form, and instantly calmed.

One of his arms was still wrapped around my waist, and it tightened when I stirred. His other arm was flung over his head on the pillow. Long, dark lashes brushed the deep shadows under his closed eyes. His lips were parted slightly and he breathed evenly. At rest, the lines of tension around his mouth and eyes had smoothed, and his trademark mischievous smile was absent. He looked peaceful and much younger than his twenty years.

I smiled as I snuggled against him, lightly tracing the contours of his perfect features. Responding to my touch, Erik absently brushed his lips across my forehead and mumbled incoherently.

"Erik?" I whispered, craning my neck so that my mouth was next to his ear.

"Sleep, Tal. I'm here," he mumbled, pulling me closer.

"Erik, I need you to get up," I said softly.

He made a couple more unintelligible noises in reply, but refused to open his eyes. As much as I hated to wake him, I really needed to. So I bit his earlobe, hard.

"Jesus, Tal," he cried, yanking his head back.

"Oh, good, you're awake!" I exclaimed brightly, giving him an innocent smile.

Erik scowled, fixing me with bloodshot eyes. I immediately felt bad for waking him. He'd stayed up most of the night to ensure that I slept; every time I'd cried out, he'd soothed me back to dreamland. Unfortunately for him, it was there that inspiration struck; my dreams of Placement Tests and encrypted text gave me an idea. I knew that I was missing some of the puzzle pieces, but the ones I did have were starting to form a picture.

"What's so important that it can't wait another hour?" Erik asked drowsily, letting his lids fall closed.

"I need to talk to a Crypto," I said, pinching the skin that covered his taut stomach muscles.

The hand behind his head shot down and long fingers encircled my wrist. "Hands off the goods, Lyons," he smirked. "You're giving me funny ideas."

I had a pretty good idea what those funny ideas were when the hand at my waist snaked up my shirt. Erik's fingers trailed over my stomach now, dipping dangerously low into the waistband of my borrowed gym shorts.

"I'm serious," I protested, swatting feebly at his chest. "I want to see some personnel records and placement results."

"I'm not Penny," he reminded me.

"Right, but you are a Mimic."

Erik's body stiffened. "You want me to Mimic a Crypto and do what, exactly?" he said slowly.

"Some of the files I want are probably restricted. If I ask Mac to get them for me, then he'll want to know why, and I don't want to say anything to him until I'm sure."

"So you want me to mimic a Crypto, break into the database and get the records for you?" Erik's eyes flew open in alarm. "Tal, I can't do that. I explained this to you last night – I'll be able to mimic the Brain's Talents, but I wouldn't even know where to begin once I'm in."

"I don't want you to mimic the Brain's Talents. I want you to mimic mine," I replied calmly. I'd thought this through already. "You can use my Manipulation to control the Crypto and get him to retrieve the files."

"Not that I don't want to help," Erik began evenly. "But why can't you just control him yourself? Wouldn't that be a lot easier than having me mimic you to manipulate him? No offense, Tal, but this plan seems pretty convoluted......" Erik shook his head and settled back against his pillow. The hand at my waist had stilled when I told him what I wanted, but now began scrawling lazy lines across my stomach.

"I won't be able to control him," I said quietly, hating to admit the weakness.

"You can control anyone. Don't play the feel-bad-for-me card. I've been on the other end of your Manipulation; I know exactly how strong you are." Erik sounded irritated, but he continued to hold me close. He guided my wrist to his chest and gripped my sides, lifting me so that I was lying on top of him. Erik's mouth found my throat and he nibbled his way down to the neckline of my tee.

"Erik, stop. I'm serious," I mumbled. My words came out low and throaty, and we both knew that I didn't really want him to stop.

"If you really want me to stop, make me." He flipped me over so fast that I let out a startled cry when my back hit the mattress. Erik moved over me, dipping his mouth to meet mine, the challenge evident in his amused eyes. I pushed gently on his chest to keep him at bay.

"I'm serious. I can't," I said. The playful expression turned serious as he settled on his elbow beside me. "I'm too drained from yesterday; I haven't used that much energy in months. Ever since I came back from Nevada ...I just get tired so easily, and I don't have the strength left to completely control another person."

I met his troubled gaze, and the pure sympathy made me look away. I hated appearing weak, particularly in front of him. From our first meeting, he'd been taking care of me. When I got hurt on our first mission, he absorbed the pain so I wouldn't have to feel it. After Donavon cheated on me, Erik helped repair my broken heart. During my seizure on the ledge, Erik had taken control, kept me conscious and sane. Even last night, he'd dulled my emotions and quieted my racing thoughts so that I could sleep.

Erik wiped at the tear that trickled from my tightly scrunched eye. "I wanted to do those things for you," he whispered. "Having help doesn't make you weak."

"You never need someone to pick up the pieces of your crumbling life," I sniffed. I knew I was being dramatic, but I felt like there was a pile of bricks on my chest. Receiving the injections and the constant monitoring of my blood were bad enough, but now I couldn't even use my Talents. My gifts had been an essential part of who I was for my entire life and now they were failing just like my health and sanity.

"Like I said, a Mimic is only as strong as the Talent they're imitating, and I'm stronger than ever when I'm around you. Your abilities are just as good – maybe better – than before your mission. I didn't do all of those things for you because I think you're weak. I did them because I care about you, because I want to help you. And if you want my help now, I'm there." He leaned over and kissed my tearstained cheek.

The warmth and gentleness of his words only made me cry harder. Erik held me and whispered assurances, his voice like silk encasing me in a safe cocoon. He didn't try to take the pain away; instead, he let me cry until I'd gotten it all out.

When I was cried out, Erik led me to the bathroom. I sat on the closed toilet lid while he started the shower.

"Need help getting naked?" he asked, squatting so that he was peering up at me. His tone was coy and suggestive, and I knew that he was trying to put an end to my pity party.

"I think I can manage." I smiled.

"I don't mind, Tals. I'm happy to help you wash your hair, rub soap on your back ...or your –"

"I'll be okay," I cut him off before he could voice the inappropriate images that he was projecting.

"If my services aren't needed, I guess I'll go get your clothes," he offered, standing to leave.

"Thanks, Erik," I said softly to his retreating back. At first I didn't think that he'd heard me, but his mental reply came through the closed door.

"If you let me help you shower, then you'd really have something to thank me for."

Despite my dire mood, I beamed as I climbed over the side of the tub.

My bag was sitting inside the bathroom door when I emerged from the hot water. I quickly dressed in jeans and a long-sleeved white t-shirt. As I wound my hair into a wet knot on top of my head, I tried to quash the growing bubble of dread in my stomach. I was almost positive that I would find the missing link in the records. But now that I was so close to uncovering the truth, I was more apprehensive then excited.

I definitely wanted to unmask the traitor. I wanted him to pay for what he'd done to me. The anger and frustration from the previous day remained; and I knew that when I did fill in all the gaps, no amount of deep breathing, equalizers, or manipulation from Erik was going to quell my desire for revenge. Even thinking about it made my blood boil. Still, the knot of anxiety in my stomach pulled tighter with each passing moment.

Erik sat on his bed, dressed in his standard attire – jeans and a dark green polo shirt – when I returned to the bedroom. He was playing with his communicator, but glanced up when he heard me.

"Ready?" he asked with an easy smile.

"Definitely," I replied with a confidence that didn't penetrate the surface.

Erik cleared his throat, looking uncomfortable. "Um, Donavon said to let him know when you're ready to fly out. He, um ...he said he'd be with Harris, working out ...or something."

"You saw Donavon?" I asked. I hadn't given him a second thought since landing the day before.

"Yeah, his room is next to yours. And ...well, he kinda heard me getting your things." Erik was visibly distraught talking about Donavon. I knew that if I read his mind, I'd find that the conversation between the two hadn't been as friendly as what he imparted. On the plus side, Erik appeared bruise- and blood-free, so at least their interaction hadn't come to blows.

"He also wanted me to remind you to take your medicine. Said you have a shot in your bag?"

I did have a shot in my bag, but I had yet to administer the medication myself. Dr. Thistler always gave me the injection, and just the thought of plunging the needle into my own arm made my stomach roll.

"I'll be okay until I get back to school," I said decisively. "It'd be better if Dr. Thistler gave it to me anyway." I gave him a reassuring smile.

The look in Erik's eyes – not to mention the images of me shaking on the ledge that were playing in his mind – told me that he thought waiting was a bad idea. He opened his mouth to argue, but quickly reconsidered.

"You're the boss," he said instead.

It was really early, and the night-shift Cryptos would still be on duty. I wasn't very well acquainted with many of the Brains, and hoped that the ones working would be weak-willed. Erik had demonstrated that he was more than capable of controlling even the most reluctant of minds – namely mine – but I didn't want any problems.

The Crypto Bank at Headquarters was just as sterile and impersonal as the one at School. I led Erik around a curved hallway lined with frosted-glass doors. I knocked on one at random, marked "213," and waited. Erik reached for my hand and gave it a brief squeeze as soft footsteps made their way to greet us.

"Hey," a short, skinny boy said when he opencd the door. "Are you two in the wrong place?"

"No. I don't know if you know who I am, but – " I started to say.

"Talia, right?" he interrupted. "And Erikson Kelley?" he said, turning to Erik.

"Yeah, that's right," Erik answered. "We were hoping that you could help us with something. Talia needs some personnel records."

"Oh. Well, you know, I can't really do that without authorization," the boy stammered.

Erik released my hand and stepped forward. His gaze was steady as he pinned the smaller boy's watery brown eyes with his. "You said that you know who Talia is, so you must also know that she lives with Director McDonough? He personally approved her access to any files that she needs, and you wouldn't want to upset him, would you?"

The boy stumbled several paces back under Erik's intensity, and his expression went slack. "No, of course not. Come in," he mumbled.

Luck must have been on our side; when I stepped inside the small room, I saw that the boy was alone.

"Where's your partner?" I asked.

Sick, I read from his mind, a moment before his lips formed the words.

"So it's just you today?" I confirmed.

"Just me," he agreed.

The Brain walked over to his computer chair and sat, facing the wall of electronics. Erik crouched beside him while I flanked his other side. The boy looked uneasily between the two of us, like we might attack him at any minute.

"What files do you need?" he asked Erik.

Erik glanced in my direction, and I mentally sent him the names of all the Cryptos who'd had access to my mission intel and the Instructors that I'd been investigating. *"I'm specifically interested in their Placement Exams, but get their complete records."*

Erik spoke in soft, soothing tones as he relayed my request. The boy's fingers flew noisily across the keys. I tapped my nails impatiently on the desk; the anticipation was making me antsy. I was so close to the truth; I just knew it.

"Relax, Tals. I've got this," Erik sent. When I met his eyes over the boy's head, he winked.

I laughed; he was enjoying himself. Erik loved the thrill of the hunt. This wasn't like the missions we went on as Hunters, but it was mentally demanding and possibly a little risky. If this led nowhere, I had no doubt that Mac would understand, but he'd frown on my breach of protocol. And while Erik had been vetted, I wasn't so sure that Mac would appreciate his involvement. I just hoped that when the time came for explanations, Mac would go easy on him.

"Anything else?" Erik asked me.

I debated briefly. This might be my only opportunity to get my medical records. While Mac would overlook me manipulating the Crypto to get the other Operatives' files, I wasn't confident that he'd feel the same way about mine. He'd deliberately omitted Donavon's blood transfusion and possibly threatened his son into lying to me. Those details were enough for me to be incredibly curious.

"I want my medical records," I finally sent. It was a gamble, but I had to know. *"Donavon's too."*

Erik raised his eyebrows in a questioning gesture as if to ask whether I was sure. When I nodded, he instructed the Crypto to access the information. After the boy had pulled all the files, Erik had him print hard copies and then mask the intrusion. The Crypto did as he was told. Erik walked to the printer and retrieved the ream of paper.

"Thanks for doing what you could for us," Erik said, and headed for the door.

"Yeah, man. Sorry I couldn't be more help. Protocol and all that," the Brain replied, looking bewildered by the stack of pages that Erik now cradled in the crook of his elbow.

I reached for Erik's free hand, lacing his fingers with mine when we emerged from the Crypto Bank. Rays of bright orange sunshine shone through the smattering of ancient trees, and our shadows cast long, distorted figures on the lush grass. Birds chirped their morning song while Operatives stumbled tiredly from their cabins. Today was just like any other day for them, but not for me; today I would finally learn the truth. The papers that Erik held would prove the identity of the spy; I could feel it. Even more importantly – at least to me – they held the truth about my blood transfusions. I would finally know for sure if it had been Donavon's blood that made me sick.

Chapter Thirty-One

"What are we looking for? I'll take half," Erik offered once we were sitting on his bed, the pages strewn across the comforter.

"Honestly, I'm not sure. It was something you said about the Placement Exams and how Mimics work. It got me thinking that maybe Grace isn't the only one who cheated."

As I explained my theory out loud, it sounded a little thin even to me. But the sense of urgency that caused me to force Erik awake before the birds was the same one that had me convinced now that I was right.

"Let's get started then. Want me to order breakfast?" he asked.

"Sure, whatever," I replied distractedly. Food was the last thing on my mind. I was already rifling through the first file – mine.

Unfortunately, the words in the medical file held about as much meaning to me as the encoded lines of text that scrolled across Penny's screens. The blood transfusion was documented, but that was about as much as I could decipher. The names of the experimental drugs that Dr. Thistler gave me were unfamiliar. The complex chemical formulas explaining the analysis of my daily blood work were longer than I was tall. The only words that made any sense were Dr. Thistler's diagnoses – "fair", "acceptable", or "extreme" – that accompanied the results.

Frustrated, I threw the report to the carpet and rubbed my

temples. *Great*, I thought. I'd been so convinced that once I saw the records I'd finally know why the transfusion mattered so much. Maybe Donavon was right; maybe Mac really was only angry because he'd breached protocol.

"What he did was really dangerous," Erik commented when I voiced my thoughts. *"If your body had rejected the transfusion, you could've died."*

"I know. But if it's that simple, then why didn't anyone tell me?"

"Maybe the Director just didn't think it was a big deal. I mean, he didn't tell you where the other blood came from, did he?"

"Yeah, I guess you're right," I admitted. Despite our words, neither of us really believed it was that simple, and the doubt in Erik's mind doubled my own. But neither of us had enough medical knowledge to glean anything from the records to the contrary. I resolved to confront Mac when I got back to school. If he told me that the transfusion didn't matter, that it had nothing to do with my current condition, I'd drop it.

Erik and I worked in companionable silence for hours. The room-service waiter came and went, and at Erik's insistence I ate several bites of French toast and maple syrup sausage. My fingers shook as I turned one page after another. The dull ache in my head became a full-on throbbing by the time I'd made it through Jennifer's entire life history. TOXIC's restricted personnel files were exhaustive, extensive, and – worst of all – boring.

"Maybe we should take a break?" Erik suggested when he noticed me rubbing trembling palms over tired eyes.

"No, no, it's here. I know it is. I'm just missing something." I sighed, annoyed with our lack of progress.

"Come here," Erik said, reaching across the sea of paper that separated us to take my hand. "You're shaking. Just rest for a few minutes. I'll keep looking."

I let Erik pull me to settle in with my back against his chest, but I brought Grace's written test results with me. It wasn't long before my head was bobbing back against his shoulder and my eyes wouldn't stay open. I tried to resist it, but I didn't have the strength; the page in my hand fell to my lap and I started to dream.

My subconscious knew that Erik was aiding my brain in the struggle to put me under. The darkness swirled into dreams of limbs attached to strings, a different puppeteer pulling each one. I woke with a start, jostling a neat stack of paper and sending it flying to the floor.

"Don't do that," I snapped, turning my head to scowl at Erik. "I'm not a child. I don't need you *helping* me sleep."

Erik gave me puppy dog eyes as if to say, "who, me?" Annoyed, I picked up the next report in my pile, but I didn't protest when he moved my hair to the side to nuzzle my neck.

As I tried to concentrate on the words in front of me, two caught my eye: Light Manipulator. A light bulb clicked on, cutting through the haze in my brain.

"Erik?" I asked.

"Hmmm," he mumbled into the back of my neck.

"How often do you use my Talents against me?" Erik drew back, caught off guard by the question.

"Use them against you? That makes it sound so malicious."

"You know what I mean."

"I don't know, not often. Just when you want me to," he added, sounding a little defensive. I think we had different definitions of "want."

"Do you ever do it without me knowing?" I asked nervously, dreading his answer.

Erik fidgeted uncomfortably behind me and began absently twirling my curls as if to buy some time before he answered. "Yeah, sometimes,," he finally said.

"Like when?" I pressed. I had a sinking feeling that only the captain of the Titanic had experienced before me; I was pretty sure that I'd found the missing link.

"Like when we're *together*," Erik said. "But Tal, I just want to know how you're feeling, want to make sure you're comfortable and that I'm not pressuring you into doing something you don't want to do." He wrapped his arms around me from behind and pulled me tightly against his chest. "And I like to feel your reactions."

I rolled my eyes – Erik didn't need reassurance in that department. I wasn't concerned with him reading my thoughts; despite all of my training, I was a strong projector and he'd always been more susceptible to receiving it than most. It was the compulsion facet of my gift that worried me.

"Do you ever control my thoughts when I'm not aware of it?" I whispered shakily. The feeling of dread was evolving into a full-blown panic attack.

Erik hesitated, which was all the confirmation I needed.

"I don't mean to. Sometimes you're just so upset, and I hate seeing you that way, so I do it without thinking," he finally admitted.

"I need to get back to school, *now*." I practically jumped off the bed, sending files flying to the floor in my haste.

"Wait. Why?" Erik exclaimed, grabbing for my wrist before I made it very far.

"I think I know who the spy is," I said.

"Who?"

In light of our discussion, I'd thrown up my walls and was using all my remaining strength to keep them firmly in place. I hated how vulnerable I'd become. I'd let my guard down too much around him, and apparently around at least one other person. He'd been in my head more than I'd realized, and while I trusted him, my complacency had exposed me to others. I felt violated and dirty just thinking about it. Now I knew how other people felt when I delved into their heads.

I turned to meet his earnest, terrified expression, and I debated telling him the truth.

"Tal, don't shut me out," he urged. "I'm sorry. I don't mean to be intrusive. I promise I'll stop if you want."

"I – I – I just need to go," I stammered, yanking my wrist free from his grasp and running for the door.

"Natalia, stop!" Erik bellowed. The force of his command froze my feet mid-step. Erik quickly caught up with me. "Tal," he began in a much gentler and less controlling tone. "It's just that –"

"Please don't say it," I said quietly, averting my eyes. I knew what he was going to say, and while part of me wanted to hear those three words leave his lips, I wasn't ready.

Erik's face fell and he swallowed thickly. I'd hurt his feelings, wounded his pride. I felt horrible. But once he saw what I'd just read, he'd understand. At least, I hoped that he would.

With trembling fingers, I slowly handed the incriminating report to Erik. He hastily flipped through the pages, skimming the contents as he went. His body went rigid, his fingers tearing holes in the paper when he came to the same realization that I had.

"I can't believe this. Do you think that it might be a mistake?" he asked in a low, threatening voice. I was reminded of how deadly he could be when provoked.

"Maybe, but it's more than a little suspect, don't you think?"

Erik didn't answer. Instead, he grabbed my hand and started dragging me toward the elevator. His fingers gripped mine hard enough to turn them purple. Waves of fury rolled off of him, and the air around his body seemed to vibrate. If I hadn't been so numb, I might've tried to calm him. As it was, that task would be impossible. The shock over my find was quickly turning to rage.

At the hover hangar, Erik barked orders at the attendant, and in record time we were taxiing along the short runway. Erik's hands gripped the wheel until his knuckles turned white and blue veins bulged against the backs. When I touched his arm, I could practically taste his desire for blood.

Neither of us spoke on the ride. As angry as I was, I actually had more pressing issues to worry about. It was now midafternoon and I had yet to take my medication. The trembling in my hands had spread to my arms and legs, and I wasn't sure how much longer I could fend off a seizure. A cold sweat was starting around my hairline, and soon my entire body would be damp and sticky. We'd left Erik's room in such a hurry, I hadn't even thought to grab the bag with my shot.

As if noticing how bad my condition had become, Erik's head snapped to face me. The fire in his eyes dimmed before giving way to panic. He took one of my clammy hands and squeezed it reassuringly.

"We're almost there," he promised.

"I know."

Erik shot me one more scared look and stomped on the accelerator. "I will kill that traitorous bitch," he mumbled under his breath.

Chapter Thirty-Two

"Go find Mac and tell him to meet me down there," I ordered Erik as soon as we landed.

"What? No, I'm going with you," he replied.

"I'm not arguing about this. Please just trust me, and go."

The anger and resentment had built to a crescendo on the ride, and it was invigorating my senses. I put the full force of my Talents behind my words, leaving Erik unable to protest.

"Be careful," he cautioned. He leaned down and gave me a quick kiss on the cheek before sprinting to the administrative building.

Once I was certain that he wouldn't veer off course, I set out for the Crypto Bank. I knew that Erik was indignant on my behalf. He felt my pain and fear, and had experienced one of my seizures first-hand. He'd been inside my head and knew what I went through with every episode. As angry as I was, I had so many questions; if Erik got there first, he wouldn't afford her the opportunity to answer.

I jogged across campus, and every thump of my sole against the soft grass amplified the rage building inside of me. My hands shook when I grabbed the door to the Crypto facility, but now the tremors were driven by anger, not my illness. I covered the length of the long hallway that led to the main Crypto Bank in record time. The doors slid forcibly apart with a loud, echoing bang as I neared.

"Talia!" Penny exclaimed in surprise when I burst through the opening.

Gemma's bushy head snapped around to catch sight of me.

"Get out," I barked at her. At first, she was too shocked by my violent entrance to move. "I said get out!" I screamed. Tripping over her feet as though they were too big, Gemma finally clambered from her computer chair. She shot me one last terrified glance over her shoulder before exiting.

"Talia, what's going on?" Penny asked in a low, even voice. It was the same voice that I used when I was trying to take control of someone; the same voice that Erik had used with the Crypto boy earlier that day. The voice she'd probably used on me a hundred times before.

Erik wasn't the only person who'd convinced me to divulge things. He wasn't the only one who'd always seemed to know what I was thinking and feeling. I recalled all of the conversations where I'd been so intent on keeping my thoughts bottled up inside, only to find the words tumbling from my mouth, and I hated her more.

I'd wanted to tell Penny everything and had felt so comfortable around her. She'd made me feel safe and happy when no one else could. Being around her had given me the same comfortable peace that Erik gave me. Now I knew why.

How could I have been so stupid? How could I have trusted her? Every time I'd even thought about reading her mind, I'd instantly dismissed the idea – it was too intrusive, and she was supposed to be my friend. Why hadn't I ever wondered why she was the only person who never projected even a single thought in my direction? No one was that good at blocking me.

"Don't you dare!" I shrieked at my supposed best friend. "Don't you dare use my abilities against me!"

Penny shrank back, wilting like a flower in mid-summer heat. Understanding sparked in her bright eyes.

"How could you?" I hissed.

"Tal, please," she begged. "You don't understand. You weren't supposed to get hurt. It wasn't supposed to happen that way, I swear. Just calm down and let me explain."

Tears illuminated her lime-colored eyes and began falling down her deathly pale face, landing in fat splotches on the tiled floor. If it had been anyone else, I would've attacked right then. But she wasn't just anyone; Penny was my best friend, my confidante. *She is also a traitor*, I had to remind myself. She was the reason that I was sick. She was the reason that I'd nearly died at the hands of my parents' killer.

Pain and rage swirled inside of me, and I flashed to a similar scene between myself and Donavon – windows shattering, shards of glass flying. Then Mac's words played in my head: *Sometimes, the people closest to us are the best at deceiving us. You of all people should know that.*

"Tal, let me explain. You have to let me explain," Penny wailed.

The glass breaking wasn't only in my memory. The wall next to us exploded, bits of hard plastic spewing across the room. Computer monitors splintered, and electrical fires sparked from the screens. Penny covered her head, screaming.

"Explain what?" I spat. "How you sold me out to Ian Crane? How you set me up to be tortured and killed? How you betrayed the person who was supposed to be your *best friend*?"

"No, no," she sobbed. "He wasn't going to kill you. He just wanted to talk to you. He wanted you to understand what TOXIC is really about – what they do to people, what they've done to you."

Her words seemed to hurtle through the air and assault my ears. They were similar to the ones that Crane himself had spoken in Nevada – words that sliced through skin and bone to hit a nerve. As my fury dimmed, spasms shot through my arms and legs, nearly crippling me. I briefly entertained the notion that I'd been struck by one of the sparks from the monitors. Then I realized that it was a seizure. *No, no, no,* I thought. *I need to stay conscious.* I grasped for my fury from just moments before. It was the only thing holding me together. It wasn't hard to catch. The mental and physical anguish that I'd experienced over the past couple of months were fresh in my mind.

My temper flared as Penny's tears continued to fall. They were like gasoline fueling the fire until it blazed like an inferno.

I bared my teeth. The sharp points of my canines pricked my lower lip, and I tasted blood. I wanted Penny's blood. I wanted her to hurt to pay for all that she'd cost me. My fingers curled into claws, the nail beds seeming to elongate. The transformation sent a trickle of fear through me, but the brief flare of panic was quickly doused by my escalating rage.

Alarm bells screeched overhead, and I knew that Erik and Mac would be here shortly.

"TOXIC gives special children a place to feel normal," I hissed, making my way forward. My voice came out in a growl that was unrecognizable to me. It sounded primal, ferocious.

"No, they don't," Penny moaned as I closed in on her. "And I think that deep down, you know that."

"What I know is that you are a traitor. You cheated on your placement exams. You befriended me. You made sure that the intel about Crane's visit to Nevada would be intercepted. You knew that Mac would send me there for my solo mission because of my past with Crane. You knew that he'd need a Manipulator to get onto the compound. Then, under the pretense of being my friend, you helped me gather intel so that you would know exactly what I was planning to do once I got there. Crane knew who I was that night in the pub because you told him what I looked like. You told him that I'd be there." I stopped my rant when I felt a tug on my psyche. "Stay out of my head!"

"I'm n-n-not in your head," Penny stammered. "Please, listen to me. You need to get away from here. You need to find Ian. You aren't safe. He did know who you were that night in the pub, but not because I told him."

"Tals, are you okay? We're coming." It was Erik forcing his way into my head. He was somewhere close by. I could feel him.

Heavy footsteps thundered overhead, cutting through the wailing alarm as they trampled down the corridor to the destroyed room. Penny and I now stood inches apart. I was close enough to hit her, but I didn't. I couldn't.

Penny didn't take her focus off me. I wasn't sure if it was because she couldn't hear the approaching men over the alarm, or because she just didn't care.

"What did Crane inject me with?" I hissed.

"I don't know," she cried, reaching tentatively for me. I snatched my arm away from her grasping fingers. Now that we were so close, I didn't want to touch her. I didn't even want to be in the same room with her anymore. I might have left then – Erik and Mac were nearly there –but I needed to know one more thing.

"How does he know my father?" I didn't mean to phrase it that way; I'd meant to ask her *if* he knew my father. But sometime between Nevada and now, I'd come to believe that he did. The only question left was how.

Penny glanced nervously toward the open door. She could hear the men coming for her. She was scared, but not for herself. Her concern was for me.

"Talia, listen to me. Look inside of yourself, all of the answers are there. You just need to be willing to accept the truth."

I didn't get a chance to ask her what that meant. A team of Operatives, led by Mac and Erik, stormed into the ruins. Mac and another man seized Penny, forcing her to the floor. Erik pulled me out of the way.

"You can't trust him. You can't trust any of these people," she screamed in my head. *"Please just listen to me. Find Ian. I promise, I've always been your friend even before we met in Hunters Village."*

I shook my head, trying to clear Penny's voice as it forced its way in. All of her mental barricades were down, and the rush of thoughts and images was suffocating. It suddenly became hard to breathe, like her memories were physically crushing my lungs. The weight of her mind caused my knees to buckle, and I fell to the ground. Broken glass tore through my jeans and ripped my flesh. The pain brought the room back into focus, but I couldn't hold on to it.

Erik's arms encircled me from behind, cradling me to his chest. The room no longer existed. All I saw were Penny's memories dancing like clouds through my head.

"Force her out," Erik whispered in my ear.

The sound of his voice helped me summon the strength to do just that. I pushed against her mind until the weight of her consciousness lifted, the effort causing me to collapse into Erik's arms. A low keening started in my throat and built to a blood-curdling scream that tore my vocal chords as I processed what I'd just seen. Erik tried to calm me, but I was past the point of reason.

Mac and his men were dragging a struggling Penny to her feet. Every Operative not actively trying to contain her had his weapon trained on Penny. Her hair was quickly turning dark red from a wound on her scalp. Her cheek was already swelling from where one of the men had slammed her into the floor. When she opened her mouth to speak, Mac's elbow connected with her temple.

I watched, horrified as she slumped against one of the men holding her. I wanted to cry out, tell them to stop. But I couldn't. What had I expected to happen when I sent Erik for Mac? Had I thought that he would politely ask her to accompany him to interrogation? If he wasn't so concerned about me, Erik's hands would be around her throat, choking the life from her.

"Everything is okay now," Erik soothed, running a hand over my hair. He was still attempting to calm me, but his words had no effect. They weren't true. Everything was not okay. Everything would never be okay.

The horrible sound coming from my mouth died off as the

Operatives carried a now-unconscious Penny up the hallway. I watched their retreat until my vision blurred and the angry black dots connected. Then I passed out.

Chapter Thirty-Three

Calloused fingers tickled my arm. The sensation was pleasant, and I didn't want it to stop. I felt a slight tug on my head while someone played with my curls. I smiled. Erik must be impatient, waiting for me to wake up so that we could go have breakfast. I turned into him, reaching for his warm body. A sharp stinging sensation shot up my arm when the back of my hand made contact with cold metal. My eyes shot open, and clear blue irises fluttered into focus. Not Erik. Donavon. Antiseptic filled my nostrils, but when I tried to wrinkle my nose, I found that I couldn't. Something was in it. Frantically, I clawed at the plastic tubing.

"Easy, Talia," Donavon whispered.

"Am I in Medical?" I asked drowsily.

"You are. You have been for a couple of days now," he answered, still stroking my arm.

"A couple of days? Why does this keep happening?" I moaned.

Donavon chuckled softly. "Dr. Thistler said that the overload of emotions, coupled with the fact you hadn't taken your medicine, sent you over the edge."

"Overload of emotions? But we just kissed," I said, confused. I thought back to the night on the ledge. Erik was right; he did overstimulate me. I smiled at the thought. Erik was going to have to learn patience. Where *was* Erik? I frowned. If he was the reason that I was now in a hospital bed, hooked up to an IV and a breathing machine, the least he could do was sit by my sickbed. A serious talk about his priorities was in our future.

"Kissed?" Donavon asked, looking confused now.

"Where's Erik?" I demanded.

Hurt clouded Donavon's clear eyes. His jaw hardened and his lips pursed into a thin, angry line at the mention of the boy who he considered his rival.

"We're on lockdown. Dad sent him back to Headquarters until further notice."

Wasn't I at Headquarters? Then I remembered Donavon saying something about Dr. Thistler; if she was treating me, then I was probably at school.

"What is the last thing you remember?" Donavon asked, speaking slowly, enunciating every word.

I had to think. I remembered being in Erik's room at Headquarters. We were lying in his bed, kissing. There was paper everywhere. Then I remember standing in the doorway to his room. He was about to tell me that he loved me, but I'd stopped him. Why had I stopped him? What could've been more important than hearing those words come from Erik's lips? Penny......

"Oh, my God," I gasped, trying to sit up. The machine next to my bed emitted a long, alarming screech. The beeps on the heart monitor stopped being individually distinguishable. Every excruciating detail came rushing back.

"No, no," I moaned, the all-too-familiar tears stinging the backs of my eyes.

"Shhh. Just relax. She's where she belongs," Donavon said, wiping at the tears with his rough fingers.

"How could she be a spy?" I wailed.

Donavon didn't get the opportunity to answer as Medics rushed into the room, responding to my out-of-control vitals. The first one through the door shoved Donavon aside. The Medic reached for my IV and plunged a syringe full of yellowish liquid into the port. The medicine quickly reached my bloodstream, and my flailing limbs stilled, now heavy with the chemicals. Suddenly, moving required too much effort. I sought out Donavon, now standing against the far wall. He smiled and nodded reassuringly.

Once my vitals returned to acceptable levels, the Medics retreated just as quickly as they'd come. Donavon moved back to my side.

"Why don't you try to sleep?" he suggested gently.

I shook my head vehemently, fighting the drowsiness. "I don't want to. No more sleep," I slurred. It was a losing battle.

"It's better this way," Donavon whispered, stroking my cheek.

Out of the corner of my eye, I noticed the two scars on his palm. "Sorry I bit you," I mumbled.

"It's okay, I deserved it," came his quiet reply.

Then I lost consciousness again.

I spent another week in Medical. Most of my time there was spent in a drug-induced slumber, under Mac's orders; he thought it best that I recover my strength without unnecessary distractions. He didn't allow me many visitors, and I felt like I was back in my bedroom at his house, cut off from the outside world.

Donavon came every day. By unspoken agreement, we didn't discuss our fight further and put our mutual, lingering animosity aside. He sat with me while I slept. Even though I was barely conscious, I always felt his presence, and I actually welcomed it. In one of my more lucid moments, he told me that he'd talked to Erik and let him know that I was okay. He passed on Erik's sentiments of concern, despite the fact it obviously pained him to do so. I regretted that I'd been too chicken to just tell Donavon the truth from the beginning that we would never get back together. I wanted to call Erik myself, but Mac wouldn't approve it. He said that once that I was feeling better he'd reconsider.

Mac came every day, too. He congratulated me on uncovering the spy. He informed me that TOXIC had launched a full-scale investigation to determine how deeply the Coalition had penetrated. So far, Penny hadn't cracked under psychic interrogation, but he assured me that it was just a matter of time. Mac had the good grace to refrain from suggesting that I question her myself, and I was glad. The thought of being in the same room with her caused my blood to boil and my heart monitor to spike.

Gretchen came to visit several times as well. She didn't say much. Mostly she just sat with me, but I appreciated her company when I registered it. She was the least stressful visitor that I could 've asked for. When we did talk, she never mentioned Penny. Instead, she teased me about my relationship with Erik. If it had been anyone else, I probably would have thought she was being nosey, but I knew that she was just trying to improve my mood. She'd always hoped that I would marry her son, but really, she just wanted me to be happy.

Dr. Wythe made a couple of very unwelcome visits. He asked probing questions that I didn't feel like answering. I usually fell asleep midway through our sessions, and when I woke, he was gone. I knew that I wouldn't be able to avoid him forever, but the drugs at least helped to prolong the inevitable.

Donavon snuck Kenly in towards the end of my stay in Medical. She rambled on about all the training she'd been doing in my absence, and assured me that Donavon was a suitable substitute until I was back on my feet. Despite the progress that Donavon insisted she was making, I knew in my heart that she would never be ready in time. Her crowning achievement – preventing me from breaking my leg – hadn't been hers at all. I now knew that it had been Penny who kept me from falling. I enjoyed Kenly's visit, but she reminded me too much of my ex-best friend; I asked Donavon not to bring her again.

When the trifecta of Mac, Dr. Thistler, and Dr. Wythe were finally convinced that I could function without the help of drugs or machines, they agreed to let me move back to Mac's house. It wasn't my first choice, but it was certainly better than the hospital. Dr. Thistler insisted that I be under constant supervision, so returning to Instructor housing was out. In the aftermath of what happened with Penny, I was still in no condition to go before the Placement Committee, so returning to the Hunters was not in my immediate future either.

As soon as I was settled in my old bedroom, I begged Mac to let me call Erik; I needed to hear his voice. I wanted to tell him about the accusations that Penny made before he and Mac had barged in – the accusations that nearly mirrored Crane's. But I knew that I couldn't. All of my communications were being monitored and recorded, and I had no intention of making the statements part of the official report. If I'd thought that Mac had me on a short leash before, now I would be nearly tethered to his side.

Surprisingly, Mac agreed to grant me phone privileges, on the condition that I use his communicator. I didn't see the point, but my own had been confiscated – ostensibly to review all the messages that I'd ever exchanged with Penny. Mac assured me that it wasn't because I was under any kind of suspicion; it was, after all, protocol.

"Hello? Tal?" Erik's relieved voice came through the communicator.

Tears welled up in my eyes when his tiny holographic image appeared. I couldn't speak. I didn't even know what to say.

"How are you feeling? The Director won't let me come see you. We're on lockdown here until after the sentencing. They even recalled all the Hunters out on missions."

"I'm okay," I sniffed. "I wish you were here."

The words that Penny had spoken before the cavalry arrived were still ingrained in my mind, but the images she'd projected were fading. They were becoming dim watercolors of the originals, and I wanted to tell Erik about them before they were completely erased from my memory. Somehow, it was just like the way that I couldn't clearly recall what had happened after the bullet struck me in Nevada.

"I know, Tal," he soothed. "I wish I was there, too. I wish that I could hold you."

"I wish that you could do more than hold me," I said.

"Why, Talia Lyons, are you trying to have phone sex with me? And on the Director's communicator, no less. You should be ashamed of yourself," he teased. "Some Brain is going to appreciate an earful of very graphic details, if that's the case."

I gave a thin laugh. Only Erik would say something so ridiculous right then.

"That's not what I meant, and you know it," I chastised. "I wish that you could take the pain away." Right now, I didn't care how weak needing him made me. I liked the numb detachment that the drugs provided me, and I knew that Erik could give me the same feeling without the side effects.

"If I was there with you in that big bed, there wouldn't be any pain. Just never-ending pleasure," he said suggestively.

"How did you know that I was in a big bed?"

"I've got a good imagination. Want to know what you're wearing?"

I laughed again. I was pretty sure that whatever Erik's overactive libido pictured me wearing would give the listening ears way too much good gossip for the rumor mill.

"Thanks, Erik," I said softly.

"For what? Making you blush?"

"No. For being you." Though I was indeed blushing.

"As soon as the sentencing is over, I'll be there. The Captain and Henri have agreed to grant me some leave to stay with you. Even the Director said that it would be okay," he promised.

I was shocked. Mac had agreed to that? He must figure that the best way to keep an eye on us would be if we were under his own roof. I almost couldn't say that I blamed him after the way our earlier conversation had gone.

"What do you think will happen at the trial?" I asked, abruptly taking the conversation in a sharp turn toward serious.

Erik didn't answer right away. I could tell that he was measuring his words carefully, trying to find the best way to tell me what I already knew.

"Well, um......" he cleared his throat loudly. "There probably won't be a trial. People accused of treason don't usually get trials. And they'll have at least some of the security footage from the ...confrontation. They know that she basically admitted to being a spy."

"I see. Will I have to go?" I really didn't want to be there.

"Probably. She'll also be charged with conspiracy to commit murder."

Oh, right, my murder.

"I've already asked for permission to go to the sentencing with you. Henri doesn't think that the Director will grant it, but I'm trying."

"Thanks," I said, tears filling my eyes again. Dr. Thistler had ordered extra doses of my medication to dull the out-of-control rage that I'd been experiencing, but it actually left me more emotional than ever. I kept crying for no reason. At least that's what the doctors and Mac told me. Secretly, I thought that without my anger, I was left with only the wounded feelings of betrayal and the loss of someone that I'd considered my best friend.

Neither of us spoke for several long moments, but I didn't want to get off the phone with him yet. Just hearing his voice made me feel so much better.

"So ...about that phone sex. I'm thinking that you're wearing something see-through. Purple, of course. Lacy, definitely lacy," he said thoughtfully.

I choked on the mixture of my laughter and tears.

"I love you, Erik," I whispered. "You don't have to say it, too," I hurried on, not giving him the chance to reply. "I know you were about to before, but I just wanted to tell you now, like this. I wanted you to know that it's for real, and not because of anything that either one of us makes the other one say or do."

343

"I love you, Natalia," he said in a confident tone. Then he laughed softly. "Man, I've never said that before. To anyone. Feels kinda weird. Weird in a good way," he assured me.

"I'll see you soon," I said tiredly. I wasn't ready to say goodbye, but my eyes were starting to close.

"Call me whenever the Director lets you. I'm doing everything that I can to be there ...at the sentencing. Either way, I'll be there before you know it."

"Okay. I'll do everything I can to convince Gretchen that I need something purple, see-through, and lacy," I said.

"Don't make promises that you can't keep," he playfully warned.

"I never do," I mumbled, my exhausted body sinking deeper into the soft inviting mattress. After a week in the hospital, my old bed felt like heaven.

"Bye, Tals. I love you."

"I love you, too."

Mac let me sleep late the next day before impatiently barging into my bedroom without knocking, Janet in tow.

"Morning, Mac," I greeted him sluggishly. I was still exhausted, and so not ready for his company. "Hey, Janet," I greeted her more warmly.

"It's afternoon, Natalia. And I need you to give an official statement now. We really cannot put this off any longer. The sentencing is in a couple of days, and the Judge will need it. It's protocol," Mac insisted. I hated protocol.

"And you didn't think that bribing me with breakfast might get me to talk faster?" I said sarcastically.

"I shouldn't have to bribe you. It is your duty as a TOXIC Operative to give a report when you are involved in an incident. Under the circumstances, I have let it go for longer than normal, but it cannot wait any longer." Mac was definitely short on patience this morning, and I didn't blame him. The whole ordeal had been a nightmare for both of us. He'd been making daily visits to Tramblewood to question Penny, but always made sure to return at a decent hour so that he could see me while I was awake. I was sure that he wanted the incident behind him almost as much as I did.

"Fine. Where do you want me to start?" I replied shortly.

"At the beginning, please. Mr. Kelley was interrogated before he flew back to Headquarters, but I would like to hear your version of how you breached protocol and forced a Crypto to access classified information instead of asking me." Mac's tone was pure disapproval.

"Erik's not in trouble, is he?" I demanded. I felt horrible; if he were, it would be my fault. Sanctions usually accompanied breaches of protocol. Crap, I *really* hated protocol.

"No. Under the circumstances, I have excused Mr. Kelley's behavior. He's promised to exercise better judgment in the future."

"Thanks, Mac," I sighed. "I really appreciate it."

"You can thank me by abiding by the rules set in place." Mac rolled his eyes in a rare show of normalcy. He never did something so human. The gesture told me that he knew the chances of getting me to follow TOXIC protocol in the future were slim. While I hated that people begrudged me his special treatment, I rarely let that stop me from taking advantage of it.

"Why don't you start with how you discovered that Ms. Latimore may have cheated on her Placement Exams?" Janet suggested gently, getting us back on track.

So, I started at the beginning. Mac already had the tapes of my interrogation sessions with Cal and Jennifer, so I only reiterated the finer points. I glossed over what I'd learned from Grace and Rider. I explained how after questioning the four other Cryptos, I'd become convinced that Penny also must have known that there was something wrong with the encryption; I just hadn't been able to figure out why she didn't tell me.

All of the others had given assorted reasons for the omission, but none were applicable to Penny, particularly since it was my mission. I considered that maybe she hadn't really known, but I didn't see how that could be true ...unless she wasn't an Elite-level Higher Reasoning Talent.

I recounted Erik's explanation of how the Placement Exams essentially worked. I told Mac and Janet that I hadn't realized that the Manipulator on my panel was actually a Mimic. I recounted how I hadn't known what Erik's Talent was because I'd never met someone like him, or at least I thought I hadn't.

Mac actually smiled at that. He'd hand selected Erik for my trials as a true test of my fighting abilities since he had known that I wouldn't be able to control him the way that I had the others. At the time, I'd thought it was a dirty trick, but now I was glad that he had; it was my fight against Erik that had guaranteed my spot with the Hunters. Plus without it, I might never have met Erik.

Next, I explained how, if I'd been unaware that Erik and the panel member were Mimics, it might be possible that I had encountered others as well. At that point, I still hadn't made the leap to Penny being one, but I was suspicious enough to want a look at her Placement Exam results. I wanted to look at the others' records, too, just in case.

Initially, I'd thought that I was wrong when I looked at Penny's results; everything seemed on the level. Both her written exam and her physical demonstration indicated that she was exactly what she purported to be – an Elite-level Higher Reasoning Talent. Despite that, the whole Mimic thing still nagged at me. I went back further and reviewed all the suspects' intake evaluations. That was where I finally found the missing piece.

When TOXIC first found Penny, she was at Mrs. Gubbard's Home for Orphaned Children, and she wasn't the only Talented child there. Two other kids were collected at the same time – an eight-year old Light Manipulator boy, and a ten-year old Higher Reasoning girl. The Operatives who had collected Penny wrote down on her intake form that she was a Light Manipulator, but once Penny arrived at school and was formally tested, she was declared a Higher Reasoning Talent. At first, I dismissed the original evaluation as a clerical error. Then I remembered when we'd been in the city for Festivis someone had made Ursula's chair disappear. I'd thought that it was Cadence, but that didn't really make sense since she was the only one there besides Erik who was really friends with the girl. I'd dismissed it, thinking that maybe Cadence had a devious side, but the fact that Penny had originally been classified as a Light Manipulator made me wonder if it hadn't been her. I didn't understand how Penny could be a Light Manipulator ...unless she were a dual Talent. That theory didn't feel right either, though, because there was no reason for her to hide being a dual Talent.

I explained that Erik's imitation of my abilities and the whole Light Manipulator mistake on Penny's intake form made me review all of the interactions I'd had with her since we'd met. I described how I always felt safe around her and had told her things that I wouldn't otherwise talk about; how I'd never read her mind because every time I considered doing so something stopped me; how Erik told me that he had used my Talents on me and I didn't know it. I thought maybe that was what Penny had been doing to keep me from reading her mind. And if that were the case, it left only one option: Penny was a Mimic.

I shifted my position in the bed and took a deep breath before launching into an abridged version of how Erik frequently mimics my gifts and uses them on me. Mac and Janet exchanged knowing glances.

"He doesn't do it to get me to talk about, like ...confidential things," I said defensively. The last thing I wanted was for Erik to come under investigation.

"I think we all know exactly what Mr. Kelley uses your manipulation for," Mac assured me dryly. Janet gave me a sympathetic look.

"Right," I stammered as heat rushed my cheeks.

The way he said it left me no doubt that he'd been privy to my personal conversation with Erik. I obviously knew that he would be; I just didn't think he'd be so bold as to mention it. I should've known better.

I hurriedly started recounting how I'd realized that the chair incident at Festivis wasn't the only time that Penny had mimicked someone else's Talents in front of me. I told them about the water glass she'd caught at Captain Alvarez's dinner, and how she'd saved me from a broken leg when I'd tripped over the baton. These incidents further solidified my belief that she was a Mimic.

"When I confronted her in the Crypto Bank, she admitted that she was the reason that Crane knew I was coming," I finished.

"Did she say anything else?" Janet asked. "We weren't able to salvage any of the security footage."

I looked guiltily at Mac. He'd said that I wasn't in trouble for breaching protocol, but he hadn't mentioned the destruction of property ...millions of dollars' worth of property.

"It's been taken care of," he assured me, answering my unspoken question.

I relaxed.

"No, Janet. She just kept saying that TOXIC was bad, that's all," I lied easily.

Mac looked unconvinced, but he didn't press the issue.

"I still don't understand exactly how the low-level encryption plays into everything," I said. "Did she plant it?"

"Not exactly. The intel did originate from the Coalition, but the encoding was purposely crude so we'd be sure to decipher it. As far as I can glean, she arranged to have the communication sent when she would be working, so that her team would handle all of the intel for the mission. She knew that you still hadn't been assigned your solo Hunt and banked on my sending you because of your specific Talents," Mac explained.

"But how did she know that the others wouldn't say anything about the encryption?"

"She could not have known for sure. I am assuming after

spending so much time with Mr. Simmons, she knew how ambitious he was. Likewise she knew how weak Ms. Eisenhower was. As for the verification team, I can only assume that she got lucky. Of course, she was in classes with Ms. Howard, and as a Mimic, she might have realized how low level the girl's abilities really are." Mac gave me a pointed look. Apparently he'd figured that detail out on his own; so much for my promise to aid true love.

"There is nothing to indicate that she knew Ms. Howard and Mr. Trindel would be working that evening, but she may have. It would not have been hard to know ahead of time which Crypto units would be on duty at School. Honestly though, Natalia, I may have done a few things differently, but I still would've sent you for him. The intel would have been scrutinized more closely and I would have sent an entire team, but TOXIC had not had an opportunity to go after Ian Crane like that in years. I would not have let the opportunity pass."

"I see," I said. "What's going to happen to her?"

Erik had already told me, but Mac's confirmation would make it real.

"She will be executed," Mac said bluntly.

Apparently, he didn't share Erik's affinity for sparing my feelings. Then again, Mac probably didn't think that I should care about her impending demise; he probably thought that I should be advocating performing the deed myself.

"Right, of course. I figured," I replied quietly. I bit my lip to keep the tears at bay. I didn't want them to see me cry for Penny. Neither of them would understand.

"You will need to be at the sentencing. Technically, you are her accuser, and it is protocol for the accuser to be present," he continued.

Man, I *really, really* hated protocol.

"What about Erik? Are you going to let him be there as well?" I asked, practically begging Mac to do so.

Mac studied me for several long moments before answering.

"No, Natalia, I'm not. You may see him once all this unpleasant business is behind us."

I nodded, the urge to cry becoming harder to suppress. How was I going to face her without him by my side?

"However, you may continue to speak with him on my communicator. And I do intend to grant his leave request so that he may come and stay here with you. There is one condition for that, though." Mac paused, and I held my breath. I could usually handle conditions, and I'd do just about anything he asked if it meant that I could see Erik.

"Sure. Anything." I smiled tightly.

"While the Cryptos might appreciate hearing about your and Mr. Kelley's private affairs, I do not. In the future, it would be much appreciated if you kept your conversations less ...explicit."

The color returned to my face, the fire under my skin so intense that I thought spontaneous combustion a real possibility. Thankfully, Mac didn't wait for my reply. He turned and motioned to Janet, and they left me alone with my humiliation.

Chapter Thirty-Four

Erik and I spoke frequently in the ensuing days. We kept our conversation light and trivial, neither of us mentioning Penny, the sentencing, or the inevitable execution. Despite Mac's warning, Erik continued to make sexual innuendos in an attempt to keep me laughing. I longed for him. As much as I dreaded facing Penny in court, the day couldn't come soon enough; once it was done, I would finally see Erik.

Donavon kept me company in my room most days. We talked and joked about people we had both come to know over the past few months at school. We mostly watched movies on my wall screen, but on my more adventurous days we walked around the campus grounds. He'd taken over training Kenly since I had neither the energy nor the desire to finish what I'd started. I observed their practice sessions, but usually grew tired midway through and returned to my room before they finished.

My relationship with Donavon would never be like it had been before. I knew that whether I had Erik or not, I'd never love Donavon that way again. He'd hurt me so much when he cheated on me, but it was more than that. I still gravitated to him because he always comforted me and made me feel safe, without the complication of romantic feelings. I was close to getting past his indiscretion; after what Penny had done, Donavon's infidelity paled in comparison.

We never talked about Erik. He didn't ask, and I didn't offer. I figured that he preferred not knowing any details. However, every night when I talked to Erik, I told him about the time I spent with Donavon. After all of the lying and deception in my life over the past two years, I needed to have someone who I could be completely honest with.

Erik didn't try to hide his jealousy. He gently let me know exactly what he thought about my spending so much time with Donavon, but he never asked me to stop. He said that he understood why I couldn't write him out of my life completely. Erik might not like the friendship, but he tried to be the bigger person. Despite that, I had a sneaking suspicion that Erik wouldn't hesitate to flaunt our relationship in front of Donavon the first chance he got.

Dr. Wythe came to see me every morning. Our sessions were as taxing and pointless as they'd been the last time he'd treated me. Sometimes I felt as though we were having a staring contest, each of not wanting to be the first to blink. Other times he practically interrogated me about what happened in the Crypto Bank. Even if I wanted to tell him the truth – which I didn't – the memories had become like dreams, distorted and nonsensical. I could no longer recall the exact details.

Early on the morning of Penny's sentencing, I was restless and agitated. Today was the day that I would stand beside Mac while Penny's charges were read in open court. The Judge would pretend to deliberate before delivering the punishment. Today was the day that I'd watch my ex-best friend condemned to die. Despite the fact that the sun had yet to rise, I called Erik.

"How ya holding up?" Erik's tiny holographic form asked.

"Not so good," I admitted. It was the first time that we'd talked about her since Mac had given me permission to call him.

"I wish that I could be there," he said sleepily.

I envisioned Erik clad only in pajama bottoms, snuggled under his plaid comforter, his hair disheveled and eyelids heavy from sleep. I could almost feel his arms around me. When I inhaled, I swore that I could smell the woodsy musk and pine soap that was Erik's scent.

I sighed heavily. "Soon. Only a couple more hours until this is all over," I assured him.

"I know. Are you nervous about seeing her?"

I was nervous, but I wasn't sure if I should admit that on the record, so to speak. I found myself second-guessing everything that I said and did these days.

"Eh, not nervous. Angry mostly," I answered. Anger was a safe emotion. And I *was* angry - a little sad and very confused, but mostly angry. I wouldn't need to fake any outrage or resentment in court. "What are you going to do today?" I asked, changing the topic.

"Same thing I do every day. Sit around looking good," he joked.

I laughed. "Good luck with that."

We bantered back and forth for another few minutes before I reluctantly disconnected. I needed to get dressed unless I wanted Mac banging on my door demanding to know why I wasn't ready.

Perversely, sentencings were formal affairs. I would be expected to wear something decadent. I selected a long, black gown from the plethora of plastic-encased dresses that Gretchen had ordered for me over the years. The silk cascaded over my skin as I pulled it from the bag. The bodice had a lace overlay, square neckline, and capped sleeves. I laughed almost manically as I ran my fingers over the lace, recalling Erik's lingerie comment. The mounting anxiety over what was happening in a few short hours was making me crazy.

I took my time straightening my hair, and I dabbed small amounts of neutral-colored shadow on my eyelids. After I was satisfied that the evidence of my sleepless night was hidden beneath the makeup, I decided that my hair should go up. First I tried sweeping it into a ponytail. Too casual, I decided. Next, I braided my long tresses down my back. But that wasn't right either. Frustrated, I wound the pieces of now-wavy hair into a severe bun at the base of my skull. Finally gratified, I glanced at the clock.

Crap, ten minutes until departure. If I didn't hurry, Mac would come looking for me. I hastily stripped off my pajamas and zipped myself into the black dress. The material hung loosely on my too-thin frame. I stared at myself in the full-length mirror, and my stomach rolled in disgust. No matter how I felt about Penny and everything that she'd cost me, there was something inherently wrong with wearing a formal gown to watch another human being be condemned to death. *At least I am wearing black*, I thought to myself. It was somber, like my mood.

When I finally exited my bedroom and wound my way through the McDonoughs' house, I found Mac and, to my surprise, Donavon waiting for me in the foyer. Mac gave my outfit an approving once-over. Both father and son wore tailored black suits; Donavon had chosen a charcoal gray shirt and black tie to go with his, while Mac wore his customary white shirt and red tie.

"Ready, Natalia?" Mac asked, his voice lacking any emotion.

I nodded, unable to speak for fear of getting sick. Then I turned to Donavon and gave him a questioning look.

"Dad thought you might want a friend. I know you'd prefer that it was Erik......," he sent.

"I'm glad you're coming," I sent back. And I *was* glad. Donavon was no substitute for Erik, but at least I wouldn't be alone with his father. Mac wasn't exactly the touchy-feely type and provided little comfort; I expected that he would treat the entire event with the same cool indifference that he treated everything else unpleasant.

I followed the two men through the front door and into the waiting road vehicle. Silently praying that no one would try to engage me in conversation, I clasped my hands in my lap. At the hover hangar, we boarded a luxury craft with TOXIC's logo emblazoned on the side. I quietly took a seat in one of the four cushy armchairs. A stewardess instantly appeared and asked if she could bring me a drink. I started to shake my head no, then decided that I actually did want a drink – a strong one.

"Vodka," I said.

The stewardess nodded her bobbed auburn head. Mac arched his eyebrows in surprise.

"Really, Natalia? You aren't supposed to have alcohol, particularly not for breakfast," he said mildly.

"Today, I think that I'm entitled to it," I said to Mac. Then, turning to the stewardess, I repeated, "Vodka."

She glanced nervously between me and Mac. When the Director nodded his acquiescence, she finally left to fetch my drink. She returned moments later with my drink, and coffees for Mac and Donavon.

The clear liquid burned my mouth and throat when I sucked hungrily through the small cocktail straw. The instant that the vodka hit my empty stomach, it grumbled a protest. I didn't care. The alcohol would dull my emotions, and just then that was all that mattered.

During the half-hour ride to the city, I stared glumly out the window and continued to down drinks. I could feel Mac's disapproval, but it meant little to me. I hoped that if I drank enough on the flight I would be numb by the time we arrived. My plan worked. When we landed, my head was spinning from the three drinks that I'd managed to consume, and my insides felt hollow.

Mac held firmly to my upper arm, guiding me down the slippery metal steps and toward the waiting car. My mind buzzed and my legs wobbled from the combination of alcohol and anxiety. Mac helped me through the open door of a TOXIC road vehicle with darkly tinted windows. Donavon clambered in behind me. He reached for my hand, and I gave it willingly. He squeezed my fingers gently.

"Hang in there," he sent.

I didn't respond, just stared straight ahead.

Three armed bodyguards climbed into the row of seats behind Donavon and me while a fourth took the driver's seat. Mac sat shotgun. The vehicle started moving through empty city streets. Numbly, I watched the passing Government buildings, wondering where all the people were.

"The city is under Martial Law today. Citizens aren't allowed to leave their homes," Donavon answered my unspoken question.

I nodded that I understood.

Mac and the driver spoke in low tones, but I didn't pay attention. I didn't really care what they were talking about.

The driver turned on Fifth Street and continued to a building with "National Courthouse" engraved in a marble slab that hung atop magnificent marble columns. He brought the vehicle to a stop in front of the gleaming black steps. The bodyguards exited first. One held up a hand indicating that Donavon and I should wait. Their huge guns were drawn as they scanned the area surrounding the courthouse. I followed their line of sight and saw snipers perched on every building in view. I shuddered at the scene. Once the bodyguards were satisfied that there was no imminent threat, they motioned us out.

One offered me his gloved hand and helped me out of the car. He stayed firmly at my side while we ascended the stairs. A second guard fell in step, flanking my other side. Neither looked at me; instead, their eyes darted warily in every direction.

"What's going on? Why are they so vigilant?" I sent Donavon. Even through my alcohol-muddled brain, I felt disquieted and a little scared by all the security.

"Dad's afraid that the Coalition will strike today. Depending on how high Penny was in their organization, they might come for her."

Great - another encounter with Ian Crane. I really wished that Mac had warned me.

Once our group made it safely through the front doors, the

bodyguards relaxed slightly. Our footsteps echoed through the white marble corridor. The sterility of the hallway made my apprehension spike. The building held no warmth, and it was almost as if you could feel that bad things had happened here.

My right foot slipped, skidding briefly across the smooth floor, and I let out an involuntary yelp. The bodyguard on my right grabbed my arm to steady me. I smiled gratefully at him. His large, square jaw spread into a thin smile and he gave me a small nod. *Focus, Talia,* I ordered myself. *Just another hour, and this will all be over.*

At the end of the corridor were double wooden doors with armed men on either side. They pulled the gold handles as we neared, and I caught my first glimpse of the courtroom beyond. As my bodyguards dropped back, Donavon hurried forward and took my hand. Together we followed his father through the entryway.

A hundred or more faces turned in our direction when we entered. A black-robed woman sat elevated behind a beautiful lacquered bench. Her eyes were a cold, steely gray when they fixed on me. I swallowed thickly. One person sat on either side of her, their platforms slightly lower. The rows of benches in the gallery were already filled with high-ranking government officials dressed in opulent finery.

TOXIC hadn't publicly convicted a traitor in years. And the current of excitement that ran through the room was demonstrative of how much the practice had been missed. The occupants were like eager spectators at a highly anticipated sporting event, their eyes gleaming with eagerness that no one tried to hide. The charged atmosphere sent a wave of disgust rolling over me. I hated how much pleasure they were getting from the pain of others.

I stopped and met their gazes head-on, refusing to show how intimidated I was. In truth, the courtroom terrified me; now that I was here, I wanted nothing more than to leave. I didn't want to see Penny. I didn't want to hear the charges against her, didn't want to remember everything that she'd put me through. The alcohol was wearing off; a potent cocktail of fear, trepidation, and rage was taking its place.

Donavon tugged on my hand, urging me to walk forward. When I still didn't move, Mac placed his hand on the small of my back and forced me down the aisle. The only empty seats were in the first row. Every eye in the room followed my movements, and their thoughts buzzed angrily in my head. Most held looks of open curiosity. A few seemed to pity me. I blocked them all out, and took my seat between Mac and Donavon.

The murmurs that had quieted when we entered started up again once we were seated. In a rare show of emotion, Mac wrapped his arm protectively around my shoulders. I gave him a weak smile, a gesture that he surprisingly returned. Donavon held tightly to my hand as much for my benefit as for his; he seemed no more eager than I was to watch the impending charade.

The dull hum in the room swelled to a near roar, and I craned my neck to see what all the commotion was about. My heart skipped a beat when I saw her. Sorrow and rage warred for control of my emotions. Mac "tsked" in disgust when he, too, caught sight of Penny.

"It will all be over soon," Donavon sent.

"I know."

I couldn't tear my gaze away from where she stood at the start of the aisle. She was flanked by four impossibly large guards. Their guns were all pointed at her as if she might make a run for it at any moment. Penny's flame-colored hair hung limp and dirty down the back of a bluish-gray jumpsuit. The material looked rough and uncomfortable, and swallowed her gangly frame. Both her wrists and ankles were shackled. I watched with a mixture of wide-eyed fascination and repulsion as she shuffled to the front of the courtroom.

The gazes in the room were split between Penny and me. I kept my expression neutral; I knew that showing empathy for a traitor would be as good as signing my own death warrant. While

I'd been the one to discover her treachery, I'd still been her best friend. If it weren't for Mac, I would have spent the days following her arrest in an interrogation room instead of the hospital. Not everyone believed that I'd been naïve enough to not know what she was the whole time.

As she neared my row, I noticed that her limey-green eyes were hard, defiant. They held no trace of the weakness she'd displayed in the Crypto Bank when she'd begged me to understand. Despite everything, it warmed my heart to see her this way. I wanted to hate her lack of remorse. I wanted to begrudge her the self-assurance that she showed, particularly since I felt none. But I couldn't. I only felt sad for her, for me, and for everyone whose lives she had ruined.

Penny's movements were slow and jerky, hindered by her restraints, yet she radiated a confidence and poise that I'd never seen before. She paused when she reached my aisle. I boldly met her eyes, and I swear that she winked. I smiled in spite of myself. When she started shuffling again, I thought that I might have imagined the gesture because neither Donavon nor Mac seemed to have noticed.

The guards led Penny to a glossy, wooden table in the center of the space that separated the gallery from the Judge's platform. They moved off to the sidelines but kept their weapons trained on her. One of the Judge's underlings cleared his throat and began to read from an electronic tablet.

"Penelope Latimore, you are accused of Spying for the Coalition, Treason against the United States of America, and Conspiracy to commit murder of TOXIC Operative Natalia Lyons."

I blanched when he read my name. No matter how angry I was, I hated being associated with her charges.

The underling continued reading off the litany of evidence against her. When he read a transcription of my statement, Mac's arm was the only thing that kept me from slipping right over the edge of the bench. Donavon's pressure increased on my hand. I tried to return the gesture, but my fingers were numb. My face remained a mask of cool composure, even though internally I wept for the plight of a girl I'd once called my best friend.

When the underling finished, he turned his eager eyes to the Judge. The tension in the room was palpable, everyone waiting for her to speak ...everyone except for me. I dreaded the words that were undoubtedly about to leave the Judge's pursed lips. My stomach twisted in knots, the vodka sloshing sickeningly around my intestines.

After several long, breathless moments, she spoke, her voice low and raspy. "Penelope Latimore, for your crimes, you are hereby sentenced to death by lethal injection."

Cheers erupted in the courtroom, rippling through the gallery like a tidal wave. The spectators wanted blood, and they'd gotten it. My reaction was the exact opposite. I had to swallow a scream gathering in my throat. My body shook as I tried to contain the tears pushing painfully against the backs of my eyeballs. I yanked my hand free from Donavon's and wrapped my arms around my midsection. Desperately, I tried to keep my disgust and the vodka from coming out.

"Natalia, pull yourself together," Mac hissed in my ear.

I turned to face him, narrowing my eyes. "Shut up, you unfeeling bastard," I hissed back. "She was my friend. My best friend."

Mac glared at me. "She tried to have you killed. She is the reason that you will probably never be a Hunter. She is the reason that you have seizures," he said coldly.

I straightened my spine and met his challenge. He'd expected his words to invoke anger, and they did – at him. "Don't act like you're blameless," I matched his cold tone.

Fear flickered across his harsh expression. It disappeared just as quickly as it had come. Mac schooled his features back to neutral. "You are emotional, and I understand that. You have been through a lot in the past week. You don't know what you are saying," he replied evenly.

He was right; I didn't know what I was saying. I didn't *really* blame Mac for my seizures, or for anything else that had happened to me. I was upset and frustrated and angry and I needed someone to blame; after hearing the exuberant cheers of the exalted members of society, I couldn't bring myself to blame Penny.

Instinctively, I knew that it was her fault. She was a traitor. She'd admitted as much to me. Yet, a small part of me still couldn't believe that she'd actually betrayed me. I wanted so much to trust that she was always my friend just like she'd said.

I tore my gaze away from Mac, unable to look at him any longer. Whether for show, or because he knew how much I was hurting, Mac tightened his grip on my shoulders. I didn't want to cause a scene, so I didn't pull away. Donavon – who'd been quietly watching the exchange between me and his father – reclaimed my hand.

"He's just stressed, Tal. You know how much trouble this mess has been for him," he sent.

"What about me? You don't think I'm stressed? Haven't I been through a lot? Don't I deserve a break?" I snapped back.

Donavon didn't answer.

In the front of the room, the Judge rapped her gavel against the lacquered wood, effectively quieting the room.

"Ms. Latimore, do you have anything that you would like to say for yourself?" she asked Penny.

I wasn't sure what I expected Penny to do. Beg for her life? Proclaim her innocence? Make some idealistic speech? She did none of those things.

"No," she answered in a clear voice that rivaled Mac's for the iciness award.

"Very well. Guards, take her take to Tramblewood to await execution," the Judge ordered.

Penny stoically rose from her chair. She turned to face the

crowd. The set in her jaw was hard. Her eyes were now devoid of emotion, completely unreadable.

As she surveyed the room, her gaze landed on me. I didn't look away. A faint smile tugged at the corners of her mouth. Suddenly, I wanted to stand up and run to her, hug her. But even if Mac hadn't been holding me firmly in place, I don't think that I would have; I was too afraid.

"I'm sorry. I'm so sorry," I sent her. It felt odd, I'd never communicated mentally with Penny before.

"Don't be. It was worth it," she replied.

Worth it? What had she learned in her time with TOXIC that was worth her life? If the tables were turned and I was standing in front of a Coalition Judge who had just condemned me to die, I hoped that I'd think it was worth it, too. I also hoped that I would appear just as strong and calm as Penny did.

"Maybe I didn't accomplish everything that I came here to do, but I at least achieved one thing," she sent. *"You're doubting TOXIC – doubting what they stand for, what their mission really is."*

I didn't know what to say. *Was* I doubting TOXIC? Sure, I didn't agree with some of their ideals – the Mandatory Testing laws had always bothered me – but they were necessary, right? And I didn't actually believe her accusations ...did I?

You have no idea what your Agency does to innocent people. If I didn't believe her or Crane, why couldn't I get his words out of my head?

"Tal, open your mind. Look into my head. Please," she begged.

The guards took up their positions surrounding her. Then, head held high, she began her death march.

"Tal, please," she urged. *"There isn't enough time to explain everything, please look."*

I didn't know what to do. I wanted to yell at the Guards to stop. I wanted to scream. I wanted to break something. My emotions were so out of control that I couldn't concentrate on any one of them. I tried to stand up, but the combined weight of Mac's arm around me and Donavon's grip on my hand made it impossible.

The guards began dragging Penny down the aisle. I knew that it wasn't her reluctance to go to her death that made her struggle; she wanted to give me as much time as she could to absorb as many of her thoughts as possible.

I lost myself in the images that poured from her consciousness to mine. I saw a place that I recognized through Penny's eyes. I couldn't place how I knew the small stone cottage, yet as soon as I saw it, I knew that I'd been there. I knew that if I concentrated hard enough, I would be able to hear the distant roar of the ocean's waves beating against cliffs.

The next image was through an inside window of the cottage. I watched through Penny's eyes as a tall man with silver hair waited in a gravel drive, his whole body rigid. Even from behind, he was unmistakable: Crane. He visibly relaxed when a road vehicle with tinted windows rolled up the drive. When the car stopped, he reached for the passenger door handle and pulled it open. A much shorter man emerged. Crane embraced him, clapping him affectionately on the back. When they broke apart, I got my first look at the other man's face. Pain rippled through me. I wanted to reach up to touch the glass pane, call to the man with Crane. His curly, nearly black hair was tousled. The olive skin of his face was marked with a smattering of freckles across the bridge of his nose. My breath caught in my throat as tears again threatened my eyes. The short man's hazel gaze turned to the window. I wanted to bang on the glass, urge him to see me.

"Daddy!" I screamed. Warm, rough hands gently rubbed my arms. The sensation caught me off guard, and I broke the connection with Penny.

I blinked back to reality. I was still rooted on the bench in the courtroom, whimpering while Donavon tried to soothe me. His were the hands that I'd felt on my arms. I could tell that he wanted to hug me, hold me, but he was terrified.

I looked back and forth between Donavon and Penny. I wanted to see more. I *needed* to go back into Penny's head. I needed to see my father again. Donavon seemed to be urging me to stay with him, here in the courtroom, but I couldn't. I wouldn't.

Back in Penny's world, Crane and my father were no longer alone; a petite woman stood with them. Her chestnut hair was piled high on her head, and vibrant blue eyes sparkled like sapphires in the sunlight. I would've cried out to her, except my attention was drawn to something in my father's arms – or rather, someone.

On my father's hip sat a small girl, no more than three or four. She had dark, curly hair wreathing her tiny head. Her face was buried in my father's shoulder. The child threw her head back in laughter as Crane tickled her chubby little belly. Then, as if reacting to a noise that only she heard, her head swiveled in Penny's direction. Her purple eyes seemed to pierce *me* when they caught sight of Penny. My body began to shake, and I reached out to steady myself. I gripped something soft and fleshy, like a hand. I didn't have time just then to ponder the conundrum; the only thing that mattered was the little girl.

Curiosity danced across her beautiful irises. The corners of her cherubic mouth curled into a huge smile.

"Hello, my name's Natalia," the little girl sent. *"What's yours?"*

That was the last straw. Hysterical screams ripped from my throat as my three-year-old self continued to smile at Penny and, by extension, me. My shrieks reverberated through the courtroom, echoing off of the vaulted ceiling. Disembodied hands ran through my hair and over my arms, feeling like insects crawling on my skin. Furiously I tried swatting the creatures away, but large fingers laced through mine, immobilizing my hands.

"Let go, Tal. Just let go," a firm voice in my head commanded.

I recognized the voice and knew that I should obey, but I was caught between my own reality and Penny's memory. Just like with Ernest, I was in so deep that our minds had woven together in an odd inter-dimensional quilt. The difference now, though, was that I didn't want to extract myself from this. I wanted to be standing in the cottage, watching my loving parents interact with their daughter. I dreaded coming back to the present time.

My throat was raw, and the ache in my chest was painful. My head began to feel like it might explode. Black spots dotted my vision like inkblots, slowly bleeding together until my family and Crane were only visible through spider-web-thin slits.

"Please, Tal, come back to me," the voice pleaded. The words increased the pounding in my head, and my desire to stay in Penny's world gave way to a silent prayer for the blackness to take over. Just when I thought that my mind would split in two, the connection broke. My muscles turned to jello, and I collapsed against something hard as I finally lost consciousness.

Epilogue

Tramblewood Correctional Facility.

With what little strength remained in her thin arms, she struggled in vain against the restraints that bound her wrists to the uncomfortable metal chair. Her fingers and toes tingled from sitting in the same position for so long. It didn't take very long for her eyes to adjust, and she could make out the faint outline of the door. The grumbling in her empty stomach reminded her that her captors hadn't fed her in hours ...or was it days? Time held little meaning for her anymore.

Suddenly, the dank space was bathed in a harsh, blinding light. She squeezed her eyes shut against the painful shock to her retinas, barely managing to suppress a groan that threatened to escape her cracked lips.

"Ms. Latimore, good to see you again," a cold voice greeted her. He paused briefly, drinking in her emaciated appearance, and she took the opportunity to open one eye just a slit and chance a glance at her visitor. "Or should I say, Ms. Crane?" he continued, cocking his head to one side in a questioning gesture.

The visitor was backlit, his features hidden in shadows, but she would've known his voice anywhere. She also knew that his question was rhetorical. He was taunting her, hoping that if he let her know that he knew who she really was, she might be more inclined to engage in the banter that had been one-sided thus far.

"You are what, Ian's niece, I assume?" he continued, taking several steps inside the room. The armed men flanking either side of the visitor advanced as well. One of his bodyguards moved to stand within arm's reach of her chair. She scowled in his direction, but the guard's face remained impassive.

"Ian never had any children that I'm aware of, so I know that you are not his daughter, and you are too young to be his wife......" The hulking blonde man crossed one arm across his still-impressive chest, cupping the opposite elbow in his upturned palm. He tapped a large finger thoughtfully against his square jaw.

"Regardless, whatever the relationship is, he must not hold you in very high regard. After all, it's been, what? Two weeks? And there is no indication that he plans to come for you."

The sinister smile that spread across his face sent chills from the roots of her hair to the tips of her bare toes. Her resolve to not rise to his baiting weakened.

The drugs that the prison guards were using to suppress her Talents had considerably weakened her gifts, but her anger and humiliation fueled a last-ditch effort. She focused every ounce of inner strength that she could muster to glom onto his morphing ability.

Slowly her right arm began to tingle, and she knew that she still had some fight left. In the blink of an eye, a bluish-gray tentacle appeared where her arm had just been. The point of the tentacle was slick and narrow; while the bones of her wrist had been too large to slip through the cuff that was holding her to the chair, her new appendage was not. She whipped her tentacle free and flung it towards the visitor, wrapping it around his meaty neck. She squeezed. His eyes bulged, and panicked gasps echoed off the stone walls.

The closer of the two guards was on her before she could even smile with satisfaction. He repeatedly struck the appendage with the butt of his rifle until the grip on her prey slackened. She was too fatigued to hold the morph any longer, and it wasn't long before his gun made contact with her wrist instead of a tentacle.

A shock of pain reverberated up her arm to her shoulder, and she yelped in spite of her resolution to remain silent. The guard quickly holstered his weapon and grabbed her forearm, twisting it painfully.

"I should break it," the guard growled, his breath hot and rancid next to her ear.

She clenched her jaw against the mounting agony in her shoulder and tried to breathe through her mouth so she wouldn't inhale any more of his noxious fumes. The guard didn't release her; instead he looked to the visitor, now rubbing his throat, for direction. The visitor nodded, and the cracking of her radius filled her ears, followed by a pain so intense that her eyes poured tears. Despite her best efforts, she began to sob.

Along with her cries, words that she'd longed to hurl at the hateful Director spewed from her pursed lips.

"You're one to lecture on the merits of a family tie," she gasped, boldly meeting his eyes. "Look at what you've done to your own son!"

The Director's laugh contained no mirth. "I have given him the chance to be great, to be special," he said quietly.

"She knows," Penny hissed as the guard finally released her now-broken arm. She cradled it in her lap, wishing that she'd go into shock, so that the limb would go numb.

"Natalia? Natalia knows nothing." Mac re-crossed his arms over his chest, and Penny could see the ring of bright red spots that her tentacle's suckers had made on his exposed throat. Pleasure coursed through her frayed nerves.

"I have made sure that she chalked your little episode in the courtroom up to the fantastic delusions of a very disturbed traitor."

It was Penny's turn to laugh humorlessly.

"You think that you have so much control over her, don't you? But what you don't understand is that deep down, she knows what you are. Once she is willing to admit that to herself, she'll run."

Danbury McDonough's eyes flickered with fear, belying the neutral tone in his voice when he shrugged and answered. "We'll see." He scrutinized her for a long moment. "Actually, I will see. You won't be around to watch me crush the Coalition and Ian once and for all."

If her broken arm hadn't been causing waves of nausea and dizziness to wash over her, she might've attempted another attack. As it was, the most that she could hope for was ruining his neatly tailored suit with projectile vomit. She cursed her weakness; she'd failed Talia too many times already. Now she could do nothing more than whimper as the man who'd been treating her best friend like a puppet for years succeeded in destroying the Coalition's last hope at getting Talia to safety.

Loud voices echoed through the hallway behind the Director. The high-pitched giggle that assaulted Penny's ears sent a fresh wave of panic through her, and she visibly trembled.

Danbury McDonough chuckled and stepped to one side to allow the new visitor and his entourage to enter the cell. The owner of the childlike voice was small, just over five feet. His boyish face was freckled and tan; his impossibly clear eyes sparkled with mischief. Penny wasn't fooled; the man might look like he was twelve, but his real age was probably closer to forty. His deceptively youthful appearance wasn't his only oddity. As a Mimic, Penny could always identify the exact abilities that another Talent possessed. But somehow, the man-boy's gifts were impossible for her to pinpoint. He wasn't a solitary Talent, that much she knew. It was the extent and nature of his abilities that confused her.

"Penelope, you remember Dr. Wythe," Danbury McDonough announced, clapping the shorter man on the back.

"So we meet again, Ms. Crane," Dr. Wythe greeted her, shoving his small hands into the front pockets of his gray dress pants.

The pain in Penny's arm paled in comparison to the memories

of the torture-filled interrogations that she'd experienced at the hands of Dr. Wythe. The sessions always ended in the same way – with Penny blacking out. The only bright spot in her otherwise-bleak horizon was that he kept coming back; it meant that, despite his best efforts to physically extract her memories, he'd yet to uncover the information that TOXIC desired.

"I just came from a delightful morning with a mutual friend of ours," he tempted, watching her closely with his unnerving eyes to gauge her reaction.

The breath that she'd been about to take hitched in her throat. There was only one person he could be talking about: Talia. His strange, nearly translucent irises seemed to widen with delight at her reaction.

"Oh, don't worry, Penelope. My methods can be painless, almost pleasant even ...if I want them to be." It was like he was reading her mind. Maybe he was – she thought that Telepathy was one of his Talents.

"Leave Talia alone," Penny hissed, renewed hatred causing her to fight against her restraints. She didn't care what they did to her anymore; they were going to kill her anyway. But the thought that he was rifling around in Talia's head was too much for her to bear.

"Maybe I will. Maybe you and I can reach an accord, Ms. Crane. Tell me what I want to know," he shrugged his narrow shoulders noncommittally, "and I'll declare Ms. Lyons cured and end our sessions."

Penny contemplated his offer for one accelerated beat of her heart. Talia would never dredge up the memories that Dr. Wythe had forced her to repress if he kept "treating" her, but Penny divulging the Coalition's confidential secretes wouldn't help her Uncle Ian reach Talia either. Penny warred with her conflicting emotions. No, Talia was strong. No matter how good the man-boy was, Talia was better. Penny would just have to trust that Talia would allow herself to remember to understand.

Penny straightened her spine, forcing her posture into a defiant and confident stance.

"You'll have to kill me first," she declared, staring straight into the man's imploring eyes.

"Don't worry, Ms. Crane, we have big plans for you," he said softly. "Now, let us begin."

ABOUT THE AUTHOR

For more information on Sophie Davis and the Talented Saga, visit Sophie's website, www.sophiedavisbooks.com

To contact Sophie directly, email her at sophie.davis.books@gmail.com.

You can also follow Sophie on twitter: @sophiedavisbook.

Thank you for taking the time to read *Caged*. Sophie loves feedback, and any reviews posted to goodreads.com, amazon.com, barnesandnoble.com, ibooks.com, or any other retail site where *Caged* is sold, are greatly appreciated.

Made in the USA
San Bernardino, CA
01 May 2014